KT-157-487

The Fallen Angel

David Hewson

W F HOWES LTD

This large print edition published in 2011 by
W F Howes Ltd
Unit 4, Rearsby Business Park, Gaddesby Lane,
Rearsby, Leicester LE7 4YH

1 3 5 7 9 10 8 6 4 2

First published in the United Kingdom in 2011
by Macmillan

Copyright © David Hewson, 2011

The right of David Hewson to be identified as
the author of this work has been asserted by him
in accordance with the Copyright, Designs and
Patents Act, 1988.

All rights reserved

A CIP catalogue record for this book is available
from the British Library

ISBN 978 1 40747 052 8

Typeset by Palimpsest Book Production Limited,
Falkirk, Stirlingshire
Printed and bound in Great Britain
by MPG Books Ltd, Bodmin, Cornwall

MIX
Paper from
responsible sources
FSC
www.fsc.org   FSC® C018575

. . . while I was painting her I felt all the time as if she were trying to escape from my gaze. She knows that her sorrow is so strange and so immense, that she ought to be solitary forever, both for the world's sake and her own; and this is the reason we feel such a distance between Beatrice and ourselves, even when our eyes meet hers. It is infinitely heartbreaking to meet her glance, and to feel that nothing can be done to help or comfort her; neither does she ask help or comfort, knowing the hopelessness of her case better than we do. She is a fallen angel – fallen, and yet sinless; and it is only this depth of sorrow, with its weight and darkness, that keeps her down upon earth, and brings her within our view even while it sets her beyond our reach.

The Marble Faun, Nathaniel Hawthorne

PART I

CHAPTER 1

It was the last Saturday of August, just past midnight. Nic Costa sat on a low semi-circular stone bench midway across the Garibaldi bridge, listening to the Tiber murmur beneath him like some ancient spirit grumbling about the noise and dirt of the city.

To his left in Trastevere ran a steady stream of cars and crowded late-night buses taking people home to the suburbs, workers from the hotels and restaurants, diners and drinkers too tired or impoverished to stay in the city any more. On the opposite side of the river, where this portion of the road bore the name Lungotevere de' Cenci, the traffic flowed towards the centre, more quietly at this time of night.

Rome was slowly, reluctantly, working its way towards sleep. If he closed his eyes he could almost imagine himself at home in the countryside of the Appian Way, listening to nothing but the distant echo of insomniac owls. Then, from both sides of the river, came the familiar sound of the weekend: loud, slurring voices, English, German, American, some he couldn't name. The many busy bars of

Trastevere and the Campo dei Fiori were beginning to disgorge their customers onto the street and for the next few hours the uniformed police and Carabinieri who worked the graveyard shift would find themselves dealing with the aftermath of an alcohol culture that was utterly alien to them. Most Romans didn't much like getting drunk. Excess of this nature was socially unacceptable, an embarrassment, though that night he'd had rather more wine than usual and didn't regret it for a moment.

Further along the Tiber he could see a noisy bunch of young men and women stumbling across the ancient pedestrian bridge that joined Trastevere, near the Piazza Trilussa, with the *centro storico*. Costa wished he had the time and energy to walk there, then further still, until he could see the Castel Sant'Angelo illuminated like some squat stone drum left behind by the forgetful children of giants. Rome seemed magical, a fairy-tale city, on a drowsy evening such as this. And there were so many memories locked in these streets and lanes, the houses and churches and palaces around him. Good and bad, some fresh, some fading into the muted, resigned acceptance he had come to recognize as a sign of age.

'May I ask again? What happened in Calabria?' inquired the woman seated next to him.

There was nothing like a *gelato* in the open air after midnight. He was three days into his summer holiday, one forced on him by the state police's

4

insistent human resources department. Already he felt a little bored. Then along came unexpected company.

Costa licked his cone, bitter chocolate and fiery red pepper, thought for a moment and said, 'It's all been in the newspapers.'

'The newspapers! Some of it. About you and Leo and the rest locking up a bunch of crooks and politicians then getting feted by Dario Sordi in the Quirinale Palace. Medals from the president of Italy.'

'It was one medal,' he pointed out. 'A very small one.'

'So why did you need a party to celebrate?'

It was a good question. He hadn't. It was their colleagues in the Questura who'd arranged that evening's private celebration at a famous restaurant near the Pantheon. It was there that, by accident, on his part at least, he had met the woman who was now by his side picking at a pistachio ice cream with mixed enthusiasm. Teresa Lupo had invited her without telling him, and winked at him like some old-fashioned comic as she arrived. He felt sure he'd blushed, and hoped no one had noticed. And then he'd scarcely talked to anyone else all evening.

'It's disconcerting,' she continued. 'I turn my back for one moment and suddenly everything's changed.'

'You've been gone for nearly two years, not a moment. Of course things are different.'

Her round brown eyes glittered beneath the single iron lamp above them.

'So I see,' she said. 'I'd like to know what happened in Calabria. To Gianni and Teresa. To Leo.' She hesitated. 'To Nic Costa too. Him most of all.'

'I laid to rest some ghosts,' he said without thinking, and realized he was happy to hear those words escape his own lips. 'Most of them really. But that's a story for another time.'

She put her small hand on his arm and moved a little closer. He was unable to take his attention away from her dark, inquisitive face, which was even prettier than he remembered, bearing the signs of make-up and some personal attention which had never been there before.

'I'm happy for you. Would you mind very much if . . . ?'

She took his arm and wound it around her shoulders. Then her head leaned against his and he felt her soft, curly black hair fall against his cheek.

He whispered, half to himself, 'I remember the first time I saw you. It was in that little outpost of the Barberini where you kept your paintings. You were a nun.'

'I was never a nun. I was a sister. I took simple vows, not solemn ones. How many times do I have to tell you this?'

'Quite a lot, I imagine. Is that . . . possible?'

He heard, and felt, her laughter.

'I don't see why not. I've only been back three

weeks. There's time. All the time in the world really.'

But there isn't, Costa thought.

'It was winter,' he recalled. Bleak midwinter. The bleakest ever. He'd seen his wife, Emily, die before his eyes. That loss, and its cruel, invisible twin, the associated guilt over her murder, had almost broken his spirit. He'd wondered for a while if he would ever put that dark time behind him. It might have been impossible without this woman's unexpected intervention. 'You wore a long black shapeless dress with a crucifix round your neck. You carried your life around in plastic bags. There was nothing in your world except painting and the Church.'

'Back then all of that was true.'

Emily's loss still marked him, and always would. But it had become a familiar, background ache, a scar he had come to recognize and accept. The sight of her in those last moments, by the mausoleum of Augustus, in the grip of the man who would kill her, no longer haunted him. Time attenuated everything after a while.

Feeling a little giddy from the wine Falcone had ordered throughout the evening, he took away his arm, turned and peered into Agata's eyes. She was still the woman he'd first met. Someone with the same intense curiosity, one which so often creased her high forehead with doubts and questions that this habit of fierce concentration had, with age, left the faintest of marks there, like scars of the intellect.

7

'The last time we met was at the airport. You were going to Malta to work for some humanitarian organization. You weren't a nun or a sister or whatever any more. Your life still seemed to be contained in plastic bags. You didn't have art. I wasn't sure you had the Church.'

'You sound as if you were worried.'

'Of course I was! You'd spent your entire life in a convent. You were going somewhere you didn't know. To a life you didn't understand.'

She folded her arms and glowered at him.

'You'd lost your wife. And you were worried about me? Someone you barely knew? This constant selflessness of yours is ridiculous, Nic. You can't worry about everyone. You have to lose that habit.'

'I have lost it. As much as I want to, anyway.'

'Well done. I didn't abandon painting by the way. Or the Church either. The first is your fault. You told me to go and see that Caravaggio in the Co-Cathedral in Valletta. *The Beheading of St John the Baptist.*'

She edged further into his arms and placed her head on his shoulder.

'Sorry,' he said. 'It's good, isn't it?'

'It's a depiction of a man who's just been executed. His murderer is reaching down to finish the job with a very small knife.' She hesitated. 'It's wonderful. I refused to go and see it for nearly eighteen months. When I went I took one look and knew I couldn't stay out of the world forever.

It's like every other Caravaggio I've ever seen: a call to life. A challenge, to face our fears.'

'And the Church?' he asked.

'I'm still a good Catholic. I simply came to understand there are more definitions of the word "good" than I'd learned inside a convent. Also I missed Rome . . .' She closed her eyes. '. . . so very much.' She smiled and looked back at the city, now growing somnolent beneath the clear night sky. 'I grew up here. This place is my life. I couldn't leave it forever. Could you?'

'Never. This job of yours . . .' He still struggled with the idea of her earning a living like everyone else. 'How did you get it?'

'Hard work! How else? I didn't sit in my cell all day, you know. I have the degree, the postgraduate qualifications, to teach the history of art anywhere in the world. Why do you think those eminent men from the Palazzo Barberini used to come to me for an opinion?'

'Because they valued it,' he said quickly.

'Quite. On Monday I become assistant professor at the Raffaello College in the Corso. It's a school for foreign students. Not a public university exactly. Perhaps that will come later. But it's a job, the first I've ever had. Teaching spoilt brats the history of art. Caravaggio in particular. You, however, may attend my lectures for free.'

'I will.'

'No. I was joking. You know as much as I do about

him. More in some ways. You can see into his head. I never will. Frankly I don't want to.'

Her hand went to his hair. She stroked his head, as if amazed by their closeness.

'Those ghosts really are gone, aren't they?' Agata Graziano whispered.

'Exorcized,' he said.

'Don't tell me what buried them. I don't want to know. It's enough that they're dead.'

CHAPTER 2

Costa felt awkward holding her. He still had a *gelato* in one hand, as did she, and it seemed inevitable that this experimental moment would culminate in a kiss. He was happy with this idea, provided the evening ended there. He needed to think about Agata's sudden reappearance in Rome a little more. In the morning, when his head was clearer, and hers too.

She noticed his predicament with the ice cream, raised a single dark eyebrow, and nodded at the ground.

'No,' he said. 'We've enough litter in Rome as it is.'

He got to his feet, took the half-finished cone from her fingers, went to the bin at the end of the bench and deposited both ice creams there.

When he got back she was standing up, a diminutive and beautiful young woman with her arms folded across her chest. She wore a tight dark jacket, a scarlet silk shirt and grey slacks. Around her neck was a silver chain with some abstract ornament – not a cross – that he'd noticed earlier. Her dusky, compact face was stiff with a familiar bemused anger. The noise of the revellers finding their way home from the Campo and Trastevere was getting louder all the time. Bellowed shouts and obscenities in foreign languages. This was the price of being an international city.

'Perhaps not all the ghosts have gone,' Agata said. 'I wonder . . .'

'Enough talking,' Costa said, then took her in his arms and kissed her, chastely almost, on the lips, holding her very gently so that she could withdraw easily from his grip.

He imagined this was the first time any man had embraced Agata Graziano, not that he had much idea of what she'd done in Malta for the last two years.

They broke for breath. Since they'd last met scarcely a day had passed when he hadn't thought about the curious little sister from the convent in the *centro storico* who had fought so bravely to find some justice for him after the efforts of the police and the judiciary had failed.

To his astonishment her eyes stayed wide open throughout.

'I'm sorry,' Costa said quickly.

'No, no, no . . . don't apologize.'

'I didn't mean . . . I thought . . .'

She waited, then said, 'Thought what?'

'I thought that perhaps you wanted me to . . .'

Before he'd finished she dashed forward, kissed him quickly and rather roughly on the lips, then pulled back grinning, looking a little wild.

'I did. And I like this!' Agata announced brightly before lunging at him once more.

The kiss was brief, the embrace longer. She stayed in his arms, smiling, her head against his chest.

'I like this a lot,' she murmured. 'Nic . . .'

She glanced up at him. At that moment, from somewhere in the network of streets on the city side of the bridge, there was a cry, that of a man in terrible pain. Then, not long after, came a young female voice calling, shouting, words that were so high-pitched and full of distress they were incomprehensible.

'You can't take your car home,' Agata declared, trying to ignore the din. 'You've had too much to drink. A taxi driver will charge the earth to take you out to that beautiful house in the country. My job comes with a little apartment.' She hiccupped, out of embarrassment perhaps. 'In the Via Governo Vecchio, believe it or not. Please . . .'

He shuffled from side to side and stared at his feet. He hadn't been driving a car lately. At the beginning of the month, when the city began to wind down, he'd decided to resurrect his father's ancient Vespa scooter from the garage. With the spare time from his holiday he'd got it back on the road. The thing was parsimonious with fuel and it was wonderful to feel the fresh air against your face in weather like this, dodging the traffic, parking anywhere. The Vespa was a little rusty in places but the engine still had noisy fire in its little belly. Now the decrepit little turquoise beast was just round the corner, waiting in a side street.

The racket from across the road kept getting louder and louder.

'In my apartment I have a . . .' She struggled for the words as her skin took on the warmth of a rising blush. 'A . . .'

'A couch?'

'I have a bed.' Agata blinked at him, wobbling a little. 'There. I've said it.' She smiled, a little bashful, perhaps even a little ashamed. 'You're happy, just like Teresa said you'd be. Finally. The Nic I always knew was there even when I could see your heart was breaking. My Nic . . .'

'You're babbling,' he said, reaching forward and taking her shoulders. 'Do you have a couch?'

'I am *not* babbling. Of course I've got a stupid couch. I live in the Via Govermo Vecchio.'

'Good. Then . . .'

The unseen girl was screaming again, at the top of her voice. There was real agony and fear in her cries, not the drunkenness and violence he'd come to recognize over the years. He could see his concern reflected in Agata's shocked features.

'There's something wrong,' she said, her eyes wide and glassy with trepidation.

'Stay here, please,' Costa ordered.

Then he ran across the riverside road and down

14

towards the tortuous web of lanes and alleys that meandered in every direction out from the ghetto like a tangle of veins and arteries wound around the human heart.

CHAPTER 3

The commotion was in the first street on the right after he crossed the Lungotevere de' Cenci. In the half light of a single street lamp he could see a body lying on the ground, legs apart in a broken, unnatural fashion, the upper torso in darkness at the foot of a tall residential building.

Something was next to the figure, a pale shadow in what looked like child's pyjamas, faint pink. This was the source of the keening, wailing scream that had brought him here.

He took out his phone, called the control room, identified himself and ordered an emergency medical crew.

'We've had a call already,' the operator told him. 'Didn't leave a name. Do you know what happened?'

'No, but someone's hurt.'

'Need anything else?'

The figure in the pyjamas fluttered out into the light like a moth struggling to break free of a spider's web. It was a girl, Costa thought immediately, and there was blood on her, on her chest, and in the loose, flapping fabric around her legs.

16

'Make sure there's some backup,' he said, without quite knowing why. This was a complex, rambling part of town, on the very edge of the ghetto. There were people closing in, attracted by the noise. No blue flashing lights. Not a sign of a uniform, police or Carabinieri.

He was off duty, unprepared, a little heady from Falcone's wine. But there was no one else around.

Crossing the street he called out, 'Signora.' Then looked more closely as he approached, saw her fully in the light, crying, distressed, quite beside herself, blood sticking in a messy smear across her slender chest and thighs.

'Signorina,' Costa corrected himself as he approached. 'Police.'

He reached her, stopped, a little breathless. The girl was perhaps fifteen or sixteen. Her long blonde hair was the colour of old gold under the lamps and hung in thick tresses around her shoulders as she twisted and turned, trying to see what was around them, glancing anxiously at the shape on the ground. She had a beautiful, pale, northern European face, trapped between womanhood and the world of a child, innocent yet on the verge of knowledge.

There was a strange noise from somewhere nearby, like the trickle of water or sand.

'Daddy,' she mumbled in English, looking at the stricken body on the ground.

'Signorina . . .' Costa took her skinny bare arms and held her. This was odd. There was still the

17

sharp sense of danger somewhere close by. 'Tell me what happened.'

She looked into his eyes and he found himself lost for a moment.

'He fell,' the girl said simply and glanced at the building behind them.

Costa looked at the figure on the black Roman cobblestones. After a decade in the force the rules came back without a second thought. Protect the living, protect yourself. Then, and only then, think of the dead. And this man was gone. He could see it, in the shattered skull, so broken he didn't want to peer too closely, and the unnatural, agonized way the corpse was sprawled on the hard ground.

A handful of people were beginning to gather from the riverside road and the streets that entered from the ghetto. They grew quiet as they approached, encountering the invisible dread that came from meeting mortality out in the open, on a hot, idle August night. From somewhere came the sound of someone retching and he wondered whether the cause was the broken body on the paving stones or drink, or both.

The girl crouched down again, next to the dreadful shape. Her long, straight hair fell on the bloodied torso there. She kept mumbling one word over and over, in English, 'Daddy, Daddy, Daddy . . .'

It sounded wrong somehow. Too young a cry to leave the lips of a teenager.

Costa took in the way the dead man, a tall, skinny individual of late middle age he guessed, was leaking blood out into the cracks in the cobbles.

Around the body stood a pile of shattered rubble, old stone and cement. A few steps away lay a single piece of metal scaffolding and some planking. A thin trickle of pale dust was falling in a vertical line onto the ground next to what looked like fresh rubble close to the fathomless pool of darkness that was the entrance to the building behind them.

He looked up and saw the same beautiful, starry sky he'd been sharing with Agata Graziano only a few moments before. The man seemed to have fallen from an old, decrepit palace that stood a good five storeys high, one of the tallest on this side of the street. Against the moonlit night he could make out that the top floor had a balcony running the width of the building, with scaffolding attached for part of its length, suspended on cables that led to some apparatus on the roof. The nearest corner, almost directly above them, was gone entirely, both metal railings and terrace ripped away, leaving a line of broken tubing, cracked concrete and ragged wire clinging to the stone façade.

The contraption was moving perceptibly in the darkness.

The steady trickle of fragments of stone and sand grew stronger, depositing a growing pile of rubble on the ground.

Four years before he'd been called to a tenement in Testaccio rented to illegal immigrants, the
clandestini who performed the jobs that Romans
had come to believe were beneath them. The
building had been denied maintenance for years,
against the city statutes. On one grim December
day an entire wall had collapsed, burying those
unlucky enough to be inside. He'd never forget
clawing at the rubble to get to a child, or the relief
he'd felt when he was able to retrieve a single
young soul from that bloody, choking mess.

His head cleared very quickly as he turned on
the growing crowd of bystanders, many of them
foreign, some of them drunk, and yelled, 'Police!
Get back! This is a building collapse. Clear the
area. Now!'

CHAPTER 4

A few of them obeyed, a few others retreated into the darkness of a narrow alley opposite that seemed to run uphill, in the lee of a vast, hulking palazzo. Costa yelled again, in English this time, then took the young girl's arm as she knelt by the corpse on the cobblestones. The falling trickle of sand and brick and plaster had turned into a growing stream that made a rising, relentless rattle as it reached the earth.

'Please,' he begged. 'I've got to get you out of here.'

'My father!' she said, turning, looking into his eyes. There was such pain and despair in her pale face it sent a chill through him. She didn't move, not a millimetre.

He crouched down by her side.

'My name's Nic Costa. I'm a police officer. You are . . . ?'

'Scusami?' she said in Italian so easy and natural she sounded like a native. Her hands were on the man's bloodied chest. She bent down, placed an ear next to his unmoving mouth, listening.

Costa gripped her arm and made the girl look at him.

'Your name!'

'Mina.' She glanced at the terrace above them. 'I think he went out for a cigarette. There was a noise. Like . . . a whip cracking. The scaffolding . . .' She put a hand to her mouth. It was covered in blood. Her eyes were very large, bright and lustrous with tears, like jewels. 'He's dead, isn't he?'

'Stand on the far side of the road, Mina. When you're there I'll carry your father over. Please do this now. If the building falls and we're still here I can't help anyone.'

He looked up. The man must have tumbled five floors from the balcony. No one could have survived such a fall onto the ancient stones of Rome.

'I need you to move,' he said with more force.

She stayed on the ground and gripped his arm.

'You'll bring him . . . ?'

'I'll do as I promised. When you're safe. I can't carry two of you.' Costa quickly snatched off his jacket and wrapped it round her bare shoulders, over the bloodied pyjamas. 'Now stand on the other side of the road.'

Slowly, she got up and wiped her brow with her arm, casting towards him an expression so sharp and full of expectation he wondered how old she really was.

The girl was tall, almost his own height, and sylph-like. She crossed the street then walked into the dark alley opposite. A familiar female shape was there, a shorter one. Agata had followed him and immediately approached the distraught teenager the moment she arrived, coming out of the crowd of bemused and distant bystanders to help. He watched as she placed her arms around the girl and held her.

Something the size of a small rock landed no more than a metre away, followed by a steady rain of pebbles. A sharp object cracked against his skull then a line of metal tubing clattered noisily to the ground next to him, bouncing around in a manic dance across the cobbles.

Costa steeled himself. It was wrong to move the man. Wrong medically, if by some miracle there were still some faint flickering light of life. Wrong from an investigative point of view too. But this was an accident, not a crime scene, one that was not, perhaps, entirely finished. Besides, it was a way of getting the girl to move, perhaps the only means he could find. *Protect the living.*

He pushed his arms beneath the bloodied torso, reaching forward as far as he could until his own face touched the stained and dirty shirt that enclosed the fractured body in front of him. It was impossible to ignore the smell of violent injury, though at least this awkward position, so close he had to turn away his own head as he strained to lift the body upright, meant that he didn't have to look at the shattered skull.

Then he took a deep breath and began to lift the girl's father off the ground.

The body felt unexpectedly light in his arms. Something warm and liquid trickled onto his neck. He didn't want to think about what it might be. Steadily, making sure he didn't stumble, Costa crossed the street and staggered towards the alley opposite. When he felt sure he was sufficiently distant from the palace behind, he lowered his burden gently onto the pavement. The girl and Agata were a few steps away. The daughter watched him for a moment then withdrew herself from Agata's grip and came to stand at the end of the cul-de-sac, her eyes on the building opposite.

The stream of rubble was turning into a torrent. Costa looked up and saw that a good five metres of scaffolding at the end of the balcony had begun slowly to tear itself from the front, dangling downwards, swaying from side to side like some timber and metal pendulum struggling to mark the passage of time as it dispensed itself and the fabric of the balcony onto the street below.

Finally there was a siren. He turned and saw the mirrored flash of a blue emergency light on the Lungotevere de' Cenci. Costa made a frantic call to the control room to warn them about the state of the building and demand an emergency construction crew. A police van turned into the head of the lane and found itself blocked by parked cars. It stopped, and some men got out and began to walk directly towards the area of the collapse.

Ignoring the continuing torrent of debris raining down on the street, Costa stepped out and waved at them to stop. At that moment the final segment of hanging terrace and scaffolding began to give way and tumbled to earth in a deadly rain of metal and timber and concrete that shattered on the black cobblestones a few metres in front of him. He retreated quickly, trying to find safety, listening to what sounded like the crackle of gunfire.

'Nic . . .' Agata was by his side, peering anxiously into his face, as he reached the pavement. 'Are you all right?'

'Yes.' She was alone. 'Where's the girl?'

'Here.' Agata Graziano turned to look behind her. The crowd had retreated into the alley when the balcony began to collapse. Now they were cautiously starting to return. Agata put a puzzled hand to her head. 'Well, she was . . .'

He heard that young, almost childish voice again, and this time it bore something different, something he hadn't expected. Anger. Fury. Perhaps even blame.

'Robert! *Robert!*'

The girl was back in the road, walking towards the inky pool of darkness around what he assumed was the palace door. Costa found the questions kept coming. Why had no one else in the building noticed what was happening here? There were no lights on the lower floors, only in the windows close to the collapsed balcony. No illumination over the entrance itself, where surely there should

25

have been at the least a set of lit bell pushes of the kind that sat outside every apartment block in Rome.

'OK,' he murmured, half to himself. 'I am past persuasion.'

He marched into the road, stood in front of the girl and ordered her to return to the safer side of the street. She ignored him completely, her eyes fixed on the palazzo, calling someone's name again and again.

Costa sighed, seized her by the waist then threw her over his shoulder the way a father did with a recalcitrant child. She weighed more than he expected but she didn't protest, just kept calling that single name, plaintively, out of fear, he thought, nothing else.

Robert . . .

'Don't leave here again,' he ordered as he let her down onto the pavement.

She went quiet and shut her eyes briefly. Then she looked at him and Costa felt his heart skip a beat. There was something she wanted to say, and wouldn't, out of fear, perhaps. Or something else. He knew it. Could feel it. Understood, too, that there was nothing he could do to persuade her to speak what was on her mind, in her heart.

'My brother's in there somewhere,' she murmured. Then, shouting again, 'Robert . . . !'

Another shape came out from the darkness by the entrance. It stayed in the shadows. Costa could just make out a tall figure walking through the continuing shower of dirt and stone as if it didn't matter.

There was a gun high in his right hand, waving towards the stars. Costa felt his heart sink. Quickly he held out both arms, told those around him to retreat further back into the alley behind, and tried to think.

A good half-dozen uniformed men were slowly working their way up the street, wary of the building. They saw what was happening and took positions by the parked cars, reaching for their weapons.

The girl tugged on Costa's arm.

She stared into his face, pleading.

'It's my brother. He's not . . . bad.'

'Please go back to where you were.' She didn't move. 'Mina . . .'

'Don't you dare hurt him,' she said, retreating.

He stepped out onto the cobblestones, arms held high and open, trying to assess what he was seeing.

'Robert,' he said firmly. 'We need to get medical attention for your father.'

The brother was half in shadow. From what Costa could see he was wearing a bloodied T-shirt and jeans. His free hand still kept the gun high in the air. A stray and ludicrous thought went through Costa's head: he's running away from home, the way children sometimes do.

All that the uniforms would see was a man in possession of a firearm. They would be quietly telling themselves to waste no time or niceties in bringing this confrontation to an end, and Costa couldn't blame them for that.

'Your sister needs you,' Costa added, watching him closely.

He wished he could see the face of this figure in the shadows, read some expression there. But the youth stayed back in the darkness, as if afraid. Only the gun was in the half-light, wavering.

'She's safe now,' a stony voice said in English.

Costa found his head was beginning to hurt.

'I'm sorry?'

'Robert?' the girl cried in a begging, childlike tone from behind. '*Robert . . . ?*'

Another explosion ripped through the warm Roman night and this time it was a gunshot. Costa found himself blinking, cowering instinctively, unable to see what had happened, where the weapon was aimed.

Then a memory. Another time. Another shot, by the grim walls of the mausoleum of Augustus, one that had taken his wife from the world.

He wheeled round anxiously, dark images rising in his head. Agata was there, with the girl. They stood backed up against the wall, eyes shiny with fear. Unharmed.

'Thank God for that,' Costa muttered to himself, and heard the uniforms moving swiftly, heard shouts.

When his attention returned to the street it was empty save for the taut, determined shapes of five or six cops working their way through the lines of parked cars, cautiously, step by step, making sure to stay on the safe side of the street.

The brother was gone, fled into the spider's web of lanes that ran throughout the ghetto in this labyrinthine quarter of the *centro storico*.

A uniformed officer he knew walked over, gun in hand, pushed up his helmet visor and asked, 'What the hell was that about? The kid could have got himself killed.'

It almost seemed as if that was the idea, Costa thought.

'Did he fire at me?' he asked.

'No,' the officer said, shaking his head. 'He took a shot at that . . .' A nod at the decrepit palazzo behind them. 'Then he was off. I've got two men going after him. For what it's worth. This place is like a rabbit warren. Besides . . .' He eyed the girl, who was now on the ground next to her father, sitting quietly, cross-legged in the dirt, Costa's jacket still round her shoulders. She was holding the dead man's hand, rocking to and fro, eyes listless, focused on nothing. 'We've got a name, haven't we? English? Been . . . ?' He made a familiar gesture with an imaginary bottle. '. . . knocking it back?'

'I've no idea,' Costa admitted. 'I'm off duty.'

The uniform man smiled and said, 'It's my case then.'

'What? It's a collapsed building. And a dead man.'

'If some scary-eyed kid waves a gun in your face . . .' He shook his head. 'It's a case.'

29

Costa wasn't listening. The girl called Mina was watching him from beside her father's body on the other side of the street and there was an expression on her beautiful young face – a pained, resigned sadness so profound, so innocent, it gave him a chill.

He walked over and crouched down next to her.

'Mina,' he said, trying to look into her face, though it wasn't easy.

'What?'

'Is there something we should know? Something you want to tell us?'

It was the hesitation that struck him. She waited a good two seconds, staring at the ground, then mumbled, 'What kind of thing?'

'I don't know. I just wondered.'

Then she did look at him and he found he couldn't interpret the expression in her eyes at all.

'Where's your mother?' he asked.

'I called her. She said she'd be here soon.'

Agata put an arm round her and glared at him. He wanted to say to her: *this is my job, this is what I do*. Notice things. Little things sometimes. Though not now, not when he was on holiday, with little to occupy him except bringing an ancient Vespa back to life.

'I'll ask someone to look after you,' Costa told the girl, got to his feet, and took a look around him, trying to remember what he knew about this part of the city.

The memory came back suddenly, like a ghost emerging from behind some long-forgotten door.

A name. That of a beautiful, tragic young woman. One notorious enough to have earned her a legacy close to the Lungotevere, the stretch of busy road by the river here. Even to the very place where Mina's father had died.

There was a sign on the corner of the palazzo with the shattered scaffolding. The street was the Via Beatrice Cenci. His eyes refused to leave the girl called Mina as Costa found himself recalling a tragedy from another age.

PART II

CHAPTER 1

The following Sunday morning, more than twenty-four hours after the incident in the ghetto and his encounter with the strange young English girl, Costa found himself downstairs on the sofa in the living room of his home near the Appian Way, flicking through two old history books of his father's which retold the tale of the Cenci family.

It was almost seven thirty. The Questura would be slowly coming to life, such as it was on this last weekend of August. Someone, perhaps Leo Falcone, would be looking at the previous day's report of the building collapse, wondering if this was in any way the business of the police.

The media didn't think so. The TV bulletins ran brief stories that told of a tragic accident, one that had taken the life of a foreign academic. Knowing the way these things worked, Costa felt sure their verdict came directly from the authorities. The dog days of August were the slowest, most enervating time of the year. The crime figures fell through the floor in these scorching, exhausting weeks. Any Romans who had the time and money fled

the city for the beach or the mountains, somewhere cool to relax. Those who remained drifted
through the weeks until September arrived, with
a sluggish return to work and, at some point, a
welcome hint of autumn.

He'd spent the previous day alone at home,
tinkering with the Vespa, sleeping, thinking about
tackling some of the persistent chores that the big,
old farmhouse he'd inherited seemed to demand
with an ever-increasing frequency.

Thinking about Agata Graziano too, wondering
what exactly he should do about her unexpected
reappearance in his life. Their brief semi-drunken
embrace had happened a little too suddenly.
When he'd gone out to the party that Friday night
he hadn't, for one moment, expected to meet the
woman who'd flitted through his life so quickly, yet
with such intensity, two years before. He didn't want
to lose touch with her again. Equally he didn't
want to rush anything, to add one more complexity
to her return to Rome, and a life quite unlike that
of the cloistered sister she had been.

The accident had ended messily. Police, construction crews and paramedics had descended on the
Via Beatrice Cenci. After a little while the girl's
distraught mother emerged from the night and
went with her in the ambulance to the hospital in
San Giovanni. Exhausted, dirty, confused, he'd
seen Agata to the door of her little apartment in
Governo Vecchio then, perhaps foolishly, taken his
little scooter home, only to sleep for ten solid hours

and wake with a single name ringing round his head.

At first he'd been unwilling to listen to its siren call. He'd called Agata, had a slightly strained conversation about the night before, and made a tentative arrangement to meet later in the week. Still there was another name that wouldn't leave him, that of Beatrice Cenci, a young woman whose fame and notoriety were commemorated both in an old and narrow street in the heart of Rome and a body of literature and art that spanned centuries and continents.

She was there, on the table, her face in front of his eyes, very much alive in the famous portrait from the Barberini gallery. A young girl executed by the Vatican in circumstances that still had the power to haunt those who came across her story. Beautiful Beatrice, muse to poets and writers and artists, captured forever by the artist Guido Reni, a defiant symbol of youthful innocence punished with unimaginable cruelty for avenging the sexual tyranny of a parent.

He looked again, recalling that shocking incident in the early hours of the previous day and his conviction, which had not waned more than twenty four hours later, that the daughter had wanted to tell him something. This long-dead face, staring out from the canvas, beseeching the viewer in silence, was disturbingly close to that of Mina, the frightened yet defiant figure in the bloodied pyjamas, bent over the broken corpse of her own father. It was more than a physical similarity. Something in the eyes of Reni's Beatrice seemed to have carried over into the expression of the English girl, some guileless, mute acceptance of the harshness of life, a burden borne with the serene stillness of a saint awaiting martyrdom.

How had he first encountered the Cencis? It was in his teens, when questions, about the world, about the imperfection of his parents, began to cast a shadow on a life he had previously thought perfect. Around the time his own mother died after a long illness, Costa found himself briefly obsessed with Beatrice, compelled to read these two books, trying to understand her fate.

Through her story he began to appreciate that men held an ambivalent attitude to women, one that praised and adored their beauty while condemning, and punishing on occasion, their courage and individuality. It was a failing commonly acknowledged, but always in silence, unmentioned, unmentionable. And so Beatrice Cenci cast a long shadow across Rome because her story came to embody this very human frailty in a way that allowed it to be expressed and exorcised, century after century.

After her execution thousands had followed her coffin along the Via Giulia, across the Ponte Sisto, up the steep hill in Trastevere to the little church of San Pietro in Montorio at the foot of the Gianicolo hill. There she was buried in an unmarked grave beneath the altar. Costa knew the church, though not well. This quiet little place was rarely visited except by those seeking Bramante's haunting little temple which was supposed to mark the site of St Peter's martyrdom, not the last resting place of a childlike girl butchered as a common criminal. Even there Beatrice found no peace. Local rumour had it that Napoleon's troops, when they ran riot in Rome at the end of the eighteenth century, exhumed her famous corpse and played football with the severed skull.

For a few brief, agonizing months of his mother's illness Beatrice was rarely from Costa's head, a distraction and a nagging reminder of another approaching tragedy, one much closer to home. He could still recall walking past the Ponte Rotto, the ruins of the imperial-era bridge stranded in the river near Tiber Island, which Beatrice had offered to rebuild from her own fortune, if only the Church would let her family survive. It had seemed to his young mind utterly savage that the tyrant in the Vatican should have refused her offer and instead taken her life, and those of her brother and step-mother.

Beatrice was a victim, one transformed into a heroine by her indefatigable will and serene beauty, and her refusal to bend to the power of the Pope who, some sources claimed, pursued her for his own reasons, among them the seizure of the valuable Cenci estates.

Buoyed by popular stories and Reni's portrait of a tortured innocence, her savage end came to touch people far beyond Italy. Painters had been drawn to it for centuries. Some had even depicted Reni and the girl together in prison the night before she was beheaded, the artist at his easel, she sitting quietly, patiently, without fear, but with a muted sense of fatalistic resignation that would be captured on canvas for eternity. On the opera stage and in the theatre, in the exquisite Victorian photography of Julia Margaret Cameron, the story of the virginal Roman girl caught the imaginations of poets and writers and musicians. Alexandre Dumas had told her tale before moving on to *The Count of Monte Cristo* and *The Three Musketeers.* The American Nathaniel Hawthorne made her fate a focal part of the moral argument in his book, *The Marble Faun.*

Fifty years before Hawthorne, the English poet Shelley had seen Reni's portrait in the Barberini and set down a description of the doomed girl which, for Costa, summed up the general conception of her character and its perennial appeal.

'There is a fixed and pale composure upon the features; she seems sad and stricken down in spirit, yet the despair thus expressed is lightened by the patience of gentleness,' Shelley wrote.

Costa couldn't shake from his head the idea that the selfsame words could so easily be applied to the English girl, Mina, doggedly staying by her dead father, eyes brimming with tears, afraid, yet refusing to move until he agreed to her demand to carry the man's broken body to safety.

And the words of her brother, fleeing into the night after firing a gun, apparently at the building where they'd lived.

She's safe now.

Safe from what? The collapse of the building above her? Or something else altogether?

In the eyes of the world Beatrice Cenci was a righteous criminal, guilty of a just conspiracy to murder the father who oppressed, beat and raped her. A young woman guilty of the heinous crime of patricide in concert with her brother, stepmother and two henchmen, who had hammered a nail through Francesco's skull then – and this element troubled Costa as the detail came back to him – thrown the battered body out of the window, hoping to pretend to the world that he had died accidentally from the fall.

It had taken the investigators of the Vatican to discover the truth, through means the sixteenth century thought normal: torture, in all its forms. He had shivered as he read again how the young woman's arms had been ripped from their sockets as her inquisitors hauled her to the ceiling on ropes, fighting, and failing, to extract a confession. Giacomo, her brother, was less brave, and through his cowardice and unpredictable behaviour doomed them all. Under duress the truth, and the admissions, emerged, though never from her. Beatrice's father, a rich and cruel nobleman, was a monster who sexually molested his daughter over a period of months, forcing her to take part in vile trysts with her own stepmother and with other men as he watched. His murder was the patricide of a heartless tyrant, hated by all. But patricide nonetheless, a crime the Pope of the day saw fit to punish with the utmost severity.

And so, on 11 September 1599, Giacomo was paraded through the streets of the *centro storico* in a tumbrel as torturers tore the flesh from his body with red-hot pincers. When they reached the piazza by the Ponte Sant'Angelo they bludgeoned him to death with a mallet to the temple. His corpse was decapitated and dismembered, the four quarters of his body hung from the bridge on butcher's hooks for all to see. Beatrice's stepmother followed to the same scaffold. Finally, watched by her younger brother, the only member of the Cenci family allowed to live, Beatrice walked impassively to the block, her head held high in front of sympathetic crowds that lined the bridge and the banks of the Tiber, all screaming for mercy for a sinner surely more deserving than most.

They fell silent at the final moment. The executioner raised his blade and the hooded monks of the Confraternita di San Giovanni Decollato, the Brotherhood of the Decapitated John the Baptist, waved their images of Christ in her face. She died from a single blow of the sword, refusing to admit her guilt or confirm a single detail of her father's criminal and incestuous abuse. Thousands of mourners followed her bier to San Pietro in Montorio that evening. Even now the anniversary of her death was marked each year by a faithful few, and there were those who claimed her ghost haunted the environs of her old Roman home in the ghetto, the Palazzo Cenci, and the bridge in front of the Castel Sant'Angelo close to where she died.

Why this obsession that spanned centuries and continents? Perhaps because her fate asked awkward, unanswerable questions. How compliant was she in the death of her father? Did she initiate the attack, and spur on the murderers themselves when they faltered, as Giacomo had hinted? Or was she the silent victim, resigned to her death, simple and profound in her fatalism, as she had been to her depraved father's abuses until, in the eyes of her admirers, finally she chose to place her rights as an individual above the harsh, inflexible tenets of the law?

There was, he thought, more to the enduring attraction of this story than met the eye. The sympathy the Cenci case aroused seemed to stem also from a general sense of unease surrounding the taboo of incest, a crime that always generated extreme emotions. Costa had been a police officer long enough to understand that sexual abuse within the family was more common than many appreciated, and usually went unreported and unpunished.

'Daddy,' he said quietly to himself, remembering the night before.

CHAPTER 2

He got himself a coffee and something to eat. Outside the kitchen window the vines were beginning to grow heavy with fruit. Another ten days of inaction remained. He could call Agata, ask her out for lunch. Or tinker with the Vespa's temperamental two-stroke engine, work on the field, tackle so many things that needed his attention.

The book lay on the table, the cover, that evocative image of Reni's, uppermost.

There were questions that needed to be answered and he wondered if, in the stifling dying days of August, anyone would notice.

At a quarter to nine he phoned the Questura. Falcone was on duty. The inspector sounded cheery if a little tired.

'You can't keep out of trouble, can you?' Falcone observed when he had listened to Costa's questions.

'So you'd have walked away?'

'We're not on duty permanently, Nic. What exactly do you want?'

'I'd like to know what's happening. Whose case is this?'

44

Falcone grunted something inaudible. There was the sound of fingers clacking on a keyboard.

'Not ours, that's for sure. The city building inspectors are going to look at the contractor and the works records. If there's a criminal prosecution it's theirs, not ours. We don't do construction work.'

'The brother?'

'Narcotics are handling that. They knew him already. Strange family. English. The father was an academic, quite well known in some circles. The mother a part-time office worker and musician. The daughter a saint, it seems. And the son a dope dealer to all those charming foreign kids who hang around the bars on the Campo. Takes all types.'

'He had a gun.'

'Fired it in the air, or so the witnesses said. Did he look popped up?'

Costa tried to remember.

'I didn't see him very well. I got the impression he was scared.'

'He should have been. He left behind enough dope to put him in jail for a year or two. The kid wanted out of there with no one chasing him. The drugs squad can do this kind of thing. It's beneath us.'

'The autopsy . . .'

'It's Sunday. There's not the slightest suggestion this is anything but an accident. Half of Teresa's team are off work, as is the lady herself. It can wait until tomorrow.' There was a note of impatience in his voice. 'Do you really have a single reason to think this is suspicious?'

'Has anyone even bothered to look inside the apartment?'

'Yes. Narcotics and the construction people.'

'If this is a crime scene they'll leave it in a pretty state.'

'If, if, if . . . A man steps out onto his balcony for a cigarette and falls five floors from some rickety scaffolding. He was, by the way, drunk too. Uniform found a quarter of a bottle of Scotch in the girl's bedroom when we looked.'

'The girl's bedroom?'

'He had to go through there to reach the balcony. Kindly give me some reason to pursue this further or go back to taking a holiday the way normal people do.'

'If there's anything wrong here and the city construction people march right through it . . .'

'Then someone will kick my backside,' Falcone interrupted.

'Let me into the building. I can be there in half an hour.'

Falcone hesitated then asked dryly, 'Is Agata Graziano's company really so tedious? You do surprise me.'

'None of your business, Leo. Do I have your permission?'

Costa waited. He'd pushed the right buttons. The building department people could

46

be guaranteed to wipe out anything useful if it existed. The fall-out from that kind of mistake could be painful.

'If you can convince Peroni the two of you can go and waste your time in there,' Falcone said in the end. 'I'm sick of him malingering around here, moaning about the heat.'

The line went quiet. Peroni came on. His voice sounded croaky and weak.

'You want to do what?' he asked after Costa explained the idea in detail.

'There's a little cafe in Portico d'Ottavia. You know it?'

'No. It's Sunday. Are they open?'

'It's the ghetto, Gianni. Remember? I'll buy you a coffee.'

'Sounds promising.'

A memory came back of that part of the city: the first time he took Emily there, and the childlike smile on her face.

'And some Jewish pizza too.'

'Thanks for that,' Peroni mumbled, then hung up.

CHAPTER 3

One hour later they met in the little place in the ghetto. Costa liked this area. The mundane mingled with the remains of the magnificent, the past with the present. A few strides along from the humble cafe where they met stood the remains of the arch Augustus had erected in honour of his sister Octavia. It was an interesting part of Rome, a mix of grand, sometimes crumbling palaces, humble homes, some Jewish buildings and organizations, and a few restaurants that didn't look down on a vegetarian like him.

Peroni fell onto a stool in the cafe with a sigh then placed his head in his hands. The burly, middle-aged cop had lost his customary smile. His scarred, friendly face was wan and bloodless. Judging by the mournful look in his bleary eyes he had very little confidence that the large, strong coffee and slice of *pizza ebraica* in front of him would do much to change the situation. He was wearing a pale brown jacket that had seen better days, an ill-matching pair of blue trousers, and a cheap, whitish shirt, the necktie bunched together in a half-knot at the open neck.

'Why is it you look so bright and breezy when I feel awful?' he asked, poking at the pastry on the plate. 'And why are you wearing an office suit? It's Sunday. In August. You're off duty.'

'I don't want to look off duty, do I?'

'God, I hate enthusiasm. It's so exhausting. Like this heat. I told Teresa. We should have gone on holiday like everyone else, instead of sweating like pigs in Rome.'

Costa went to the counter and got two glasses of tap water then returned and placed them on the table. He'd looked at himself in the mirror that morning while shaving, thinking about Beatrice Cenci. Just turned thirty, he still ran from time to time. He was fit, a little skinnier than he once was. His dark hair didn't seem much interested in changing colour or disappearing in the near future and his face fell into a smile a lot more easily than it had for a few years. Nor did the heat bother him. Unlike Peroni, he'd grown up in Rome. He expected the dog days to be like this. Were it not for the nagging thoughts that kept bothering him about the incident in the Via Beatrice Cenci he would have described himself as a contented man.

'It was a great party,' he said. 'Memorable.'

'Memorable for the hangover I had yesterday.' Peroni lifted the little pastry and stared at it. 'What on earth is this?'

'Jewish pizza,' Costa said, taking a bite of his own. 'You'll like it.'

'That's not pizza.'

'It's sweet.'

'I don't do sweets.' Peroni breathed deeply, took a bite and nodded, as if half-impressed. A few raisins, some candied fruit and a stream of crumbs began to trickle from his mouth to the floor.

'Are you sure you wouldn't be better off at home?' Costa asked.

'No, no, no.' Peroni shook his big head very carefully, as if it might fall off. 'The air conditioning's packed in. Teresa's there and she's worse than me in the heat. That wouldn't be a good idea, honest. What are we doing here again?'

Costa explained in more detail about the incident in the ghetto, the girl called Mina, the dead father, the son running away after firing off a single aimless shot. He didn't mention anything else, not even when Peroni kept staring at him as if he was wondering, 'Is that it?'

'Nic,' he said finally. 'The building inspectors went straight in there yesterday morning. Those people are good. They'd let us know if there was something wrong.'

'There was something wrong. The son pulling out a gun, shooting it in the air then running off into the night. With his father dead on the ground. His sister there too.'

'Dope.'

As if that explained everything.

'It needs looking at.'

'It is being looked at. By the drugs people. They

knew the kid anyway. And the building inspectors can deal with the structural stuff.'

'The girl . . .'

Costa didn't elaborate. Peroni was a very smart man. It was hard to keep anything hidden when he was poking around.

'What about the girl?'

'Where is she now?'

Peroni pulled out a notepad and looked at it.

'With her mother round at the academic place where her father worked. Some institution called the Confraternita delle Civette. Near the Campo. Heard of it? I haven't.'

The Brotherhood of the Owls. The Little Owls, to be precise. Costa had been an avid birdwatcher when he was young, and knew where to find these charming little birds when they nested in the ruins and bosky corners of the Appian Way.

'No,' he replied. 'New to me.'

'It seems they're being very generous in the circumstances. Providing the family with accommodation. Uniform interviewed the mother and the girl, as you'd expect after an accident. They're pretty upset, naturally. Didn't have a lot to add. The girl was at home on her own for most of the evening. Father came back around ten. They spoke briefly. He seemed cheerful. She got dressed for bed then went into some music room they had and spent most of the night practising. Got a concert coming or something. She thought her father was going to read a book then go to bed. Some time after

51

midnight she heard a shout and a noise, saw what had happened, went outside. The rest you know. The father didn't like to smoke in the apartment. He'd got into the habit of stepping out onto the balcony.'

'Even when it's covered in scaffolding?'

Peroni looked a little annoyed, which was unusual for him.

'Don't you have better things to do on your holidays? The whole block was being renovated. That was why they got the apartment on the cheap. They probably never even saw it without scaffolding. Why would they worry?'

Falcone had looked into this after all.

'Did she see the brother that night?'

Peroni scanned his notes.

'He was out drinking with his friends in the Campo. Where he was most nights. The sister says she glimpsed him in the downstairs hall when she was rushing out after her father fell. Must have been on the way back and got caught up in the whole thing.'

'The father's dead on the ground. The mother's God knows where. And the son doesn't even step out of the shadows to help his own sister?'

'The mother was playing in the orchestra at an amateur concert. From what we know she came as soon as she could. The son was maybe drunk. Doped up. Who knows? People get funny around death. I've seen cops scared of going near a corpse. So have you.'

'Yes, but . . .'

'Narcotics say he was a runner for one of the Turkish rings dealing stuff to the foreign kids. They had him on their radar for a little chat soon. He'd dumped a very valuable stash of coke and heroin in the doorway. The narcotics people found even more in his room.' Peroni thought about this for a moment. 'The question you might want to ask is: why did he stay around at all? And did his sister know what he was up to? She didn't tell you he was there for quite a while, did she?'

That didn't add up.

'She was more concerned about her father. Here's another question. Would you walk out onto scaffolding five floors up for a cigarette?'

'You never smoked, did you? Of course I would, particularly if I had a wife who hated the smell of tobacco in the house. The scaffolding ran the length of the balcony. It was the sort they suspend from the roof on arms or something. You can see that from what's still up there. Seems pretty stable to me. Looks like it's been there forever. Too long maybe. Perhaps it got rusty. The construction people will know.'

Costa sighed and said, 'You've been there already?'

'Walked past on my way here,' Peroni admitted with a grin, then called for another coffee, coughed a couple of times, and straightened up as if he felt a little better. 'We do get the job done without you, believe it or not. If there is a job. Which there isn't. So what's really on your mind?'

'Beatrice Cenci,' Costa muttered, not expecting a response.

The man opposite stiffened.

'What the hell has that poor girl got to do with it?'

Costa blinked.

'You know who I'm talking about?'

'I'm not a complete idiot. There was a play about her a few years back at the Teatro Sistina. Teresa took me.' He frowned and the foreign expression made his big, friendly face age several years. 'I bawled my eyes out. Then she told me it was all true and I bawled them out again. What a horrible story. Want another piece of the funny pizza?'

'Not really.'

'I'll take one for later.'

He turned, smiled at the woman in the head-scarf at the counter, and got himself some more.

'The man died in the Via Beatrice Cenci,' Costa went on, and knew how ridiculous that sounded.

Peroni looked at him and raised a single eyebrow.

'The daughter,' Costa continued. 'Mina. She had blood on her pyjamas.'

'Her father had just fallen five floors. She was bent over him when you arrived. His blood, don't you think?'

'Do we know that?'

'No,' Peroni admitted. 'Are you really suggesting there's more to this just because it happened in the street where the Cenci girl lived, what, five, six centuries ago?'

'Four and a bit actually. No, of course I'm not.' There had to be more to it than that. 'Sometimes you see things, Gianni, and you know they're wrong. You don't understand why. Or what it is you're half-seeing either. But you know.'

'Oh yeah, you know.' Peroni peered at him across the table. 'And a few days or weeks or months later you get to understand that, half the time or more, you were just an idiot. We've all been there. It can turn out nasty. Particularly when it involves kids.'

Costa bridled at that remark.

'And the other half?'

'You're on holiday. Leave it to someone else.'

'I'm not in the habit of asking favours. Let's just go there and run through the basics.'

'Uniform and narcotics have done that already.'

'Uniform think this is nothing more than a building collapse. Narcotics see what they want to see.'

'And we'd be different?'

'Maybe,' he said hesitantly. 'I don't know.'

Peroni leaned forward and peered into his eyes.

'Maybe you're bored. Or turning suspicious in your old age. You're on holiday. It's sunny out there. Why aren't you taking Agata somewhere? Not trying to turn some terrible accident into a crime scene?'

It was the second time he'd heard this suggestion. Costa knew a conspiracy when he saw one.

They could have told him in advance that Agata was going to be there that Friday night. It might have saved some embarrassment.

'Don't presume to organize my life, please. And pass that message on.'

Peroni folded his arms and said not a word.

'One quick look inside the apartment,' Costa suggested. 'Indulge me. Then we're done.'

'You're . . . off . . . duty,' Peroni said emphatically.

'And you're barely fit for work. We make the perfect pair.'

The big man looked him up and down.

'Fine talk coming from you. That was a nice suit once. Not a Sunday suit but a nice one. Have you noticed you've got oil stains and dirt on your trousers?'

Costa looked down, saw the problem and tried to brush off some of the marks. It just made everything worse.

'This is that grubby old scooter you told me about, isn't it?' Peroni asked.

'It's a Vespa Primavera ET3. Not a grubby old scooter. If it was good enough for my father it's good enough for me.'

'Vespa-pa-pa-pa-pa-pa-pa,' Peroni sang suddenly, in a rather good baritone. The woman at the counter clapped her hands and joined in, and together the two of them chanted, 'Vespa-pa-pa-pa-pa-pa-pa . . . *subito*!'

Costa sat there feeling like a fool.

'It was a TV advert for those things,' Peroni

explained. He glanced at the woman at the counter. 'Back when we were young.'

She laughed, called him a mildly rude name and sang again, 'Vespa-pa-pa-pa-pa-pa-pa.'

'Ah.' Costa got it. 'The sound of the engine.'

'That's an engine? Please. You're going through a second childhood and that's the truth. You won't call Agata, then?'

'In my own time. She was there, with the girl, and the father. She saw more of Rome than she wanted. Our Rome. Not hers.'

'That could be a good reason for you to talk to her.'

'My business . . .'

Peroni sighed. Then he folded the extra piece of sweet pizza into a napkin, stuffed it into his jacket pocket, got up and went to the door. It was for Teresa. Costa just knew.

'Thirty minutes. That's all you get,' he said. 'Then I'm back to the Questura for a nap. The street's still closed, by the way. You'll need your ID. And don't you dare bring that stupid scooter.'

CHAPTER 4

The ancient cage lift was out of order so the two men had to walk up a long and grubby winding staircase, past bare timber planks and sacks of cement, the detritus of building work. On the fourth floor Costa paused to let Peroni catch his breath, then called Falcone. There had to be more background on the family who'd been living here above what was essentially a construction site, empty save for the topmost storey.

Falcone told him what he knew. The dead man was an English university professor named Malise Gabriel, sixty-one years old, a peripatetic lecturer who had moved to Rome nine months earlier from Madison, Wisconsin. The name rang a distant bell, though not one Costa could immediately place. Gabriel was attached to the academic organization called the Brotherhood of the Owls, which was based in the Palazzetto Santacroce, a few minutes away on foot, near the Campo. His wife also worked there as a part-time personal assistant to the director. The daughter was older than Costa had first thought. She had turned seventeen three weeks earlier, something of a prodigy according to the uniformed officers, fluent in several languages, taught at home by both parents, never at school, though she attended lectures in art, music, literature and history at a variety of city colleges. She was also a volunteer with local charities, for animals and the homeless, and, in spite of her youth, understudy organist at the great church of Santa Maria in Aracoeli on the Campidoglio, the Capitoline hill overlooking the Forum.

Her brother Robert, though just three years older, seemed to belong to an entirely different family. He had been cautioned, though never charged, over two fights in the bars near the Campo, and had no apparent job. Nothing had been seen of him since he fired that single shot into the night and fled the scene of his father's death. According to his mother, who seemed concerned, though scarcely beside herself, his absence was not unusual. For the past few months he had lived at home sporadically, spending the rest of the time with 'friends' she didn't know.

'What does the morgue have?' Costa asked.

He could hear Falcone tapping away at his keyboard.

'It says here that the injuries are consistent with a fall from a substantial height. Gabriel had been drinking. There are no apparent suspicious circumstances, at least from a cursory examination. As I keep emphasizing, this is Sunday and August too . . .'

'Teresa needs to see him.'

'Teresa isn't here. Tomorrow she may take a look.'

He knew Falcone well. The man was not going to budge.

'I'll let you know what we find,' Costa said and started to climb to the top floor of the building.

He leaned over the banister and looked down five storeys to the ground-level entrance. The *centro storico* had its share of old buildings like this, unappealing grey stone leviathans built in the sixteenth or seventeenth centuries, cold and empty homes to rich and bickering clans like the Cenci.

The customary closeness of family meant little in the world that enclosed Beatrice Cenci. The murderous plot that had begun with one nobleman's vile treatment of his daughter had taken root in the Palazzo Cenci just around the corner, a vast, hulking pile by the side of the little alley into which Mina and Agata had retreated when the scaffolding began to collapse. These grim mansions were sometimes little more than prisons, invisible to the world beyond their shuttered windows. Francesco Cenci's mulish will had run unchecked through the many floors and rooms of the building he came to regard as his own private kingdom, a solitary and perverted paradise where he was God, able to do whatever he wanted. Behind these thick stone walls, invisible to humanity, strange passions flourished.

Peroni finally reached the top, coughed three times, pulled himself upright and managed a cheery smile.

'Thirty minutes,' he repeated. 'Not a second more.'

The door to the Gabriel home was open. Costa pressed the bell and walked in.

CHAPTER 5

The apartment extended across the entire top floor of the palace. It consisted of a spacious living area, an attached open kitchen, and five or six rooms off, bedrooms, bathrooms, it was impossible to tell at a glance. The furniture was old and worn, the walls badly in need of paint. There were no carpets, only scratched floorboards that hadn't seen polish in years and a few threadbare mats. The dining table was the kind of cheap plastic stuff sold by the discount warehouses. There was a battered, baggy sofa, with a woman on it, sitting back, eyes closed, listening to music from the speakers of a portable audio player in her lap. Jazz. Costa recognized the familiar tune: Mingus's *Good-bye Pork Pie Hat* played by a piano trio.

To add to the confusion, gangs of men Costa assumed were from the city construction department were wandering to and fro carrying instruments and cameras, treading the dirt of the building work from the lower floors into the bare floorboards and occasional scattered rug. Two of them came out of the furthest room in the corner, the one where he assumed Malise Gabriel had stepped out onto the balcony. They were talking in low tones, looking bemused.

The music came to an end. The woman pressed a button to switch off the player, looked at them and asked, 'Can I help?'

She was about forty, very thin with short blonde hair and a pained, mannish face. Her eyes were raw and pink. Costa guessed she'd been crying very recently. He thought she looked a little anxious. Nervous. Scared even.

'We're police,' Costa told her.

'I've already spoken to the police.'

She had a curious accent. The Italian was good but not native.

'You're with the construction company?' Peroni asked.

'I *am* the construction company.' She pulled out her card and passed it over. It said: Joanne Van Doren, CEO, Cenci Enterprises.

'You speak good Italian,' Peroni noted.

'My mother came from Rome. My father was on Wall Street. I grew up in New York. Some strange sense of belonging, a recovered memory maybe, persuaded me to come to Italy and try to do my own thing.' She stared around at the apartment. 'More fool me, huh?'

'I'm sorry,' Costa said. 'I don't follow. Your people were responsible for the scaffolding?'

'I'm responsible for everything. I own this entire block. Bought the dump for a song five years ago, when songs cost a lot more than they do now. I employ the construction crew. I design what's supposed to become of this place. That's what I am, really. Or was. An architect. This . . .' One more caustic glance at the bare, grim apartment. '. . . is meant to be one of the most prestigious condo blocks in Rome. If I can get ten thousand euros per square metre I might even manage to scrape a profit.'

She ran a lean hand through her hair and stared at them.

'What do you think? Interested?'

'A little out of my range,' Peroni said. 'Not that I'm looking.'

'Who is?' she asked. 'I'm the person everyone sues, of course. The banks when I default on payments. The city when they think I screwed up over something as simple as a suspended scaffold. Oh, and Cecilia Gabriel, who seems to have decided I'm responsible for poor Malise's death. You'd think she'd have waited a day or two before threatening me with the lawyers. I let her family have this place for next to nothing. I know enough not to expect thanks from the English aristocracy but even by their standards she seems a little eager with the ingratitude.'

'You've spoken to Signora Gabriel?' Peroni asked.

'She was round here at ten thirty this morning. Picking up things. Telling me she wouldn't set foot in the place ever again. Oh, and saying she'd be serving a writ real soon.' Joanne Van Doren licked her lips. 'You mind if I see if there's a beer left in their refrigerator? This has been one hell of a weekend.'

They followed her into the kitchen where she found a bottle of Moretti. Then they came back and sat down in the living room, listening as she talked freely and frankly about the Gabriels, her tenants.

It was the kind of story Costa had heard before. A foreign family coming to Rome, the parents hoping to forge a fresh life in the city, to chance upon some thread of luck, some new opening in their lives that had never been there elsewhere. The American woman seemed to like them, in different ways. The father was friendly, intellectual, a little intense. The mother seemed quiet, committed, perhaps a controlling influence, she was never sure. The son, Robert, was wayward, unpredictable, but never caused any trouble that she knew of.

Joanne Van Doren's face lit up when she said the girl's name.

'Mina,' she said, beaming, 'is a doll. If I were ever to have a kid, which seems somewhat unlikely, I'd pray for one like her. Bright as a button, interested in everything, so talented it makes you sick. Put her in front of a piano and you can lose a couple of hours of your life. Same for drawing, books, poetry, literature. Malise and Cecilia can take the credit for that, I guess. They taught her at home. Said it was the only way.'

'They did that with Robert too?' Peroni asked.

She thought for a moment and said, 'No. Now you mention it. Robert said he went to some boarding school in Scotland, the same one Malise got dumped in when he was a kid. Perhaps that's why he turned out the way he did. These snooty families have strange habits. You could never send Mina away. It'd be too painful to have her out of the house. Let me show you something.'

They followed her into a room at the far end of the floor, as distant from Mina's bedroom as it was possible to be. There was a digital piano there, the kind that could be played in silence through headphones. Alongside was a violin case, a classical guitar and a little laptop computer.

'Cecilia played violin in some amateur orchestra. Good, but Mina left her behind as a musician long ago from what I gathered. Listen.'

She hit the keyboard of the computer. A kind of software Costa didn't understand came up. A few more taps and deep, powerful organ music, very familiar, began to emerge from the headphones.

Joanne Van Doren flicked a switch and it came out of the little speakers seated on the desk.

'Bach,' she explained. 'Touch cheesy, I guess, though that's because it's been so misused over the years. *Toccata and Fugue in D minor*. Or the voice of God in human form as someone once said, hopefully not within earshot of Malise. Mina had scarcely been here four weeks before she'd talked

66

her way into understudying the organist at the church on the Campidoglio. This is her playing there. She'd record it on the computer then bring it home to listen, try to make it better. Can you believe that? Also she speaks Italian better than I ever will, and for the life of me I don't actually recall Cecilia even teaching her. God, I love that kid. This is my old laptop. I gave it her. Bought her the music kit too. Malise and Cecilia didn't have two pennies to rub together.'

Costa was thinking.

'She'd work on her music in here? With her headphones on?'

'Usually,' she agreed. 'Mina was very particular about not disturbing people. Incredibly thoughtful. Not your average teenager at all.'

He closed the door.

'Like this? So she wouldn't know if someone came or went from the apartment?'

The American woman looked puzzled.

'I guess. So what? How is Mina? They said she found Malise outside. Jesus . . . it doesn't bear thinking about.'

She reached for a tissue, dabbed at her face, then apologized.

'I just can't believe it happened here. Then Cecilia blames me . . .'

'People don't think straight in situations like this,' Costa said. 'She'll feel differently in a day or two.'

'You don't know her.'

67

Costa bent down and looked at the computer. In an open window there was a piece of notation, one that looked as if it was being worked on recently. He hunted round the menus until he found a way to pull up some information about the piece. It had last been saved at a quarter to midnight on Friday evening. The girl had told uniform she was practising when her father died. The computer seemed to corroborate this.

'Can we see her bedroom?' Costa asked.

'Sure. It's a mess, mind. Not Mina's fault either.'

They followed her to the door at the far corner of the building. The men in city council overalls were still in there, peering out of the window at the shattered scaffolding tubes and cables. Peroni showed some ID and asked them to leave for a moment. Costa glanced at his colleague. The room was filthy with dust and dirt. There were boot marks on the single bed by the wall, stamped on the sheet, which had a distinctive design: white and green, with a repeating square pattern like an antique Roman mosaic. Books and CD covers lay scattered on the bare floor. These men were interested in the outside only. Nothing within.

A poster on the door had fallen down at some stage and now lay crumpled on the bed, covered in shoe marks. He picked it up and found himself looking at Guido Reni's portrait of Beatrice Cenci from the Barberini, the one from the books, a good print which brought out the sensitive, sad beauty of the subject.

'She liked that story,' Joanne Van Doren said. 'Found out about it soon after they moved in. I'd never even heard of it. Mina took me all over Rome, to places that had connections with Beatrice. We thought it might be good publicity when I got around to selling the condos. That's why I put the Cenci name on my company. Mina was going to be the guide for potential buyers. I promised her a little pocket money.'

There was a bookshelf on the wall opposite the bed. Costa bent down and looked at the titles. One shelf was entirely devoted to works on the Cenci and their time: Dumas, Stendhal, Shelley, Moravia. Then he shook the duvet on the bed. Dust and dirt and bits of plaster and rubble fell on the floor. He threw back the cover and examined the sheet underneath. Fresh boot marks apart, it was spotlessly clean, newly ironed. Newly changed.

Costa was about to move on to the mattress beneath when Peroni coughed loudly and gave him a black look. This wasn't the time.

The older cop walked towards the window, glanced out, then asked, 'Why did the scaffolding collapse?'

Joanne Van Doren shrugged.

'If I knew I'd tell you. Whether it's the fault of my workmen or not. Do you imagine I feel good about this? I liked Malise. He was a decent, caring man. I guess that's why Mina turned out the way she did.'

'The scaffolding . . . ?' Peroni persisted.

She didn't like being pressed.

'Do you have a head for heights?' Joanne Van Doren asked. They didn't have time to say anything. 'Good. Then follow me.'

CHAPTER 6

There was a set of external metal stairs at the back of the building. They climbed up the steps to the roof. The view was extraordinary, a sweeping prospect of Rome stretching from the Campidoglio to the Gianicolo hill and St Peter's across the Tiber.

A heavily built man in council overalls was clambering over some bulky apparatus at the front. Joanne Van Doren walked over and said to him, 'You've got company. The police are back and want to know what happened.'

He was about fifty, with a brutish, ill-tempered face and a grey moustache. He didn't look as if he wore an overall often, particularly on Sundays.

'Signor Di Lauro is the building inspector in charge of the investigation,' she explained with a friendly wave. 'I am, of course, offering all the help I can.'

'Any ideas?' Peroni said, flashing his card.

'Don't you people ever talk to one another?' Di Lauro grunted. 'I went through this with those guys I spoke to this morning. I really have better things to do.'

'Please,' Costa interrupted. 'Just briefly.'

'Briefly.' He climbed down from the mechanism he was looking at, a complex set of wheels and pulleys and platforms, and put his hands on his hips. 'This is what's known as a suspension scaffold. That means the strain is taken by the anchorage and counterweights you see here. On the roof.'

'How much can it support?' Peroni wanted to know.

'This apparatus is licensed for a load of three hundred and fifty kilos. Three men.' He waited to see if they understood. 'So if there was just one man on it . . .'

'Got you,' Peroni replied. 'And . . . ?'

'And what?'

'Why did it break?'

Di Lauro closed his eyes as if in pain.

'I don't know. Maybe structural failure in the scaffolding itself. Metal fatigue. Or maybe someone did their job wrongly. It happens.'

He grimaced. Something didn't seem quite right.

'Often?' Costa asked.

'This scaffolding was erected by Signora Van Doren's own people. They worked on it. They stood to suffer if it went wrong. No. Not often. Scaffolders are meticulous men. The paperwork's in order. The tiebacks, the counterweights . . . this seems to be a professional job.'

Costa grabbed hold of a piece of loose cable, took one step towards the edge of the roof and peered

72

down over the edge at the distant cobblestones below. The view down to the street made him feel a little queasy. He looked at Di Lauro and asked, 'Would it be easy to make it fail deliberately?'

The council man sighed.

'No. Possible. But not easy. You'd need to know what you were doing.'

'Nobody has access to this roof,' Joanne Van Doren cut in. 'The building's empty except for my workmen and the Gabriels. Trust me.'

'So when will we know?' Peroni asked.

Di Lauro shrugged.

'Impossible to say. A week at least. Possibly longer. We've taken away the debris from the ground. Tomorrow I'll find some people to look at it.'

'Tomorrow?' Costa asked.

The man sighed. 'It's . . .'

'Sunday. I know. And August.'

'Listen,' the council man snapped. 'You do your job. I do mine. I will find out what's happened here. If it's negligence, there could be criminal charges, Signora Van Doren.' He didn't look at her as he said this. 'In cases of extreme negligence it can be manslaughter.'

'I was at home drinking a glass of wine in front of the TV,' she said with a wan smile. 'That would seem a little cruel.'

'The last case of this kind took three years to come to court. It got thrown out after four months.' Di Lauro shook his head. 'None of this is easy.'

73

'More lawyers,' the American woman grumbled.

'Thanks,' Costa said, and led the way back downstairs. He was glad to be inside again. Joanne Van Doren was starting to look impatient with their presence.

'What are you going to do with this building now?' Costa asked.

'Try to sell something,' she said, as if the question were idiotic. 'Get this damned apartment finished so I can put it on the market. I need the money. Otherwise everything goes to the bank and I'll be as broke as my old man back home. These aren't good times for the private sector, gentlemen. Haven't you noticed?'

She looked briefly ashamed and for a moment seemed on the verge of tears. It struck Costa that this woman appeared genuinely affected by the death of her tenant, though she did not, perhaps, want this to show.

'I'm sorry,' she said. 'I shouldn't have snapped at you like that. This is nothing next to what Mina and her mom are having to deal with. Malise loved them. I can't imagine what life's like without him. You know . . . instead of poking around here you might be better off trying to help them get through the next few days.'

Costa nodded, then watched as some new men arrived at the door.

'I'll pass that on to the appropriate authorities,' he murmured as she walked away to greet them.

Peroni was poking around in the living room, going through the newspapers and magazines that were piled in a jumble on the glass table in front of the sofa.

'This is where he must have been drinking last night before he stepped outside,' the big man said. 'There's a ring from a glass here. Just one.' He bent down and sniffed it. 'Whisky. Got spilled too. Good point you made back there.'

'Which one?'

Peroni started at him, surprised.

'If that kid was wearing headphones in that music room a small army could have walked through here and she'd never have noticed. Also, there's this. I don't get it.'

He stood up, a thick book in his hands. It was an old edition, a fat, tall paperback. The title was *All the Gods are Dead*. The author's name was Malise Gabriel. Bells were ringing in Costa's head again.

Joanne Van Doren saw what they were doing and came over.

'I put that under the table myself,' she said. 'We had to sit down and use it when the council people turned up. They wanted to see some plans. I should have told Cecilia when she came round. She was looking for all the little personal things she could find. The conversation got a little . . . tense. I kind of forgot.'

Peroni flicked open the book and glanced at Costa.

'So this is what he was reading,' Peroni said. 'His own book? And it's . . .' He turned to the front and checked the date. '. . . twenty years old. Why would someone read a book they wrote themselves? An old one?'

'Maybe to remember the good times?' the American woman suggested. 'Who knows? Excuse me. I really need to talk to these guys.'

She crossed the room and began addressing the newcomers in overalls. Costa couldn't hear a word she was saying.

Peroni was flicking through Gabriel's book.

'You know something, Nic? I doubt I'd understand a word of this even if my English were better. It's all jargon and academic-speak. Almost makes *me* want to step outside for a cigarette. Do you have the faintest clue what "non-overlapping magisteria" means? Or why it should be a bad thing?'

'I'd have to say no on both fronts. How do you know he was reading that chapter?'

'Bookmark,' Peroni replied, and showed him the page.

There was what looked like a postcard in it with a line in Italian, the script in a cursive, elegant hand, *'E pur si muove.'*

Peroni stared at the words in front of him.

'Now I'm an uncultured oaf. But the way I'd spell that is "*eppure si muove*". Maybe these foreign academics aren't as clever as they think. Funny thing to write on a bookmark, though. "And yet it moves". What moves?'

'No idea,' Costa said. He picked up the bookmark, stared at it, thinking about the words. Then he turned it over, saw what was on the back, and felt his heart sink.

'That's unusual,' Peroni said, his broad, pale face wrinkling with puzzlement.

This wasn't a real postcard but a black and white photo from a domestic printer. It showed a naked girl writhing on an off-white crumpled sheet, her slight frame posed artfully, the way a sculptor might have placed it. There was a visible stain next to her thigh. Her willowy body was that of a teenager, with pale, perfect skin, thin legs crossed and turned, so that the lens saw only her thighs and a side view of her navel, nothing else. It was if she was struggling to hide. As if some inner sense of shame or shyness wished to protest, to say that what was happening felt wrong.

The picture was cut off at her neck – decapitated, he thought for a moment. In the topmost portion of the image two taut sinews stretched up towards the smooth white skin of her throat, as if extended by pain or guilt. There was a tantalizing lock of hair in shadow cast by a light or an object out of view. It was light hair, fair or blonde perhaps.

'Is that the daughter?' Peroni asked.

'It could be.'

'Could be?'

'Yes,' he said with audible impatience. 'Could be.'

The American woman had stopped talking to her workmen. She was watching them and Costa didn't like the curiosity in her face.

'Let's talk about this outside,' he suggested.

CHAPTER 7

It was a brief conversation. The narrow street was empty, with barricades at both ends and pedestrains allowed through only down a narrow route on the far side. Costa looked up at the scaffolding and the broken balcony, understanding the form of the building better than he had before. The place looked different in the bright light of day. More ordinary. More unremarkable.

They talked briefly about what they'd seen and the options.

'I'll call Leo and get things started,' Costa said, reaching for his phone.

'Whoa, whoa, whoa. We didn't agree to that.'

He bridled.

'May I remind you I'm the senior officer here?'

Peroni beamed, placed a huge hand round Costa's shoulders and squeezed.

'By all means. When you're on duty. But you're not, are you? Right now you're nothing more or less than my dear friend, Nic, casting around for something to do. If this is going to turn formal it's best it's kicked off by a working police officer, not someone who's just got nosy all of a sudden.

And if it turns out to be a wild goose chase and we find ourselves accused of picking on some unfortunate grieving family . . .'

'I don't need protecting, thank you,' Costa protested, though he found himself talking to the big cop's retreating back.

There was nothing to do but wait. Wait and look at the building, grey and grim, like some empty shell of a fortress. He couldn't shake from his head the photo Peroni had found, the bookmark for the chapter Malise Gabriel was reading before he tumbled to his death just a few steps away, to a street now swept and washed clean by the city workers struggling to reopen it to the public.

Costa wondered what bothered him most. The evidence that was already being lost under the feet of the building inspectors. Or the pale, thin body in the photo.

Peroni came back, his face devoid of expression.

'Something has to happen,' Costa said, assuming the worst.

'Tomorrow we'll talk to the mother and the girl. Teresa will look at the body. We'll quietly examine what we've got to see if a more formal investigation is justified. Leo doesn't want to rush into anything and I agree with him.'

'And today?'

'Today we're going to have dinner together.' Peroni brightened. 'I get to choose the place.'

'Dinner? We're going to discuss a potential investigation in a restaurant?'

'No. We're going to discuss . . . what was the phrase in that book? "Non-overlapping magisteria". Or rather Malise Gabriel, who's rather more interesting than I assumed. Sora Margherita in the Piazza delle Cinque Scole at eight o'clock.' He pointed up the street. 'It's just round the corner.'

'I know where Cinque Scole is.'

'Good. It'll be Leo, me and Teresa, who may still be a little bad-tempered what with this heat and our non-existent air conditioning. I've warned you so don't get snappy with her.' Peroni glanced at his watch. 'I'd best be off. Got to check something at the Questura.'

He peered at Costa then pulled two plastic evidence bags out of his jacket.

'The book and the postcard please.'

Costa handed them over without protest.

After a few steps he turned, remembering something.

'Oh yes,' he said, walking slowly backwards. 'Agata's going to be there this evening too. Best go home and change into something decent. You look as if you slept in that suit. In a garage.'

PART III

CHAPTER 1

He didn't go home. Costa bought a bottle of mineral water and wandered the ghetto, renewing his memories of an area he'd had little reason to visit professionally over the past few years. Then he walked into the open space of Largo Torre Argentina, a chaotic, semi-excavated pile of temples and imperial-era buildings next to a line of busy bus and tram stops. This was one place he did know well. He recalled the day he'd taken his late wife there and pointed out the columns of Pompey's Theatre near the tram stops where Julius Caesar was assassinated. Nothing marked the location of this momentous murder. In the modern world the area, which was once as important as the Forum itself, was best known to many for the cat sanctuary that resided between the pillars and shattered head-stones through which emperors once walked.

He was leaning on the railing, staring down into the walled-off area of the refuge when he saw her. Mina Gabriel was there in a T-shirt and jeans, crouching down feeding three strays near the furthest wall, close to the columns associated with Caesar. Two women in their thirties were talking

85

to her, with grave and sympathetic faces. The girl got up, turned, smiled briefly, kissed them both, smiling gently, and said something that looked like '*grazie*'. Then she came back to the entrance, picked up a leather music case and began to walk up the steps to the street level.

Costa strode quickly over and met her.

'Mina?'

She looked tired. Her guileless brown eyes were pink and watery, her young, intelligent face drawn. She'd tied back her hair into a simple ponytail so that she now looked much younger than he recalled. With the music case slung over her shoulder like a satchel she could have been one more Roman schoolgirl.

Head cocked to one side, a little wary, she looked at him and said, 'Yes?'

'Nic Costa. I was the police officer. The other night . . . Your father. I wish I could have done more.'

She thought for a moment and asked, 'The man in the street? You carried him across the road?'

'The man in the street.'

The girl nodded.

'You carried me too. When I wouldn't get out of the way. I'm sorry if I behaved badly.'

'You've nothing to apologize for.'

She looked around, as if trying to work out whether he was alone. He couldn't help but notice there were scratches on her hands. Old ones, the blood dark red.

'Are you here to interview me?'

'No, no. I was just passing. I'm on holiday at the moment. I saw you. I wanted to say . . . to offer my condolences.'

'Everyone's so kind here,' she said, staring at him, her eyes very steady and focused. 'Even though they don't know us. The women at the sanctuary. The people at the church.' She held up her music bag. 'They're going to let me play there. In front of the public. At five o'clock.'

'Are you sure you want to do that?'

'Why not?' she replied with a shrug. 'I can't sit at home all the time, thinking about what happened, wondering if I could have changed something. My brother's still out there somewhere, I don't know where. Mummy's talking to Uncle Simon about organizing a funeral in Berkshire. Not that that's going to be an easy conversation. He hated Daddy.'

'Why would your father's brother hate him?'

She shrugged and said, 'I don't know. We've never met Simon. I just hear what goes on. He's a banker in London. Filthy rich and materialistic. Nothing matters to him except money. Exact opposite to us. It doesn't matter. Mummy wants to deal with all that. I can't sit around moping. Daddy wouldn't. He was always doing something.'

She had forty minutes before the appointment in the nearby church of Aracoeli.

'Would you like a coffee? We can talk if you want.'

Mina Gabriel stared at him more intently, and he was aware of being judged, perhaps by a child,

87

perhaps by someone with an older, more informed intelligence.

'A Coke would be nice,' she answered. 'It's so hot here in August. I never expected it to be like this. None of us did.'

'It's hot,' he agreed. 'A Coke. An ice cream if you like.'

She smiled and said, 'Just a Coke, thanks. I'm not a kid.'

They began to walk towards the piazza.

'Your hands,' Costa said. They were fine and slim, with long, musician's fingers. The scratches extended from the knuckle almost to the wrist on her right. 'You've hurt yourself. Can you play?'

'Cats,' she replied. 'Horrible little things, sometimes. Ungrateful. It's nothing. I can play.'

CHAPTER 2

He let her do the talking. About her father, about life in a family led by an academic gypsy, moving from post to post, in America, Canada, the UK and Australia, never staying anywhere long. Costa didn't ask why they never settled down. As he listened to her chatting, noting the way the conversation came round to Malise Gabriel with almost every turn, the answer seemed to become obvious. It had to do with his obdurate, independent character, the way the man would always stand up for what he believed in, whatever the cost. Mina simply called them 'the arguments'.

Then came Rome.

'This was supposed to be the last place,' she said. 'Somewhere we settled down. We had connections. Daddy's maternal grandmother was Italian. She was called Mina too. I'm sort of named after her. In Italian it's short for Wilhelmina. Daddy put Minerva on my birth certificate. The goddess of wisdom. Don't ask me why. There's no one in the family left here, I don't think. It was supposed to be a good move for Daddy, not working inside a

89

university ever again. Just some little academic institution. Fewer people to fall out with.'

'What did he do?' he asked.

'Write. Talk. Edit academic papers.' She picked at a discarded napkin on the counter. 'I think it was beneath him, really. But he had to do it. There was nowhere left to go, really. We had to live.'

'I talked to Joanne Van Doren,' he said.

'I thought you said you were on holiday?'

'I am. But I was a witness. I had to be involved a little.'

He didn't like lying to her, and he wasn't sure it had worked.

'Joanne's very kind. She bought me some musical stuff we couldn't afford.'

'She said you did a lot of research about Beatrice Cenci.'

'You know Beatrice?' Her face lit up for the first time.

'I was born here. It's one of those Roman stories you pick up if you read a lot of books. But foreigners . . .'

'How could I not know? We were almost opposite the palace where she lived. The street. The name of the *vicolo*, the piazza. Do you think they'd still be called Cenci if it weren't for her?'

'No.'

'We had a plan. When Joanne had the apartments ready she'd use the Beatrice connection to sell them. Not that the building had anything to do with her, but . . . Business, I suppose.'

'What did your father think?'

She looked briefly guilty.

'I never told him. He'd have been cross. He hated business. 'Filthy lucre', he called it. We were an academic family. We were supposed to be above that.' She glanced at him. 'Joanne would have paid me. There's nothing wrong in that, is there?'

'Nothing,' he said, and this seemed to reassure her. 'What would you have done?'

'The Beatrice tour. All the places in Rome that were connected to her. The Barberini. Montorio.' Her face grew serious. 'A few others too. You're a Roman. You must know.'

'I don't actually.'

He remembered how he'd held back from visiting the sites when he was younger, which was against his nature. He loved his native city. Normally he wanted to know the history of every last corner, every brick and cobble. But with Beatrice Cenci, the interest seemed prurient, wrong somehow.

'Is your mother coping? Does she need help?'

The girl scowled.

'How would I know? Mummy thinks I'm a child. I need to be protected from all that. There's no point in arguing. We're not a . . . conventional family. Also . . .' There was a subtle though noticeable change in her expression, a coolness he had not seen before. 'She's got Bernard to help her. She doesn't need me.'

'Bernard?'

'Bernard Santacroce. He runs the organization Daddy worked for. Filthy rich. Our benefactor. He gave Daddy the job in the first place. I imagine we're dependent on his generosity now.'

'He's Roman?'

She frowned.

'Bernard's English really. Of Italian stock, as he puts it. He claims he's one of the old Santacroces. They hated the Cenci. He bought the palazzetto off a relative, I think, and got the Brotherhood of the Owls running again. It had fallen apart a bit.' She wriggled upright on her little stool in the cafe, looking like a schoolgirl who'd found the right answer. 'The Santacroce claimed they were descended from Valerius Publicola, one of the original founders of the Roman republic. They even added the word "Publicola" to their full name. The Cenci had to retaliate, of course, so they said they were descendants of the Cincii, another famous republican family. Seems a bit petty to me. You live, you die. Who cares except the people who knew you? Your parents. Your children. Then they're gone too.'

'How do you know all this?' he asked.

She looked at him as if the question were stupid.

'I read books, of course.'

'I know that, but . . .' He'd felt this way himself at her age. Then something got in the way, something he didn't want to mention to her. His own mother's illness had pushed him towards the Beatrice Cenci story. Her premature death had

92

made it too painful to pursue his curiosity all the way, to visit those last mournful places that marked the young girl's end. 'But why?'

She thought for a moment.

'Dunno really. When we came here it just seemed the natural thing to do. It's not like America. Or Canada. Or anywhere else. Rome's a little world, all its own.' She glanced out of the window of the cafe by the Piazza Venezia, at the busy square beyond, and its monumental buildings, Aracoeli, the Capitoline museums, the hideous Vittorio Emanuele monument the locals called 'the type-writer', the 'wedding cake' and much worse. 'All that history . . . it sort of swallowed me. I felt at home, and I'd never felt that about anywhere before.'

Mina sucked on the straw of her Coke.

'I talked to Daddy. I told him this was what I wanted to do when I grew up. To write about Rome. To tell people about all the things they never saw. To open their eyes. He said . . .' Mina Gabriel seemed to be trying to recall his exact words. 'He said I should let this place infect me as much as I possibly could. Haunt me. Like a ghost. Or a . . .' One more hunt for the correct term. '. . . succubus. Something that possesses you. You won't understand. If you grew up here you'd take it for granted. I know I would.'

Costa didn't say anything. He was stealing a glance at her right hand again, wondering if the scratches there were really the work of a cat.

93

She leaned forward and looked up into his face. 'I could show you if you like,' she said. 'Tomorrow.'

'Show me?'

'Yes. The places. Beatrice's places.'

'You'll have things to do.'

'I told you. Mummy won't let me. We could go on the tour I invented for Joanne. It would be good to get out. To talk to someone new. I hate sitting around doing nothing. I get that from Daddy. Everyone said we were alike. Peas from the same pod. There were two things he loathed more than any other. Idleness and hypocrisy. Please.'

Costa couldn't think of a way to say no. In his head he was trying to frame a different question.

'How did you get on with your father?' he asked.

She stared straight into his face, her wide, young eyes unblinking, and said, 'I loved him. And he loved me. That's how it's supposed to be, isn't it?'

'Exactly,' he said.

CHAPTER 3

Mina Gabriel checked her watch then picked up the music case.

'I've got to go to the church now. I'm doing this for him. Daddy adored this piece. Odd really. It's religious. Everything Messiaen did was. Look.'

Mina opened the bag and showed him the music: *Transports de joie d'unne âme devant la glorie du Christ qui est la sinenne.*

'*Ecstasies of a soul before the glory of Christ, which is its own glory,*' Mina translated. 'A very long title, if you ask me. Ridiculously so. We just call it *Transports de joie.*'

She finished her Coke then went to the counter and bought a chocolate bar, ripping off the wrapping, taking a big bite.

'Want to come and listen?' she asked, mouth half-full.

'I'm not a Catholic.'

'Me neither. It's just music. Got to feed the cats at ten thirty tomorrow. We can meet afterwards if you want. Up to you. I don't mind being on my own. Honest.'

They crossed the Piazza Venezia together, dodging the fractious traffic, then ascended the broad sweep of steps that led up to Santa Maria in Aracoeli, St Mary of the Altar of Heaven. It was one of his favourite Roman churches, in part because its name alluded to another, pagan past. Perched on the Capitoline hill overlooking the Forum, this was once the site of an important imperial-era temple. Images of the Emperor Augustus and the Tiburtine Sibyl still stood on the high altar, commemorating the legend that Augustus had received a vision of the coming of the Catholic Church from the Sibyl herself, in his temple on this very spot. Rome's distant and near pasts, two different though related kinds of superstition, converged in the darkness of this quiet and holy place, and lived there happily, side by side.

The organ stood in a dark corner of the cavernous church. Mina Gabriel disappeared behind some nearby curtains and returned wearing an ecclesiastical gown that made her look like a choir girl. Then she climbed onto the long bench in front of the instrument. He watched how she positioned herself easily over the keyboard, the stops and the vast array of pedals beneath her feet, as if coming home.

He took a seat at the end of a row, half-hidden in the shadows. The low, sonorous growl of the instrument grew out of the persistent gloom of the nave, seeming to come from everywhere. The music was like nothing he'd ever heard, both harmonious and discordant, free-flowing, without the conventions of time and melody which he expected. There was something ethereal yet disturbing in its clashing tones. As he watched, the girl seemed to become a part of the device, one more complex component of the vast, incomprehensible machine in front of her.

The sun shifted position. A ray of sunlight burst through one of the high church windows. It fell on her left cheek and he saw that the white skin there was wet with tears, awash with some released emotion she'd kept back for the shade of the basilica.

The sight of her touched him, more than he expected, more than he wanted. Costa found his own eyes growing damp as he followed her anxious, taut body flying over the keys and stops and pedals of the ancient organ, extracting from the instrument the composer's tortured paean to an invisible yet omnipresent creator, a frail young girl trapped entirely by its mechanisms and the effect they produced.

He wiped his face with his sleeve and quietly walked out by the side door, to the little staircase that led up to the more familiar Campidoglio, the summit, a stage in stone set by Michelangelo to mark the *caput mundi*, the head of the world.

The early evening was airless and hot. There was no time to return home before the meal Peroni had organized. He sat in the piazza, in the shadow of the great bronze statue of Marcus Aurelius on horseback, waiting, thinking, wondering.

CHAPTER 4

Peroni's choice of restaurant was always likely to prove controversial, with Falcone at least. When Costa arrived, feeling more than slightly grubby and sweat-stained, the small gathering was standing in the Piazza delle Cinque Scole, directly opposite one side of the squat mass of the Palazzo Cenci on its little hill.

'There must be somewhere else,' Falcone complained, arms folded, face suffused with heat. He had looked a little leaner of late, which made his silver goatee seem somewhat theatrical, almost like that of a stage wizard. In a pale linen suit, stiff with outrage in this modest corner of Rome, his anger seemed almost comically petulant, a point not lost on Agata Graziano, who stood to one side with Teresa, scratching her petite dark nose to hide her mirth. Agata and Falcone had enjoyed a long, secret and somewhat strange bond. She was an orphan child who grew up in a convent school. As a young cop Falcone had secretly donated part of his salary to charity, perhaps out of a sense of guilt at the failure of his own marriage. It had been used to pay for Agata's education. When

99

Falcone discovered this, ever curious, he had arranged to meet the young girl, liked her, and the two had come to form an odd bond, close yet detached too, both grateful to the other for something they rarely acknowledged. Unconsciously, perhaps against his own wishes, Falcone had become in some sense a substitute yet distant parent. The relationship allowed her rather more leeway with him than was afforded to most.

'I like the look of it, Leo,' Agata said cheerily. 'You don't have to eat in a fancy restaurant every day, do you?'

'It's not even a restaurant, really, is it?'

Costa pitched in.

'My father used to bring me here. He said it's real working-class Roman food.'

Falcone shot him a filthy look, up and down the grubby suit, and grumbled, 'My point exactly.'

'You said I could choose,' Peroni pointed out, waving a handful of tickets. 'And we're members now.'

In one sense at least, the grumpy old inspector was correct. Sora Margherita was no longer a restaurant. The city authorities had complained about the lack of facilities in the tiny dining room set behind a small door in the ghetto and, amidst local outrage, forced the place to close. Then the owners discovered a loophole, and reopened as the 'Associazione Culturale Sora Margherita'. A dining club, membership free, fees charged according to how much one ate and drank. At which point the city gave up and culinary life in the ghetto returned to normal.

Costa walked round to Agata and Teresa, kissed them both on the cheek, took his membership ticket from the set proffered by Peroni and led the way inside. Within fifteen minutes they were in a quiet corner away from the only other group braving the scorching night, seated in front of some of the best *carciofi alla giudia*, deepfried artichokes, he'd ever encountered. The wine was from Velletri. The staff were charming and quite unperturbed by the argument at the door. Even Falcone began to smile after a while. Then the conversation started in earnest.

The topic was Malise Gabriel, a man with a curious first name, Gaelic it seemed. He was an ethologist, a scientist specializing in the study of animal behaviour, who graduated from Cambridge and won a readership there before he turned thirty. Ten years later he wrote the book which Peroni found in the apartment, *All the Gods are Dead*. The title came from Nietzsche's *Thus Spake Zarathustra*, though Gabriel's work made Nietzsche's attack on the Church appear mild. It was a calculated, prolonged and highly detailed assault on organized religion and religious thought, a broadside that had managed to offend Catholics, Muslims, Protestants, Buddhists and Hindus alike, while selling millions and entering multiple translations. For one brief year the book had been everywhere: cited as a cruel and corrosive diatribe

101

by its critics and a brave and perceptively fresh analysis by its supporters, the first shot in a war in which secularism would reclaim the moral high ground for good, dispatching religion to the fantasy world of superstition where Malise Gabriel felt it belonged. Then this controversial academic fell abruptly out of the public eye, resigned from Cambridge and left the country, to embark upon the shifting and footloose academic career, much of it spent with inferior institutions, which had led him ultimately to Rome.

Falcone was not idle that afternoon. He had pieced together some of the story and what he had to reveal gave Costa pause. Cecilia Urquhart was, like Gabriel, part of a long-established English aristocratic family, hers Protestant, his originally Catholic. A bright and precocious pupil at school, she had won a place at Cambridge when she was eighteen. It was there, months later, that she met Gabriel, there that she fell pregnant. Gabriel resigned from the university to avoid the ensuing scandal and Cecilia lost what appeared to be a promising academic career. He never wrote another book and became something of a wandering pariah. His last post in Wisconsin ended the way of most of its predecessors: summary dismissal over an undisclosed internal argument. After that, he came to Rome, employed principally as an editor with the curious institution known as the Confraternita delle Civette.

'Ridiculous name,' Peroni grumbled.

Teresa sighed and said, 'You know, you people amaze me. There's a million television programmes about the history of art and politics and society. But something about science? Never.'

Pasta arrived from a beaming waiter, simple and delicious with tomato sauce.

'The Brotherhood of the Owls was one of the oldest and most revered scientific institutions in Italy,' the pathologist went on.

'Was?' Costa asked.

She squirmed a touch.

'I thought it had packed in a few years ago, to be honest,' she admitted. 'Apparently some Englishman came back and rescued it. All the same it's still odd you've never even heard of it. This is your history too.'

Costa recalled what Peroni had said about Teresa and hot weather. It seemed spot on.

'What about Galileo?' she asked. 'Anyone heard of him?'

He remembered the bookmark, and the curious words written on the flip side of what looked suspiciously like a photo of the naked Mina Gabriel. Their origin had come back to him that afternoon as he sat on the Campidoglio, beneath the statue of Marcus Aurelius.

'"*E pur si muove*",' Costa said. '"And yet it moves". Galileo said that when . . .' He fought to recall the precise circumstances. 'When he was in a tight corner or something.'

Teresa Lupo put down her fork. Always a bad sign.

'"In a tight corner"? The Catholic Inquisition put him on trial for his life. All because he had the temerity to prove, beyond any reasonable doubt, that the earth moved round the sun, not the other way round, whatever the Pope of the time thought. They made him choose between being burned alive at the stake as a heretic, as the Vatican did with another awkward genius, Giordano Bruno, in the Campo dei Fiori a few years before. Or renouncing his beliefs, which he knew absolutely to be true.'

'I remember this story,' Peroni announced, waving some *bigoli* around the table, spattering sauce everywhere. 'As Galileo walked away from the Inquisition he muttered, "and yet it moves". Just to let everyone know he hadn't really changed his mind.'

'Precisely.'

'Brave man,' he added.

'Why would Malise Gabriel write that on a book-mark?' Falcone wondered. 'And what does this have to do with the Brotherhood of the Owls?'

Teresa cast a savage look in his direction.

'A lot. Let me tell you something. At the beginning of the 1990s I was a student at La Sapienza. A Cardinal of the Catholic Church came to give a lecture about religion and science.' She shook her head, as if still unable to believe what she was about to disclose. 'He turned up and told us that the outrage among the scientific community about Galileo's treatment, his forced recantation on pain of death, was somehow our problem. Something to do with the self-doubt of the modern age. And who was that Cardinal?'

She leaned forward and looked at Agata, who was sitting quietly picking at her food.

'None other than one Cardinal Ratzinger. Your Pope!'

'Not my Pope,' Agata replied. 'The Church's Pope. Everyone's. Bookmark? What bookmark? I don't know what you're talking about.'

Teresa harrumphed, folded her arms and stared at Falcone.

'I'm not sure, either,' she declared. 'I merely give you some facts. The Brotherhood of the Owls is a scientific academy of like-minded men founded by the supporters of Galileo around the time of his trial, one which made him a member, not that he asked for it, or perhaps even appreciated the honour.'

'So,' Peroni asked, trying to understand, 'they would be on Galileo's side? Malise Gabriel's side?'

'Not exactly,' Teresa continued. 'The Brotherhood was formed to try to persuade the Vatican there was a middle way in dealing with Galileo. That the Church and science could live happily alongside one another, agreeing on occasion to disagree. They wanted to say we should leave science to the scientists and religion to the Church.'

She looked at each of them in turn.

'They were fools. The Pope wasn't interested in common ground. He did as he pleased, and Galileo spent the rest of his life under house arrest, simply for telling the truth.'

Peroni ordered some meat and an extra plate of vegetables for Nic. And more water. It was getting hotter in the little restaurant.

'I still don't see the bookmark . . .' Falcone began, fishing as always.

'This is what Malise Gabriel was writing about in his book,' Teresa explained. '*All the Gods are Dead* was a concerted argument for the idea that science could and should investigate and, if need be, destroy, anything in its path, however painful, however awkward, whatever the damage. The quest for knowledge was everything, and could accept no boundaries. The position of the Church was that unbridled curiosity was none of Galileo's business, and it would take his life if he insisted it was. The Confraternita delle Civette, on the other hand, held that science and religion were separate fields, which could on occassion overlap, but without the need for conflict. Malise Gabriel kicked life back into one of the biggest and most bitter scientific debates there's ever been. Without him we might never have had Richard Dawkins and Stephen Jay Gould going head to head the way they did. Gabriel was a wrecked genius, one rather more tragic than Galileo by the sound of it. But the odd thing is he ended up in the territory of . . .'

She put down her knife and fork, unhappy with something.

'I was about to say the territory of the enemy. But the Confraternita aren't that. They're just not as extreme as he is. They were always intent on reconciling science and religion. Not raising one to the heights and destroying the other. Odd place for him to fetch up. The middle ground. Not much room for that kind of thinking these days. We tend to be one thing or the other. I was amazed somebody had revived the old beast, to be honest with you.'

They went quiet. Then Agata said, 'I remember some of that. Galileo stayed at the Palazzo Madama for a while, as Caravaggio had earlier. Science and religion weren't enemies. Galileo believed he was pursuing knowledge in order to become closer to God. He wasn't an atheist, like this man Gabriel.'

'Given how things turned out, does that really make a difference?' Teresa asked. 'Truth is truth, whether you believe in a god or not. The earth isn't flat. The sun doesn't revolve around us and never has. People die and that's it.'

They looked at one another, wondering who would have the courage to protest. It was Agata who spoke.

'You don't know about that final point,' she said quietly. 'No one does.'

'Come and spend a day with me some time,' the pathologist shot back. 'See what you think then.'

Agata Graziano put down her knife and fork.

'I'm out of my depth in these things. Why are

we here? That poor girl in the street . . . her father died. Whether he was controversial, or a man who got into some scandal, what's it matter? Malise Gabriel was still with his wife and family twenty years later. He surely loved them. There, at least, he must have found something he could believe in.'

'That's true,' Falcone agreed.

'The photograph . . .' Costa began.

Peroni and Falcone began coughing simultaneously, glaring at him from across the table.

Agata watched them, then got up, saying, 'Excuse me. I need a breath of fresh air.'

They were silent as she walked out, then Peroni nudged Costa's elbow and murmured, 'Go and have a word, will you?'

'And say what? Sorry we insulted your faith and everything you believe in?'

'Tell her the sweets are fantastic. That usually works with women.'

Teresa groaned and let her large head fall into her equally large hands. Falcone was holding his wine glass up to the light, muttering noises full of approval and a genuine surprise.

August, Costa thought.

CHAPTER 5

Agata was leaning against the wall, eyes closed, looking tired. A pretty young woman in her early thirties, doubtless worried about the job she'd start tomorrow, the first real employment she'd ever had. It was thoughtless of Falcone to invite her out, especially on dubious pretences. He'd clearly briefed Teresa fully before the meal, and was fishing for more information about Malise Gabriel and his background in the Confraternita delle Civette.

'It's stifling in there,' Costa said as he joined her.

'What is this?' she asked with a touch of anger. 'Why am I here? If you wish to have meals to discuss your cases, do so. But please tell Leo to leave me out of them. I saw enough of the world you live in two nights ago. I don't want to meet it again. Not for a long time.'

He glanced at the piazza, and the Cenci building opposite.

'It's still there, though. "And yet it moves".'

It was a very strange thing for someone to write on a bookmark.

'You dragged me into one of your cases once before. I don't want it to happen again.'

109

He took a deep breath and said, 'I don't recall that you needed much dragging. Nor is this my case. Or any case as far as I'm aware. Leo's just . . . being inquisitive. He's interested in this man. And that message. These strange institutions. I can understand why he'd want to know more. Can't you?'

'It's none of my business.'

'I'll let him know. Sorry. Can I walk you home?'

'No,' she murmured, looking down the street towards the Via Arenula and the way back. 'Tell them thank you for the meal.'

'Can I . . . come by some time? To see how the job's going? I am on holiday.'

'You're at a loose end?' she said with a welcome smile.

'Precisely.'

'Well, I'm not.'

She took out her little phone and waved it at him. Agata was very well dressed for a hot Sunday night: grey slacks, a cream shirt, a necklace. Her curly black hair was no longer unruly, and once again her petite, dark face wore make-up. She looked beautiful and he wished this were the time to tell her so, though he felt scruffy and realized why both Falcone and Peroni had cast caustic glances at his oil-stained suit earlier.

'Call first, Nic. You promise?'

'Promise.'

She was gone so quickly there wasn't time even for a friendly embrace. He watched her disappear back into the ghetto, the way Robert Gabriel had presumably taken when he fled after his father's death. It seemed a distant and unreal event on a beautiful, lazy evening like this.

The rest of them tumbled noisily out of the door, Falcone and Peroni fighting each other for the privilege of picking up the bill.

'Was it something I said?' Teresa asked.

'What do you think?' Costa demanded abruptly. 'She's still a Catholic, you know.'

'The truth hurts, I imagine. I still can't believe what Ratzinger did. He tried to come back not long ago. The academic staff put a stop to that one. Wouldn't even let him through the door.'

'Well, there's freedom of expression for you,' he snapped. 'None of this was Agata's fault, was it?'

Teresa's broad, intelligent face fell.

'Oh dear. I'm sorry, Nic. I never meant to offend her. Anything but. It's this awful heat. She doesn't look like a nun any more. I thought . . .'

She shrugged and looked very sorry.

'She never was a nun,' Costa pointed out. 'And who cares about a speech from twenty years ago?'

'When it tries to belittle the persecution of a brilliant man for telling the truth, I care. We all should,' she insisted. Then she paused and asked, 'Did we learn anything tonight? Really?'

The two older men stopped bickering and looked at him, waiting for an answer.

'I learned that Malise Gabriel was an intriguing man who made enemies very easily,' Costa said.

'That he died in curious circumstances that may, if you look closely enough, prove to be suspicious. And also . . .' He thought about Mina Gabriel. '. . . that he was a soldier in some kind of war, maybe. One most of us wouldn't even understand. He must have lost all those jobs for a reason. That's it. I'm a cop. What more do you expect?'

Teresa grinned, pecked him on the cheek and said, 'Nothing. I wish I hadn't upset Agata. I'll call her and apologize. Take her out for a coffee.'

'She's busy.'

'I'm persistent. I told you. It's August. Drives you mad. And what happened at La Sapienza – it still gets to me after all these years.'

'Do you have a case?' Costa asked Falcone straight out.

The inspector smiled and patted him fondly on the shoulder.

'Thanks for coming to dinner, Nic. You must excuse us. We've a busy day tomorrow. Enjoy your holiday. Any plans yourself?'

He thought about it and said, 'Not really. I thought I might mess around with the Vespa. I can show you if you like. She's round the corner.'

Falcone gazed at him in horror.

'Quite. Sadly I have to go now,' the inspector said. 'Good evening.'

PART IV

CHAPTER 1

There was a knack to bringing to life the little engine on the thirty-year-old Vespa. It involved depressing the kick-start halfway, hesitating a second before pumping hard twice, sometimes three times. Then he would wait for the pop-pop of the primitive ignition to kick in and light the fire that would despatch a brief blue-grey cloud of two-stroke smoke into the atmosphere. After that the machine would settle into a dyspeptic rumble, kept alive by blips on the throttle. This all required care. One pump too many and the carburettor filled with fuel, demanding a wait of up to five minutes, or, if he became impatient and tried again too soon, a messy strip-down.

All the same he loved the little beast and the sense of freedom it brought. On its worn plastic saddle, wearing a pair of thick-rimmed sunglasses, he could almost ignore the sweltering heat that was Rome. Costa had bought two brand-new helmets and, on this bright, humid Monday, picked out some old casual clothes – a polo shirt and some ancient jeans – for the trip into the city, weaving through the traffic with ease, making the journey in half the time it took by car.

Mina was in the refuge already, placing dishes of food on the ground near the shattered columns of Pompey's Theatre, talking to the older women who ran the place.

He watched her, asking himself why he was doing this. Leo Falcone was intrigued by what had happened in the Via Beatrice Cenci in the early hours of the previous Saturday. That much was obvious from the sly way the inspector had been extracting opinions about Malise Gabriel the night before, exploring the background to the English academic who, twenty years ago, had been something of a brief and controversial sensation. If Falcone saw signs of a criminal act then a swift investigation would follow, even in the enervating heat of summer. But it occurred to Costa that Mina Gabriel would, perhaps, be the key, and there Falcone's robust and conventional approach might fail. The solitary inspector was never at home in cases that involved family, children in particular. They depressed and embarrassed him, more than they did most officers. And Costa couldn't shake from his mind the impression he'd gained in those first moments when he saw Mina Gabriel next to the shattered corpse of her father. The idea that she wanted to speak out, to reveal something that troubled her. Surrounded by strangers, with no one to talk to and Leo Falcone pressing for answers, she might be lost. Unless

116

he established some bond, some measure of trust.

This strategy concerned him nevertheless. It was a dangerous trick to play with a witness who might turn into a suspect should it be proved that Malise Gabriel's death was not the accident it seemed. He wondered what lawyers would make of his attempt to get close to a girl who had just turned seventeen, barely beyond the age at which she could be interviewed formally – and even then only in the presence of her mother.

'There's no case and I'm on holiday,' Costa told himself as he sat on the scooter, waiting for her. 'I can do what I like.'

Then step away should anything untoward emerge, he thought.

He was still trying to convince himself of this when she climbed up the steps and smiled at him, the two helmets in his hand, and then at the little machine, mostly turquoise paint, though with a modicum of rust and restorative plain grey primer, parked on its foot-stand by the pavement.

'A scooter?' Mina asked, wide-eyed.

Another cheap T-shirt, perhaps the same pair of jeans. Her long blonde hair hung loose over her shoulders. She looked like any of the thousands of foreign students who wandered Rome all year long. Perhaps prettier, more engaged than most though. Her eyes had an acuity he hadn't noticed before. They were no longer touched by recent tears. The scratches on her hands were beginning to fade too.

With them, perhaps, evidence, he thought, and felt immediately guilty.

'It was my father's,' he said without thinking.

She took the helmet from him.

'What do I do?'

He showed her the footrests and said, 'You hang on. Where are we going first?'

'To see the painting,' she said. 'To the Barberini. You know the way?'

'I think I can find it,' he said, and climbed on the machine.

The Vespa started after two kicks and then they were threading through the hectic traffic and the back streets, crossing the busy shopping street of the Corso, heading uphill towards the Barberini, Mina Gabriel clinging tightly to his waist.

CHAPTER 2

osta flashed his police ID and was allowed to park the battered Vespa in a staff area next to the patio of the imposing marble palace on the hill, though not without a few raised eyebrows from the security officers at the gate. They entered through the porticoed entrance and marched up Borromini's winding helicoidal staircase into the stately residence of the Barberini. He followed the girl as she strode through the vast halls and glittering corridors of a palazzo with which she was clearly familiar. In Rome it was impossible not to stumble over an unexpected nexus in places like this, some snaking, unforeseen connection between events that were, on the surface, unrelated. The most famous member of the Barberini family was Maffeo, Urban VIII, the very Pope who had forced Galileo to recant his beliefs on pain of death. He was a despot, pillaging Rome for his own purposes, removing the precious bronze girders from the portico of the Pantheon in order to make cannons for his army. Knowledgeable Romans still muttered a cynical Latin saying that had been repeated in the city for nearly four centuries: *quod non fecerunt barbari, fecerunt Barberini.* What the barbarians didn't do, the Barberini did. The clan was now extinct. It was ironic that their principal legacy in Rome was a palazzo famed for its rich art collection gathered by others, with Raphael's supposed mistress *La Fornarina* and Holbein's portrait of Henry VIII among its treasures.

Mina walked as if he wasn't there, heading straight for the early seventeenth-century portraits. It all came back. Guercino's *St Matthew and the Angel. The Flagellation of Christ.* A minutely detailed Annibale Carracci wooden altarpiece. And behind, high on the wall, with some other, lesser works, the face he'd come to recognize as the girl who died on the scaffold in front of the Ponte Sant' Angelo.

She was as he remembered, a solitary figure mainly in white, set against shadow, staring back at her audience over a shoulder wrapped in pale material like a shroud, her face luminous, sad, dark eyes intent on the viewer, unyielding. Over the centuries this image had become Beatrice Cenci, for the public, for an army of poets and writers and artists. These features had come to sum up the very essence of the young woman's character: defiant yet submissive to her fate, an innocent forced to resort to the ultimate sin in order to defend her own dignity and independence.

Just then he glanced at Mina. The resemblance

between her and the portrait was, he now saw, fleeting, more a matter of a look, an expression, an attitude. Yet there was a connection between them, a bond visible in the way this modern girl's eyes were fixed on the painting with an avid intent so heated that Costa wanted to walk straight out of the room, out into the scorching, sunny day and forget everything he knew about the Cenci, their prison in the ghetto, the terrible family intrigue which had led to Beatrice's tragedy.

'You see what they've done?' Mina asked, dragging him back to earth. 'They hide her up there, so you can't see her eyes, her pain and how she forgives them too. All of them. So they make you stand back, hoping you won't see the truth. When Shelley was here . . .' He caught sight of her hands. Her delicate long fingers were balling into tense, angry fists. 'That picture wasn't high on the wall like that. He could look her straight in the face. Read the books. He was allowed to see. It's as if they're still ashamed. Four hundred years later.'

'The Barberini has a lot of paintings to show,' Costa said, and that was true.

She was chewing gum like any other teenager, thinking, looking like any other teenager. There was a music player and a set of cheap headphones poking out of her jeans pocket. She squinted at the canvas and said, 'Thanks for reminding me.'

Then she dragged him by the arm back into the room they'd just passed quickly through, and he knew exactly what they were going to see, understood that she had made the very link that had occurred to him some fifteen years or so before, when he was around the same age, mooching in these great chambers, staring at the dead faces on the walls.

Caravaggio's *Judith Beheading Holofernes* was a canvas on a different and darker scale. A large painting, it occupied much of its wall in the adjoining hall, tenebrous and violent, screaming to be seen, to be witnessed. It depicted the young woman, Judith, in a virginal white smock as she decapitated the naked Holofernes, the warrior she had seduced in order to save her city from destruction. The savage, shining blade had hacked through most of the screaming man's neck as she grasped his hair, pulling, holding tightly. Bone and tissue were visible. Blood flowed freely onto the crumpled sheets beneath him. By Judith's side stood a servant, a cloth bag in her hands, ready to seize the severed head and return it to the city, proof its tyrannical besieger was dead.

Mina stared at the work, a thoughtful finger to her lips.

'This was painted the year, maybe the year after, Beatrice was executed. When she died, all of Rome was there. Caravaggio must have been among them.' She waited, watching him. 'You don't sound surprised.'

'He wouldn't have missed it for anything,' Costa said quietly.

She hesitated for a moment, her expression quite impenetrable, then asked, 'So is this a version of what he saw? The death of Beatrice painted through some kind of mirror? I don't mean the physical details. They're unimportant. Look at Judith's face.'

He saw what he always did when he came into this room. A woman forced to commit a terrible act out of duty, not desire. There was shock, regret, even shame in her pained features, which were not dissimilar to those of Beatrice Cenci in the adjoining room.

'What do you want me to see?' he asked.

'That she's sorry! Holofernes was the general sent to wipe out her people. By killing him she saved them. Why would she pity him?'

'Because in the classical tradition a woman was thought to be more compassionate, gentler, more merciful than the man.'

'Weaker, you mean?' Mina muttered. She glanced back to the portraiture room and repeated her question. 'What do you think? Is this her too?'

'I think that, without Beatrice's execution, Caravaggio wouldn't have painted this Judith. That the two are linked. One dependent on the other.'

'Action, reaction,' she said in a low, unemotional tone.

'Precisely.'

The girl said nothing. She walked out of the room, and Costa followed.

CHAPTER 3

Around the time Costa and the girl were walking up the grand winding staircase of the Palazzo Barberini, Gianni Peroni was gazing mournfully at a more modest and grubby set of steps, those inside the grey shell of the building in the Via Beatrice Cenci, wondering how many more times he was going to have to climb them before the questions surrounding the death of Malise Gabriel were resolved. He and Falcone were in their fifties. They needed modern conveniences like lifts, particularly on a hot, airless Roman day.

'You mean there's no one else living here?' Falcone asked as they began to march up the first set of stairs. Some floors were empty, stripped bare and midway through the process of renovation, full of timber, copper piping, sinks and WCs waiting to be installed.

'Not a soul, apparently. The American architect who owns the place is trying to gut it and turn the place into some fancy-price apartment block.'

The woman had buzzed them in from the front door. He'd expected to hear the sound of construction: machines, men's voices, hammers. It was silent behind the block's thick grey walls.

Falcone shook his head.

'A fancy apartment block here? It's not exactly the Via Giulia, is it?'

The ghetto was an unfashionable part of the centre. The streets and alleys around the Piazza delle Cinque Scole were still modest in nature, with a busy and occasionally insular Jewish community. Outsiders, particularly foreign ones, would not be welcomed as warmly as they would elsewhere, in Trastevere or the busy expatriate streets around the Spanish Steps and the Piazza Navona, where the tourist dollar was the primary source of income. The ghetto lived to its own rhythm, a distinct and separate little community tucked into the heart of Rome, almost invisible behind the high walls of bleak, imposing palaces such as the one through which they now trudged.

'I told you she was American,' Peroni said. 'Probably got sold a pup by some local property crook who knew a soft touch when he saw one. She was in quite a state.' Almost as if she'd been bereaved herself, he thought. 'Money problems. She as good as told us she was about to go bust. The Gabriels were paying a pittance to live here and now the widow says she'd going to sue over the accident. This whole place feels . . .' He hated instinct. But sometimes it was impossible to ignore. '. . . bad.'

The tall, lean figure ahead kept on marching

125

upwards. On the third floor Peroni was forced to halt for breath. Falcone folded his arms, waiting.

'It's a long way, Leo,' Peroni grumbled. 'We're not young men any more. Also . . .' This had concerned him from the moment Falcone had outlined his thinking. 'Why's it just the two of us? Either this is a case or it isn't, and if it is . . .'

'It isn't a case. If it turns into one I'll let you know.'

'So we're just snooping?'

Falcone smiled and tapped the side of his nose.

'What's wrong with that?' He glanced up the stairs. 'This whole business . . . It doesn't fit somehow, does it? Why would someone like Malise Gabriel, a man who once had a little fame and notoriety, wind up scratching a living in some oddball academy in Rome, without two cents to rub together?'

'Because the notoriety beat the fame in the end? He was a troublesome bastard who kept on getting fired from every job he had,' Peroni suggested.

'Quite. And he had an eye for young girls.'

'A long time ago. And only the one girl we know of. The woman he married and stuck with.'

'What about the bookmark you found?'

'It's just an arty glamour picture. You can buy that kind of thing in a shop. We don't know it's the daughter. We don't know anything.'

'It wasn't bought in a shop. It was printed at home. Forensic are taking a closer look. Now come on, old man.'

Three months separated them. That last comment

seemed unnecessary. Determined to disprove the slight, Peroni did manage to keep up though, which was probably the point.

The door to the Gabriel apartment was open. Falcone stood there, a look of blank fury growing on his face. Peroni went ahead and walked through.

The entire floor seemed empty save for a single chair on which Joanne Van Doren sat, head down, fingers tapping at the keyboard of a tiny laptop computer. Every chair, every table, every book and personal effect, every last shred of possible evidence had disappeared. What had been the Gabriels' home a few days before now resembled the gutted, empty spaces in the storeys below.

Peroni went over to the woman and, when she kept on typing, coughed loudly.

She looked up at him and said, 'Yes?'

'Where's the bedroom?' Falcone asked.

'Which bedroom?' Joanne Van Doren wondered, eyes wide open with apparent innocence.

They were still pink. Peroni thought she looked even more miserable than the day before. 'Follow me,' he said.

They walked into Mina's room, the one at the corner, with the double French windows opening onto the shattered terrace. Everything was gone: the books, the shelves, the curtains, the compact desk and chair. The bed and all the sheets.

'Is there a problem?' she asked, joining them.

'You didn't mention you were going to clear the

apartment,' Peroni said, trying to quell his own anger.

'You didn't ask. Cecilia Gabriel's taken what she wanted. This is the only part of the building with working heat, power and water. I can lease it. Maybe I can even sell it if I'm lucky. The bank keep saying they need money straight away.'

'Signora,' Falcone interrupted. 'A man died here in the early hours of Saturday night. There's an investigation into the circumstances.'

'I told Di Lauro I was clearing the place. He didn't say a thing.'

'Di Lauro?' Falcone asked.

'The city building inspector,' Peroni murmured.

'A building inspector?' Falcone looked livid. 'We're police officers.'

The skinny American looked close to the edge, ready to burst into tears.

'Will you get off my back!' she screeched. 'The only people who stuck around here yesterday were Di Lauro's. I told them what I was doing. They didn't look interested. Why should they be? The accident happened outside. I haven't touched anything there.'

The inspector glanced unpleasantly at Peroni.

'Get onto the Questura. Get a warrant for this place. All of it. I want a court order barring any further construction work anywhere in this entire block until I say so. Nor do I want anyone allowed in.'

'You can't do that!' she shrieked. 'I have a buyer coming.'

His sharp eyes scanned the bedroom.

'Your buyer can wait. The things from here. Where are they now? With the Gabriels?'

'Some of them. What they wanted. Cecilia's still got a key. I told her to come in last night when we were gone and take whatever she liked before the men dumped it. Probably best we didn't meet, what with everything. Look, seriously. You can't . . .'

Peroni found this interesting.

'You paid people to clear this building on a Sunday evening? Isn't that expensive? Why not wait until today?'

Her pale face coloured for a moment.

'This is my place. For now, anyway. I can do what I want. Please. I might have someone coming round who's going to buy.'

'The bedclothes?' Falcone said. 'The furniture? The personal items? Cecilia Gabriel has them now?'

'Some, I guess. I told you. I wasn't here when she came round. She took what she wanted and the workmen got the rest.'

'Where did they take it?'

'Wherever trash goes in this city. You tell me.'

Falcone demanded the name and phone number of the contractors and told Peroni to get someone to try to track down the material.

'Talk to forensic and get a team in here to

see if there's anything they can find in this mess. We can go and see the Gabriel woman ourselves.'

'What?' the American barked. 'Did you hear a word I said? I'm desperate.'

'Why did you let the Gabriels stay here for next to nothing?' Peroni asked, trying to bring the temperature down a little. 'I don't understand. You could have got someone in paying a proper rent, couldn't you?'

'With all this construction work going on?'

'It's going on now and you think you can sell it.' The question discomfited her.

'It was a favour. OK? Bernard Santacroce, Malise's boss, asked me. They'd lodged with him at the Casina when they first came here. It didn't work out. Bernard and Malise were . . . on opposite sides of some philosophical fence I didn't begin to understand.'

Falcone was interested.

'Why should you do this Santacroce a favour?'

'Because . . .'

'Because what?'

She placed her thin hands together and pleaded with him, 'Why are you doing this to me? I need the money.'

Falcone scanned the room.

'I'm not happy with Malise Gabriel's death, Signora. You've removed what may be material evidence from these premises in circumstances I still do not understand. As long as I remain unhappy I

130

will keep the keys to this building. Why did you do these people a favour?'

She looked angry. And worried too, Peroni thought. Close to the edge. Falcone could have tackled this with a little less aggression, even if it wasn't his usual style.

'Because I felt sorry for them! OK?' The blood had drained from her face. 'I felt sorry for Mina most of all. It wasn't her fault her father couldn't walk down the street without picking a fight with someone. They were all going nuts in that crazy little place of Bernard's. They had to leave.' She got a little closer. 'Look. I'm sorry if I've done something wrong here. I didn't mean to. I can help you out. Tell me what you want. It can be fixed. But I've got to let these people in to view. If I don't . . .'

Falcone dismissed her with a wave of his hand.

'I want this entire apartment closed except to my people and a forensic team until further notice. No one is coming in without my permission. Including you.'

'Are you trying to bankrupt me?'

He wasn't interested.

'You may stay here until the forensic team arrive. After that you'll have to leave. We will tell you when we're finished.'

'This is going to a lawyer right now,' she said and stormed off.

Falcone walked over to the window and looked at the broken scaffolding. Then he leaned out and peered down to the street below. Peroni joined him. The Via Beatrice Cenci was open again now. This part of Rome looked the way it usually did, quiet, residential, a little run-down.

'Why would she clear this place so quickly?' the inspector asked. 'On a Sunday night? Without giving you a clue it was on the cards when you came here yesterday afternoon?'

'It's annoying. I wouldn't read into it any more than that. Go easy on that woman, will you? She looks in a bad way. Worse than yesterday I think.'

Falcone raised his eyebrows and said nothing.

'OK,' Peroni sighed, thinking about it. 'I agree. Something here stinks. I'll get Teresa's people in straight away and see if they can find something in all this muck and dust. One of the juniors can start hunting the dumps to see where all that stuff has gone. That may not be easy. If they've used some illegal site . . .'

Falcone closed his eyes for a moment and muttered, 'I can't believe I didn't come round myself.'

'Don't blame yourself, sir,' Peroni said and didn't regret the note of acid in his voice. He wasn't taking the blame. They had all thought this was the accident it appeared.

'I want to see Cecilia Gabriel,' Falcone said, barely noticing. 'And this girl, Mina. I want that brother found too.'

'Narcotics are looking.'

Peroni thought of the way Nic had talked about

the daughter, about how bright and sincere she was, and the pain he'd seen on her pretty young face. He wondered how Nic would feel when he realized it was his insistence on examining events more closely that would bring Mina Gabriel into a police interview room before long.

'We've got a case, haven't we?' he asked, knowing the answer.

Falcone moved his foot through the grime and rubble on the floorboards. Joanne Van Doren's voice was rising to a scream in the big room beyond. Some Roman lawyer was beginning to feel her anger. It sounded as if the man wasn't giving her the news she wanted.

The inspector's mournful grey eyes scanned the bare room, and the larger space outside, then came to rest on Peroni.

'I honestly don't know. I hate this sort of thing. It's starting to feel grubby already. I wish Nic were on duty. Perhaps if I—'

'He needs a break,' Peroni cut in. 'He needs to learn there's more to life than work. There's Agata too. We agreed on this, Leo. Remember?'

'I remember,' Falcone muttered and threw up his hands in a gesture of surrender.

CHAPTER 4

The little turquoise scooter wound its way slowly around the hot and humid streets of Rome as Costa listened to Mina unearthing the traces of Beatrice Cenci's past as if they were ley lines waiting to be rediscovered beneath the dust.

They stopped at the site of the ancient Tordinona prison, northwest of the Piazza Navona, where she was tortured. Then the Vespa worked through the back streets towards the Campo dei Fiori, to the spot in the Via di Monserrato where a plaque on the wall marked the position of another former Vatican hellhole, the jail of Corte Savella. It was in this narrow, ordinary street that she spent her last night on earth before being walked by hooded monks to the block a few minutes away by the Ponte Sant'Angelo. It had taken until 11 September 1999, four hundred years after her execution, for the city's rulers to make public their shame about her death. The words on the wall marked the site from which she had been taken to the scaffold, *'vittima esemplare di una giustizia ingiusta'* – an exemplary victim of an unjust justice, said the sign.

134

By lunch time they stood outside the Palazzo Cenci. In the bright August sunlight the place still seemed forbidding, a private fortress, built on its own little hill which, like much else around, had taken on the Cenci name. Mina showed him the tiny pink-walled church in the intimate little piazza at the summit of the modest mound, in the shadow of the palace. The tablet on the façade marked its reconstruction in 1575, thanking 'Franciscus Cincius', Beatrice's own tormenting father, for the work. Inside the closed building, Mina said, was an unmarked tomb originally planned for Francesco. It now contained the quartered remains of Giacomo, his son and murderer. The father himself was hurriedly buried in the countryside where he was killed, in the hope that the crime would never be discovered.

'Every September the eleventh,' she said, looking back at the palace, 'there's a mass here for Beatrice and her family in the chapel. I want to go if I can.' She looked at him. 'Some Romans still love her.'

'It was Romans who killed her,' Costa pointed out.

'Not the ordinary people. They approved of what she did. Standing up for herself.'

'Do you?' he asked.

She sat down on the bonnet of a Fiat saloon parked lazily in the road and toyed with her long, blonde hair again.

'Yes, I think she was right. What choice did she have?' She took a piece of gum out of her pocket, popped it in her mouth and said, 'You know an awful lot for a policeman.'

CHAPTER 5

Next the Vespa went to the bridge where Beatrice died, now little more than another traffic-choked stretch of road by the Tiber. Mina pointed out what she believed to be the place: in the middle of the busy Lungotevere where pedestrians crossed to walk onto the foot-bridge of the Ponte Sant'Angelo. He parked the scooter outside a cafe in a little lane. They waited for the lights then walked to the cobbled stones that led across the Tiber to the vast, hulking shape which had once been the mausoleum of Hadrian. The Castel Sant'Angelo's soft brown stone, a vast cylinder towering over the river, seemed to shimmer in the midday heat. The girl dragged him past each of the angels on the bridge, fanciful, heavenly creatures, some bearing musical instruments, some vicious devices from the stations of the cross.

This bend in the river was one of his favourite points in Rome, a place where every aspect of the city's character, imperial, Renaissance and modern, seemed to converge. It was hard to imagine the streets thronged with crowds, silent, anticipating a hideous act to end a brief and terrible story. Yet here, by the bridge that was now a favourite place for tourists to take pictures, the city had once executed criminals with a shocking regularity.

Mina stopped him as they walked back to the scooter.

'They say that every September the eleventh Beatrice's ghost comes back here, carrying her head beneath her arm.'

Costa frowned. He'd heard so many such tales.

'Romans have a fondness for the supernatural. We're a credulous race.'

'Do you believe in ghosts?' she asked outright.

'No.'

She seemed to approve of his answer.

'I remember talking to Daddy about it. He said, if you think of all the millions of people who've died there ought to be ghosts everywhere. It doesn't make sense. We'd be surrounded by ghosts in mourning. For each other. For us. You wouldn't be able to think for the sound of their crying.'

Mina Gabriel placed a finger on the stone base of the statue of an angel in front of them, a beautiful figure, fluid and full of movement, in its hands a cruel crown of thorns.

He followed the gaze of the statue above them. The creature's blank eyes were set on the dome of St Peter's, as if seeking salvation, or some semblance of reason.

A scowl crossed her innocent face as she glanced towards the great basilica too.

'They'd kill someone just for wanting to be themselves.'

'Did you talk to your father about Beatrice a lot?'

'I was talking about Galileo. And all the others. Don't you know about the Confraternita?'

She was testing him. He was sure of it.

'No,' he replied.

'Another time,' Mina replied quickly. 'Daddy didn't talk to me about Beatrice. What makes you think that?'

'You said . . .'

'About ghosts. Not Beatrice. Not ever.'

There was a hiatus in the conversation. A stiffness. Something unsaid.

'They took her body along the Via Giulia,' she said, returning to the subject, pointing out the direction back to the street that paralleled the river. 'Then across the Ponte Sisto.' One more sweep of her arm to the old footbridge further along the Tiber. 'Then through Trastevere, up that steep hill, to Montorio. Thousands of them. A long way. Hard work. They hated what that man . . .' Her eyes flashed back towards the great dome. '. . . did to her.'

'I believe they did,' he agreed.

PART V

CHAPTER 1

Teresa Lupo gazed at the body on the mirror-bright table in the morgue, a skinny male corpse beneath a white sheet rolled back to reveal everything from the waist up. The information sheet her assistant Silvio Di Capua had provided gave the basics. Malise Gabriel was sixty-one years old, pronounced dead on arrival at the hospital in the early hours of Saturday morning, two days before. The duty morgue officer, a college intern, had examined the body, read the report from the police, and written the probable cause of death as severe head injuries consistent with a fall from a substantial height. This could not be a formal finding. She was a temporary worker. In the absence of suspicion of foul play the full autopsy would naturally be delayed due to staff shortages. Nothing much had happened since.

'Leave it to the Monday people,' Teresa grumbled. Not that there was anything to indicate the duty junior had done anything wrong. The bruised and bloodied corpse in front of her looked the way she would have expected from seeing the police

143

incident statement. There were no indications of other injuries. No obvious inflicted wounds. No cuts or abrasions that spoke of anything but a fall.

She looked at the face of the man on the table. Features sometimes changed with death, particularly an end such as this. His skull had suffered multiple fractures and there were severe injuries to his forehead and the right side, above and below the ear. Teresa had found a photograph of Malise Gabriel from his brief time in the spotlight. Twenty years before he'd seemed like the aristocrat he was, handsome, a little arrogant perhaps, with the face of a sportsman, the broken nose of a rugby player. A strong, physical man. Not like this.

'If you're thinking what I think you're thinking,' Di Capua cut in, 'the answer's no, you can't.'

She glowered at him.

'How do you know what I'm thinking?'

'I've seen it before a million times. You've got that look.'

'That look?'

'The one that means work. And trouble.'

She sighed.

'This man deserves a full autopsy, and he will get one.'

'Yes, but he doesn't need to get it from the head of the department, does he? We've got a team going into that house in the ghetto. Half our people are on holiday.'

'Yes, yes,' she snapped. 'I get the point.' She knew where this was leading. 'You want to do it, then?'

Di Capua smiled. He'd turn thirty soon. The little that remained of his hair was now close cropped. His clothes were standard white office garb. The failed hippie she'd first employed seemed to have metamorphosed into an impertinent dentist somewhere over the past few years.

'I suggest I handle this and you go round and see what's happening in the house.' He smiled. 'Let's face it. This is just one more autopsy. You can do that with your eyes closed. From what Peroni said . . .'

She'd listened to the phone call asking for a team to seal off the Gabriels' apartment. Judging by the tone of Di Capua's response, Falcone was not in the best of moods.

'They're trying to dredge up a speck of evidence in a building site,' he went on. 'Now that's going to be hard.'

'Thank you,' she said with false grace, passing him back the file. 'I was going to do that anyway. He'll want something by the end of the day, you know.'

'So what's new? I'm not promising miracles. I'll do the best I can.'

'Good. Here's a starter for you.' She leaned down and indicated the bloodied, torn scalp. 'This man is suffering from some kind of hair loss. I suggest you discover who his doctor is and get what records you can. Also . . .'

She picked up Malise Gabriel's right hand.

'There are scratches here that don't look like the kind of thing you'd get from a fall from a building. I could be wrong, but they may be worthy of further investigation.'

He nodded, with an ingratiating pleasantness that told her he'd seen all this already.

'Anything else?' he asked.

'Enough for now. We can talk later.'

She walked out of the room trying to recall those happy days when Silvio Di Capua lived in fear and awe of her. He was up to something. She just knew it.

So Teresa Lupo waited outside for a few seconds then reopened the swinging door to the morgue and poked her head back in.

Di Capua had rolled back the fabric completely. The body of Malise Gabriel lay naked on the table, white and purple and bloody. Her assistant was staring at the lower part of the torso. He jumped visibly as she banged open the door very deliberately. It was worth it just for that.

'Is there anything you'd like to tell me, Silvio?' she asked.

His large, wide-set eyes rolled upwards. The young pathologist's composure returned.

'When I'm ready,' he said.

CHAPTER 2

Peroni and Falcone spent three hours with the forensic team in the Via Beatrice Cenci as they pored over the Gabriels' apartment, picking and prodding patiently in their white bunny suits. The American woman's mood had grown progressively more downcast and sullen. Falcone had what he wanted: men and women scouring every last inch of the place for physical evidence. After a little while he had Teresa Lupo to stand over them, watching every step, every last precise action too. Not for a moment did it appear to concern him that the formal search warrant for these actions had yet to arrive from the magistrate. It was, Peroni reminded himself, that time of year.

Joanne Van Doren was in the poky kitchen when they left, skinny fingers around another beer. Peroni made a point of going up to her and asking if there was anything he could do.

'Write a cheque for fifty thousand euros?' she suggested wearily.

He tried to treat it as a joke, and to ignore Falcone tapping his toes ready to leave by the door.

'Signora, if there's something you'd like to tell us . . . it would be better now. To hear it voluntarily, rather than discover it for ourselves.'

Her eyes flashed wildly.

'What do you *mean*?'

'What I said.'

For a moment Peroni thought he was getting somewhere. Then something, some second thought, intervened and she said, 'It was an accident. I don't know what else you expect me to say.'

The place they were headed was so close it was pointless taking Falcone's Lancia saloon. The directions they had received told them to go to the Palazzetto Santacroce and ask for admittance at the door. The building lay in the warren of lanes a few minutes away on foot across the busy Via Arenula, an area much like the ghetto, dark and cramped, though rather grander in nature. The palazzetto was a grand and imposing four-storey mansion in its own cul-de-sac behind the river, close to the footbridge of the Ponte Sisto with its beautiful view of the dome of St Peter's.

'There's money here,' Peroni muttered as they walked through a brown stone entrance arch into a small courtyard with a fountain at the centre surrounded by lush, well-tended grass.

'You can say that again,' Falcone replied, pointing at the first-floor apartment visible beyond the caretaker's kiosk. Paintings, statues, grand gilt furniture, rich red velvet walls. This was another

Rome, barely touched by the pressure and poverty of the street.

'We want the Casina,' Peroni told the uniformed man behind the glass, showing his police ID.

It was only when they went through a second set of doors to the rear that he realized the full extent of the property, which ran all the way to the riverside road, making it as large, surely, as the Palazzo Farnese, the palatial mansion close by that was now the French embassy. The hidden back was almost entirely given over to garden, a rare oasis in the city, carefully laid out with shrubs and palm trees, fountains, flower beds, topiary and shady bowers with seats, all beneath high, unbroken walls which rendered the secluded refuge invisible to the city at large.

In the corner was what could only be the Casina. It was a tall, circular tower that stood above the grounds of the palazzetto like a guard post. The ground floor was completely windowless. The second possessed nothing but a few narrow slots through which, Peroni assumed, archers were expected to fire their arrows. The remaining two floors had elegant arched openings, medieval in appearance but now with modern glass windows. the roof was a crenellated battlement with embrasures in the raised portions, as if to provide another vantage point for archers. The rosy weathered building seemed more like the abandoned tower of some lost fairy-tale castle than a Renaissance palace. Peroni had never seen anything quite like it in the heart of Rome and said so. Falcone, clearly astonished, agreed, then narrowed his sharp eyes, stared at it again and said, 'The Porta Asinaria. The place in the walls near San Giovanni.'

Peroni nodded. He was right. This was a precise copy of the little-noticed gate marooned behind railings next to the busy gap in the walls near San Giovanni, through which streams of modern Roman traffic passed every day.

They were engulfed in the scent of white jasmine tumbling down in festoons around the door. It almost obliterated the stink of the traffic bustling along the Lungotevere beyond the furthest wall.

'The rich are with us always,' Peroni murmured and pressed the bell.

CHAPTER 3

Cecilia Gabriel answered the door and led them up three levels of a circular stone staircase, into a large room strewn with belongings: clothes, paintings, photos, books, sheet music on stands. She was a striking woman, tall and statuesque, with an angular face, high cheekbones and attentive blue eyes. Beautiful, Peroni thought, but in a hard, unsmiling way. Her chestnut hair was cut short in the fashion Audrey Hepburn preferred for the movie that still brought tourists to Rome more than half a century after it first appeared. She didn't seem nervous. Just . . . uncomfortable, impatient. Impecunious too, in a faded blue denim shirt and jeans that looked a little too young for her. The woman was, he knew from the records, a little short of forty. Something – strain, illness perhaps – had added a few years to that. She didn't look happy, which was understandable in the circumstances, though he felt the crows' feet at the corners of her elegant eyes, the creases around her mouth, were more than signs of age.

The place was a good step up from the bare

apartment in the ghetto. Decent, old-fashioned furniture. Long, gilt mirrors on the walls. Deep, generous carpet and a sizeable polished dining table.

Malise Gabriel's widow motioned them to two sturdy antique chairs and sat down gracefully on a small sofa opposite. Her movements were feline, controlled, poised. He could imagine her as a musician, dressed in tasteful black, bent over a cello somewhere in the orchestra, a woman who would draw the admiring attention of those in the audience.

'Where's your daughter?' Falcone asked.

'Out somewhere,' she replied, looking puzzled by the question.

'When will she be back?'

She didn't know that either, and it almost looked as if she didn't care.

'Your son? Robert?' Peroni chipped in.

'Yes. That's his name.'

He could feel Falcone stiffen next to him.

'Where is he?' the inspector asked. 'Do you have any idea? Have you heard from him?'

'Robert came round to our old apartment for something to eat the afternoon of the accident. I haven't heard from him since. I wish he'd get in touch but it's his decision. There are practical things we need to discuss, apart from anything else. I'm not his keeper. He's twenty years old.'

'Are there places you know he stayed when he

wasn't with you? Somewhere we could look?' Falcone asked.

'He never talked about his friends. He liked the bars in the Campo. I imagine you know that.'

'I believe we do,' he agreed, shooting Peroni a sideways glance.

She sighed then said, 'Inspector. My husband died in an accident two days ago. I'm struggling to deal with all manner of things I never knew existed. Life insurance. Funeral arrangements – not that I know when you will allow me to reclaim his body.' She hesitated and started at him. 'Grief. Mine. My daughter's. Helping you put my son in jail over some stupid drugs habits isn't high on my priorities.'

'There are a number of questions surrounding your husband's death,' Peroni told her.

Her head crooked to one side and she stared out of the window. There was a palm tree there, its green crown resplendent against the perfect blue August sky, the under-surface a vivid orange.

'What kind of questions?'

'Unanswered ones,' Falcone said then patiently, persistently, began to extract from Cecilia Gabriel her version of events on the night her husband died. She said she had played at a semi-professional concert in front of several hundred people at the Auditorium Parco Della Musica. The party afterwards had gone on into the early hours. She knew nothing of the accident until she received a phone call from her daughter. Then she went immediately to the street and saw Malise Gabriel being taken away by the paramedics.

'I went to the hospital with Mina. Not that there was much point. Then . . .' Peroni saw the briefest flicker of emotion on her narrow face. 'We couldn't go home. To that place. Not after what happened. I called Bernard and he agreed we could use our old accommodation here. It was very generous of him.'

'Why did you leave in the first place?' Peroni asked.

She didn't appear to appreciate the question.

'This apartment didn't come with Malise's post. It was kindness on Bernard's part that allowed us to stay here when we arrived. There was never the slightest suggestion this would be anything but temporary.'

'I gather they didn't get on,' Falcone said.

Her face hardened.

'People talking already? It's no great secret that my husband and Bernard had differences. Philosophical ones, to do with the work Malise was undertaking for the Confraternita. Nothing more.'

Falcone told her he wanted a full list of all the items she'd taken from the Via Beatrice Cenci so that they could be handed over to the forensic team.

She scowled at them.

'Are you serious?'

'I may wish to see the things you brought here,' Falcone said.

'Why? Is this really necessary? My husband's dead and you want to rifle through our belongings?'

'It may be necessary,' Falcone insisted. He stopped, watching her. 'We're looking for the items you left in the apartment as well.' He took an envelope out of his pocket. 'Did anyone have a reason to bear a grudge against your husband?'

'Don't be ridiculous.' She flashed an angry look at her watch. 'There's paperwork. I don't have time to deal with these stupid questions.'

Her words tailed off into silence. Falcone placed his card on the table.

'I need to talk to your daughter. Please ensure she calls me when she returns. If your son should get in touch . . .'

Cecilia Gabriel folded her arms and stared at them.

'Signora,' Peroni said, remembering how they'd agreed to tackle this subject. 'Your husband was reading his own book the night he died.'

'Is there a law against that?'

'Not at all. But he used a bookmark. It had a strange message written on it.'

Falcone took out the plastic evidence envelope and showed it to her, only the reverse side, with the long, cursive scrawl.

'It that his handwriting?' the inspector asked.

She shook her head.

'It doesn't look like it.'

'And the words?'

'"*E pur si muove*",' she recited. 'Galileo whispered

that after he recanted in front of the Inquisition. Look it up in an encyclopaedia.'

'We know,' Peroni said calmly. 'But the context . . .'

She laughed, as if genuinely amused by their ignorance.

'And you call yourselves Romans? The context? This is the Casina delle Civette. The home of the Confratrenity of the Owls. The society my husband worked for was formed by friends of Galileo when he fell under suspicion. It was their way of supporting him. Galileo was one of the inner circle. He used to come here. To this very building. Secretly. He didn't dare let the Vatican know. The men who built this tower . . .' She looked around them. 'They paid a price too. Not with their lives. They were too aristocratic for that. But Bernard's ancestor, Paolo Santacroce, was persecuted for two decades. This is his legacy. Their legacy. A testament to the power of truth over superstition. That was Malise's life's work and so they persccuted him too.'

'Who persecuted him?' Peroni asked, genuinely puzzled.

'You wouldn't understand,' she muttered.

Falcone said, 'I need to call the Questura. After that I would like to talk to Mr Santacroce.'

She pointed back to the circular staircase through which they'd entered.

'One floor up. I'll ask if he will see you. I work as Bernard's personal assistant.'

'Thank you.' He looked at the back of the picture.

'Signora. This is a delicate question but I regret it must be asked. We know from the newspapers, from the controversy that your affair engendered twenty years ago, that your husband was – how do I put this easily? – not averse to relationships with girls much younger than him.'

She didn't blink, didn't move.

'I was nineteen when I fell pregnant,' Cecilia Gabriel said. 'That didn't make Malise a paedophile then. Nor does it even in these supposedly enlightened days.'

'What I have to ask is painfully simple,' Falcone went on. 'Did this . . . taste stay with him through life?' He flipped the picture over. 'This was the bookmark he was using on the night he died. It was more than a message. It was a photograph. See . . .'

Falcone thrust the black and white picture in front of her. Peroni found he couldn't read the expression on her narrow, agonized face as she stared at the nude adolescent torso twisting on the crumpled sheets, face out of view, a single lock of fair hair falling down onto her slim shoulders, neck twisted as if in pain, face and head cut off by the frame. And on the fabric, the ragged damp mark of a stain.

'One must wonder,' the inspector went on. 'Because of the apparent similarity, which seems remarkable. Is this a photograph of your daughter? Is it possible . . .'

The woman lunged forward and struck Falcone hard across the right cheek with her open hand.

The noise of the blow echoed around the room and the force brought colour to Falcone's face, from the silver goattee to his cheek-bones. Gingerly he placed his fingers on the area where she'd hit him. He looked hurt.

Peroni walked forward, stood between them, looked her in the eye and said, 'I could arrest you for assaulting a police officer.'

'Do it. I can't wait to be in court and tell people the kind of accusation you scum throw at a grieving widow.'

She was utterly calm and in control of herself.

'We're attempting to find out how and why your husband died,' he reminded her.

'Malise stepped out onto the balcony for a cigarette and Joanne Van Doren's lousy scaffolding collapsed. End of story. Why do you have to make everything so complicated?'

Peroni shrugged his big shoulders.

'Because sometimes it is. The photograph, Mrs Gabriel. It's unusual. We have a job to do. It's rarely a pleasant one.'

She snatched the picture from Falcone's fingers, held it to her face and glared at them, demanding they see.

'It's me, you idiot. From twenty years ago. Malise kept it. He reprinted it from time to time. It was ours. A memory of happier days. *Sub rosa*, if you're bright enough to understand Latin. All families have their private matters, Inspector. They only look sinister to prying, evil eyes.'

158

'Privacy doesn't concern me,' Falcone said, still stroking the place where she'd slapped him. 'Death does.'

'It was an accident!'

He took his hand away from his cheek and retrieved the bookmark from her grip.

'I would like to see Bernard Santacroce now, if you please.'

CHAPTER 4

The scooter climbed the steep, winding road from Trastevere and the noise it made meant Peroni's song from the previous day – Vespa-pa-pa-pa-pa-pa-pa – rarely left Nic Costa's head all the way. They got off in the forecourt beneath the white marble façade of San Pietro in Montorio. He recalled what Mina had told him about the procession from the Ponte Sant'Angelo to this small and, by Roman standards, humble, church. It must have been a long and arduous journey, one taken by thousands following the bier that contained Beatrice's broken corpse.

Montorio was part way up the Gianicolo hill, by a bend on the busy road to the summit where Garibaldi had once fought. It was a quiet place, green, with expensive houses and views of Rome that encompassed an entirely new perspective. The dome of St Peter's was invisible. All one saw was a view back over the river to the centre which, from this height, fell into an unfamiliar panorama of distant steeples and towers.

'The Tempietto,' she declared, snatching off her

helmet, shaking her long blonde hair then popping another stick of gum into her mouth.

He followed her to the iron gate of the cloister next to the church. It was locked. The opening hours had passed. Inside he could see Bramante's tiny temple, circular with Doric columns, perfectly proportioned in a way which Palladio would consciously copy.

'It's a martyrium,' Mina told him, clinging to the bars, poking her pale, narrow face through as she tried to see more, winding her leg round the iron uprights, as a child would with a playground ride. 'That's what you call a monument that marks the site of a martyr's death. Peter, supposedly.' Her hand rose, and with it a didactic finger, as if she were practising to be the tour guide for Joanne Van Doren's non-existent condominium customers. 'They used the hill for crucifixions. That much is true but Daddy said there's not a shred of evidence Peter was executed here. Or even that he came to Rome.'

Costa recalled this argument well. It was a recurrent one when sceptics and believers locked horns.

'I think some people would challenge that idea.'

She watched him.

'Would you?'

Costa thought about it for a moment and said, 'I'm not qualified. We all have the right to believe what we want, for or against. I don't think private opinions are worth fighting over.'

'You sound like Bernard, Daddy's boss. Typical

161

liberal woolly thinking. The truth is the truth. If you could prove Peter never came to Rome, you should. However much you hurt people's feelings. They shouldn't base their lives on lies.'

'Truth can be relative. And unpleasant. Did Bernard and your father quarrel?'

Mina smiled at him and he wondered if she felt he was prying.

'Do you want the truth? Or a nice, polite answer?'

He smiled and said, 'The truth, please.'

'They hated one another. Daddy was supposed to edit some papers about science and religion. Put his name to something he didn't believe for one moment. Just like Galileo.' She glanced in the direction of the Tempietto. 'One more martyr in Rome. We may have been broke but you couldn't buy his principles. What else did he have left?'

'He had his family,' Costa said.

'Suppose so,' she said, then picked up her helmet and tripped off to the church without looking back.

It was a compact, quiet place. Two people, a middle-aged man and an elderly woman, were on their knees in the shaft of light that illuminated the nave, praying. Mina came close to Costa and whispered, pointing with her right hand, 'They never marked Beatrice's grave. Some people say it was beneath the alter. Others in the chapel there.' He caught the brief sign of an impatient expression on her young face. 'I can't believe they hated

162

Beatrice so much they'd deny her that. Then the French came.'

By the time Napoleon invaded, the Cenci story was part of Roman folklore. It was this that attracted the marauding soldiers to Montorio, and an orgy of destruction that, rumour had it, saw her remains disinterred then scattered across the hill where imperial Rome once crucified those it regarded as criminals.

Mina sat down on a bench and stared at the altar. Costa joined her. They stayed there for a few minutes in silence. Then, without another word, she got up and marched outside, crossed the forecourt and climbed onto the perimeter wall overlooking the hill, perching there like any other teenager, hands round her knees, helmet strap gathered round her wrist, gazing at the view: the historical heart of the city stretching in front of them like a magical panorama with the ragged crown of the Sabine Hills beyond.

He thought it best to leave her alone for a few minutes. Costa went and peered at Bramante's Tempietto through the cloister's bars. It resembled a monument that had escaped from Ancient Rome only to find itself locked in a beautiful prison for some reason. Finally he walked over to the wall and saw, as he reached her, that she was crying.

The tears ran in two vertical streaks down each cheek, bright and viscous. After a little while she sniffed then wiped them away with a scrunched-up tissue dragged out of her jeans pocket.

'Perhaps this wasn't such a good idea,' he said. 'I can run you home.'

'I'm not crying for Beatrice,' she spat at him with a sudden, childish petulance. 'She's been dead for four centuries.'

'Of course not. If you want me to go . . .'

'I didn't say that, did I?'

'No. If you want to talk about anything . . .'

She stared at him with cold, glassy eyes.

'That's why you came, isn't it? To interrogate me?'

He hitched himself up onto the wall, sat a little way along from her and said, with a shrug and a wry smile, 'Actually I came because you asked me. I nearly said no.'

Her head went to the city again. She was silent for a while then she murmured, 'I'm sorry for being hateful. It happens sometimes. Mina, the perfect child. Not so perfect really.'

'I meant it. If you want to talk, fine. If not . . .'

'I don't.'

He waited. For all the knowledge that Malise and Cecilia had crammed into this bright and unusual girl, for all her skill with words and languages, she was still a teenager. Sullen and joyful in turn, unpredictable, uncertain of herself and the world around her. Grieving inwardly for a father whose death she, perhaps, failed to understand too.

'Somewhere there,' she said finally. Her arm was sweeping the glorious panorama in front of them.

'In that dip to the right of the Vittorio Emanuele monument . . .'

'Yes?'

She wouldn't look at him. She was uncertain of saying this somehow.

'There's another church, Santa Francesca Romana. Next to the Forum. It's white. Pretty brick campanile. Somewhere behind the Palatine, close to the Colosseum. You know it?'

'There are so many churches in Rome,' he said, trying to recall that section of Mussolini's broad and insensitive highway cutting through the core of the imperial city. Then it came: a small, elegant building perched on a ridge next to the fence marking off the Forum, and a memory of traffic jams in spring.

'You mean the car drivers' church?' he said, remembering. Santa Francesca was the patron saint of motorists. On her feast day in March hundreds would converge on the area to have their vehicles blessed.

She stared at him, full of doubt. Costa explained.

'I suppose that's the place,' she said, listening to his description. 'Daddy told me a story. About Simon Magus, the wizard, and St Peter. It's as true as anything else.'

She clasped her hands, fingers gripping one another tightly. Telling stories helped her somehow.

'Nero,' Mina Gabriel began, 'was the emperor and ordered a debate, a contest of miracles, a trial of the powers of Peter and the wizard. Simon called on his masters and flew. Levitated.' She gestured with her hands. 'Right in front of everyone. The emperor. The people, thousands of them, because they'd come to see. It was magic, wasn't it? Everyone wants to believe in magic. So Simon flew.' Her hands unclasped, her fingers rose to the blue summer sky. 'High up. Like a bird. Like an angel.'

Her eyes went back to the distant line of steeples and towers.

'Peter's miracle was to kneel down and pray to God to bring the magic to an end. It wasn't God's magic, you see. It was someone else's and that was *not* allowed. So Simon fell to earth, died on the stones in front of Nero. Broken. Gone.'

Tears again. He waited. The tissue came out. She coughed, struggling to regain her composure. Then she gestured towards the city.

'In Santa Francesca Romana, on the right, next to the main altar, there's a stone with some hollows on it. They say they're the marks that Peter's knees made as he prayed to God, with such force he could move rocks, kill a man, do anything. This was God's magic, wasn't it? Nero was furious. He had Peter crucified.' She nodded towards Bramante's Tempietto. 'Perhaps here. Who knows? But you see the point?'

The story was new to him yet it seemed so Roman, so cruelly apposite.

'Not exactly.'

Mina's round, liquid eyes, too sad, too worldly

for someone of her age, held him. Costa felt he was being slow.

'If you believe this story,' she went on, 'Peter wasn't crucified for being a Christian. He was tried for murder. His prayers sent Simon crashing to his death. He killed someone because they were different. And now . . .'

Her gaze strayed towards the Vatican, hidden by the hill.

'. . . look where he is.'

'Rome's full of stories,' Costa told her. 'Full of beauty and barbarity too. That's what we are. A kind of magnifying glass for humanity. All the best parts, all the worst, out there in the light of day for everyone to see. Not so much of the barbarity any more, though. Usually, anyway.'

'Daddy told me that story. He said it comes from the Acts of Peter. They're apocryphal but it's the same source that says Peter was crucified upside down. If you believe that . . . and most of the world does.'

She closed her eyes, remembering something, then, in a pure soprano, sang out loud the foreign words . . .

'*The day thou gavest, Lord, is ended*
The darkness falls at thy behest.'

Mina watched him, her eyes dark with some inner fury.

'At *thy* behest,' she said, back in Italian again.

167

'All Peter did was pray. He didn't murder Simon Magus. God did.'

Mina Gabriel wiped away her shining tears, snatched up the helmet and pulled it down over her golden hair.

'There's one place left,' she said.

CHAPTER 5

Bernard Santacroce was about fifty years old, perhaps a little more, shortish, fit and handsome in an expensive dark suit, pale pink shirt and grey tie. He had a full head of reddish hair and the tanned, unlined face of a banker or a surgeon, knowledgeable, confident, content with himself. The man sat behind a vast wooden desk, polished until it looked like a mirror, in a study at the summit of the tower that was the Casina delle Civette. Beyond the window stood two majestic palm trees, feathery fronds swaying in the light breeze. There was a glorious view down to the garden, and across the river to the Vatican. Peroni had never been anywhere so solitary and peaceful in the centre of Rome. The tower was magnificent and unique, one reason, perhaps, why Santacroce looked so pleased with himself as Cecilia Gabriel led them in.

Falcone's cheek had lost a little of its colour. The heat was still inside him, though. Whether she knew it or not, the Gabriel woman had guaranteed that he would not turn aside from what she presumably believed was merely a tentative inquiry into a death in suspicious circumstances. He had his pride too.

Santacroce waited for her to leave then bade them sit down.

'I don't need to be a genius to understand what this is about,' he said ruefully. 'It's Malise, isn't it?'

'Some simple questions, sir,' Falcone replied.

'Nothing was simple with that man, unfortunately. Odd really. He was constantly telling me God was dead. Now God says the same of Malise. One wonders who to believe.'

Peroni took his chair and engaged Falcone with a raised eyebrow, nothing more.

'Mind you, I'm a Catholic. So I won't have to wonder for long,' Santacroce added with a smile. 'And an Oxford man. Fortunate to have acquired all this . . .' He swept his arm around the room. '. . . as well as the palazzetto, which furnishes both a home and an income. I imagine it was inevitable that Malise, being a vitriolic atheist, of Cambridge, and now dirt poor, would despise the likes of me. Though given the generosity I showed him and his family, it still seems a touch ungrateful. I'm sorry he's dead, Inspector, but I'm afraid I'm rather too old and comfortable to pretend I much care. Cecilia and Mina deserved rather better than he gave them but please keep that to yourselves. They're both rather tender at the moment.'

Falcone made a few scribbles in his notebook then asked, 'Where were you exactly around midnight on Friday?'

170

Santacroce stiffened, as if astonished by the question, placed his chin on his hands and stared across the desk, like a professor considering some weighty problem.

'Why on earth would you want to know that?'

'I'm trying to understand the precise circumstances of Malise Gabriel's death,' Falcone said. 'It's important we establish the whereabouts of those who knew him.'

The man toyed with a well-chewed fingernail, watching them, then pointed back to the main building.

'I was in my apartment. Alone. From the close of play here, around six o'clock, until early the next morning when Cecilia phoned me with the terrible news. I immediately agreed that she and Mina could come and stay in their old apartment in the Casina. They were not the reason I asked them to leave in the first place.'

'The son? Robert?' Peroni asked.

'Never met him. He arrived in Rome, from London I think, after they moved into Joanne Van Doren's place.'

Santacroce's bland face creased in a frown.

'I must confess I don't understand the reason for these questions. Malise's death was a shocking accident. Why the interest?'

They didn't respond. Falcone pushed, instead, for information on Gabriel's recruitment to the small academic institution which Santacroce headed. This was obviously a subject the man enjoyed; it allowed him to display his knowledge and magnanimity, and to boast about an organization which one of his own ancestors had created four centuries before, and he himself had revived after a successful career in the City of London.

Peroni listened and made notes, realizing that in such circles he was hopelessly out of his depth. The Confraternita delle Civette, as far as he understood it, was a self-elected brotherhood of scientists from around the world whose primary function was to pat each other on the back and hold the odd meeting in exotic locations. Its stated purpose was to promote the importance of science, and the role of Italy and Rome in the field particularly. There was no budget for actual research, no formal set of focused principles. From time to time the organization would publish papers by its members, but these would normally be philosophical works on the nature of science itself, not academic reports. It was, it seemed to the old cop, a rather intellectual and upper-class dining club, one paid for through Santacroce's generosity and bequests from members over the years, with a small staff and, latterly, Malise Gabriel to handle the lazy flow of publications that emerged from the Confraternita and its members.

'Was he good at his job?' Peroni asked.

The man behind the desk stared out of the window for a good ten seconds before answering.

'Malise was a very capable man. He had a fixed idea of his role. It did not always coincide with

172

mine. Since I was his employer, my opinion was bound to prevail.'

'What was he working on?' Peroni asked.

'Most recently? Principally a paper of mine. Preparing it for publication. Checking facts. Establishing arguments. Proof-reading.'

They waited.

'About what?' Falcone asked when Santacroce said no more.

'Inspector. Do not take this the wrong way. These are very specialized intellectual issues. I really don't have the time to try to explain them to people who, through no particular fault of their own, cannot possibly understand them.'

'Such as . . .' Falcone began.

'Such as non-overlapping magisteria. I'm sure you take my—'

'Malise Gabriel wrote about them in that book of his,' Peroni said. 'He thought they were a bad thing. How about you?'

There was a sour smile on Santacroce's face. He didn't like being caught out.

'I think there's room for us all to get along. Church and science. Provided we keep our noses out of each other's business.' He leaned forward. 'Which is, as I'm sure you'll appreciate, a poor and clumsy summary of what non-overlapping magisteria actually means.'

Peroni nodded and caught Falcone's eye.

'So,' he continued, 'you wrote a paper saying this and asked Malise Gabriel to edit it, even though

173

he believed the exact opposite? Wouldn't that have been a bit demeaning in the circumstances? Though very welcome for you.'

Santacroce stared at the large grandfather clock by the wall. It was next to an impressive painting of a bearded man standing defiantly in front of three angry-looking clerics, a dramatic scene, full of motion and imminent danger.

'Is this really relevant?' Bernard Santacroce asked eventually.

'Probably not,' Falcone replied. 'But send us the draft of your paper, please. We have a colleague who is very interested in these matters. I'm sure she'd be delighted to read it.'

'How did Gabriel get on with his wife?' Peroni asked.

'I really think that's a question for her, officer.'

'In time. Right now I'm asking you.'

The smile and apparent good nature that had greeted them were gone.

'There's a word in English,' Santacroce said. 'Uxorious. You don't have a direct equivalent in Italian, which is odd since the derivation is Latin, of course. I suppose the closest translation would be along the lines of "*sottomesso alla moglie*", though it's not quite the same. Malise was uxorious in the sense that he was utterly devoted to her, and to his family, to the extent that he was almost beneath their thumb. Not literally. He could shout and rant for England when he chose. Nevertheless he was consumed by a fear that he would somehow fail them. Understandable really. He'd done it often enough in the past. The idea that he might stumble one last time – and, trust me, this was his final chance of any gainful academic employment – made him a little weak, to be frank. Call me old-fashioned but I believe a man should be the head of his family in all matters. Had he fulfilled that role, perhaps his unfortunate son wouldn't now be running round Rome in the company of drug dealers.'

Santacroce picked up a pen and made a note to himself on a pad on the desk.

'Let me be candid with you. I'm no fool. I've no illusions about my own talents. Without . . .' A glance around the room. '. . . all this I'd be nothing. A middling degree from Oxford gets you nowhere. Malise was a genius of a kind. A somewhat diverted one, but a genius nonetheless. Had he kept good counsel and his hands to himself, he'd probably be master of a college by now. Instead he was little more than an itinerant and very intelligent beggar dependent upon the mercy of lesser men like me. He had no discipline. No sense of politics. His emotions got the better of him and he, and his family, suffered the consequences. I did my best to help and found myself threatened as a result. They had to go. There was no option. How Cecilia coped with him . . .' For the briefest of moments he appeared almost regretful. '. . . I really can't begin to imagine.'

'Was he violent towards her?' Peroni wanted to know.

'I've no idea. Nor do I wish to know. Ask her. I will send you this paper of mine provided you agree to keep it private. It's not yet ready for publication. Malise never finished the task I gave him. Now, is there anything else I can do for you?'

Falcone put away his notebook.

'You can direct us to the office Gabriel used when he worked here. We'd like to look around.'

'The ground floor,' Santacroce said. 'Where you came in. They were the servants' quarters originally. It was the only place I could put him.'

Peroni stood up and eyed the large canvas next to the grandfather clock.

'It's Galileo, isn't it?' he asked. 'When they called him to the Inquisition?'

Santacroce nodded.

'What cultured policemen we have these days. It's a little over-dramatic for my taste but there you go. Galileo Galilei was a greatly misunderstood man. He was much more than a scientist. A philosopher too. Without him mathematics, astronomy, physics . . . none would have been the same, perhaps for centuries.'

'He still found himself arguing for his life,' Peroni replied.

'He did. Which was wrong. This brotherhood was founded to defend him, to let him know he wasn't alone. We do not forget what our cousin from Pisa did for us. Every work that appears under the name of the Confraternita delle Civette must, by order of our constitution, make some reference to him also, however slight. It's one of the few rules we have. My own paper, the one that Malise found somewhat obnoxious, is entitled "*E pur si muove*", a phrase that . . .'

Santacroce stopped in mid-sentence, smiled awkwardly. The attention this comment had raised in the two police officers had brought the slightest rush of colour in his face.

'It's a technical term,' he added quickly. 'You wouldn't know what it means.'

'No,' Peroni agreed. 'But my friend might. Please.' He pulled out his notebook and pen and handed it over. 'Write it down for me. I'd like to look it up. I'd like to learn.'

Bernard Santacroce passed the notebook back, the page blank.

'As I have already indicated, I will ask Cecilia to give you a copy,' he said, then gestured towards the door.

CHAPTER 6

Costa followed Mina's instructions as they wound down the hill from Montorio, back into the *centro storico*. After a while he began to understand where they were going, and the knowledge left a cold feeling in his stomach.

The Museo Criminologico was an outpost of the Ministry of Justice in the Via del Gonfalone, a cul-de-sac between the Via Giulia and the Lungotevere. This was the Italian state's official black museum, a place he had visited as a cadet, one that had filled him with horror, with nausea. He could still recall dashing out into the street, taking deep breaths, staring at a chilly winter sky, the first time he'd been forced to visit. The next, a kind of punishment for his perceived weakness, went more easily. He'd been a police officer for a few months by then, and had become . . . desensitized was the word the college instructor had uttered. It still amazed Costa that the term had been used as if it were praise. As if that was the point of the process of becoming a police officer. To feel less yet somehow see more. If anyone else noticed the contradiction they never mentioned it.

'Are you all right?' Mina asked as he leaned on the parked scooter for a moment.

'Just remembering something,' he said, and walked up to the door, flashed his ID and walked in.

'You don't have to pay for much, do you?' she said as she joined him.

Costa tried to smile when he told her, 'I wouldn't pay for this.' It was late afternoon, a little early, but right then a beer would have been wonderful. 'Afterwards I'll buy us some ice cream.'

The tears were gone. The pretty, somewhat over-active yet cerebral teenager was back.

'Or even a lollipop,' she replied, her head cocked to one side. Then she stepped inside, ahead of him.

CHAPTER 7

Silvio Di Capua frowned at the corpse on the table. The day had not gone the way it was supposed to. When he finally started on the preliminary autopsy he had begun under the impression he possessed two firm findings. Now their certainty seemed to be drowned in a sea of doubts, with insufficient time to dispel or clarify even a handful. He needed additional advice before he could proceed with the full autopsy. An expert. Nor was it proving easy to extract information from the dead man's medical records.

The young pathologist muttered a quiet curse, swallowed his pride and called her. Teresa was still in the apartment in the Via Beatrice Cenci. She'd been there for the best part of six hours and now sounded harassed and a little cross.

'Find anything?' Di Capua asked.

'Ever tried looking for evidence on a building site? The muck and dust these people leave behind them . . .'

'I have, actually. Several times. You just need to be patient and a little creative. It can be quite rewarding.'

'Thank you for that comforting advice. I'll bear it in mind. We're not having any luck tracking down the stuff that got cleared out of here either. It sounds as if a lot went to some dump out in the hills.'

'That was quick,' he said. 'I never realized the construction industry's waste-disposal people were so efficient.'

'Well, since you're so expert in these things, Silvio, I'll let you go down there to see if we can extract something out of it.'

He liked that idea and said so.

'But you did find something?' he asked.

'We've found very little really. About half an hour ago, underneath a thick layer of dust, we picked up a blood stain on the side of a radiator in the girl's room. Near the windows. I've sent someone back with a sample.'

'You won't get an answer till the morning. August, remember. It's like . . . like a morgue here!'

'If you crack that joke one more time I will, I swear, eviscerate you. With a teaspoon.'

It was an old one, he realized.

'Boring blood or promising blood?' he asked.

'It's just possible it's evidence of a struggle,' she said with an audible sigh. 'I don't know. There's no hair. No tissue. What about you? What about the photograph?'

Falcone had called from the Casina delle Civette asking them to examine urgently the picture of the unidentified naked girl and work out how old

181

the initial photo might have been. The print the two cops took with them wasn't the original. Before they left that morning Di Capua had scanned the photograph found in the apartment and run off a two-sided copy, one side picture, the other the handwritten message. Being the showman he was, Falcone wanted something that looked genuine to push into people's faces should the mood take him. The original itself had been scanned into the lab system, at very high resolution. Di Capua managed to peer at it briefly that morning, trying to interpret the mass of pixels before turning to Malise Gabriel. The first task had taken rather longer than planned.

'On the surface it looks like an image taken from silver halide film,' he told her. 'From an old-fashioned camera. A digital copy of a conventional print.'

'So it could be twenty years old, then?'

'A lot more than that for all I know. It's just a partial image of the torso of some young nude girl lying on crumpled sheets next to what appears to be a semen stain. Nothing to date it at all. There's visible film grain in the image. The photo came from a Japanese dye sub printer, really common. You can buy them down the shops for a hundred euros or less. Slip in your memory card or an image from a scanner, press a button, the picture pops out in a minute or less. I've got something similar in the lab. That's what I used to give Falcone his prop. Don't get excited. It isn't like a typewriter. Even if you find me a printer to look at I've no idea how we could say with any great certainty the picture came from that. You'd need the print material – the disposable paper it uses, which usually gets thrown away pretty quickly. I can give you the brand though and a range of models. Since we're going down the dump, we can look.'

'And?'

Teresa always knew when there was a caveat coming.

'It could be a fake. A good one. If you're handy with photo software it's very easy to make a digital original look as if it was shot on film years ago. You just turn the picture black and white, add some noise then soften it with some Gaussian blur. No easy way of saying if that's what's happened here. It could be twenty years old. Fifty even. It could be from last week. We've got a photo expert on call. I can get him in if you—'

'I'll think on it. What about you?'

He took a deep breath, knowing she wouldn't like this.

'Here's the bad news. What with photos of nude teenagers and some other things I'm way behind. After what you said this morning I wanted to get Gabriel's medical records first. I thought that would make things easier. I was wrong. The surgeon at the university hospital won't release them and won't tell me why.'

'Doctors don't have to roll over and give us everything we want.'

'I know, but they usually do. And why not? The man's dead.'

'The university hospital?'

'That's what I said. I suspect Gabriel was being treated for cancer. I tried the head man in oncology—'

'Adriano Negri?'

'Friend of yours? It didn't show. He won't cooperate. Won't show me a thing.'

'You leave him to me. Is that it?'

'Not at all,' he said patiently. It was always best to get the worst out of the way first. Teresa worked better when she finished on a rising note. 'I've got two things for you. Scratch marks. Some on his hands that could be evidence of a struggle. There are similar parallel marks on his lower back too. Fingernails. Three. Recent. Someone defending themselves. Someone having fun. Could be either. If you could locate a suspect and get a good look at their hands it's possible we might still find some tissue underneath the nails.'

'Fun?'

'Fun. Don't ask me to put a time on it but shortly before he died, anywhere between a few minutes and a few hours, Malise Gabriel had sex. No question about it.'

He paused, aware that her practical medical knowledge was immeasurably greater than his, since Teresa Lupo had worked as a doctor before becoming a pathologist.

'Are people with cancer much interested in . . . you know? Intercourse,' he asked.

'If they can!' she snapped. 'They're still human beings. Good God, Silvio. Depends on the condition. Treatment or the disease can affect the sex drive. It doesn't mean the desire disappears. They're just sick people. For pity's sake . . .'

Di Capua added quickly, 'There's trace evidence of a condom, which is one more reason why I'm a little behind here. I don't know the brand yet. There's nonoxynol-9 spermicide residue which could help there. I've also got traces of water-based lubricant. Maybe intercourse was difficult for some reason. Or it was just something he . . . they liked. No way of knowing. But again, there could still be something on the partner if you can get her or him into an examination room.'

He heard her begin yelling at someone to examine the toilets for condoms, then issuing another string of orders: checks for tissues, toilet paper, all the usual means by which semen might, with luck, be found. Di Capua knew what they really needed, though: bedding. If that was nothing more than ashes out at some dump in the hills this was not going to be easy.

'Who the hell examined this man when he came in?' she demanded.

He knew what was coming.

'Maria. One of the university interns on work

185

experience. It was Saturday. In August. He was an accident victim. Do you remember being young and naive and way too scared to cause trouble? I do.'

A florid curse lit up the line.

'You want me to fire her?' he asked.

'Don't be ridiculous. It's not her fault it took us two days to realize we had a murder on our hands. I'm the head of the department. If you want to blame someone, blame me.'

Typical, he thought. Their omissions were regrettable but scarcely case-threatening.

'Praiseworthy but unjustified,' he told her. 'We rely on the police to alert us to these things. They were asleep at the wheel. It's not our fault they didn't wake us as a result.'

'That's the most pathetic excuse I've ever heard,' she grumbled. 'I'm calling Falcone. Then I'm coming back to take a look at this myself.'

CHAPTER 8

The black museum was one more place she appeared to know by heart. Mina Gabriel walked straight through the winding corridors of the ground floor, past models of men being torn limb from limb by horses, display cases full of knives and mallets and cruel instruments of torture. It was like reliving a nightmare. An executioner's blade with a lion's head handle, used to gouge out eyes, to cut off ears and noses and fingers. The Milazzo cage, an iron shell containing a human skeleton, a victim for once of another nation's cruelty, in this case the British who had executed a deserter in Sicily by first mutilating the man then letting him starve to death locked inside the contraption. A spiked collar, a gossip's bridle, pillories, stocks, whipping blocks. The ghoulish red cape of Mastro Titta, Rome's most famous executioner, a celebrity of death, his uniform now hanging next to the axe he used to decapitate criminals in front of crowds of thousands.

Costa stared at the guillotine used by the Papal States and wondered how many lives had ended on this crude contraption of wood and metal. This place appalled him, made him ashamed of his inherited past, which was, perhaps, its purpose. Perhaps . . . There was always a morbid curiosity in people too. He knew that. It burned inside Mina Gabriel, with an urgency she appeared almost to relish. He was curious to know why.

She grabbed his arm and rushed him round one more corner, stopping in front of a long glass exhibit case. He gazed at a nest of hangman's nooses, each neatly tied. Next to the snarls of fading hemp was a note with the names and crimes of the men and women whose necks had once felt the rope's deadly embrace. By the side stood a grey hooded tunic in coarse fabric, loosely hung on the wall in the shape of a human being so that it resembled nothing less than the cast-off skin of a ghost.

'The Confraternita of San Giovanni Decollato,' Mina said, not that he needed to be told. The Brotherhood of the Beheaded John the Baptist.

'They have their own church,' she went on in a low, earnest voice. 'Near Santa Maria in Cosmedin. Do you think you could get me in? It's closed usually.'

'Why do you want to go?'

She seemed transfixed by the dusty cloak.

'Those monks looked after people before they were executed. They probably cut Beatrice's hair to make it easier for the executioner. These . . .' There was a zinc alms box bearing a decapitated head and next to it a set of small images of the

188

Virgin and Christ. 'They'd beg money from the crowd for her funeral, shove those stupid little pictures in her face to . . .' Her pretty features distorted with anger. '. . . comfort her.'

He thought he'd lost the dreadful image those final few moments had once devised in his imagination. Now he realized the memory of Beatrice was not so easily obliterated, that it was a phantasm that would return to haunt him at the least prompting. A single visual remembrance stood out more than any other, and it was not the obvious, the harsh, bloody violence of that final moment, but the grey, hooded figures dressed like this, charity from the same source that signed her death warrant, gathering around like demons as the executioner approached. One more indignity at the end.

'They keep things in that locked-up church of theirs,' she murmured, gazing at the faded grey robe in front of them. 'The basket her head fell into when she died. The hood of Giordano Bruno when they burned him at the stake in the Campo dei Fiori. Ropes and locks of hair . . .'

'Mina, Mina,' he said quickly, loudly too, against his own wishes. 'Enough. Let's get out of here.'

'Not yet,' she insisted, and dragged him back towards the exit, towards the thing that had stolen the breath from him a decade or more before.

It was about a metre long, a specialist weapon, unsuited for warfare or any conventional purpose. Behind the glittering steel stood a black and white

189

photograph of Reni's portrait of Beatrice, eyes turned to the beholder, even in this tiny print. By its side was an old book, the page open at the story of the weapon – the 'Sword of Justice' – that historians were convinced was used to behead Beatrice Cenci and her stepmother Lucrezia on that September day in 1599.

Mina stood stiff and upright in front of the display case, neither girl nor woman at that moment, her dark eyes full of outrage, fixed on the weapon, her breath shallow and irregular.

'Let's go outside,' Costa said. 'I promised you ice cream.'

'Ice cream!' she spat at him.

'Mina . . .'

'"The Sword of Justice"?' she asked, her voice full of heat. She was a child again at that moment. Full of the simple outrage that children possessed, the rudimentary innocence that classified all cruelty and hurt and neglect as wrong, never seeking to understand the reasons behind them.

'They may have meant that in the sixteenth century,' he said. 'Not today. If anything it's ironic.'

'Because we're so much more civilized now? More reasonable? More kind?'

'Next to this,' he said, nodding at the shaft of old stained steel behind the glass. 'Yes. We shouldn't bury our horrors. We should find the courage to face them.'

'That depends on the horrors, doesn't it? If

Beatrice was alive now . . . if all this happened today?'

He found his mind wouldn't think straight for a moment. She was looking directly at him, demanding an answer.

'How would you torture a confession out of her, Nic?' she persisted.

'I wouldn't,' he said immediately. 'Nor would anyone. We're not perfect but we're better than we were.'

There was an expression on her pretty, pale face that could have been the pout of a ten-year-old. He placed a hand gently on her arm and guided her to the door. It was almost six. The place would close soon anyway.

Outside the fierceness of the day was beginning to abate. The Via Giulia looked as quiet and as beautiful as ever.

'I promised you a *gelato* . . .'

'Don't patronize me,' she interrupted without looking at him. 'I want to go home.'

CHAPTER 9

Cecilia Gabriel printed out a copy of Bernard Santacroce's academic paper then left Falcone and Peroni alone to poke around her husband's gloomy office on the ground floor of the Casina delle Civette.

There were books aplenty, an office computer, some manuscripts, a music player with a collection of classical CDs, mostly Beethoven, and, on the cheap, utility desk where he worked, photographs of Gabriel's family.

The pictures sat in a line next to the computer. Peroni stared at them, wondering, aware of Falcone's judgemental gaze from behind him.

'You're the family man,' the inspector said in the end. 'Tell me.'

There were eight photographs in all. Mina Gabriel appeared in every one. The oldest showed her little more than five or six, the one next to it as a plain, somewhat gawky, very serious-looking kid, taller, staring straight at the camera. Gabriel's wife was in four pictures and didn't seem to want to smile much in any. The son appeared once, as a scowling boy of fourteen or so, tall and skinny, half-hidden behind his mother, with a head of curly brown hair that needed attention and doubtless wasn't going to get it. None of the photographs bore any obvious visual context: a holiday destination, a birthday party, a picnic. Every picture bar one depicted the subjects seated on mundane, often slightly scruffy furniture, stiff, as if posing.

The exception was a photograph of Mina alone, recent, Peroni guessed. The girl was pictured from the waist up at a stone window. She appeared to be wearing nothing but a coloured bra or a skinny bikini top and a giggly, girlish smile. Her hair was a mess, as if she'd just climbed out of bed. She looked happy in a way it would be hard to fake. Peroni guessed the shot was taken upstairs, in the apartment Cecilia Gabriel had now reoccupied. But it dated from summer. He could see that from the full, verdant palm trees, the tone of the sun and the girl's scant clothing by the open window. Given the timing of their stay in Rome this shot could only have been after they had moved out. Mina must have returned here with her father, got into a bikini or stripped to her underclothes, then . . .

The big old cop winced. He hated cases like this.

'Tell you what?' he muttered.

'Would you have a photograph like that on your desk?' Falcone asked. 'Of your own daughter?'

It was so easy to misread the signs, and the consequences for doing so could be terrible.

He looked Falcone in the eye and said, 'If you manage to peek behind the scenes of any family you'll find something that looks funny from the outside. A photo. A slap. A cross word spoken in the heat of the moment. You can't judge people's lives on the basis of a snapshot. If you did we'd all be guilty of something. The girl's probably just sunbathing. Kids do. Even smart kids who belong to academic freaks on the slide. It could be nothing more than that. Everyone takes pictures of their family when they're happy, having a nice time.'

There was a cold, disbelieving expression on Falcone's chiselled face.

'Sunbathing?'

'Why not?' Peroni pleaded. 'Can't anything be innocent any more? At what point did we start to tell people they couldn't take pictures of their kids messing about being kids without someone snooping around to take a look and asking if it's something worse?'

Falcone pointed at the picture.

'At the point they look like that. Anyone can understand . . .'

Peroni fought to keep a handle on his temper.

'Not if you're a parent! A normal one. The photo's sitting on his desk. His wife must have seen it a million times. If there was something wrong, something going on, don't you think she'd have realized?'

Falcone scowled and muttered something about

how relationships could cloud someone's vision, make them vulnerable.

'I don't remember anyone ever accusing you of that when you still had a wife,' Peroni snapped back, and regretted his outburst immediately. His colleague's marriage had been a protracted nightmare of recriminations and infidelities on both sides, one that had marked Falcone, perhaps helped make him the solitary man he was.

'No,' Falcone agreed, picking up the photo of the half-naked girl and looking at it very closely. 'They didn't. Perhaps the mother did find out in the end. Perhaps that's what happened. The mother, the brother . . . the girl maybe. I don't know. They told him to stop. He didn't. So finally they got together and killed him. Just like Nic said. They borrowed the idea from the Cenci girl, trying to make it look an accident.'

'Nic didn't say that. And besides, the Cenci all wound up dead, didn't they? Great idea to copy, I must say . . .'

'There's something very wrong here,' Falcone insisted. 'Do you really not see it?'

Peroni took one more look at the photo of the girl and issued a long, unhappy sigh.

'I don't know what I see if I'm honest. Families are just the world in miniature. Imperfect. Miserable as hell at times. Wrong too.' He had to say it. 'If you'd understood that maybe you'd still be married. Everyone's got their secrets. You have to learn to

195

live with them and keep them to yourself. It's best for everyone.'

Again he regretted his clumsy words, which were meant to inform, not accuse. Yet Falcone's face bore a brief mark of hurt. This was getting too personal, too close, for both of them. The inspector was his friend as much as a colleague and he hadn't recovered completely from the unexpected and vicious slap he'd got from the girl's mother. It wasn't the violence that shocked him. Peroni knew that. It was the hatred, the force behind it. Falcone was a decent man, trying to do a difficult, sometimes impossible, job, one that society demanded without ever asking the cost. He didn't want thanks. But he didn't expect to be detested either.

'I'm sorry,' Peroni said. 'That was uncalled for. I should never have said it. I simply feel we may be getting ahead of ourselves.'

Or was he really trying to convince himself of all this? He knew what Falcone meant. He just wasn't sure they were looking in the right place. Meeting Bernard Santacroce had bothered him, for one thing. The man was a stuck-up bastard who hadn't made the slightest effort to hide how he felt about Malise Gabriel.

'Why wouldn't that toffee-nosed bastard upstairs write out the name of his stupid academic paper for me?' Peroni wondered.

'I imagine he thought it was beneath him. Besides, we've got the paper already, haven't we? If you think that's evidence and this –' Falcone waved the photograph of Mina Gabriel in Peroni's face – 'isn't, then God help us all.'

There were times when Peroni wanted to give Leo Falcone a piece of his mind. The truth, the whole truth, nothing but. It wasn't rank that stopped him. It was simple human concern. He knew how much the man would be hurt if his fragile and lonely façade was punctured.

'May I offer a word of advice?' he said instead.

Falcone replaced the photograph then folded his arms, saying nothing.

'We're walking on eggshells here,' Peroni told him. 'If I remember correctly the only way they broke down the Cenci family was by torturing the brother. We don't have that option, even if we knew where he was. If there's a case here it may well depend on someone – the wife, the daughter, maybe even the son – deciding to tell us the truth. We won't get that out of them easily. Or by shouting.'

'I never shout!' Falcone objected, then added, more quietly, perhaps with a little regret, 'Well, rarely these days.'

Peroni opened the door to the Casina delle Civette. Evening was on its way, a lazy golden one, still full of heat.

He took Falcone by the arm, looked into the man's lined face, with its silver goatee, which was now, with age, beginning to look a little vain and said, 'Come on. Let me buy an old friend a beer. It's August, Leo. We don't need to rush things. No one's going anywhere. A little time. A little patience. Who knows how this will look in the morning?'

The inspector's phone trilled. Peroni picked up Bernard Santacroce's academic paper, placed it under his arm, and waited.

Falcone listened for a moment then hit the speaker button and turned the handset so he could hear. It was Teresa. She had news and it changed everything.

CHAPTER 10

The Vespa wound its way back along the Via Giulia then, under Mina's shouted guidance from the back, Costa turned left into a narrow side street he didn't know and brought the scooter to a halt outside an imposing Renaissance palace. To his amazement – and some embarrassment – Falcone and Peroni were walking out of the entrance arch, talking rapidly to one another with a serious intent that usually meant something had happened.

Before he could drag the little machine into the shadows Falcone's sharp eyes caught them and he was over, Peroni following in his wake.

The inspector glared intently at Costa then, as if ignoring him, spoke directly to the girl.

'Mina Gabriel?' he asked, showing his ID.

She got off, removed her helmet, shook her long, blonde hair free and said, 'Yes?'

'We need you to come to the Questura. If you want to bring your mother, please call her now. The choice is yours. It isn't necessary. There's no legal requirement.'

'What's this about?' Costa asked, to Falcone's obvious displeasure.

Falcone turned to Peroni and said, 'This has nothing to do—'

'I want him here!' Mina yelled at him. 'You can't order me around. Who do you think you are?'

'Signora!' It wasn't the right word and it was obvious from Falcone's face he knew it. She looked like a girl again, with an angry pout contorting her pale and pleasant northern features. 'I need you to come to the Questura for interview.' He glowered at Costa. 'We have our reasons.'

'Reasons?' she said. 'What reasons?'

'At the Questura—'

'Are you arresting me?'

'No,' he replied, shaking his head. 'Not at all.'

'So you can't make me?'

'I'm asking—'

'I'll talk to Mummy,' she said, and passed the helmet back to Costa. 'If she says I should come, I'll come.'

'Leo,' Costa interrupted. 'Can we please talk about this calmly? I'm sure Mina will do every-thing she can to help.'

'I want to talk to my mother,' she insisted.

'Fine,' Falcone snapped. 'Then let me ask one simple question. I wouldn't normally broach this in a public street but since it appears I have no choice—'

'What?' she demanded.

'Your father had sexual intercourse the night he died. That is beyond doubt.' He didn't look happy having to say this at all. Falcone seemed mournful, and deeply upset. 'You said there was just the two of you in the apartment all evening. So I need to know. Was it with you?'

She looked as if she'd suffered some kind of invisible, physical blow. Her slim shoulders hunched forward, her mouth fell open. Tears, of grief and indignation, began to fill her bright young eyes.

Mina Gabriel shot a glance of unadulterated hatred in Costa's direction.

'I thought you said you couldn't torture people any more,' she told him.

'You don't have to answer,' he said, in spite of Falcone's growing fury. 'We can arrange an appointment at the Questura. Tomorrow, say. With your mother. A lawyer. I can come if you want—'

'You're a police officer!' Falcone bellowed.

'Right now I'm on holiday,' Costa replied.

Mina took two steps forward until she stood directly in front of the inspector.

'I'll tell you what I told Nic,' she said briskly. 'I loved my father. And he loved me. Read that how you will, you grubby little man.'

She shook her head, dashed forward and kissed Costa briefly on the cheek, the way any young Roman girl might have done with a friend at the end of the day. Then she whispered in his ear, 'I'm sorry. Thanks for listening to me.'

The girl half-walked, half-ran into the building.

Costa wondered whether he'd done the right thing, and not just because Falcone seemed beside himself with anger.

'I could get a warrant right now,' the inspector stormed. 'We could go through every last thing they own. I can take her into custody this instant. Her and the mother.'

Costa waited for a little of the heat to abate.

'If you do that,' he said quietly, 'she'll never tell you a thing. I can't believe what I just saw here. How could you do that? How?'

'What choice did I have?' Falcone roared.

'Some,' Costa replied quietly. 'Why the rush, Leo?'

'I thought that's what you wanted, wasn't it? You're the one who brought us into this case.'

'If it is a case,' Costa said. 'And if it is you're going to have to take this very carefully indeed. You're dealing with a family here. Not some street crook who's thrown a brick through a jeweller's window.'

Peroni added mildly, 'I tried to explain that to him. Also, to be perfectly frank, I'm not sure you could do any of those things you suggest, Leo. Not on the little we have.'

Falcone shook his fists, exasperated, and Costa realized he understood this last point too.

'So what do we do?' the inspector asked.

'How about that beer?' the big man suggested cheerily. He caught Costa's eye. 'And some explanations.'

PART VI

CHAPTER 1

Falcone loathed the idea of an ordinary cafe or bar so they found themselves in an enoteca he knew called Angolo Divino on a corner near the Campo dei Fiori. It was early. They were the only customers. The inspector lost a little of his fury as the three of them walked there from the Palazzetto Santacroce, Peroni making discreet and inconclusive calls back to the Questura and Teresa Lupo along the way. The position was not improving. Robert Gabriel, Mina's elusive brother, remained missing. The magistrate approached for a search warrant for the apartment in the Via Beatrice Cenci had thrown out the request on the grounds of insufficient cause, and maintained her refusal even when forensic added the evidence of Malise Gabriel's recent sexual activity. It was, accordingly, clear that, without fresh evidence, any bid to seize the Gabriels' belongings in the Casina delle Civette would be refused too.

Costa recognized this mood in the man who was both his superior and his friend. Insular reflection did not come naturally. He preferred to act inside the moment, to work with the rhythm of the case. In the absence of such motion he felt lost, powerless. Whatever had occurred during this difficult day had left him stranded with few options. This was never a position likely to generate harmony.

There was also something personal here. Families made Falcone nervous. No one knew much about the man's own. The inspector's past was not so much secret as invisible. Even his ill-fated marriage, which had ended years before Costa came to know him, remained a topic to be avoided. The prospect of dealing with the intimate intricacies of the Gabriel clan perhaps amplified this sense of isolation. Falcone's one attempt at some kind of familial bond had occurred years ago when, as a newly divorced officer determined never to commit himself to a direct relationship again, he had sponsored Agata Graziano through school and college, which was how she had come to be involved in the earlier police investigation that introduced her to Costa. Now even that tie, fond and awkward in the same breath, seemed a little tenuous as his former ward struggled to make a life of her own outside the enclosed world of the Church.

'Explanations,' Falcone said again as they sat down.

Three glasses of beefy *primitivo* from Puglia and a plate of cheese and cold meat appeared then Costa told them about his day. When he was done Falcone looked at him and said, 'You might have mentioned last night that you'd arranged to meet Mina Gabriel.'

'Last night it was difficult to get a word in edge-ways. Also I was rather more concerned with Agata's state of mind, to be honest. She didn't appreciate being dragged into things like that. Besides, I'm on holiday. I can do what I like. There didn't appear to be a case. Mina looked like a sad and lonely kid in need of company. She asked me to provide it. How could I say no?'

'Funny way to spend the day,' Peroni noted. 'Following in the footsteps of that poor Cenci girl.'

'She said she planned to earn some money taking Joanne Van Doren's customers on a history trip. Softening them up for the purchase. I was her guinea pig for when that happens.'

'Don't you mean if?' Falcone asked. 'That place is months away from being saleable. Years even. The way the woman kept going on about the bank . . .'

'I thought that was genuine,' Peroni intervened. 'She looked very upset.'

Falcone scowled.

'Or guilty. She'd just cleared out the last trace of any possible evidence of a crime. Do you think the Gabriel girl was genuine, Nic? That's all this Cenci connection is? A hobby?'

Costa thought back on the day, and the deep discomfort he'd felt at times.

'Up to a point. Perhaps she believes that herself. But I'd say its clear she's obsessed with Beatrice for some reason. The detail she knows . . .' He remembered her standing stiffly in front of the sad, accusing face on the wall in the Barberini, the tantrum at Montorio, the way she stared avidly at the sword in the museum, drawn to its ancient, stained blade. 'It's . . . morbid. Abnormal. She must have spent weeks, months researching it.'

'Why?' Falcone interrupted.

Peroni played with a slice of the fatty Florentine salami called *finocchiona*. Costa could smell the fennel in it from across the table. His own father had adored the stuff.

'Teenagers get obsessions,' Peroni said. 'That is one obsessive story. Someone like you wouldn't . . .'

He stopped, aware of the sudden chill.

'I wouldn't understand, naturally,' Falcone replied with an acid smile. 'I don't have feelings, do I?'

'Gianni wasn't saying that,' Costa cut in quickly. 'Besides, I don't understand Mina Gabriel either. Sometimes she's astonishingly bright and confident. Then, at others, quite unworldly and unsure of herself. Mature one moment, juvenile the next. And . . .'

He remembered the fond way Joanne Van Doren had talked about her. There was no easy way to explain this. It had to be seen, in the caring, worried expressions of the women at the cat sanctuary, in the faces of the church wardens in Aracoeli, watching from the shadows as she bent over the organ there, trapped in the mechanisms of the gigantic instrument, eyes streaming, intent on playing the piece her father had loved, one that was both haunting and resonant.

'She has this . . . aura. I don't know how to put it. There's a personal magnetism you don't expect to see in someone of that age. Or anyone really. She's special. People love her.'

'She's an attractive teenager, Nic,' Peroni said. 'Intelligent, likeable, considerate. You don't get that so often. It doesn't mean she's not trying to work out who she is, just like any other kid. There's nothing unusual there, not really.'

Costa shook his head.

'I disagree. She's worried. Frightened, maybe. Hiding something. I thought that when I saw her in the street the night her father died. It's as if she wants to talk but can't. Whether it's because she's afraid, ashamed, or maybe just hasn't found the right person to tell . . .'

The three men fell silent over their food and drink. Costa wondered what the *finocchiona* tasted like. The smell . . . He grabbed a slice of pungent seasoned pecorino and pushed the thought aside.

'So here we are,' Falcone grumbled. 'The three of us wondering what to do. I hate August. I don't have the manpower for some complicated investigation even if I had the evidence to justify one. Half the people who are any good are on holiday.' He glared at Costa. 'Including you.'

'What's the rush?' Peroni asked. 'No one's going

209

anywhere. Give us a week or so and we'll be back to normal.'

Falcone sighed and said, 'We could be looking at murder.'

'Could we?' Costa asked. This point had been bothering him for the last hour. 'We've no evidence that Malise Gabriel's death wasn't an accident. The only reason we have doubts is because of the way we're interpreting how his family are behaving. I see the look in Mina's face and think there's something wrong. What could be evidence disappears for no good reason. It's intriguing. Infuriating. But it doesn't add up to anything circumstantial, let alone substantive.'

'Here's something,' Peroni chipped in. 'That American woman looked much more worried than the real widow. Cecilia Gabriel seems as hard as nails. I couldn't wait to be out of there, and she didn't hit me.'

Falcone muttered something inaudible then added, 'All the more reason why I should be doing more than I am.' He glared at Peroni. 'Shouldn't I?'

'Doing what? We're trying to prise open the lid on one of the most private things anyone owns. Their family. Cecilia Gabriel and her daughter don't seem keen to help. The son's nowhere to be found. This isn't going to be quick or easy. Besides, do we have a choice? We could be in trouble already.'

'Facts,' Falcone protested. 'On the evidence we've

210

been given Malise Gabriel was alone in the house with his daughter. Logically, circumstantially, he had sex with her, not that we have any firm proof. Even if she agreed to a physical examination . . .'

Costa shook his head and said, 'She won't do that. Not now. Why would she? She isn't making a complaint.'

'I'm going to have to ask for one, aren't I? If she's innocent, where's the problem?'

Peroni caught Costa's eye and said, 'The problem is she'd have to go into a room with a complete stranger and let herself be prodded and poked as if she were a rape victim. Allowing you to do that is as good as an admission that something untoward happened, isn't it? Nic's right. She won't agree.'

'It could clear her!' Falcone pointed out. 'And her father.'

Costa thought of the words she'd used outside the Palazzetto Santacroce.

'Mina identifies with Beatrice Cenci. If you ask her to go through an examination she'll equate that with some kind of torture, of duress. Understandably, perhaps. Beatrice never confessed to a thing, even when she was hung up from the ceiling until her shoulders were dislocated. If Mina sees herself as a modern-day Beatrice she'll ignore every question you throw at her as a matter of principle.'

Falcone scowled.

'Why? Her father appears to have been murdered.

211

He had sex before he died. There were scratch marks on his back. If we could examine her nails . . .' Costa and Peroni were shaking their heads in unison. 'There was blood on the radiator by the wall. A sign of violence, possibly. Perhaps the brother chanced on them and lost his temper. Perhaps it was planned in advance.'

He put his glass on the table and murmured a low curse. Then he glanced at Costa, as if seeking support.

'If I pull in Mina Gabriel tomorrow, with or without her mother, and put her through an aggressive interrogation – no physical examination, just questioning – do you think she might break?'

'No,' Costa said immediately. 'She's very smart and very cool. When she wants to talk, she'll talk. Not before. Nothing's going to change that. Not unless you can break her story somehow. You're also forgetting that she spent most of that Friday night in the room she used for music. Practising, wearing a set of headphones. She only saw her father briefly, later in the evening. That was how she knew he was there.'

Falcone looked interested and said, 'So?'

'So if you're practising music, very intricate and difficult music, with headphones on . . . surely anything could have happened outside the door of her room. Someone else could have walked in and gone to bed with Malise Gabriel, then left without Mina noticing.'

'Please,' Falcone told him. 'You know nothing

of affairs. No one would do such a thing if there was a family member in the next room. Headphones or no headphones. It's ridiculous.'

'They would if the girl knew the affair was going on,' Peroni said slyly. 'If it was their secret. Daddy's friend's coming round. Best not disturb us.'

'Well, there's one more reason to bring her in.' Falcone glanced at his watch then drained his glass. 'Unless the girl tells us something I see only two ways forward. Forensic can come up with something concrete from outside the house. Or we can find the brother. I'm sick of waiting on narcotics. We can at least try to locate Robert Gabriel ourselves. Agreed?'

Costa shrugged.

'It's not for me to agree or disagree. It's your case.'

Falcone's acute grey eyes flashed with displeasure.

'Oh no. You're involved already. You spent the whole day with Mina Gabriel. She trusts you. We can use that. It may be one of the few advantages we have.'

'I'm on holiday, Leo.'

'I know. But you can do what you're doing now. Hanging around. Talking to her. If she trusts you that could help us.'

Peroni grabbed some more cold meat with a wordless grumble.

'Is that wise?' Costa asked. 'Doesn't the question of entrapment bother you?'

'Not in the slightest. She needs a friend. It seems to me she has one.'

He half-expected this. Costa knew the direction the man's mind took when opportunities were scarce.

Falcone tapped Peroni on the knee.

'Also I like your idea. Let's wait until we've something solid. Then, when we're ready, we'll bring in the girl and her mother. Who knows? Maybe the son too.'

Peroni blinked and said, 'You liked my idea? You're following my advice?'

'I always listen. Give me credit for that. Besides.' Falcone's face fell serious for a moment. 'If we go nowhere near them for a day or two perhaps they'll think they've got away with it.'

'Whatever *it* is,' Costa added. 'Anything else?'

Falcone smiled and held up his wine glass. He looked satisfied finally, if not exactly happy.

'One more round of drinks, Nic. Then I'm going home. Best make it quick. The price goes up at seven.'

CHAPTER 2

Costa bought them another glass and stuck to water. Then, when they left, he picked up the Vespa from outside the Palazzetto Santacroce and rode round to the narrow lane of Governo Vecchio. It ran from the old talking statue of Pasquino near the Piazza Navona towards the river, a cramped, cobbled route that was once one of the pilgrim streets to the Vatican. Falcone had owned an apartment here, close to the famous wine bar Cul de Sac, before moving to a quieter place in Monti. Near Navona it was busy with tourists and Romans alike. As it progressed towards the Ponte Sant' Angelo, where Beatrice Cenci had been executed, it became quieter and more local, one more shady, constricted alley among many. Governo Vecchio was a convenient place to live, and pricey too. Agata's new private college seemed very generous.

Her address turned out to be a single bright red door on the corner that led to one of his favourite churches in Rome, the baroque little temple of Santa Maria della Pace, a classical jewel in the midst of the area's sprawl of palaces and apartment buildings. There was a florist's opposite. Costa caught the woman as she was locking up and managed to buy her last few flowers: a rather limp-looking selection of tulips. He stood on Agata's doorstep, bouquet in one hand, crash helmet in the other, ruffling his hair to try to look a little more presentable after the long, eventful day.

It took a good minute for her to answer and when she did he'd no idea what to say. So he just stood there, extending the flowers, smiling awkwardly. Agata was wearing a short and sleeveless black cocktail dress. Her hair was newly fashioned in a way that, to his eyes, looked a little too serious and old. She was struggling to fasten a rather heavy pearl necklace round her dusky throat and there was a look in her intelligent eyes that he couldn't quite interpret except, perhaps, as embarrassment. The apartment, from what he could see through the half-open door, looked beautiful: modern furniture, large art prints on the wall, an airy individual residence hidden behind the thick walls of a building that probably went back to the seventeenth century or earlier. She didn't make a move to let him in.

Costa thrust the flowers out a little more, and realized as he did so how sorry some of them looked.

'I asked you to call first,' she said.

'Busy day.'

'Busy? Doing what? You're on holiday, aren't you?'

There was something in the way she spoke, a tone that was almost accusing. He didn't understand.

'All sorts.'

Her attention had gone beyond the flowers to the tatty Vespa on its stand on the cobblestones.

'That's your scooter, is it? The one Leo told me about?'

'That's her,' he said proudly. 'Look. You're living just up the street from one of the best pizza places in Rome. Da Baffetto. We don't need the scooter. You have to queue usually but . . .' He pulled out his police ID card. 'Sometimes I have ways.'

She sighed then turned round. He got the message, tucked the bad bouquet under his arm, then gripped the clasp of the pearl necklace and closed it against the warm dark skin of her neck. It was the first time he'd performed this simple act since his wife had died and the closeness of it, the pointless intimacy, made him feel wistful and a little sad.

A tall, muscular man, bald, intellectual-looking, with fashionably heavy black plastic glasses and a haughty pale face, came into view from behind her.

'Agata won't be eating pizza tonight,' he announced in a clipped Milanese accent.

Costa looked at him, trying to understand. The newcomer was about forty-five, handsome in an arrogant, patrician way. He wore a silvery grey suit, silk perhaps, very expensive, and eyed the little Vespa as if it were poisonous. Still looking at

217

the scooter he pulled out a set of car keys and pushed a button. There was a grey Alfa Romeo saloon parked thoughtlessly along the road. It made a loud beep then the lights flashed and the doors clicked.

'I'll drive us to Testaccio,' he announced, then placed a proprietorial arm around Agata's shoulder. 'The table is booked for eight thirty at Checchino's. We shouldn't be late.'

'Checchino's?' Costa knew the place, a little. One of Rome's most pricey restaurants, not that its speciality – offal – was something he'd touch. 'Nice if you like that kind of thing.'

'She will,' the man interjected with a sardonic smile before almost pushing her out of the apartment.

'Bruno's my new boss,' Agata said as she turned and locked the door, embarrassed in a way that made Costa feel deeply guilty. 'We've got to talk about work. I'm sorry. If you'd called . . . If I'd guessed you were at a loose end. I never knew. From seeing you today . . .'

'No problem,' he cut in with a smile, then wondered what she was about to say. 'You saw me?'

She didn't answer and the man had got her out of the apartment so quickly there was no chance to ask again.

As Bruno bustled her off she turned and made the gesture of a phone, surreptitiously as if she didn't want him to notice. Costa clung to the bunch of flowers and nodded, still smiling.

'Of course,' he said to himself as she climbed into the shiny Alfa. Its powerful engine roared with rather more noise and vigour than was necessary. Then Bruno drove briskly away along the narrow, congested street.

An elderly woman in a cotton dress, an ancient checked apron and saggy stockings was sweeping up outside the tiny pasta shop next to the florist's. Costa walked over and said, 'Signora?'

She looked at him in a knowing way that suggested she'd followed every moment of this little encounter.

'Some flowers,' Costa said, offering her the bouquet.

Her lined face brightened.

'You're a kind young man. A lady appreciates that. *Grazie.*'

'*Prego.*'

'One word of advice,' she added, waving a finger.

His heart fell. Romans, even complete strangers, had a way of telling you frankly what they thought, however unwelcome the message.

'Yes?'

'Kindness is all well and good. But remember that saying? All's fair in love and war?'

'I never really understood it,' Costa admitted.

She patted his arm as she took the bouquet and said, 'It shows.'

He shrugged then went and sat on the Vespa, watching the people come and go down the Via Governo Vecchio. Young and old. Couples and families. Queuing patiently for Baffetto's cheap and excellent pizzas as they did every night, even in the rain. Ordinary men and women, the kind he liked, the kind he wanted to work for, to protect, wandering around on a lazy late-August evening, seemingly without a care in the world. Very few of them, he noticed, were alone.

It was stupid to turn up like that. Selfish to think she would be waiting there, for him alone. Agata Graziano was a beautiful, intelligent young woman discovering a new life in a city where she'd grown up behind the enclosing walls of a convent. An attachment to a solitary cop fumbling through the years, one so lacking in direction that he thought rebuilding an ancient Vespa was a worthwhile venture for a man turned thirty – this was surely the last thing she needed.

Costa looked at his watch. He'd be home in twenty-five minutes, back behind the walls of the farmhouse where he grew up. Somewhere that wasn't a part of the city, didn't belong to its ungainly mass of awkward humanity. The place was a kind of escape. A sanctuary. Somewhere to hide. He didn't mind that at times.

'Home,' he said to himself, and, without thinking, popped the scooter kick-start four times in a row then, to compound matters, absent-mindedly jerked on the throttle.

The two-stroke engine coughed once, sputtered, choked and died.

Flooded. That meant waiting an hour or so. Or taking out the spark plug and fiddling with the carburettor, which involved tools he hadn't brought along.

The old woman was still watching him, holding the bouquet, shaking her head.

At that moment his phone buzzed; he felt grateful and stared at the screen. He'd given his number to Mina Gabriel in case she needed it. Now she'd sent a message. It read, 'Do you believe what that horrid man said? Do you think I'm guilty of something?'

He sighed, gave up entirely on the Vespa and phoned her back. From the sound of her voice she'd been crying.

'Mina? It's Nic. Are you all right?'

She mumbled a simple, tetchy 'Yes.' Then nothing.

'Listen to me. Don't read too much into what happened this afternoon. Leo's a good man. He's my friend. He wants to help. We all do.'

'Help?'

He tried to imagine her, alone in the tower Peroni had told him about.

'Help,' he repeated. 'What can I do?'

'Nothing.'

'Tell me, Mina!'

'Can't.' He thought he heard a noise, then understood what it was. She was closing a door, perhaps to her bedroom. Trying to make sure she wasn't heard. Then she whispered, 'Don't

221

believe what anyone says about me, Nic. It's not true.'

'No one's saying anything . . .'

'I am not some monster!'

'I know that.'

'No, you don't.'

The petulant tone of a child again. There was another sound. A louder female voice. Her mother, he thought immediately. Shouting. Angry. Words he couldn't quite understand, though he knew what they meant. Then a shriek of pain accompanied by what sounded like a physical blow, and the line went dead.

Families. He thought of Peroni and his love of everything to do with that word. Of Falcone and how the very mention of such a secret, insular closeness could place a dark cloud in the eyes of one of the most decent men he knew. These tight, sometimes cloying ties encompassed the best of humanity and, on occasion, masked the worst of it.

'I am not some monster,' Costa repeated to himself and wondered: who is? Who would ever admit to that fact? The most vicious and brutal criminals he'd met never saw themselves in that light either, not quite. They felt justified in their actions, possessed of some moral compass, and if the rest of the world failed to understand, then so what? Lives were made, not inherited or handed down. Usually.

The phone buzzed again.

'Mina?' he asked anxiously.

It was a message from a number he didn't recognize. He stared at the words on the screen: 'Meet me in the Campo. The Lone Star. Be alone. Robert Gabriel.'

CHAPTER 3

Costa knew this place well, from work, not pleasure. It was one of the busiest bars in the Campo dei Fiori area: a grubby dive serving cheap alcohol to a predominantly international and young crowd. The Lone Star was where the students and backpackers from America and England congregated of a night. To drink, to flirt. To feel free of the restraints of home. He'd lost count of the fights he'd dealt with, the number of drug busts he'd seen recorded among its customers. All just a few short steps away from the plain, upright building that had once been home to the mistress of Alexander VI, the Borgia Pope, her presence still marked by a small crest on the wall of the house where Lucrezia and Cesare Borgia came into the world.

He wondered if any of the kids around him knew how much history lay just outside the door, and what the offspring of Rodrigo Borgia, no strangers to debauchery themselves, would have made of the Campo dei Fiori five centuries on. The bar was packed. A hundred youngsters or more. The music was deafening, the voices predominantly English: drunk, elated, expectant. He scanned the faces, looking for one that might jog a memory. Costa was aware that he hadn't got a good look at Mina's brother that night in the Via Beatrice Cenci. All he remembered was a tall figure, a head of bushy hair and that curious remark before the gunshot: *She's safe now*. Words that had set him wondering in the first place.

After fifteen futile minutes he asked the barman if he knew an English kid called Robert Gabriel. No luck. After half an hour he was ready to go home. Then the phone beeped again. Not a call, just another text message: 'I wanted to see you were alone. Meet me in the apartment. Via Beatrice Cenci. Fifteen minutes.'

He was here. He had to be. Costa found himself gazing across the sea of bodies again. He stopped at a tall figure in the far corner, near the side door that led to the little lane connecting the Campo with the Piazza Farnese. The kid was watching him, interested, maybe a little afraid. Robert Gabriel looked different somehow. Just as tall, and the hair was long, though a little lank, unwashed. His complexion was darker than Mina's, his expression bleak and unintelligent. He was wearing a bleached denim jacket over a black T-shirt.

Costa shrugged at him as if to say: we could just talk here.

We could even talk on the phone, he thought.

But then he was gone, out through the side door into the street.

Costa got out as quickly as he could but it was no use. The ancient square, with its hooded statue of the executed monk Giordano Bruno at its centre, had taken on its night-time identity: loose and noisy. Watching the crowds of young men and women meandering between the bars he found himself wondering why Mina Gabriel had never thought to join her brother in this perennial ritual. It seemed easy, natural for the foreigners who came to Rome to study, to spend an enjoyable year pretending to be Roman before real life, with its cares and demands, came to claim them.

The sky was a dark sweep of velvet punctured by stars and the lights of passing aircraft. Fifteen minutes. He tried to call Falcone but the inspector was on voicemail. No one at the Questura would assemble any kind of support in the time he had. Either he went along with the invitation or he walked away from the whole affair, went back to the Vespa in Governo Vecchio, hoped the ancient carburettor had cleared enough to take him home.

He found himself thinking of Mina Gabriel, picturing her that night in the Via Beatrice Cenci, staring at him, needing something.

Costa pushed his way through the shifting, aimless throng in the Campo, and started to walk back towards the ghetto, a route that would, he realized, take him directly past the Palazzetto Santacroce from which she'd made that last, scared call, its message opaque and impeded by some intervention he failed to understand.

CHAPTER 4

The door to the building was open, the entrance hallway dimly lit with low security lights that wound up the long staircase like decorations left over from Christmas. He shouted the brother's name. Costa's voice echoed round and round the winding steps, dying somewhere near the summit. He recalled that long climb the previous day, with Peroni stopping to catch his breath on every floor.

The thought of making that journey again was starting to fill his head with dismay when a loud, metallic clang shook the floor beneath his feet. It took a moment to realize what it was. The lift, the small, old-fashioned open iron elevator with the out-of-order sign on the doors, was ascending from below with an asthmatic rusty wheeze.

One more lie, Costa thought as he listened to the rheumatic squeal of the cables and pulleys straining against one another. Then the cage arrived with a heavy, clattering bang. Nothing happened. He walked over and could see, in the dim light of the interior bulb, that it was empty. The buttons were within reach through the collapsible door. Someone had sent it for him.

He got in and waited. This was a vast, empty place. Robert Gabriel could be anywhere. After a few moments there was another rattling sound and the cage began to move uncertainly down, descending into the thick, airless dark, a dead space rank with the smell of damp and decay. Instinctively Costa patted his jacket, the empty spot where his gun would have been if he were on duty.

'One of those days,' he said to himself.

The lift came to a halt with a rickety jolt. The only thing visible was a single dingy light bulb dangling from a cord beyond the cage. He threw the door open with a clatter and got out, calling once more. Another light came on, then a third. His eyes began to adjust. The basement was full of building material. Sacks of cement, planks, a wheelbarrow, boards covered in hardened plaster. From somewhere in a far corner came the scurrying sound he associated with rats. Close by he could see a single heavy door which looked as if it might lead to some kind of 'garden' apartment, the accommodation that was always the cheapest in these places.

He walked ahead. There was a thin line of yellow light beneath the door.

'Robert,' he said calmly and turned the handle.

There was no reply. He walked in and found himself in what appeared to be a photographic studio. A small forest of professional-looking floodlights was set against one wall, several of them lit so they cast a dazzling white field of illumination across the room. They were all aimed in a single direction: at an ornate double bed covered in crumpled scarlet sheets, set against a wall decorated with a sea of cavorting cherubs, winged chubby creatures, the kind Raphael once painted, though not quite like this.

The tiny creatures, like miniature angels, leered lasciviously as they coupled and licked and squeezed and squealed on the cloudy pillows of a perfect blue sky, eyes down, always, to the bed beneath them.

Pornography, he thought immediately.

'Robert,' he called into the darkness, then realized he could smell something.

A memory returned. The forensic department when Teresa Lupo was just one more junior in a time before the world had turned entirely digital. The police photographers then used film, loved the stuff, would wind off frame after frame getting every angle of a victim, recording each death for posterity, unable to see the results until they returned to the Questura and ran their work through chemicals in the dark. Life before digital was finite, circumscribed by its own limits, by cost. No more than six films per case unless someone wanted more. Now, when photos and videos came for free, they could shoot to their heart's content, fill the

Questura's screens with a million images, each demanding interpretation.

It was easier in some ways before. Paucity, the very fact that the information to which one had access was limited, could pull a complex investigation into focus. And focus smelled like this. There was a darkroom somewhere nearby, one of those small, enclosed places with sinks and mysterious equipment from which, with a little luck, a spark of enlightenment would emerge on the face of a damp piece of photographic paper held between the teeth of a pair of plastic developing tongs.

If Robert Gabriel was there, on this hidden floor in the basement of the house in the Via Beatrice Cenci, he didn't want to make his presence known.

Costa walked up to the bed and thrust aside the top sheet. The fabric beneath was freshly crumpled. There was the faintest trace of a stain, like the one next to the adolescent torso in the photo in Malise Gabriel's book, the pale young skin that might or might not be Mina's.

He took out his phone and glanced at the screen. No signal, not even a flicker. He was underground, deep in the belly of a stone fortress. The modern world didn't want to intrude into this place.

His fingers fell on the stem of the nearest floodlight. Costa began to angle it around the room. The walls were bare. In the corner was a small and narrow door, just ajar. He took one step towards it and the chemical smell became stronger.

Acid. Fixer. Hypo. He hadn't heard those terms in years but each one came with its own distinct scent as he remembered the times he'd spent in the darkroom, watching, waiting for some image to emerge on the paper as it swilled slowly in the plastic baths.

He got to the other side of the room and pushed his hand through. There was a black curtain, just as he expected. And somewhere beyond, the most precious, most dangerous thing of all in a darkroom, the string pulley for the light switch. One jerk on that at the wrong moment and any film, any unfixed print would be rendered useless in a second.

Costa remembered the way the Questura had a red light outside its own processing unit, warning anyone thinking of entering to stay out until the mystical process of turning invisible silver halide into some black and white representation of reality was complete. There was no such sophistication here. In the basement of the ancient palazzo, next to what gave every indication of being some kind of secret pornographic studio, perhaps there was no need.

His hand fumbled against the inside wall, hunting for the string. Nothing. He edged through a little further and something brushed against his face. It was always somewhere you didn't expect it. Costa pulled the dangling cord, blinked briefly as two strong fluorescent tubes began to flicker violently into life above him, found himself walking forward in the brief flashes of illumination they afforded, then screamed, couldn't help it, as his arm bumped into something, sent it swinging away like a pendulum that disappeared for a moment and came back, fetching up against his right cheek with the plain, heavy physicality of a corpse.

Cold skin, cold clothing, another, more organic smell, the stink of death.

The tubes hit full power. The room was awash with bright, cool light. His face was level with the chest of a human being moving gently in front of him. He looked up and found himself face to face with the dead features of Joanne Van Doren, her pale, thin features distorted by the rope around her neck, eyes bulging, tongue lolling, like the mask of a slaughtered clown.

'Jesus,' Costa whispered and tried to turn away.

The hard, metallic nose of a gun edged onto the back of his neck.

'Keep looking,' said a young English voice beside him. 'At her. Not me.'

Costa fought to think, closing his eyes for a moment. Then, when he knew he had to look, he forced himself to stare at the dishes and the gear by the developing sinks, not the body swaying in the bright light just in front of him.

'What do you want?' he said finally.

'I want you to see. I want you to understand.'

233

'Understand what?' he asked and tried to turn. It was easier to talk if you could see someone. 'I can't . . .'

'Don't look at me!' the English kid screamed, and stabbed the gun hard into Costa's skull.

Pain. Fear. Incomprehension.

'What do you want, Robert?' he repeated.

Strong fingers wound into his hair, forced him down over the evil-smelling sink.

'Leave my sister alone,' Robert Gabriel hissed in his ear. 'This is nothing to do with her. Nothing. Tell them that.'

'And you?'

'What about me?'

He was scared. Angry. Full of the same petulant doubt Costa had witnessed in Mina at times.

'Where are you going to go? With no money. No home.' The pressure of the barrel on his neck eased. 'Where are you going to run? With friends like yours, you're a liability now. All they're interested in is business, whatever they told you. Liabilities worry them. They won't hide you. Not forever.'

The grip on his hair increased until it hurt. Robert Gabriel was strong.

A punch to the face, a blow with the body of the gun. Costa stumbled to the floor, lost his balance and found himself scrabbling on concrete.

'I said, don't look!' the voice above him screamed.

He waited, listening to the steps recede into the studio beyond, and then disappear into the black maw of the building.

When there was silence Costa got up and went over to Joanne Van Doren. She'd been dead for a few hours. The rope went round a black heating pipe in the ceiling. Next to her was a plain chair, like the one in the studio, on its side on the floor, as if kicked there. He remembered the pained expression on her face when he came here the previous day. Perhaps he should have noted that more, asked someone to call. But she was just the owner of this block, not someone involved in the story. Or so it seemed.

'I'm sorry,' he murmured, and walked out of the corridor, found the stairs, went up them one by one, clutchig the banister in the dark, watching his phone all the way, waiting for some sign that he was back in the world beyond once more.

PART VII

CHAPTER 1

Teresa Lupo looked at the corpse on the gurney in the basement studio, scratched her straight brown hair, screwed up her broad, pale face and said, 'Well, I can tell you one thing, Leo. You've got your murder now.'

It was nine fifteen. Costa felt dog-tired after a few restless hours at home. Just before seven Falcone summoned him to the Questura for a questioning that carried much of the same mute aggression he would have used on any witness. Then a team of officers assembled, Peroni among them, and he was ordered to join them and the forensic team that was already working in the basement of the house in the Via Beatrice Cenci.

The morgue people had made up their minds long before Falcone arrived. Costa could see it in Teresa's body language, the insistence with which she'd made them all climb into white bunny suits before setting foot inside the scene, the way she was getting her team to mark out the whole of the basement area. She'd been a fixture of the Questura for as long as Costa had been a cop, a bright, occasionally incandescent spark of intelligence, intolerant of laziness, generous to those she admired, kind and sympathetic to the bereaved who passed through her department. The relationship with Peroni, almost fifteen years her senior, had mellowed her somewhat. But no one would dare take her for granted.

'You're sure of that?' the inspector asked.

She was a cautious worker, never one to rush to judgement. It was unusual for her to reach a conclusion before returning to the Questura and a careful consideration of all the options.

'Absolutely. See for yourself.'

Peroni coughed and went to stand by the doorway leading back to the lift cage. Falcone and Costa joined her by the gurney. She was pointing at Joanne Van Doren's neck. The insubstantial white nylon noose, washing line he guessed, had been removed to reveal a mass of livid bruises, more than Costa would have expected.

'The technical term is "ligature furrow",' she said. 'The mark the rope makes on skin, under pressure. If this woman had committed suicide by hanging herself I would have expected to see just one. Diagonal, like an inverted V. It's there.' Her gloved fingers traced the lines of some pinkish marks on the American woman's neck running from her throat back into her scalp. 'But it's not alone, is it? She was already dead when she got that.'

Another strip of bruising ran horizontally around her neck, joining the fainter one at the front, separate as it ran round to the back of her head, the two lines joined by what looked like grazed skin.

'Horizontal furrows are what you get from strangulation. Someone . . .' She stood up, turned her assistant Silvio Di Capua round, and made to slip an imaginary noose over his head. '. . . came up behind her, dropped the rope over her head, tightened it on her neck.' A brief demonstration. 'And pulled till she was gone. Then he ran the rope over that heating pipe in the ceiling and suspended her next to the chair he'd kicked over. That's why we've got abrasions running from the original furrow to the one she got from being hanged like that. The rope dragged when she was hauled upright.'

'He?' Peroni asked.

'Well,' she said with a shrug. 'Someone with a lot of strength, anyway. I'd guess a man. Asphyxiation is a man thing. Women tend to be either more direct or more subtle.'

Costa couldn't quite work this out.

'And then he tried to make it look like suicide?' She nodded.

'Pathetic, isn't it? I can give you more proof once I have her back in the morgue. Really, you don't need it. How anyone could think they'd get away with a trick like that, I can't begin to imagine. I'll take a look at the Englishman later on today and see what we can come up with there. But this one, I guarantee, is murder, pure and simple. I'd guess he wore disposable surgical gloves. You can smell the latex on the rope. If we're lucky he dropped them somewhere around here. If we find them I can give you something from the lining.'

Falcone didn't look terribly hopeful.

'I want to go through this whole building,' Teresa told him. 'Floor by floor, room by room. Top to bottom. If we'd done that yesterday we'd have found this little secret studio of hers. Perhaps things would have turned out differently.' She frowned at the corpse on the gurney. 'Maybe if our American friend had been a little more co-operative and candid she'd still be alive.'

'Do whatever you think is necessary,' Falcone said, then glanced at Costa. 'We need to find the brother.'

'I can understand that,' Costa agreed.

'Seeing that you managed to let him go last night . . .'

'Managed? He had a gun on me. I tried to call you, Leo.'

'You might have left a message. Since you didn't see fit to tell any of us you were meeting him . . .'

'It was one of his conditions!' Costa felt embarrassed, on shaky ground. He shouldn't have agreed to the meeting without telling someone, even if he was off duty, on holiday, at something of a loose end. 'I'm sorry. I made a mistake. I should have told you. It was a long day. I was tired. Confused.' He recalled the brief meeting with

Agata and the way she disappeared with her slick boss inside his silver Alfa Romeo. 'Not thinking straight.'

Falcone allowed himself the briefest of smiles then patted him on the shoulder.

'Well, now you can make amends. The holiday's over, *sovrintendente*. Consider yourself back on duty. It seems to me we have a suspect.'

Costa sighed.

'Why would Robert Gabriel bring me here in that case? He was trying to tell me something.' He glanced at the bed, which was now being pored over by men and women in white suits. 'He wanted to say this was nothing to do with them. His father's death too. Joanne Van Doren gave them a home when Santacroce kicked them out. She was Mina's friend.'

Peroni was at the door, watching, listening, expressionless.

'She wasn't the mother's friend from what I saw,' he said. 'Someone needs to tell the Gabriels this has happened, by the way. Someone sympathetic.'

Falcone brightened.

'Good idea. Go back to the Questura and get what you can out of narcotics about Robert Gabriel. Then break the news about this to his mother and sister. The two of you. See what their reaction is. I want the brother.'

'I'm sure you do,' Costa murmured. He still couldn't reconcile what he was seeing in this strange subterranean lair with the family who'd been the only people to live there, several floors above. 'What is this place?'

'Porn palace,' Silvio Di Capua announced cheerily. 'A very well-appointed one too, I'd say. The darkroom out the back is fully functioning and ready to go. Used very recently. Popular place. Look.' The young pathologist got them to bend down and peer at the bed, showing them the promising signs – stains, traces of hair, possible tissue. 'It's like Christmas down there.'

'When will you know whose it is?' Falcone demanded.

'A day. Two maybe. Matching it, well . . . We've got a couple of bodies we can check. When it comes to the living, that's down to you.'

'Precisely,' Teresa added with a smile. 'Now, unless you have some other questions, I'd be grateful if you could get out of the way.'

Falcone instructed some of the other officers to pressure narcotics about Robert Gabriel's contacts. Teresa issued a series of orders to her own people then looked up at the ceiling and said, 'This is a big place, Leo. We're going to need a few days to go through every floor. Can you find us some help?'

He stared at her. She shrugged and said, 'OK. It's that time of year.'

In the far corner of the room, near some metal filing cabinets, someone squealed with glee. They all looked. Costa recognized one of the young work-experience trainees, the same girl who'd been alone on duty at the weekend when the dead Malise Gabriel was taken into the morgue and tagged as a simple accident victim.

She was plump with a ponytail and a bright, happy face.

'Look what I found in the cupboard!' she said, full of juvenile pride.

In her gloved hands was a large old-fashioned camera, black and box-like, the type with a pop-up viewfinder. Unusual, which was why she was playing with it in an injudicious way, flicking up the top, turning the big eye of the lens.

Di Capua wandered over, making admiring noises on the way.

'Oh . . . my . . . God,' he sighed. 'Pornographers with taste. How often do you see that?'

'What is it, Silvio?' Teresa asked. Then, somewhat testily, 'Maria, will you kindly stop messing with the thing like that?'

The trainee seemed fascinated by the object, as if it had come from another age. In a sense, Costa thought, it had. He hadn't seen anything like it in years.

'Hassy 503,' Di Capua crooned, holding out his hand. 'Hasselblad to you. Pentaprism with a one-twenty back. The Americans used adapted versions of this to take pictures on moon-shots, for pity's sake. Though if I'm honest . . .' He stopped and scratched his bald head. 'I'd imagine it's pretty damned perfect for a porn studio too. And . . .'

Costa caught a glimpse of something yellow on the back. A memory returned.

'It's got film inside,' he said.

Silvio Di Capua looked at him and grinned.

'Film! I love film!'

The girl holding the Hasselblad pressed a couple of buttons. The back came off. Then, as Costa watched, she somehow managed to unlatch the cover and he caught a glimpse of dull grey emulsion.

'Remind me,' she said, looking a little puzzled. 'Film?'

Age could prove a terrible divide on occasion. A good half of the people in the room were already staring in horror at the brief length of exposed stock in the Hasselblad, open to the bright light of the floods that was already wiping away any image it might once have held. The rest looked baffled, as if trying to retrieve some distant memory of a time when photographs didn't appear instantly on the back of a little digital screen.

Di Capua was on her in a flash, snatching away the camera back with a ferocity that left the trainee shocked and reeling, then fumbling it back onto the body as best he could.

'Did I do something bad?' she asked, suddenly close to tears.

'Again,' Di Capua snapped. 'Get in there.'

He pointed to the door in the corner.

'The dark place?' she asked.

'The dark place,' he agreed, half-pushing her ahead of him.

Costa put a hand on his shoulder, stopping him, and asked, 'How much is a camera like that worth, Silvio?'

The young pathologist paused for a moment, thinking, turning the camera round and round in his gloved fingers.

'Late eighties, 503CW. Eighty-millimetre planar lens.' A closer look, an admiring glance. 'No scratches. Not a sign of fungus.' He winced. 'You've got to be looking at a thousand euros. You could pay that new for the lens alone. This thing's mint. Doesn't look as if it's ever set foot outside this place.'

'Thanks.' Costa looked at Falcone and knew the inspector had to be thinking the same thing. A piece of equipment like this was surely beyond the reach of Malise Gabriel.

'Men and their toys,' Teresa said. 'They can be starving and their families near destitute. But if something's shiny and smells of sex . . .'

CHAPTER 2

Narcotics owned most of the west wing on the third floor of the Questura, a chaotic, rambling network of rooms where uniforms were rare and it was often difficult to tell the difference between police officers and their clientele. Costa was surprised to see that he already knew one of the two officers assigned to brief them. Rosa Prabakaran looked hollow-eyed and exhausted, thinner than the last time they'd met. She was wearing the kind of clothes, a short skirt, a tight and bright-checked thin sweater, that passed unnoticed in the places where Costa guessed she now worked. Rosa had been part of Falcone's team until recently. She had served alongside Costa before, most recently during a terrorist attack on the city during a G8 summit. After that case, ambition took her elsewhere, to external courses and then another department altogether, the standard route to promotion. Costa had lost touch with her, which he regretted. Roman-born to an Indian father, she'd cut a solitary and private figure in the Questura. Her colleague was new to Costa, a cocky Venetian of

248

thirty or so called Gino Riggi, stocky, with the physique of a rugby player, close-cropped dark hair and a stubbly face that smiled often, without humour or sincerity.

Peroni cleared his throat after the four of them sat at a table in the one empty interview room and said, 'Robert Gabriel. What we need—'

'Wait,' the Venetian interrupted, grinning. 'Let me get this straight. You . . .' He pointed straight at Peroni. '. . . are the *agente* here. And you . . .' Costa. '. . . are the *sovrintendente*?'

'Correct,' Costa said. 'But really I'm on holiday. So just answer the questions, will you? I'm a good listener.'

He'd taken a rapid dislike to this man for some reason. Judging from the way Rosa gave Peroni some sideways glances, she felt much the same way.

'Sir!' Riggi said with a mock salute. 'What do you want to know?'

'Where can we find him?' Peroni asked.

Riggi shrugged.

'No idea. Can't help you.'

'Gianni—' Rosa began.

'Can't . . . help . . . you,' the Venetian cut in, his voice getting louder.

Peroni folded his arms and stared across the table.

'Got a picture of him?'

'Never had the reason.'

'A list of addresses for his friends?'

249

'I don't keep his diary.'

'Details of who he worked for?'

'Details?' Riggi frowned. 'Not really.'

Rosa said, 'We think he was tied to one of the Turkish gangs. The Vadisi. The Wolves. Selling. Delivering. He's just a low-grade street kid. Really, not the kind we'd take much interest in usually. He was active. Pushing a lot. But if you pick them up they won't tell you a thing. It's too dangerous. Besides, what've we got to offer them? The Turks give them money. Dope. Girls. I think they've got some places where they can stay. Maybe . . .'

'We don't know where he is,' Riggi insisted.

Costa leaned over the table and said, 'He's the prime suspect in a murder.'

The slick-looking cop shrugged.

'You're looking in the wrong place. He's just some stuck-up English kid who's making a little money passing pills and smoke to his buddies. Didn't have it in him to kill someone. You got proof that says otherwise?'

'Early days,' Peroni replied.

'I thought not. Listen. I'm telling you. Look somewhere else. Robert Gabriel isn't a murderer. You're wasting your time. And mine.'

Peroni caught Costa's eye then said, 'We could always requisition the informants' register if you like. Or shall we just save everyone some time and hear it from you right now?'

Riggi let loose with a vile curse then slammed his fists on the table.

'What is it with you people?' he yelled. 'Do you have any idea of the kind of work we do?'

'Did it myself, son,' Peroni snapped back. 'Twenty years ago. Don't get smart. There's only one reason for you to protect this Gabriel kid.'

'Twenty years ago was different! You had . . .' Riggi looked lost for a moment, as if trying to remember something that had long eluded him. 'There was some kind of sense of right or wrong out there. Listen to me. It's gone. We're trying to police people who don't want to be policed. Victims and bad guys. None of them trusts us. None of them thinks we belong out there.'

Costa sighed and said, 'Do you really think it's different for anyone else in this building?'

'Yes,' Riggi replied. 'And if I get someone who just might talk to me now and again I will *not* hand him over on a bunch of stupid coincidences.' He scowled. It suited the stubble somehow. 'Even if I did know where he is, and I don't. Listen. Gabriel has been mildly useful to me, to us, in the past. In the future he could be a lot more help. Maybe take us to some of the Turks who are bringing this shit into the city.'

'He's a murder suspect,' Peroni repeated.

'I told you that's not possible.'

Costa thought of Mina and her insistence: *he isn't bad.* And that scared tone in the kid's voice the previous night, as he pressed the gun barrel into Costa's neck and told him to look at Joanne

Van Doren's swaying corpse because it was nothing to do with him or his family.

For some reason he couldn't quite explain, Costa felt Robert might be telling the truth. Or a part of it anyway.

'Does he have any idea of the risk he's taking?' he asked. 'Playing both sides? Informing against people like that?'

The Turkish gangs were among the most ruthless in Rome. They didn't think twice about maiming or killing someone who offended them. There was none of the hood etiquette, the pseudo-religious sense of guilt and responsibility, that could still have a restraining effect on a few Italian mobsters.

'It's not my job to walk some dumb English adolescent across the street,' Riggi said.

'Nic.' Rosa reached across the table. 'Really, we don't know where he is.' She shot a bitter glance at Riggi. 'If I had an idea, you'd know. I promise.'

'Teamwork, teamwork,' the cop by her side muttered. 'We're so good at that around here.'

'What about pornography?' Peroni asked. 'Was he involved in that? These Turks?'

'Porn?' Riggi asked, astonished. 'Is this some kind of bad joke?'

'No,' Peroni told him. 'This woman we think he killed died in what looks like some kind of porn studio. Hidden away, with its own darkroom. Has to be a reason for that.'

The Venetian threw back his head, laughing, wiping imaginary tears from his eyes.

Rosa Prabakaran scowled and said, 'They're not involved in porn, Gianni. Why would they be? Porn's so . . .'

'Turn on your computer, man,' Riggi cut in. 'You get more porn for free through Google than you could buy for a fortune in one of those little places near Termini five years ago. It's saturated market. There's no money there. Not on the scale these guys can make. Besides . . .' He hesitated and, for a moment, seemed almost reflective. 'What is it now? Five euros a month on your credit card. Straight. Gay. Violent. Kiddies. Animals . . .'

He looked at his watch. Then, in a tone that told them this interview was over, he said, 'Even a low-grade runner like Robert Gabriel could make two, three hundred a day shifting pills and smoke. How many Polish hookers do you have to pimp to bring in that kind of bread? No. I told you already. He's not your man. Not for murder. Or anything else.'

Rosa stared at Costa.

'Porn's for old people,' she told him. 'If you think that's relevant somehow. Trust me, you really are looking in the wrong place.'

'And that's it,' Riggi said, getting up from the table. 'That's all we have to tell you.'

CHAPTER 3

The chemicals were fresh, the film still within its use-by date according to the box tag on the camera. Silvio Di Capua had weighed up his options. The Questura no longer possessed its own photographic darkroom; that corner of the forensic department had been handed over to a whirring server farm for the office network. Rome still had a few specialist photographic developing companies for the dwindling band of professionals who refused to use anything but film. But they'd take their time, cost money, and . . . and . . .

He caught the eye of Maria the intern, smiling at him in the red glow of the safety light, looking both pretty and extraordinarily gullible. Di Capua was developing the film from the camera in the darkroom next door to the makeshift porn studio for no other reason than because he wanted to. A good five or six years had passed since he'd last laboured over the delicious and demanding task of bringing emulsion to life through a patient mix of chemicals and skill. He missed that tactile experience, and since the equipment and the facilities were here on the spot already it seemed ridiculous not to use them.

Maria came close to him and stared at the dishes, sniffing the acrid aroma of old-fashioned photography, seemingly impressed.

'How do you know . . . ?' she began to ask.

'School,' he said. All those years ago, when he was twelve or thirteen, learning how to develop black and white film – colour was too hard and a little . . . common was the word that came to mind.

Outside the firmly closed door a couple of inquisitive morgue monkeys were chatting as they worked the scene by the scarlet bed. This was a little unusual, Di Capua thought. But Teresa didn't screech at them to stop. She had enough problems of her own, finding the resources to perform a basic forensic job and manage the caseload back at the Questura.

'Watch,' he said, then read the instructions on the bottles, just to make sure he remembered correctly. 'And pray there's something still left that didn't get ruined.'

It took time. It was gradual, revelatory. Silvio Di Capua realized that, at the age of thirty, he'd somehow forgotten how to appreciate these slow and tantalizing processes.

'How old are you?' he asked.

'Twenty. Nearly twenty-one. I went to college a year early. I'm bright.'

Ten years, enough to create a gulf between them.

So much had happened, so much had changed, while she was still little more than a child.

'Of course you are. How much longer are you with us?'

'A month.' Her eyes sparkled. 'Unless there's an opening . . .'

They all wanted jobs. Decent jobs, the kind they thought they were owed. Di Capua had walked out of college to find the world at his feet. A good degree, a bright, inquisitive brain that could see him through any interview. Academia, finance, science; so many opportunities lay open to him when he was fresh to the market. Today they were all desperate, chasing a narrow and diminishing number of opportunities. Over-educated, over-qualified, young men and women praying they could find some niche to save themselves from the dull drone of badly paid service-industry jobs. And most of them never made it, just slumped into routine, dreary positions, hoping that one day the economic climate would improve and provide them with the kind of middle-class career they thought would arrive at so easily.

He wondered about Robert Gabriel, the brother they sought, the one they assumed had murdered the woman not far from where they now worked. Was he like that too, a kid who'd slipped through the cracks? And if he was, how might he have turned out a decade before? If there'd been work and hope to keep him engaged, too busy and too involved to waste his life in the dive bars of the Campo and Trastevere, where the drink and the dope led nowhere?

'I'm getting old,' Di Capua murmured. Worse than that, he thought, he was starting to think old.

'No, you're not,' Maria said with touching, sweet enthusiasm.

He felt the briefest twinge of interest and fought to stifle it. Then he swilled the developing tank once more. The timer sounded and he embarked upon the once-familiar round of processes that would first reveal then fix the silver halide on the negative stock inside the plastic barrel. He didn't think about Maria, didn't think about anything else. Her inexcusable clumsiness out in the studio, beneath the floodlights, had wiped at least a couple of frames from the film. That was certain and, as they waited, he told her so again.

She stared at him in the eerie red light of the darkroom lamp.

'You mean there's no way of going back?'

'What? Like some kind of undelete?'

His words shocked him, mostly because he sounded so like Teresa Lupo. Yet, to this young woman, the question was utterly logical. In the digital world there was always a way back, even if it was one that only lasted for a few steps. The notion of permanent loss, of something precious becoming irretrievable, was a ridiculous anachronism. Like polio and fax machines and last year's fashions.

'If it's gone, it's gone,' he said, and then the second buzzer went off and he was able to unscrew the tank and take out the film.

Silvio Di Capua pinned the strip to the line, let it dangle over the sink to drain and asked Maria to turn on the light, the real one. She hesitated, double-checked she understood, scared there'd be another accident. Di Capua reassured her and then, when the fluorescent tube came on, looked up and down the strip, reaching for the hairdryer next to the nearby socket, getting ready to play a careful stream of hot air onto the surface to hurry up the process of making this fragile, damp film stock turn into something solid.

The portion that had been exposed to the light was gone forever, two, perhaps three frames turned into nothing but black mush by Maria's ignorance. But there was a half-frame of something left as the exposed film rolled into the hidden part of the camera back. And five more frames beyond that, each perfect, each depicting close up in negative the kind of physical act he associated with places like this.

Porn palace had turned out to be the right phrase, he thought, scanning the negatives, trying to imagine what they'd look like when he ran them through the enlarger at the end of the table and turned them into prints.

There was something else he'd forgotten too. How it was always impossible to recognize faces in negative, even people you knew very well, members of your own family. This inverse image was like a code, locking up the truth, scrambling it until you switched black to white and vice versa and finally got back to the image that the camera lens had seen some time before.

The individuals there were unidentifiable. The subject matter was easy to see.

'Maria,' he asked. 'Are you . . . er, religious? I mean when it comes to sex?'

There was an alarming sparkle in her keen brown eyes.

'No. Not at all. Not one little bit.'

He still wasn't sure. And this part of the process would be quick too. In a matter of minutes he'd have a result. He'd know who was in these photographs, would put faces to the entwined bodies that were anonymous in negative. Falcone had refused to return to the Questura. He was outside, poking around the building, annoying Teresa's army of forensic officers in bunny suits. In half an hour or less the inquisitive inspector could have a set of prints in his hands.

Di Capua scratched his bald head and didn't look at her when he said, 'It's just that . . .'

'Silvio,' she interrupted, standing so close he felt her bunny suit rustle against his. 'I just watched a dead woman, a murdered woman, get cut down from the ceiling. I know why I want to do this job. Honestly.'

She touched his arm. He wasn't sure what he felt at that moment.

'OK,' he said. 'Well, in that case, turn out the lights again. Let's find out what we've got.'

CHAPTER 4

There was a crowd outside the Questura. Women mainly, five, six deep. They were shouting and waving banners from one of the left-wing groups that campaigned against sexual violence. The day promised to be the hottest, most humid yet. The black shapes of a few wannabe storm clouds were beginning to dot a brilliant sky that seemed to weigh down on the city as if ready to fall. Rome could turn bad-tempered on mornings like this, though these people were there already.

Costa looked at the sea of faces blocking the Questura entrance and the gates to the car pound, turned to Prinzivalli, the old uniform sergeant who was monitoring the demonstration, and asked, 'What the hell is going on?'

'You haven't turned on the TV recently, have you?'

'We've all been a touch busy,' Peroni said.

Prinzivalli glanced at his watch then led them back into the entrance hall and gestured at the TV in the side office with the words, 'Just in time for the midday news.'

They listened in silence. The lead story concerned the deaths of Malise Gabriel and Joanne Van Doren. But the picture on the screen was a snatched shot of Mina, head down, tears in her eyes, striding into the Santacroce Palazzetto, turning briefly to face the photographer's lens. Costa felt his blood run cold. She looked so innocent, so damaged. Everything he'd come to feel about this young woman was captured in that single image: the mix of strength and vulnerability and, most of all, the impression that somewhere beneath her simple, beautiful features there lay a secret waiting to be uncovered. It was the kind of shot the media would seize upon, the kind of story too, one that mixed death and sex and mystery. And something unique.

He watched as the newsreader handed over to a reporter standing outside the Gabriels' former home in the ghetto and listened to a phrase he knew would come to signify the investigation from this point on.

'They are calling her,' the female journalist said briskly, 'the English Beatrice Cenci. How much did she know of her father's suspicious death? What was her relationship with him? Did someone consciously copy the murderous plot of Beatrice, the young Roman girl who lived across the road from here, five hundred years ago? And if so, is her family also involved, as was Beatrice's? These are the questions we understand the police are beginning to ask. For the people of Rome?

Another reason, I think.' A theatrical pause for the camera. 'Four hundred years ago we executed a young woman for taking vengeance against the man who abused her. What would we do today? This is . . .'

'Turn it off,' Costa ordered.

The uniformed *agente* in front of the set looked at him, puzzled.

'Turn it off!'

'Nic,' Prinzivalli said, putting a hand on his arm. 'We have to watch the news. It's the rule. Besides . . .' The grey-haired uniformed officer, a calm and sensible man, a rock inside the Questura at times, looked at him. 'This is out there now. You have to deal with it. We all do.'

'Where the hell did they get all that nonsense from?' Peroni demanded. 'I mean . . .'

His words trailed off. The Questura was always leaky when there was a controversial case around. Cops, forensic people, civilians working the offices and the phones . . . If the death of the Englishman did come to look like homicide it was always going to be difficult to keep the investigation quiet. The murder of Joanne Van Doren had perhaps simply accelerated a process that was inevitable.

The officer at the TV switched channels and got another long and detailed report, one that had taken up the selfsame line.

'The English Beatrice!' Peroni was outraged.

Yet it seemed logical to Costa, not that he liked to admit it. The media was an imitative beast, one that fed on itself. Mina Gabriel lived opposite the Cenci palace, a short walk from the private church at which the family had worshipped. She was a little younger but possessed the same air of youthful innocence. Somehow the media had picked up the gist of her response to the police too. They knew that she was refusing to discuss any sexual relationship with her father on the grounds, the reporter said, that this was an insult both to her and to him. Then there were the circumstances of Malise Gabriel's death, which were remarkably similar to those of the dreadful Francesco Cenci.

'Who the hell put this story out there?' Peroni wondered. 'Is this the mother getting her defence in first?'

'What makes you say that?' Costa replied. 'It could be anyone. Someone here. Forensic. Those building inspectors, even. They must know something's going on. We've been pressing them hard enough.'

'You haven't met her yet,' Peroni muttered. He glanced at Costa. 'There's something . . . calculating about her. Scared the life out of me. As hard as nails.'

Costa thought of the shouting when Mina called the previous night, and what sounded like a slap.

'But why, Gianni? What possible advantage can she get from having an appalling accusation like that out in public?'

There was a moment of silence.

'We're on the defensive now, aren't we?' the old cop grumbled. 'Let's go ask her.'

'You'll need to walk,' Prinzivalli said. 'Since that story broke those nice people out front have been blocking the vehicle exit. I'm trying to reason with them. It would be best to avoid any arrests. If I can . . .'

'We don't need a car,' Costa said, as he walked across the corridor and took a spare police motor-bike helmet from the cloakroom, then retrieved his own from the storage area. 'Here.'

He threw the spare helmet at Peroni, who stared at the thing in horror.

Prinzivalli followed them outside, chatting with some of the women protesters in a friendly, almost supportive fashion. Costa listened for a while, then, when they were distracted, wandered over to the corner of the square where the Vespa was parked.

He climbed on, took great care to start it properly this time, then sat there with the little two-stroke engine rumbling happily as Peroni gripped his blue police crash helmet, standing to one side, staring at the machine, thinking.

'The tyres are barely legal,' he complained. 'Does the horn work?'

Costa pressed it.

'Sounds like an asthmatic duck. I could drown you in tickets right now.'

'Only if you were a traffic cop. Which you're not. Now get on, *agente*. And don't squirm about back there. It may upset my balance.'

265

The scooter felt quite different with Peroni on the back. Costa navigated the piazza very carefully then headed for the ghetto. He couldn't help notice Prinzivalli watching them leave, and that the man in uniform seemed to be shaking with laughter.

CHAPTER 5

Teresa Lupo walked out of the house in the Via Beatrice Cenci, glad of an excuse to get away from Falcone's beady eyes, pushed her way through the barriers and the hordes of newspaper and TV reporters, then headed round to the little cafe in Portico d'Ottavia that Peroni had told her about. The search of the building was in good hands. Silvio Di Capua had his photographs. Slowly, steadily she was beginning to assemble some basic shreds of evidence. And one hour earlier she'd had the report from an outside specialist she'd brought in to take a look at the corpse of Malise Gabriel. It confirmed what she'd begun to suspect the day before. So she'd called Adriano Negri, the oncologist who'd brushed off Di Capua's inquiries, and made it clear she wanted to see him, immediately.

He was waiting in the cafe already. Teresa kissed him on both cheeks then got a couple of slices of Jewish pizza for them both.

'Is this healthy?' asked Negri, a handsome man in his late thirties, tall with a distinguished academic face and long, dark hair.

'How many sick Jews have you seen lately?'

'Quite a few.'

'Not through eating this stuff.' She smiled at him from across the table. 'You look well.'

'Thanks. You too. I hear you're . . . settled.'

'Settled?'

'With a cop. An old cop.'

She took a bite of the pastry and wondered why they'd never discovered this stuff before.

'The man I love,' Teresa said. 'That's how it's supposed to be, isn't it?'

'You could have been choosy.' He hesitated. She could still picture him twenty years before, at La Sapienza, the university where they first met. He had long hair then, money and a wonderful if unconvincing smile. 'Maybe even me.'

'You know, it was the constant presence of that "maybe" that was the problem, I think. Also, I *am* choosy.'

He shrugged, in that exaggerated way, with the downturned mouth, that had always annoyed her.

'But a cop. An old cop . . .'

'Malise Gabriel,' she interrupted.

'Can't talk patients.'

'He's a dead patient. Probably a dead murdered patient.'

'That doesn't . . .'

'Actually, it does make a difference. Legally, ethically, morally. If you withhold valuable information from us it would be inexcusable. Possibly rather difficult too, were I to make it so.'

'Don't threaten . . .'

'Malise Gabriel was suffering from pancreatic cancer. I know he saw you several times. I need to understand his condition. If there's anything else you can tell me . . .'

The consultant drained his coffee and tried a little of the pastry. He was a decent-enough man. Arrogant, self-obsessed, destined to be single probably. But a talented doctor, one who wanted to help people.

'Am I to be quoted?' he asked.

'This is just a private conversation between the two of us, Adriano. If it came to a court case I can bring in an expert witness instead. Save me some time now, please. I will be grateful.'

He didn't look happy. But she watched the way he squirmed and knew she'd won.

'It was diagnosed when he was living in America,' Negri said. 'The insurance wouldn't cover him over there. I suspect that's one reason he came to Rome. He thought because he had a UK passport—'

'That he was covered? He was, surely?'

Negri shrugged and said, 'If only it were that simple. There are rules about residency. Malise hadn't lived in Europe for two decades or more. He was effectively stateless, at least as far as medical insurance was concerned. I did what I could for a while. He found money from somewhere. At first, I assumed paying for treatment wasn't a problem. He had a manner about him. Aristocratic. A little overbearing. One didn't wish to ask. But . . .' He seemed embarrassed. 'Treating a disease like that is extraordinarily expensive if you have to pay yourself. A few weeks ago he told me he had no more money left. Or rather no way of *finding* more. It didn't come from him. He always paid cash, very large sums sometimes. I didn't pry.'

This puzzled her.

'Do many private patients pay cash?'

He was squirming again.

'No. Generally speaking only the ones from Naples or Sicily, if you know what I mean.'

Crooks, she thought, not that he wanted to say it.

'I tried to find funds for him,' Negri went on. 'I suggested he approach his academic colleagues for support, but that was beneath him. I'm sorry.'

'Are you telling me a dying man was refused treatment because he had no money?'

'You sound surprised. Why? Oh yes. Now I remember. You haven't worked in medicine for years, have you? That's the regime we have now. Every last thing costed, justified, analysed. Ten years ago I would have treated Malise Gabriel to the best of my ability without a second thought, knowing that someone, somewhere would have picked up the bill. Not today. We live in mean times. Mean in spirit. Mean in other ways too. I'm sorry. I couldn't treat him any longer. Even if I waived my charges, someone would have to pay for the rest of the treatment and there was no one. So I had to tell him it was at an end. Not that I could have made much difference to his condition anyway.'

'How long did he have?' she asked.

'I would guess six months. A year at most. Possibly less. Untreated, it's difficult to tell.' He laughed, without mirth or feeling. 'You know the ridiculous thing? I'd arranged for him to enter a hospice for palliative care close to the end. Getting money to keep him alive was impossible. Finding some altruistic sisters of mercy who would ease his suffering – I had a dozen to choose from.'

He looked so mournful she felt guilty.

'You know who he was?' she asked.

'You mean the books? Of course.'

'He'd have gone into a church hospice?'

'You'd be amazed how many rediscover God at the end,' Adriano Negri said. 'The pain, the fear.' He thought for a moment. 'Not that I saw much of that in Malise. He was a remarkably easy patient, if I'm honest. A strong man. Opinionated. Angry, not about himself, I think, but about others. A terminal disease can manifest itself this way sometimes. The sick take it out on the healthy, as if they're to blame somehow. I can't imagine Malise would have been easy to deal with at home.'

'You've seen the news?'

'I'd rather not think about it.'

'Did you meet his wife?'

'No. The girl came with him once or twice. Sat in the waiting room. Pretty kid.'

His eyes didn't leave her.

'Well?' she asked.

'They seemed very close. Not like father and daughter.'

'Like what then?'

'Friends,' he said after a while. Then he drained his coffee. 'Are we finished here? I have patients to see.'

Negri had been at La Sapienza the year the then-Cardinal Ratzinger had visited. He was as incensed as everyone else about the statements that had been made, the implication that somehow a scientist like Galileo had deserved his treatment at the hands of the Vatican.

'Did he talk to you about his work? At the Confraternity of the Owls? About his attitude towards that?'

'Of course. I read his book. Didn't we all? I think this job he had troubled him. There was something he was being asked to do . . .'

'He was being ordered to add his reputation to a paper that said Ratzinger had a point. I read it last night. Bernard Santacroce wanted Gabriel's name on the front page. As joint author, not just editor.'

Negri frowned. He seemed genuinely sorry.

'I rather thought it must have been something like that. The work upset him. He obviously needed the money. I don't think they had anything else. All the same I can't imagine Malise would have gone along with it.'

'"*E pur si muove*",' she murmured.

'What's Galileo got to do with this?'

'I don't know. Perhaps Malise Gabriel empathized with him. Believed he was being persecuted in a similar fashion.'

A short, dry burst of laughter.

'And his daughter thought she was that poor, sad girl from the ghetto,' he scoffed. 'Or so the news would have us believe.'

'How did she feel about his illness?'

The oncologist shook his head.

'I doubt she understood how bad it was. Malise didn't want anyone to know the seriousness of his condition. He was adamant about that. He seemed to care about them deeply, I must say.'

'Would he still be interested in sex?'

He thought for a moment and said, 'Yes. We had that conversation. The condition may affect libido, of course. And the medication. But if the desire's there . . .' He sighed. 'Malise was determined, as much as possible, that he would lead a normal life until the end. The daughter was under the impression he came to me for routine checkups for a condition that was in remission. Work apart, he seemed cheerful, full of life. Active in every way as far as I could see.'

Negri recalled something.

'One thing. He never mentioned the son. In fact I didn't know there was a son until I heard the news. That surprised me.'

'You'd be amazed what goes on inside families, Adriano.'

'No,' he said quickly. 'I wouldn't.' The handsome oncologist looked lost briefly. 'Or what happened inside Malise Gabriel either. There was something . . . dark there. I can't put it any other way. I wanted to help the man. I admired him. His courage. His determination. But . . .'

He stopped and she had to prod him.

'But what?'

Adriano Negri's eyes met hers and she realized, for the first time, that there was a bleak, intense sadness in them. At that moment Teresa Lupo remembered why she'd never accepted any of his advances. He was intelligent, charming, a decent, respectable man. But unlikeable too, detached from his own emotions and those of others. They very opposite of Gianni Peroni.

'I was always glad when he left.' He pushed away the coffee cup and the plate with the Jewish pizza on it. 'I never really knew why. It was something to do with his presence. Do you know what I mean?'

'I think so,' she said.

CHAPTER 6

Costa pulled up close to the Palazzetto Santacroce and saw the nose of Falcone's sleek Lancia saloon poking out from a nearby alley. There was a bad-tempered crowd of photographers, TV crew and hacks outside the arched entrance to the building and a few uniformed cops to hold them back. He held the scooter tight as Peroni slowly got off the Vespa, grumbling all the time, then popped the machine onto its stand next to a line of bikes and other scooters.

Falcone wandered over, eyebrows raised, the faintest of smiles on his face as Peroni struggled to get the motorbike cop's helmet off his head.

'I decided to string along,' he said. 'What took you?'

'Not easy getting in and out of the Questura,' Costa said by way of explanation. 'There's some kind of demo outside. You heard?'

'Oh yes.' He flourished a large brown envelope in his hands and seemed strangely energized. 'Not to worry. And the brother?'

Peroni stowed the helmet beneath his arm.

'Narcotics are being less than helpful. He was an informer.'

Falcone thought about this for a moment, then led them through the crowd of hacks, refusing to answer a single question, or rise to their aggressive taunts, and went up to the caretaker's window of the palace.

This was Costa's first visit. The sunny open space beyond the confined entrance of the palace surprised him, as did the sight of the Casina delle Civette when they walked through into the garden beyond, with its geometric flower beds and the gaudy colours of late summer: red and yellow and blue.

He looked up at the windows of the castellated tower. A single face was there, pale and young and beautiful. Mina Gabriel awaiting their arrival.

She looked scared.

CHAPTER 7

They sat in Bernard Santacroce's study, beneath the picture of Galileo and his accusers, players in another inquisition, one that, to Costa, seemed as nebulous in its search for the truth as their own faltering inquiry into the deaths of Malise Gabriel and Joanne Van Doren. Mina's eyes were pink with tears. Her mother said they'd heard about the death of the American woman on the TV, and the rumours about the police investigation. Cecilia Gabriel seemed passive, stoic, unmoved by anything but anger. Santacroce wore a benevolent, proprietorial gaze, the look of a reasonable man dragged into an awkward situation he'd rather avoid.

'Are we accused of some kind of crime?' Cecilia Gabriel demanded. 'If so, what exactly? This nonsense on the news . . .'

'I'm not responsible for the media, Signora,' Falcone replied calmly. 'Joanne Van Doren was murdered last night. Your son clearly knew she'd died and was in the vicinity. It would be rash of me not to regard him as our most viable suspect.'

'That's not true!' Mina cried. She was wringing

her hands constantly, eyes damp and darting around the room. 'Joanne was our friend. Robert would never . . . never . . .'

Costa looked at her and said, 'Mina. You spoke to him last night after you talked to me. That's why he got in touch.'

'I told him he could trust you!' She cast a fierce glance at Falcone. 'You're not like . . . them.'

'What did Robert say?' he asked.

'Nothing. He was upset. He wouldn't tell me why. He sounded frightened. I—'

'Your brother,' Falcone interrupted, 'may well have just murdered someone.'

'No!' Her voice was high-pitched, childlike. Cecilia Gabriel made not the slightest effort to comfort the girl next to her. Not a word. Not a touch. Instead Bernard Santacroce walked out from behind his desk, pulled up a chair and placed an arm briefly round her hunched shoulders.

'Inspector,' Santacroce said. 'Is this your idea of how to treat the bereaved? Malise . . . Joanne . . . We were all close to them in one way or another. Have some decency, please.'

Falcone scowled.

'It's very difficult to talk about deceny when we're dealing with a murder, possibly two, sir. Signora Gabriel here was going to sue Joanne Van Doren. As to the relationship between the dead woman and Signora Gabriel's husband—'

'This is unacceptable,' Santacroce cut in. 'If you wish to proceed in such a fashion I will bring in a lawyer. At my own expense. Perhaps that would be for the best in any case.'

'Do it now,' Falcone agreed. 'Then we can continue this interview at the Questura. Each of you in a separate room. If you'd prefer.'

'Ask your damned questions,' Cecilia Gabriel told him.

'Where's your son?' the inspector demanded. 'I need to speak to him and I must say I fail to understand why you show no apparent interest in his whereabouts. *Where is he*?'

The Englishwoman closed her eyes. For once she seemed affected by the subject. Mina had spoken a little about her mother the previous day, and Costa had read the skimpy reports in the Questura. Cecilia Gabriel was an only child in a fading and impoverished aristocratic English family. Her brief time as a student had shown great promise, but that had been removed by the needs of family. She seemed, to Costa's eyes, worn yet a little fiery too, like some lean bird of prey backed into a corner, ready to fight if necessary.

The woman was not prepared to speak at that moment. It was left to Mina, who looked across the room, directly at Costa, and said, 'Mum.' She took her mother's hand. 'Tell them. You have to.'

'It's none of their business,' Cecilia Gabriel muttered between gritted teeth. 'Any of this.' Her aquiline head came up. She glared at Falcone. 'This is my family you're talking about, Inspector. You will not crucify them.'

'Your son, madam.'

'Robert's my son in name only,' she said simply and left it at that. The room went quiet. From the look in Bernard Santacroce's eyes it seemed this was a revelation to him too.

It was Peroni, typically, who broke the ice.

'Signora Gabriel,' he said. 'We have to ask these questions in such circumstances. For your sake, for Robert's sake. This is a criminal investigation. It's important we know the truth, especially if the boy's innocent. Try to see this from our point of view. If that's the case, where is he? Why doesn't he come forward?'

The approach, calm and unthreatening, appeared to have an effect. She relaxed a little and said, 'I can't tell you. All I know is that he's frightened of something. These people he's involved with. And . . .' The briefest glimmer of regret crossed her angular features. '. . . I imagine I'm not the first person he'd choose to come to if he needed help.'

Mina wound her fingers in her mother's and whispered something.

The woman breathed a deep sigh and continued.

'Our son, our *real* son, died when he was two years old. A swimming pool accident. In France.' Her eyes were misty, unfocused. 'Things weren't going well in Cambridge at that point. That book of Malise's was too clever for our own good. The controversy. Then the scandal when I got pregnant. The baby was Robert. *Our* Robert. Then he was gone. Malise blamed himself. He took his eyes away from the pool for a moment. It was enough. We were on the point of falling apart. There were argument. There always were. The college dismissed him. He found some work in Canada.'

'I can't imagine what it must be like,' Peroni said honestly. 'To lose a child. They talk about closure . . .'

'Psychobabble. Claptrap,' the Englishwoman muttered. 'The death of your child's an open wound, one that never heals. We were desperate. A little crazy, I think. So we adopted a little boy and, since we were of good, academic stock, the authorities didn't really notice the state we were in, didn't care that we changed his name to that of the son we'd lost.' She looked at them. 'Malise was always good at hiding his pain. Englishmen are, in case you haven't noticed. Robert . . .'

The words drifted into silence.

'Robert's my brother,' Mina said quietly. 'And he's still your son.'

The older woman patted her once on the back.

'That's true. But there was always a gap, some distance. I don't know how but he knew it was there, almost from the beginning. He understood we wanted it to disappear, more than anything, though I don't think we ever managed to convince him of that for some reason. Inspector.' She glanced at Santacroce. 'We've told people, you perhaps, that Robert was at college in England until he joined us here. That's not strictly true. We tried to keep him at home. It was impossible. He'd run away.

Get into fights. So we sent him to boarding school, not that we had the money. He was expelled from there when he was seventeen. As far as I know after that he lived in squats in London. Earning money God knows how, when he wasn't begging off us. He came to Rome when Malise told him there was no more. Nothing left. He had the choice of living with us or . . .' She shrugged. 'Disappearing for good, I imagine. We didn't want that. We wanted to be a family. But there was no more money. He tried. We all did.'

'And his relationship with your husband?' Falcone asked.

'They adored one another,' she replied immediately. 'Sometimes it was impossible to believe Robert wasn't really Malise's son. They had the same temper. The same stupid enthusiasms, the same ridiculous, impetuous urges. And when they argued . . .'

Mina took her arm. The woman couldn't go on.

'You know the kind of people Robert mixed with?' Costa asked.

She shook her head vigorously.

'No. I didn't want to know. They were criminals. Drugs were involved, I imagine. Not that Robert took them, as far as I knew. It was for the money. Nothing else.'

'Is it possible Robert was in the apartment the night your husband died?' Costa went on.

'I told you!' Mina cried. 'I was there. Just the two of us. I saw Robert in the hall downstairs when I ran out to see Daddy. He was coming home.

I think he was a bit drunk. Scared. He didn't want to come with me into the street. He didn't know anything.'

Costa shook his head.

'You were in your music room. Someone could have arrived without your knowing. That's possible, isn't it?'

'No!' she insisted. 'I wasn't listening to music all the time. I heard Daddy screaming when he fell, didn't I?'

'Do you know why the media are pushing this story about Beatrice Cenci?' Falcone asked the Englishwoman straight out.

'Because you leaked it to them,' Bernard Santacroce interrupted. 'As a way of placing pressure on Cecilia, I imagine. It's obvious, isn't it? I have to say I find all this distasteful in the extreme.'

'No,' Costa told him. 'We didn't.'

He was puzzled by Santacroce's intervention. It seemed misplaced.

'Their interest – and I must confess I share it – stems from the fact your husband had sex shortly before he died,' Falcone said without emotion. 'The evidence is very clear. If your daughter insists no one else was in the house, the only possible conclusion—'

'Don't be ridiculous!' Cecilia Gabriel shrieked at him.

Falcone glanced at Mina and retrieved a print from the envelope. It was the photograph from the book Gabriel had been reading the night he died.

'We found this in your father's book, Mina.'

She glanced at the print, at her mother, went white and shook her head.

Falcone, perhaps out of embarrassment, flipped the photo over and showed her the brief written message, Galileo's whispered denial of his recantation in front of the Vatican's Inquisition. A brief chill ran down Costa's spine when he realized, from the history he'd been given, that the great man must once have been inside these very walls.

'Do you know who wrote this?' Falcone asked. 'Do you recognize the writing?'

'No.'

The curt, aggressive tone, that of a teenager, made him turn it over. She stared at the naked figure, head cut off by the print, turning as if to hide some shame.

'Did your father ever make a sexual advance to you?' Falcone went on.

'Mummy told you about that photograph,' she snapped. 'Why don't you believe her?'

'Even if I do, the question still stands.'

'Daddy loved me.'

'Yes, but—'

'I told you!' Cecilia Gabriel interrupted. 'That picture is me. This whole idea is ridiculous. Malise hadn't felt well for some time. We didn't . . . Not often.'

'He had sex the night he died,' Falcone insisted. 'There's no possibility of a mistake.' He glanced at Mina. 'If we'd been able to examine anyone he'd been with—'

'Don't be disgusting,' Bernard Santacroce spat at him. 'This conversation is at an end, Inspector. If you wish to talk to Cecilia and Mina again it will be in the presence of my lawyers.'

Falcone reached into the envelope again and took out a set of large black and white prints, fanning them across his lap.

Bernard Santacroce's eyes grew wide. Cecilia Gabriel gaped at them and swore, an Anglo-Saxon curse, beneath her breath.

Mina closed her eyes for a moment then stared at the window. Costa found himself looking at the prints, wishing he didn't have to. Malise Gabriel was there, painfully thin, hollow-eyed, anxious, writhing on the bed with Joanne Van Doren, struggling awkwardly to get into the kind of position one associated with cheap pornography, staring at the lens from time to time as if trying to understand something, puzzled, unhappy. The monochrome pictures were utterly joyless, bleak and without any feeling whatsoever.

'There's a photographic studio hidden in the basement of your apartment block,' Falcone went on. 'Did you know that?'

Cecilia was shaking her head, glancing at her daughter.

'It is at least possible,' Falcone went on, 'that the person your husband slept with on the night of his death was Miss Van Doren, which rather destroys the story being put around by the media. From my point of view it does, of course, provide motive.' He stared at her. 'Where were you last night? After we left?'

The woman didn't answer. Her eyes were locked on her daughter.

'Mina?' she murmured.

'Mummy,' the girl replied, looking out of the window at the palms swaying in the soft, hot breeze, a distant, cold tone in her voice.

Cecilia Gabriel flew at her daughter in a flurry of fists and nails. Costa was there in an instant, separating them, getting his arm round the girl, turning his back to the furious woman screeching at her own daughter in a voice full of hatred and pain.

When he turned Peroni was holding back Cecilia Gabriel whose eyes were bright with anger and tears.

'You knew?' she shrieked across the room. 'You knew he was screwing that dirty little American bitch all along?'

Mina was shaking in Costa's arms. Bernard Santacroce got to his feet, going red in the face, worried, embarrassed, stuttering excuses and demands.

'Daddy never wanted to hurt you,' the girl cried. 'Never!'

Costa looked at Falcone, then at Mina.

'Did Robert know?' he asked. She was staring at her mother, sobbing. 'Mina?'

'Yes,' she said weakly.

'Signora Gabriel,' Falcone insisted. 'Where were you last night?'

Bernard Santacroce's face was puce with rage.

'She was with me, Inspector. We had dinner together. Mina was here in the Casina, on her own. She was upset. So I kept Cecilia company. It seemed the kindest thing to do.'

'Kindness,' Falcone repeated. 'Well . . .'

Mina Gabriel huddled close to Costa. He could feel her sobbing breath, her tears against his neck.

'Excuse us,' Costa said, and took her over to the far side of the room. They stood by the window, just able to hear the continuing rumble of argument from behind. He held her shoulders, stared into her eyes.

'This is important,' he said. 'Please tell me the truth. How did Robert react when he found out about your father and Joanne?'

She pulled back from him, her pale face puffy with tears, creased in a childish pout.

'You're just like the rest of them, aren't you?'

'No,' he said. 'I'm not.'

She stayed stiff and still in front of him, face to the floor.

'Is that what you wanted to tell me all along?' Costa asked. 'About the affair?'

'Who said I wanted to tell you anything?'

'Don't play these games.'

She squeezed her eyes tight shut for a long moment then opened them and stared up at him.

There was something about this child, this girl, this woman, that he found compelling. Some magnetic quality in her beautiful young face, a melding of innocence with some imminent sensuality that drew him to her.

Her lips came up to his ear and she whispered, 'What game do you want me to play, Nic?'

He felt like shaking her, trying to make her see something outside herself, beyond the confines of this strange stone tower, an unreal folly hidden away in the seething core of the city.

'One that involves the truth,' he said.

'"*E pur si muove*",' she murmured. 'There's truth, of a kind.'

Then she pulled herself from his grip and strode back to stand beside her mother.

CHAPTER 8

Gino Riggi had never liked the Indian woman they'd given him. She'd worked with Falcone's people too long and it showed.

The two of them were back in their dishevelled corner on the narcotics floor, running through the intelligence records she'd pulled to try to help in the Gabriel case. He looked into her dark, sceptical eyes and said, 'What's the problem now?'

'We're supposed to be on the same side.'

'Did you tell them that?'

'They know already.'

'Here.' He flipped the computer screen back to her and threw the keyboard across the desk. 'You go through all this crap. It's for your friends.'

'Oh thanks, Gino! And you're going to do what, exactly?'

'Cop stuff,' Riggi murmured then walked out and got in the lift.

The noisy crowd outside the Questura seemed to be getting bigger. They didn't look twice at him. Dressed the way he was they'd never believe he was police.

'What's the deal?' he asked some beefy-looking woman yelling obscenities into thin air. She had bright red hair and was waving a banner bearing the name of one of the far-left groups the Questura dealt with from time to time.

She looked him up and down a couple of times then rattled off some stupid story she'd heard on the news. Riggi listened carefully. This was interesting. Worrying.

'So the cops are trying to fit up this poor girl?' he asked.

The woman nodded and said, 'Yeah.'

'Bastards. And they really think she killed her old man? For messing with her?'

'No,' someone else cut in. 'They think her brother did it. But maybe she egged him on. And the mother.'

'Happy families,' he said with a sardonic smile.

'Violence against women . . .' she began.

'. . . is a very bad thing,' he interrupted. He flicked a thumb back at the Questura. 'Give 'em hell from me.'

Then Riggi walked out of the Piazza San Michele, bought a copy of the evening paper and kept on going until he reached the tiny square in front of the church of Santa Maria sopra Minerva. There he struck a match on the strange statue of an elephant with an obelisk sprouting out of its back, lit a cigarette and began to read the front page story. It was wild stuff. With pictures too. A pretty middle-aged American property developer,

290

a cute-looking kid. The kind of thing the Italian media loved.

There was a lot to consider here. He stared at the crowds in front of the Pantheon, a straggle of foreign tourists mulling around in the heat. Riggi looked like any other impoverished visitor in Rome at that moment. This was, he felt, a good disguise.

He took a look round then pulled out the list of numbers he kept on a single rolled-up sheet of paper in his pocket, each with just an initial next to it, the letter three places along in the alphabet, a simple code he used as a precaution.

Robert Gabriel was at the end, filed under 'U'. The English boy had four different mobile numbers, more than anyone else on Riggi's list. He was a nervous type, with a high opinion of himself. Nothing could be simple.

Riggi called and listened as a quiet, uncertain voice asked, 'Yes?'

'How many times do I have to tell you? You don't answer the phone like that here. Makes you stand out. When are you going to learn? Try again.'

'Who is this?'

'Gino. Who d'ya think? Try again, you moron.'

'*Pronto.*'

Riggi took another sweep of the crowd to make sure no one was watching.

'I did not appreciate receiving that text from you earlier. Do not contact me again. I don't care if it's from a number I've got or not. They can still

291

trace you. Do not call. When I need you, I'll find you. Is that understood?'

'I . . . I . . . I . . .'

The boy always stuttered when he was scared.

Riggi cut in with a sharp, mocking tone, 'I . . . I . . . I . . . What are you? Some scared little girl or something?'

'What's going on?'

'You're wanted for murder. That's what.'

The line went quiet. Then Robert Gabriel said, in a voice that, to Riggi's surprise, seemed a little calmer, 'They don't think that. Not really.'

'They don't know what to think. This is a mess. All I know is you're turning into a lot of trouble. Where are you gonna be around seven thirty? We need to talk.'

Another long and unexpected silence.

'Can't make seven thirty. Has to be eight.'

Riggi laughed. It was ridiculous.

'Oh. I'm so sorry. Am I interrupting your social schedule here? Some moron on the run? Do I need to make an appointment to try and keep you out of jail?'

'Can't explain. Eight's fine.'

'Where?'

Riggi listened to him reel off the name of the meeting place and thought: I might have guessed. The kid didn't have a single original idea in his head.

'Eight then,' he said. 'Oh. By the way. You should buy yourself a paper. They've got some pictures of your sister. Big ones.' Not a word. Funny how you could hear anger down the line, though. 'You know something? She's really hot. Thin girls. Gotta love them, huh? I can see your old man's point. Who couldn't?'

'Eight,' the young, scared voice repeated, and then the line went dead.

'Children,' Riggi murmured.

He didn't want to go back to the Questura. This all felt bad. So he walked round the corner and bought himself a macchiato in Tazza d'Oro, weighing up his options as he sipped at the powerful little cup of coffee.

The problem with informers was always the same: ownership. As long as Robert Gabriel was his, Riggi could control him, filter the information he fed into the Questura in return for a steady flow of money. Gabriel was a timid little kid but he was no idiot and maybe a little trickier than Riggi had suspected. He knew this was a sport that was played in multiple directions. Not all the leads that Riggi had leaked into the system had proved accurate. A few, a significant few, were false to begin with, and had led the Questura's narcotics team into blind alleys when they should, by all rights, have been closing down a case.

Riggi meant what he'd said to Falcone. It was easy for some stiff, middle-aged inspector in a suit to get pompous over rights and wrongs. In the street, surrounded by people who cared nothing for the law and everything for survival, the world was more grey, less inclined to divide itself into right and wrong, good and evil. This was a lesson Gino Riggi had learned for himself the hard way when he entered the Roman night on his own, in the tattered disguise of a street punk, looking for answers, finding all too often nothing but questions.

Survival.

That was what it came down to. Nothing else. The English kid was predictable, easy to master when he was just one more unknown face in a Trastevere bar whispering in the ear of an under-cover cop. Minions like him helped keep the balance between two sides that had always been there, order and chaos, competing forces that needed to be kept in check, and on occasion learn to work together too. All that was now gone. Gabriel was out in plain sight, a name on the front pages, unidentifiable at the moment, it was true, but still known to those whose lives revolved around the bars and drug dens of the Campo and the back-street dives across the Tiber and beyond.

Robert Gabriel was vulnerable and that meant those who knew him were too.

Riggi walked outside and went to stand by the fountain in front of the Pantheon, with its fierce-toothed dolphins and sweating tourists trying to finish fast-melting ice creams. There he pulled out his list and found the number, one he rarely called, and never lightly.

'Cakici,' he said, holding the handset close to his mouth. 'It's your friend in blue.'

'Which one?' the Turk asked.

'Yeah. Funny. Like you're running over with them.'

A grunt. A curse. Then, 'Maybe I should be. Real friends.'

'Look, this is nothing to worry about.'

'I don't like seeing people I know in the papers. It could be embarrassing. For both of us.'

'I was starting to think that way. Listen, we can handle this.'

A pause on the line.

'"We"? Did I hear you say "we"?'

'It's in both our interests this goes no further.'

'We have nothing in common.'

'I . . .'

'Deal with this child,' Cakici ordered. 'Yourself.'

'Listen to me.'

'No. You listen to me. If your colleagues, your honest colleagues, find him first, what do you think will happen? How long will he keep his mouth shut? You expect me to go to prison on the word of an infant? No. Deal with this yourself. Or I shall deal with you.'

Then silence. Riggi looked at the nearest dolphin, its teeth bared in the bright sun, a snarl on its features, violence in its eyes. He patted its head. The stone was hot and grimy, rough to the touch, like the skin of a petrified corpse.

Death was everywhere in Rome if you looked for it. He wondered if Robert Gabriel appreciated that fact.

CHAPTER 9

Towards the end of the afternoon Costa, Falcone and Peroni stood on the roof of the house in the Via Beatrice Cenci waiting for the arrival of the building inspector Di Lauro. Teresa sat nearby, going through some documents, head down, absorbed. Some eighty police and forensic officers were now in bunny suits searching the floors below, sifting through dust and building debris for the most part, finding little they hadn't picked up already.

Costa gazed at the Cenci palace on its little hill across the street. Now it was one more apartment block in Rome, of the kind the late Joanne Van Doren had hoped to create: doubtless full of elegant, private residences behind its stylish arched entrance. The vast bulk of the building was easier to appreciate from this height. Behind he could just make out the pink-washed wall of their private church, the place where the dismembered remains of Beatrice's brother Giacomo had been interred, in the grave meant for his father. The place where a select band of mourners would, in little more than a week, assemble to mark the anniversary of the young woman's execution by the bridge to the Castel Sant' Angelo.

He turned round and realized that he could also see, beyond the rooftops running by the river towards the Via Giulia, the summit of the Casina delle Civette, surrounded by palms, little more than half a kilometre away. The tragedy may have possessed a foreign cast but it also owned one truly Roman characteristic. This case was local, interior, close. A family affair, or so it seemed.

They'd all watched the media coverage. In spite of denials from the Questura, the story continued to grow, to the extent that it was beginning to slip beyond Falcone's reach, out into the public imagination. Mina Gabriel had been transformed into 'the English Beatrice'. One of the later editions had even morphed her picture over Guido Reni's supposed portrait creating a *trompe l'oeil* image that fused the past with the present. These were the dog days for hacks too, Costa reminded himself. There was little else to fill the pages, except this story of love and death and sexuality.

A little hard evidence was beginning to emerge, however, and it only seemed to add to the mystery.

Teresa Lupo sat on a dead air-conditioning duct a few metres away, flicking through some medical research on her laptop, reading out loud a list of obscure terms, none of which he understood.

Falcone let her finish then asked the question they all wanted answering: 'He was dying?'

'Pancreatic cancer. Final stages. Matter of months.'

'Well, that rather complicates things,' Peroni suggested. 'Why would somebody murder a dying man?'

'The family didn't know it was that serious,' Teresa said. 'At least that's what the consultant told me. Gabriel was very specific about keeping them in the dark. Didn't the mother confirm that too?'

Peroni scowled.

'Sort of. But you don't believe her, do you? She must have suspected. You can't hide something like that, not from your wife and children.'

Falcone sighed, unable to decide which argument made more sense.

'Let's try and find a question we can answer, shall we?' he said. 'What are the consequences of his illness? How would he behave? What effect would it have on the Gabriels?'

'Ask his wife and daughter,' Teresa suggested. 'Theoretically he'd be in the usual cycle – denial, anger, acceptance. Where was he on the scale? Who knows? From what I've heard it sounds as if he didn't have to go far to find the anger part.'

'And sex?' Costa asked. 'Would he be interested in that?'

'You've seen the pictures from the basement. The disease would affect his desire. There are drugs that can help.'

'He couldn't afford drugs,' Peroni said.

'Didn't he have a son with pharmaceutical connections?'

'There's no mention of drugs in the autopsy,' he pointed out.

'I am trying to help here,' Teresa barked at him. 'No. Clearly he didn't take drugs the night he died. Perhaps he didn't need them. Malise Gabriel wasn't an invalid anyway. Not yet.'

Costa wasn't happy with this idea. They'd peered at Silvio Di Capua's pictures, trying to see whether there was more information to be extracted from them. But what? Two naked bodies, coupling. Joanne Van Doren looking a little blank, as if drunk, or drugged, or guilty. And Malise Gabriel, his face contorted by an expression that could as easily have been pain as ecstasy. There was something anxious, almost staged in the way they splayed their bodies for the Hasselblad camera that had so caught Silvio Di Capua's attention.

'Well,' Peroni said, 'at least we can rule out the daughter, can't we? You've got pictures of her father in bed with Joanne Van Doren. It's pretty obvious who he had sex with that night, isn't it?'

Falcone and Teresa had got together beforehand, while Costa and Peroni had been checking the roof again. Something had passed between them.

'Gianni,' Teresa said. 'I'm afraid that doesn't stack up either. Joanne Van Doren was having her period. That doesn't mean she didn't have sex with Gabriel that night. But I would have expected to have seen some sign of menstrual blood some-where in this building. On Malise Gabriel. On the sheets. *Somewhere*. Also, why would he have used

299

a condom in that case? She couldn't get pregnant. I don't get the impression this was some highly promiscuous sex ring. Would they have been worried about disease? Sorry. Don't see it. This is all infuriating, I know.'

The big old cop murmured a groan of deep despair. Costa looked at Peroni's face and knew what his friend and colleague was thinking. Sweat. Spit. Semen. Blood. All the bodily fluids. The tell-tale physical stains of humanity. These were the keys to unlocking the secret of the palace in the Via Beatrice Cenci, or so it seemed. What offended Peroni, all of them, perhaps, was the idea that the perpetrator of a vicious murder could not be unmasked by decency, honest intellect and diligent inquiry alone, that justice required this prurient and microscopic search into the baseness of life.

Someone coughed. The building inspector, Di Lauro, had walked in on their conversation, so quietly no one had noticed.

'I'm sorry,' he said. 'If this is private . . . ?'

'You said you had something,' Falcone replied, ignoring the question.

'Perhaps,' the stiff, middle-aged man from the council agreed. He looked unhappy, with the company, and with what he had to say. 'I don't know if this is of any use or not. I've never seen anything like it in my life. It's why I asked to meet you here. Not inside. You need to see. To comprehend. Or not.'

He strode over to the edge of the building. They followed, Costa feeling the fluttering of vertigo in his stomach. Di Lauro was in a grey office suit but leapt onto the mechanism of the scaffolding structure as if he were still the builder he'd surely once been.

'You must understand,' the man said, banging a fist against the rusting pulleys that had once held the timber platform which had collapsed beneath the weight of Malise Gabriel, sending him plunging to the hard cobbled street. 'I can only tell you the facts. Nothing more. How any of this could happen . . .'

'What?' Falcone asked impatiently.

'These ties,' Di Lauro said, indicating some rusty hook-like mechanisms that seemed designed to hold the ropes that bore the strain of the structure below. 'They're incomplete. I couldn't quite believe it when I saw them. I asked Signora Van Doren – she was an architect. She found this as baffling as I did.'

'Incomplete?' Peroni said.

'That's what I said. A small part of the mechanism is simply missing. It's supposed to fix the rope to stop it running through. I could only imagine that perhaps the workmen had taken them away after the accident for some reason. Otherwise I would have told you earlier, but I needed to speak to Signora Van Doren's team to be sure. It seems such an extraordinary omission I couldn't believe it was accidental. But we've now interviewed all of the men. They all say the apparatus had not been changed since it was first assembled six months ago. So the pulleys were secure when they finished work on the day before the accident happened. In which case . . .'

He shrugged, as if the conclusion were obvious.

'In which case what?' Falcone demanded.

Di Lauro looked at him as if the question were stupid.

'In which case it wasn't an accident. These things were removed. Once you do that this end of the platform will collapse under the slightest weight. Immediately. It had nothing to hold it in place except the residual tension in the rope itself. A cat might have sent those planks tumbling to the ground. A man certainly.'

'These workmen could be lying to cover up their own incompetence,' Teresa said.

'No. They're decent people. I know them. Professionals. If there'd been some kind of mistake I would have expected the missing pieces to be around here somewhere. They're not.'

He frowned as he stared at the stork-like rusting mechanism that protruded over the edge of the roof.

'This was deliberate?' Falcone asked. 'Sabotage? Murder?'

Di Lauro shrugged.

'I'm a building inspector. I can only tell you what I find. This is something entirely new to me. I cannot and will not say in my report that this was an accident. Nor will I allow Signora Van Doren's men to take the blame, since I do not believe in my heart that they could possibly be responsible. It's unthinkable they would do such a thing, as a prank or anything else. Any one of them, more, could have died if they'd stepped onto that scaffolding in this condition.'

Falcone looked at Teresa and said, 'Get a description of these parts he's talking about. Pass it on to your people. Let's find them.'

The council officer stood there, shifting awkwardly from foot to foot.

'Is there anything else?' Falcone asked.

'You saw the blood?' Di Lauro asked. 'Downstairs? In the girl's room? The smear on the radiator near the window?'

Teresa came and stood in front of him and asked, 'Yes?'

'I didn't think this was important. Perhaps it isn't.'

'Yes?' she repeated.

'When I first came here we walked into that room together, Signora Van Doren and I. This was early the Saturday morning. When . . . it was just an accident, nothing else. She was dreadfully upset. There was still . . . in the street . . . you could see where the man had fallen.'

They were all looking at him.

'When we walked in the first thing she saw was the blood on the radiator. The unfortunate woman burst into tears. There was a lot of it. I

303

thought perhaps some hair too. At least, something dark. Signora Van Doren seemed a good woman. I felt embarrassed. So . . . I thought this was an accident.'

'So you what?' Teresa asked.

He licked his lips and said, 'I tried to clean it as best I could with my handkerchief. It seemed only kind.'

'Oh my God,' she began. 'You stupid man. How on earth . . . ?'

Di Lauro pulled a clear plastic bag out of his pocket, the sort used in a freezer. A crumpled bloodied hankie was inside.

'I managed to get it before my wife put it in the wash. Only just,' he said. 'I'm sorry. I'd no idea you would be dealing with something so horrible. If I'd known . . .'

'We weren't supposed to know, were we?' She stared at the stained handkerchief. 'You do realize that thing is now of intellectual interest alone? If I had to stand up in court and prove there was no contamination . . .'

'Thank you,' Falcone cut in, and removed the plastic bag from Di Lauro's hands. 'Go downstairs, find one of my officers, and make a statement. Then it's best you left.'

They watched him go. Falcone phoned the Questura and called for orders demanding search warrants for the Casina delle Civette and the examination of the Gabriels' financial and medical records.

When he'd done he looked at them and said, 'We should assume Robert Gabriel murdered his adoptive father and Joanne Van Doren. One way or another we have to try to understand how much Cecilia Gabriel and her daughter were involved. I'm damned certain one of them knows where that kid is. We're going in there.'

Costa looked at his watch. It was getting late and he said so.

Falcone nodded then said, 'Fine. Let them sleep as easily as they can. We can take the mother and daughter back to the Questura while we search the premises. Bring along Santacroce too. I doubt we could exclude him.'

Peroni looked sceptical.

'What are you saying, Leo?' he asked. 'That the newspapers got it right? It is the Cenci case all over again?'

'I don't care about the newspapers. Look at the facts.'

'What facts?' Peroni demanded. 'A few blood and semen stains and a lot of possibilities that don't join up. Are those really reason enough for tearing this family apart? I don't think you have sufficient reason. You may find a magistrate thinks so too when we send a lawyer for that warrant. Nic?'

Costa hated taking sides. Both men had a point.

'We need to talk to them,' he said. 'Separately, together. I don't know. Joanne Van Doren was murdered. Robert Gabriel clearly has material information about her death. There's enough here for a formal interview. We'd be remiss if we didn't carry it out.'

'Fine. And until then?'

Falcone glanced at his watch.

'Forensic can keep going here. Keep trying to find the trash that was taken out by the builders. You two can go home. Tomorrow may be a long day.'

CHAPTER 10

The door was at the end of the garden of the Casina delle Civette, hidden in an algaed corner that was overgrown with twisting serpents of ivy. It was kept locked, always. The key was in Bernard Santacroce's desk. She'd taken a copy months before, when they first lived in the Casina, and kept it carefully in her bag.

At the end of the afternoon Mina Gabriel slipped out into the deserted garden and sat on the bench seat in the leafy, fragrant bower of bergamot and lemon trees, rereading Shelley next to the crumbling fountain and its soft, liquid song.

The finale. Beatrice in her cell, awaiting the last call for pardon from the Pope, knowing in her heart this ultimate plea was futile.

The young English girl held the play in her hands, acting out the final tragic scene in her imagination, something she had done many times before. Her hands moved through the thin air with its traffic fumes and specks of dust. Her voice, clear and precise, each word enunciated with care, rang out from the citrus grove and over the spike of red and yellow canna lilies that sat like a sea of antique gold before the laden grape vines that adorned the southern wall.

Beatrice's words from Shelley's pen, hers too now:

> *'Sweet Heaven, forgive weak thoughts! If there*
>   *should be*
> *No God, no Heaven, no Earth in the void*
>   *world;*
> *The wide, grey, lampless, deep, unpeopled world!*
> *If all things then should be . . . my father's*
>   *spirit,*
> *His eye, his voice, his touch surrounding me;*
> *The atmosphere and breath of my dead life!*
> *If sometimes, as a shape more like himself,*
> *Even the form which tortured me on earth,*
> *Masked in grey hairs and wrinkles, he should*
>   *come*
> *And wind me in his hellish arms, and fix*
> *His eyes on mine, and drag me down, down,*
>   *down!'*

She stopped, looking up at the long, vaulted windows of the Casina. On the top floor was her mother, stiff at the glass, next to the imposing figure of Bernard Santacroce, his arms folded, magisterial as always.

Mina's head went down, she pouted, hating the way they followed her.

Down, down, down . . .

A long minute staring at the cracked paving of

the Casina garden, spoiled by dark moss, teeming with insects: ants and beetles and earwigs, denizens of another discrete world that ran from century to century, unheeding of mankind, creatures of the wide, grey, lampless deep.

Her gaze returned to the stone tower where Galileo had once listened to Bernard Santacroce's ancestors pledging their allegiance, if only he might concede some dishonest accommodation with the Pope across the river.

'"*E pur si muove*",' she murmured, and wondered why she'd said those words to Nic Costa. He was an honest, likeable man, someone who cared. There weren't many like that.

The faces at the window were gone. They'd taken the hint. She pulled out her phone, checked the list of numbers she had for Robert, each tied to a specific day, for safety's sake, chose the right one and called.

He sounded breathless. Tired. Crabby.

'I need to see you,' Mina Gabriel said.

'Why?'

'Robert . . .'

A long, weary sigh.

'OK. Don't nag. Where?'

'The bridge. Where else?'

She took one more look to make sure they'd stopped spying on her. Then Mina Gabriel dragged back her long, blonde hair behind her head, pulling it away from her face as much as possible, securing the locks with a band. She retrieved from her bag a pair of cheap, heavy black plastic sunglasses bought the previous week from a hawker near the Campo and placed them on her face.

'Minerva Gabriel,' she said, in a pompous grown-up voice that mocked her mother's harsh patrician tones. 'What *do* you look like?'

The girl got to her feet and reached up and squeezed the open-pored leathery skin of an ageing lemon on the nearest tree, breathing in its aroma, citrus scent and the stain of stale, dank traffic.

'Anyone, mother. Everyone,' she whispered.

Then she strode through the sea of red and yellow cannas, found the door, unlocked it with her illicit key, and let herself out into the street.

CHAPTER 11

He had sunglasses too, the same cheap kind. A black T-shirt that was tight over his muscled torso. The familiar old faded denim jacket. Fake Adidas sneakers going to ruin. It was poverty that drew this family together more than anything, she thought, and as they slipped further into penury and uncertainty the bonds grew ever closer, so tight they had long felt ready to snap.

The tourists had gone to eat, to drink. The Ponte Sant' Angelo was almost deserted: two men selling postcards and souvenirs, a tramp with a German shepherd on a piece of rope, slumped with his dog beneath the statue of a grieving angel. But there was always a steady stream of traffic thundering over the worn patch of asphalt that stole its way into her imagination every time she passed this place.

Robert Gabriel took hold of her skinny shoulders and kissed her on both cheeks. She responded. Not too much. That was never a good idea.

They walked up and down the bridge, beneath the gaze of the angels, talking, thinking, exploring.

She told him about Costa and the visit of the police. She listened to his stories, his fears. He said little of any moment. Robert never changed. Still, it was good to speak.

Finally she made him stand by the angel with the cruel flail and said, 'I wish Joanne was still alive.'

'Me too,' he answered, and didn't look her in the eye. 'I liked her. We both did.'

'I try to like everyone,' Mina told him. 'Even when it's not easy. Especially when it's not easy.'

'St Mina of Rome,' he said, a sarcastic smile on his strong, handsome face. 'They'll make you that, when it all begins. That thing. The process. What's it called?'

'What?'

'All that mumbo jumbo about making a saint. I used to laugh about it with Malise.'

He would never call him 'father', even when he was young.

'I think they call the first step beatification. It means someone has reached a state of bliss. I don't see that happening soon, do you?'

'When you're dead, St Mina, they'll light candles. Put your T-shirt in a glass case by the altar.'

'Don't be so stupid!'

'I'm not. You deserve it. You've got the looks. That pale, pained innocent face. The sacrificial maiden.'

'Shut up, Robert,' she said, cross, beginning to regret this.

He persisted. He never knew when to stop.

'No. I mean it. Look at the papers. That photograph.' He burst out laughing, clutching his stomach like a bad actor. 'The one where they put your head on her portrait . . .'

'I'd nothing to do with that.'

'You'd everything to do with it. You painted yourself as her, didn't you? What did you expect? What did *we* expect?'

That was a question she could answer.

'Freedom,' she said softly. 'The chance to live. To breathe. Security, I don't know.'

The very things Beatrice Cenci had sought too, only to finish her days beneath the flash of an executioner's sword a few short steps from where they now stood.

'So it's all worth it, then?' he asked, and stood closer to her, backing Mina's willowy body against the stone parapet of the bridge across the Tiber.

'Worth what?'

He leaned against her, leering, nudged his lips against her ear and whispered something coarse and common. His fingers fell to the belt of her jeans, slipped below, stroking the tender skin beneath her navel.

Mina Gabriel pushed him back and said, 'Cut that out.'

'Sorry. I forgot. You're a saint.'

'And you're an animal.'

'Animals are useful too, aren't they? A bit more than saints, I'd say.'

She walked away from him, back towards the lost place of execution and the endless stream of cars. This hadn't been a good idea. It wasn't worth the risk. He was, she realized, beyond hope, beyond advice.

Robert followed her, struggling to voice some pathetic excuses.

'What are you going to do?' she asked as they reached the shops and houses that led into the *centro storico*. 'Where are you going to stay?'

'Best you don't know.'

Mina Gabriel wished more than anything she could make him take off those opaque sunglasses, could do the same herself. That they could look straight into each other's eyes, just this once.

'Robert,' she said. 'Be serious, please. They're going to come for us. Just like the papers are saying. You act as if it's all some kind of a joke. Everything.'

'A joke,' he repeated. 'Not even a very funny one either. You as Beatrice. Me as Pangloss. Watch and wait. And remember . . .'

He slapped her backside, hard.

'All is for the best in the best of all possible worlds. See you, sister. Take care.'

The blow hurt. She felt her eyes begin to sting, heard some tiny little voice start to chant inside, the vicious, pained refrain that had been absent for a little while, along with all those familiar words she never dared utter out loud.

Don't touch me, don't hurt me, don't, don't, don't you dare . . .

PART VIII

CHAPTER 1

Costa wasn't ready to listen to Falcone's orders. There were too many questions buzzing around his head. So he went back to the Questura for a few hours, checking to see if forensic had picked up anything new, and whether there was any more information about the missing brother. It was early evening by the time he'd finished, none the wiser. Falcone's determination to pin everything on searches and formal interviews with Cecilia and Mina Gabriel the following day was starting to make sense. There seemed no other way forward.

Around six thirty he went outside and perched on the scooter, checking the messages on his personal phone, looking forward to some time at home. Someone prodded him on the shoulder. It was Rosa Prabakaran, looking glamorous in her evening uniform: short dress, skimpy T-shirt, gaudy jewellery. She sashayed in front of him and said, 'Oh my, Nic. A Vespa. You need me on the back, don't you? Complete the look.'

'I'm a little old for that,' he replied.

'Don't be ridiculous.' She was smiling in a way

319

she hadn't when they'd met earlier, with Gino Riggi. Costa had always liked this smart, difficult woman, and was aware his feelings had, on occasion, been reciprocated, perhaps more than he wanted. 'We'd make a good pair together down the Campo. You've never worked that beat, have you?'

He had, back when he was a young *agente*, and said so.

'Ten years ago? It's different now.' The smile disappeared and she looked like the pretty young Indian woman he first got to know a few years before. 'Lots of things are different. It's important to notice.'

He still didn't understand why she'd wound up in narcotics. Rosa was back studying for her legal degree in her spare time. She had all the makings of an ambitious officer, one who'd rise swiftly up the ranks. The drugs squad was an important unit in the Questura, but a career in itself, one that usually excluded other areas. It seemed a sideways move.

'Have a nice night with your friend,' he said.

'Gino Riggi is not my friend,' she replied straight away.

Costa became aware that there was a side to this conversation.

'Colleague, then.'

She didn't reply. There was an awkward look in her deep brown eyes, one he thought he recognized. Costa tried to remember the circumstances of Rosa's departure from Falcone's unit. It had happened quickly, with no fuss, no recriminations. And she didn't turn up in narcotics straight away either.

'I would really appreciate it if you came with me tonight,' she said with a sudden, earnest intent. 'It could be in your interest, just as much as mine.'

He looked around. They were outside the Questura, in the Piazza San Michele, beyond the tiny crowd of demonstrators still waving banners in support of Mina Gabriel and women's rights.

'Are you looking for Riggi?' he asked straight out.

She raised her trim shoulders slightly and frowned.

'Him. And Robert Gabriel.' He watched as she tried to stifle the briefest moment of embarrassment. 'Why do I tell you things I'm not supposed to? Things I don't tell anyone else?'

'I imagine because you want to.'

'Yes,' she said, exasperated. 'But why?'

He shrugged and waved the phone.

'Got to make a call. Private. Where do you start and when?'

'The Coyote. Seven. You know it?'

'Oh yes. I'll be there.'

'Thanks.'

She started to walk away. He caught her arm gently.

'Does Riggi have any idea he's under investigation?' Costa asked. 'And that you're the one who's trying to nail him?'

Rosa looked worried, uncertain of herself, and that was rare.

'I wish I knew. He's a slippery bastard. I've been with him for a month now. I don't know half the people he deals with. What he does most of the time.'

He thought about this and asked, 'What about Robert Gabriel? Have you met him?'

'Met him? I haven't even seen him. Riggi insists he deals with the English kid alone. No one else goes near.'

'Thanks,' he said, and watched her go.

He looked at the phone. There was a missed call from a number he recognized. He returned it, heard Agata answer, and the relief in her voice, followed quickly by indignation.

'You never called,' she said.

He closed his eyes and rested his head against the battered stone wall of the Questura.

'It's only been a day. Also, I seem to be back at work. Sorry.'

He didn't say what was in his head: this wasn't a good idea, she was better off if he stayed out of her life.

'Can you come round, please? Now?'

He felt tired and grubby. His head ached. Costa checked his watch, calculated he had forty minutes before the appointment with Rosa at the Coyote, took a deep breath and said, 'Of course.'

CHAPTER 2

F ive minutes later he was in the Via Governo
Vecchio dragging his scooter onto its stand.
He got a lascivious wink from the old woman
who was once again sweeping up outside as he
knocked on the door of the ground-floor apartment. Agata answered the door still in her office
clothes: a smart blue suit. She didn't look him in
the eye as she let him in.

The place was a beautiful little studio, an elegant
home packed into no more than a hundred square
metres. A gigantic print of Botticelli's *Venus* ran
along the main wall. A tiny kitchen was tucked
into the far corner. The timbered floor was covered
in fashionable ethnic rugs. At the end of the room
an open staircase with a banister led up to a double
bed set in a gallery suspended directly over a small
dining table. Once this had probably been no more
than a storeroom for the house above. Now it
was transformed into a sophisticated compact
apartment just a few steps from the Piazza
Navona, home to the young woman who sat opposite him, in front of Botticelli's ill-proportioned
goddess rising naked from her scallop shell, a pale,

northern figure set against Agata's darker, Sicilian features.

Something linked them, though. An expression of doubt, anxiety even, at the circumstances in which they found themselves.

'How's work?' he asked. 'Did you have a nice meal with your boss?'

'I didn't ask you here to talk about that,' she said very quickly. 'It's this case of yours. That poor girl in the street. Mina Gabriel.'

Costa privately cursed the media and asked, 'What about her?'

'All this talk about Malise Gabriel and Galileo and Beatrice Cenci. This picture . . .'

She had a copy of the evening paper, the one which had placed Mina's features over the portrait in the Barberini.

'You shouldn't believe everything you read.'

'Well, I might not, if I hadn't heard it from your friends first.'

She looked unhappy. The way Agata had avoided talking about work – this wasn't like her. She'd seemed so enthused by the idea of getting a job, one that was entirely about her first love, art.

'I can't really talk about a live case. I'm sorry.'

'You already have talked about it. In a restaurant, of all places.'

She watched him from her plush chair on the other side of the coffee table. He wondered if a teacher's wages would really pay for a place like this. It seemed unlikely.

'On Sunday night,' he said, 'we still thought . . . we hoped Malise Gabriel's death was an accident. That seems less likely now, and Leo certainly has a confirmed case of murder which is obviously linked to the family. The American woman who leased them their apartment.'

Her eyes grew wide with shock and indignation.

'Do you honestly think that poor girl could have been responsible for the murder of anyone? Let alone her own father? Or that a man like Malise Gabriel could have done such horrible things to his own daughter?'

Costa didn't want this conversation.

'Agata,' he said. 'The world's full of truths we'd rather not face. Evil isn't some dry, philosophical debate. Or at least not only that. It's people. Ordinary people. Decent people, given another throw of the dice. You learn to live with it.'

'I don't want to live with it! I hate it. My world . . .' He caught her naive, slightly wild expression and saw again the young, innocent sister he'd first met, bustling through Rome in her black uniform, tackling everything she encountered with a fine, sharp intellect, but always from a distance, disengaged.

'The world you lived in wasn't real,' he said, and hoped he hadn't gone too far. 'You looked at the rest of us from behind the walls of your convent. As if we were specimens. I'm sorry if people disappoint. They're just human.'

Agata waved him away with an impatient arm.

'You're missing something here. An important point.'

She picked up the paper and stabbed a finger at the photograph of Mina, superimposed upon the frail, sad figure of Beatrice in Guido Reni's painting from the Barberini.

'This,' she insisted, 'isn't reality. It's myth, manufactured myth at that.'

He didn't understand her point and said so.

'Look.' Agata walked over to the sideboard and picked up a blue folder full of documents. 'I've been doing some research. Real research. Academic research.'

'You've had time?'

'I made time. I thought it was important.' She flicked through the folder. 'If Mina and her family are consciously trying to copy Beatrice Cenci they're following in false footsteps, and they must surely know it. This painting for one thing.'

She retrieved a copy of the original portrait from the Barberini.

'It's not Beatrice,' Agata stated with the same kind of certainty she'd possessed when evaluating the mysterious lost Caravaggio that had first brought them together.

'According to the Barberini,' Costa began.

'I know what the Barberini say and they're wrong. The best they should offer is an attribution. The work didn't even appear in any known catalogue until the late eighteenth century, only thirty years before Shelley saw it and gave the

Beatrice myth international appeal. Guido Reni probably never painted a single canvas in Rome until eight or ten years after her execution, so it can't have been painted from life, whatever the guide books say. Stylistically too . . .' Her fingers ran across the original's features. 'I won't bore you with the details but there are strong reasons to believe that not only is it not Beatrice, it's not by Reni either.'

This seemed interesting, but he felt bound to ask, 'Does that matter? In terms of our case?'

'Of course. Do you think this is the only fabrication?' She stared at him. 'How old was Beatrice when she died?'

He glanced at the familiar portrait and said, 'Seventeen or eighteen. I forget.'

'You've forgotten nothing. You never really knew. Here, read this.'

She threw across a single sheet. It was a printout from an academic website, a report of a book published in 1879 by a Roman historian, Antonio Bertoletti. In a former city library Bertoletti had found Francesco Cenci's own register of the births and deaths of his children. An entry in the list detailed the birth of Beatrice, in the palace in the ghetto, on 6 February 1577, a Wednesday, at eleven in the evening.

Costa tried to work this out. 'That must mean . . .' His arithmetic was never wonderful when it came to dates.

'She was actually twenty-two when she died.

Not that you'd believe that from Shelley or Stendhal or any of the other great fabricators. Now . . .'

Another page from Bertoletti's account. It was a codicil to Beatrice's will, lodged in Rome just a few days before her execution. The change was made to give a bequest of one thousand scudi to an unnamed 'poor boy'. This was a substantial amount of money. Beatrice was a wealthy woman. Earlier she'd divided her fortune predictably among her surviving relatives. Only when the Vatican confirmed her death sentence did she bring in an annuity for this anonymous child, with an instruction that he be given complete control of the capital if he survived to the age of twenty.

According to Bertoletti the money was intended for Beatrice's illegitimate son, fathered by the married servant, Olimpio Calvetti, who was known to be her lover, and one of Francesco Cenci's murderers. Bertoletti went so far as to suggest that the reason Beatrice was banished from Rome to the distant Cenci castle where Francesco died was to hide the pregnancy.

Costa glanced at the picture he'd assumed was Reni's portrait of Beatrice and wondered what to say.

'Rather spoils the story, doesn't it?' Agata asked. 'If Beatrice wasn't the innocent, virginal teenager, but twenty-two years old, with a child by a married servant? If, as her brother alleged, she was the focal point of the conspiracy, and forced the others

328

to continue when they were beginning to have second thoughts . . .'

'That doesn't change the circumstances of the crime.'

'Are you sure?'

It was a ridiculous thing to say and he knew it.

'There's evidence that Francesco Cenci sexually assaulted his own daughter?' Costa asked.

'I don't think you'd regard it as that. Most of the story that's been handed down to us was actually invented in the 1740s as part of a ragbag collection of fiction about life in Italy. No one disputes the idea that the father was a bad-tempered bully and a brute. But the idea of incest was only introduced into the trial by her lawyer very late on. Beatrice didn't stay bravely silent either. When she was interrogated a few weeks before she was executed she said on oath that her stepmother urged her to kill her father with these words . . .' Agata checked the page. '"He will abuse you and rob you of your honour." Note that word "will". Doesn't it suggest a threat of abuse, not the fact?'

Myths and inventions, Costa thought. Rome was full of them. Some, Malise Gabriel among them, believed the Catholic Church was built on nothing but fabrication from the outset.

'But does it matter?' he asked. 'If you tell a story often enough for people to believe it, doesn't it become real in some way? The most important way? In our heads?'

Agata's eyes never left him. He felt uncomfortable beneath the power and naked interest of her gaze. Talking to this earnest young woman was a challenge usually, no more so than now. She prompted him to think, to question matters that others took for granted. He felt too tired, too confused for that. And he needed to go. Rosa would be in the Coyote bar already.

'I'm sorry,' he answered. 'Can we talk about this another time?'

Her face fell.

'I have to go,' he added. 'There's always tomorrow.'

She sighed and seemed suddenly miserable at the thought of the following day.

'I don't know what I'm doing tomorrow yet. There's so much work. The hours . . .'

He got up and said, 'We'll work something out. This is very interesting. But to be honest I don't see how it affects Mina Gabriel.'

'No,' she said wryly. 'You don't.'

There was a touch of scorn in her voice.

'Enlighten me.'

She winced and admitted, 'I can't really. It doesn't add up. When I tried to comfort Mina that night, outside the house. When her father . . .' Agata shook her head and he was mesmerized by her quick and ready capacity for sympathy towards someone she didn't even know. 'That *scene*. I'm telling you, Nic. I know suffering when I see it. Living in a convent didn't spare me from the presence of death. I've held the hand of someone as the life slipped out

330

of her. I know that pain and I'm telling you. Mina was grieving when I put my arms around her. No one could possibly invent that. Certainly not a girl who, unlike Beatrice Cenci, really is seventeen. She loved her father. I'm sure of it. And Malise Gabriel believed in the truth, or at least his definiation of it. Truth was more important to him than anything else in the world. That's what his book's all about, isn't it?'

He wished he had more time. More insight too. There was something here, an elusive idea he couldn't quite grasp.

Agata Graziano stood in front of him, her fierce intellect working as it always did, and asked, 'Why would Mina look for inspiration in a fantasy? A fairy-tale concocted out of a squalid little domestic murder, embroidered over the centuries by story-tellers and artists? Why? Shelley said the story of Beatrice was about the most dark and secret caverns of the human heart.' She took his arms. 'But it wasn't, was it? Poetic licence, nothing more. Mina Gabriel must know that better than anyone.'

There was something there he did understand, perhaps better than the inquisitive yet unworldly young woman in front of him.

'Maybe we're just looking in the wrong cavern,' he said.

'Or there are places you're not supposed to look at all,' she told him. 'However much a man like Malise Gabriel might have hated the idea.'

He didn't understand what any of this meant,

any more than Agata did. But there was something here, something hidden inside these twin tragedies that linked them, even if it was not the obvious.

'I don't think she's guilty,' Costa said. 'Whatever Leo and the media say. The mother, brother, I don't . . .'

Agata's voice shrank almost to nothing.

'Please God, I hope you're right. What kind of place . . .'

Her small, dark hand went to her mouth. Her eyes were lustrous and damp. She was close to tears. For whom, he wondered? An English girl she didn't know? Or herself, stranded in the harsh reality of everyday life, a world she didn't recognize and perhaps could not begin to face?

They stood close to one another and he remembered that awkward moment on the bridge, with the screams rising from the ghetto as the two of them hesitantly closed towards a kiss.

'Tomorrow,' Costa said, seizing her by the shoulders, 'you will go into work and think of nothing but delivering the most astonishing lecture on Caravaggio you've ever given. Later, some time, I don't know when, this will all be behind us and we'll go to Baffetto. I will buy you the best pizza in Rome. Who knows? Maybe I can even entice you onto my battered little Vespa. It's not an Alfa Romeo, I know . . .'

'Don't joke about that,' she said sullenly.

He wondered what to say, whether to pry further.

Then his phone rang. Costa found a mild curse slipping his lips and immediately apologized.

It was Rosa. He had to go.

CHAPTER 3

The Coyote Bar was in a side street between the Campo dei Fiori and the Via Giulia, a grubby little dive that scarcely seemed to be in Italy at all. The drinks were two-for-one until nine, the music deafening rock and reggae, the clientele almost entirely foreign, pushing and shoving to get the free pizza and couscous that had just been placed on the bar.

Rosa sat on a high stool sipping what looked like a mojito and picking at a slice of flabby dough covered in bright red tomato sauce. She didn't see Costa at first so he was able to watch her for a minute or two as she alternately smiled at and insulted a couple of young men trying to talk to her, all the while wearing the jaded and arrogant expression that seemed *de rigeur* for women in places like this. She'd always been a good cop, one who could shrug off the uniform and become someone else without so much as a second thought. It was a talent and a curse too sometimes.

A persistent American kid, tall and strong, like a football player, was standing over her, getting pushy and mouthy when Costa finally walked over.

'Nic,' Rosa said brightly, glad to see him arrive. 'Meet my new friend, Jimmy.'

Costa looked at the gignatic youth towering above him. Jimmy had a crew cut and a blank, unmemorable face. He was wearing some kind of sports shirt with huge numbers on the chest and a baseball cap on backwards.

'What are you doing in Rome, Jimmy?' Costa asked, briefly shaking his hand.

'History.'

Costa looked more closely at the shirt. The logo made out that it was from the Raffaello College football team, the academy for foreign kids in the Via Corso where Agata taught.

'Is it fun?'

'My old man made me do it. History sucks.'

'That's an interesting point of view. A friend of mine just started work at the Raffaello. Agata Graziano. She teaches art.'

His small, piggy eyes lit up.

'Oh wow. The new one? Black-haired chick? She's a babe. You gotta introduce me.'

Costa frowned and said, 'I think you should tell her she's a babe yourself. Now . . .' Costa picked up a slimy, limp slice of pizza, placed it in Jimmy's paw-like hand and waved at the far corner where a bunch of similarly attired kids were standing slack-jawed beneath a TV set showing American football. 'Go over there. Eat that. And don't come back.'

The American kid looked as if he might be trouble

for a moment. Then he thought better of it and slunk off.

Rosa was shaking her head.

'You've absolutely no idea how to handle them, have you?'

'Really?' he wondered. 'He's gone, isn't he? Where did I go wrong?'

'We find things out by talking to them. Not scaring them away.'

He took her by the arm and led her to a dark and empty corner where the music was just a little less loud, though still of sufficient volume to afford a curiously noisy form of privacy.

'We find things out by talking to Robert Gabriel.' He looked into her eyes. 'Or Gino Riggi. Isn't that right?'

'If only,' she grumbled.

Costa didn't have much patience left. He asked her for the background to her assignment: watching the cop from narcotics. Slowly, carefully, Rosa outlined what she knew, with the rigorous precision he'd come to associate with her.

It wasn't a pretty story, or a rare one. Riggi was one more cop who'd spent a little too long beneath the surface, so much that he'd failed to remember where the lines were drawn. Internal investigations suspected him of taking money from the Turkish gang, the Vadisi, playing both sides.

'We think his contact there is called Cakici,' Rosa said. 'Robert Gabriel's some kind of intermediary who runs between the two. If I could lay my hands on the English kid I'd offer him a deal. Immunity from prosecution in return for what he knows. *If I could get close to him.*'

She raised her slight shoulders in desperation.

'Of course that was before Leo decided he was wanted for murder. Now, I just don't know. He doesn't sound a lot like his sister, does he? Not from what I read in the papers? She's all sweetness and light.'

'Adoptive sister,' Costa said. 'Robert was adopted. Apparently he never quite fitted in.'

'Ah.' Rosa nodded.

As if that explained everything, Costa thought. He glanced around the room.

'You think we might find Robert Gabriel here? Or Riggi?'

'The *centro storico* is the Vadisi's territory. They like dealing with the foreign kids. Here one minute, gone the next. It's easy. The profits are reasonable. They don't get involved in long-term deals with suppliers or addicts. The Campo, Trastevere, that's theirs. The places Romans go for their drugs – San Giovanni, out in the suburbs – they're still pretty much Italian. Though I have to say our own people are getting muscled out over time. The Turks, the Balkan gangs, they're a lot tougher, a lot meaner. They'll contemplate things that your average Italian hood would baulk at. No need to go to confession afterwards, is there?'

He'd heard that story in so many places. It was part of the changing face of Italian organized crime.

'You don't know what Robert Gabriel looks like?'

'Just Riggi's description,' she said. 'Lanky, muscular kid around twenty with black hair, lots of it. If he's got something to sell around here . . .' Her finger ran across the crowd in the bar. '. . . they'll know him. The way it works is you walk around, look interested, talk to people. Don't do anything obvious like asking where you can score.'

'Thanks for the advice. I appreciate it.'

'I'm trying to help! If we bump into Riggi then you and I are out on a date.' Her big brown eyes focused on him. 'Is that OK with you?'

'Wouldn't be the first time we've played that game, would it?'

'No.' She didn't take her eyes off him. 'Comes naturally.'

'How many bars are there? Like this? The places the Gabriel kid would have worked?'

She looked at the ceiling, counting the answer off on her fingers.

'Around here, seven. Near Navona, another five or so. Couple by the Pantheon. Six, eight, maybe more, in Trastevere.'

So many? Costa was surprised. This was a side to Rome he, like most citizens, rarely saw. It happened off camera, in places they never visited, a hidden undercurrent in the city's busy tide of daily life.

Rosa raised her glass.

'Soda water and fresh mint. Long evening ahead. Are you ready for it?'

'Until midnight. Maybe not even that.'

She turned serious for a moment and her made-up face suddenly seemed a lot older.

'I need you to understand this, Nic. We've got a case against Riggi already but it's fragile. I have to find a little more. Or to put it another way, I need to make sure we don't lose anything we already have.'

He got the message. Her news about Riggi wasn't an accidental revelation, some personal favour Rosa had idly slipped to him as he sat on his Vespa outside the Questura. It was her way of warning him off any action that might impact upon her own case.

'We'd better split up and start talking, I suppose,' Costa said.

Rosa Prabakaran smiled. Then, as he watched, she changed again, found a sultry smile from somewhere, a walk, a posture that seemed to fit this loud, overheated temple to a form of twenty-first century hedonism he found deeply tedious.

She ambled over to the counter and started chatting to the barista shaking cocktails. Costa wandered outside, said hello to a couple of pretty girls enjoying the fading sun, then slipped round the corner and called back to forensic. Di Capua was still on duty. Costa was glad of that. Teresa's deputy seemed to understand these things better than most.

'I need you to look up the personal mobile-phone number for a plain-clothes officer,' Costa told him. 'After that I'm going to call it and I want a trace to where he is now. Is that possible?'

Di Capua laughed.

'Are you serious? This is kindergarten stuff. Beneath me. Let me put you over to my new friend, Maria. She can handle it.'

Costa remembered the accident with the camera and the rumour that the same girl had seen Malise Gabriel's corpse at the weekend and noticed nothing untoward.

'You mean the Maria who . . . ?'

He didn't have time to finish the sentence. A bubbly young woman was on the line asking a series of detailed questions. Costa steeled himself. She seemed to know what she was doing.

It took a minute to get Riggi's number, then another three to set up the trace. Costa sent up a little prayer that the bent narcotics cop wasn't on voicemail then walked back round the corner, stood next to the pretty girls outside the bar, and dialled, withholding his own number.

After four rings a bad-tempered male voice barked, '*Pronto*.'

'Hey, Sergio!' Costa said in a loud, crude voice. 'Where the hell you been? We're waiting for you. At the bar. The girls are here and they look gorgeous. Girls? Say hello to Sergio!'

The giggly kids had been listening. They raised their mojito glasses and yelled, 'Sergio!'

'I can't believe you're late again, you idle jerk,' Costa said. 'You got your head on right?'

'What're you talking about, moron?' Riggi yelled. 'I'm not Sergio. Check the damned number next time.'

Then silence. Costa smiled at the girls and shrugged. He walked back round the corner and waited. It was Silvio Di Capua who called back.

'If you tell me your new girlfriend screwed that up,' Costa told him, 'my reputation for possessing a forgiving nature will be sorely tested.'

'New girlfriend. I wish. Maria's one smart kid. You just have to keep her away from touching things. Physical stuff. Anything breakable.'

'That doesn't bode well for a developing relationship. Where was the call from?'

He listened. It was a rough fix, based on the mobile network's cell. But if he married it up with Rosa's knowledge . . .

Costa walked back into the bar and pulled her away from a couple of loud and bleary-eyed Australians.

'Do you mind?' she said, dragging his hand off her bare arm. 'I might have been getting somewhere there.'

'Were you?'

'I said might have been.'

'Trastevere. The names of the bars Riggi frequents.'

She looked puzzled but rattled off the ones she knew.

Di Capua said the call came from somewhere near the Piazza Trilussa, the tiny little square on the other side of the Ponte Sisto, the pedestrian bridge that ran across the river from close to the Palazzetto Santacroce. There was one obvious dive on her list. It was a long walk.

He went over to the coat stand in the corner and picked up the helmets he'd left there, thrusting the spare into Rosa Prabakaran's hands.

'What the hell's going on, Nic?' she demanded.

'You said we'd look good on the Vespa,' he told her.

CHAPTER 4

Kids, Riggi thought. You had to use them. No one else was stupid enough to do the job. But dealing with their idiocy, their unpredictability, their flakiness – these things drove him crazy sometimes.

He sat on a stool outside the bar in the back street near the Piazza Trilussa watching the streams of brightly clad adolescents wandering into the centre of Trastevere for the evening. A long night usually, one that might not end till three or later, till daylight, when some would find themselves on a bench by the Tiber, exhausted yet popped up with chemicals, munching cheap pizza, wondering what came next.

Riggi's uncle had lived in Trastevere. When the cop first came to Rome from Venice he'd lived with the old man for a while, in a narrow, winding street that ran up the Gianicolo hill, all the way to the church of Montorio and beyond, towards the piazzale dedicated to Garibaldi. This was only eight or nine years ago, but it seemed a lifetime away. So much had happened since, in Riggi's life, in that of Trastevere. His uncle had sold his little house for a fortune to some banker in Chicago who'd sliced it into apartments that he now rented over the Internet to tourists. Most of the neighbours had done the same so the streets that once were alive with Romans now had an anonymous, shifting population, without ties, without history.

When Riggi first came to Rome his uncle had proudly told him how Trastevere was the last true neighbourhood in the centre of the city. A solid, tightly knit community of families, most of whom had been staking their claim to these tapering streets of modest, cramped houses for centuries. Now many of the locals had taken the tourist dollar, moved out to new apartment blocks built on the flat estuarial land near Fiumicino. Places that came with easy parking and supermarkets nearby, fast trains back into the city for those who needed them. All the conveniences of modern life.

And Trastevere was slowly transformed, the Roman elements of it mutating into museum pieces for the crowds of wandering foreign tourists, the houses sold on for sums of money that men like his uncle, a dignified but impoverished print worker, could never have dreamed of attaining through their daily labour.

He hated the place. He loved it too. The kids here, gullible youngsters like Robert Gabriel, were his to control, to use, to master.

Riggi sipped his beer and thought of the ones he'd dealt with over the years. Most, in the early days, had wound up in court, busted for small amounts of dope, silent, always, about where the stuff came from. Two weeks later they'd be back in the bars, their tiny fortunes stored in plastic bags and rolled-up balls of foil. He hadn't changed a thing by arresting them. It was like brushing away the flood water back home in Venice. The *acqua alta* always returned. Why? Because this was where, when the season chose, it belonged.

So he came to the conclusion it might be easier to win their confidence, to let them think he was as crooked as they were, given the opportunity. This way he got to glimpse the men behind them, the shadowy, dark figures who lived far away in pleasant suburbs, with wives and children at expensive private schools, all paid for by a pricey pinch of chemical that went into some foreigner's nostril or mouth or vein late on a Trastevere night.

At some unnoticed point over the years the dividing line between him and them had disappeared altogether. Why? He'd no idea. He couldn't even pinpoint the moment, the event, at which the change had occurred. Sometimes the *acqua alta* turned up on schedule. Sometimes it never showed. That was the way of things.

How many bar kids pushing dope had he met this way over the years? Forty. Fifty. More. He'd lost count. Most of them looked the same anyway. Lanky, tall, pale, with unkempt hair and blank, dead faces. From time to time one of them would fail the exam, the subtle, short interview Riggi gave them before revealing who he truly was. And then they'd wind up in front of a magistrate, serving a little time, always in silence. The Vadisi understood the need for this. A cop who never caught anyone would soon attract suspicion. Statistics mattered, more and more. He needed sacrifices, just as much as the Turks did. They were necessary for all the old reasons, and practicality meant that it was easier to put the innocent and the gullible to the sword than the guilty. This was a world constantly on the edge of breaking. An occasional scapegoat, some dumb youngster putting up his hand to selling coke and heroin and poppers, kept the lid on, for a while anyway.

There'd been a time when he thought that Robert Gabriel might have been in line for this fate. But Gabriel was different, and had been from the start. Wily, cowardly, unpredictable – all the things Riggi loathed. But someone who could shift huge amounts of dope too, come back with an empty stash and pockets brimming with money, always ready for more.

Too much money sometimes, Riggi knew. The arithmetic of pushing dope was simple. Gabriel was beating the numbers and the Roman narcotics cop couldn't quite work out how. By skimming from the proceeds? That seemed unlikely and dangerous. By working for two masters? Riggi wondered about that and knew it was a conversation he and the English kid had to have. There'd been rumours of late of a new player in the *centro storico*, someone Italian, not Turkish. That idea gave him a chill. It spoke of wars, of blood, of messy public revelations.

Also . . . Riggi tried to remember. But the beer, and he'd drunk a lot of it lately, seemed to cloud his recollection.

He recalled the first time he and Robert Gabriel had met, and a curious memory returned. In a way he felt it was almost as if Robert Gabriel had recruited him. Not that this was possible. The young English kid hadn't needed bending to Riggi's will. He was there, in the mental place they both wanted, already, willing to shuttle between him and the Vadisi henchman, Cakici, without a second thought, as if this duplicitous and risky existence came naturally.

There was something about Robert Gabriel that Riggi had mistrusted from the start. Now, with a talented and tenacious cop like Leo Falcone on his tail, Gabriel was beginning to look like a serious liability. He had to get the kid out of Rome, quickly. Riggi would even buy the airline ticket himself if need be. If that didn't happen – if the kid was an idiot and insisted on staying . . .

Gino Riggi didn't see himself as a dishonest man. He'd never enriched himself much from his time working both sides of the street. A holiday in Thailand. A decent hi-fi system. Some money sent back home to his widowed mother who lived in a humble back-street apartment in Castello, too proud to ask for help. That was all this meant.

It wasn't for personal gain, not really. Riggi had rationalized this time and time again, usually late at night with a belly full of beer and a stomach complaining that a little food wouldn't go amiss either.

In a world that was fractured to breaking point the best a decent man could do was to try to keep a little equilibrium around him. He allowed the Vadisi to deal to the dumb and feckless foreign kids whose tourist dollars, largely donated by doting parents intent on giving them a brief European education, kept the economy of the Campo and Trastevere alive, if barely. In return the Turks kept away from the places where real Roman kids went to play, stayed out of prostitution and some of the nastier sides of the drug business. There was an accommodation, an awkward, illicit one that could put him in jail if it became known.

And if that happened? If the house of cards around him really tumbled down one day? Not a single gram of coke would disappear from the streets. No dealers would get busted. Nothing much would change.

He snatched the bottle of strong Moretti beer to his mouth and downed some. No one had ever been hurt in his little territory over the years. Not seriously. He didn't want that on his conscience. But if Robert Gabriel wouldn't take the hint . . .

'Stupid English kids,' Riggi said.

He glanced at his watch. It was eight thirty. At least the English were usually punctual.

A tall, dark-haired figure was bouncing down the cobblestones of the little alley with the jaunty punk walk so many of these dumb, drug-pushing adolescents thought was cool. Washed-out denim jacket, black T-shirt, jeans. The same thing a million other kids in the city liked to wear.

The morons all looked the same after a while, Riggi realized, and knew, from the sinking feeling in his stomach, he had to get out of this mess. It was wrong. It was dangerous. And one day soon he'd no longer be able to keep this creaky world afloat.

'What the hell . . . ?' Riggi began as the kid got nearer.

He stopped. His voice was being drowned out by another noise: the roar of a powerful motor-bike echoing off the tall tenement houses around him, going too fast to be acceptable, even in the rough and rowdy neighbourhood this had become.

CHAPTER 5

There was a shriek of brakes. The lanky figure ambling down the street cast a glance over his shoulder, surprised, a touch angry too. The bike rider had slowed and was now edging along at a snail's pace, booted feet rhythmically walking the cobbles as his right hand twitched on the throttle, bouncing the power of its big engine off the walls.

Riggi slammed down the beer on the table, waiting for the machine to get past, all those old phrases running through his head, the ones his uncle used to mutter before he took the tourist dollar and ran.

Kids, kids, kids. Who the hell do they think they are?

He couldn't hear himself think. Couldn't hope to exchange a word with the lean, black-haired youth approaching him, not till this deafening machine had got past.

Then the bike came close and stopped altogether, engine purring, settling into a low, happy rumble. It was a huge red Ducati, powerful and expensive. The rider was all in black, a leather suit, the kind old-fashioned racers wore. His head was enclosed in a full shiny helmet the same colour as his gear, with an opaque visor that made the man look like some kind of gigantic insect.

'Oh my,' Riggi declared, and began to clap his hands slowly, sarcastically. 'What's it they say? Big bike, little dick. Piss off out of here, moron, before I pull you off that stupid thing and give you a damned good . . .'

The cop stopped and blinked. The figure in leather had pulled down the shiny silver zip on his chest and removed from beneath it a long-nosed pistol as black and as shiny as his own artificial skin.

'Cakici?' he asked, so quietly he realized no one would have heard, not even the youth in front of him, whose face was now as white as the newly painted wall outside the bar where Riggi had bought his overpriced Moretti. *'Cakici . . . ?'*

The rider stretched out his hand and loosed a single bullet into the kid's head. A noise like muffled thunder rang round the walls of this shady, constricted Trastevere alley. The shot figure in front of him let out a brief, pained cry of outrage then jerked to the ground, body contorted and twisting as if hit by an electric shock. Two more bullets got pumped into his T-shirt.

Riggi stared at the blood and the way the kid bounced with the impact of the shots, wondering if this was real or some kind of waking nightmare.

A mess of this scale would come back to haunt him, he knew. It had to.

'Oh, wonderful. How the hell am I supposed to clean up this one?' He looked up at the helmeted figure and wanted to drag the idiot off the bike, punch him hard, scream at him. 'How the hell . . . ?'

Riggi shut up. For the first time in years he was scared, and it felt oddly vivid, as if something he'd been missing for ages had suddenly walked back into his life. Just for one last time, to say good-bye.

'Don't be so stupid . . .' he started to say.

CHAPTER 6

Costa had just crossed the Ponte Garibaldi, past the spot where a few days earlier he'd embraced Agata Graziano, when he heard the shots and saw a cloud of dusty grey urban pigeons scattering into the blue sky against the Gianicolo hill.

Rosa Prabakaran clung to him more tightly on the pillion as he tried to twist a little more power out of the Vespa's weedy guts. He broke over the lights on red, weaving through the slow-moving cars heading south-east, away from Trilussa, ignoring the blare of horns and the angry shouts. Rosa had to tighten her grip around his waist as the Vespa mounted the pavement, scattering a couple of bums who tugged at grimy lengths of rope to get their dogs out of the way, then rattled down the cobbles of the tiny horseshoe piazza.

The movement of the people on the street guided him. The source of the gunfire was two alleys away running north. A group of shocked bystanders was starting to gather round two dark, stationary shapes on the ground. Costa slewed the scooter to a halt, turned to Rosa and said, 'Deal with it.'

She dismounted in a flash, ripping off her helmet, and was down with the figures on the grey cobbled street. Costa snatched off his own head-gear too and started to ask questions.

'Him,' said a young kid, no more than sixteen, in a bright purple shirt.

The youth was pointing back across the piazza they'd just crossed to a street that dipped down by the side of the Lungotevere and led back towards the bridge.

There was a red motorbike there, a serious machine, the rider anonymous in black, carefully weaving his way through the early-evening crowd that had ground to a halt, puzzled by the nearby commotion.

'The bike?' he asked.

The kid nodded.

Costa wheeled the little scooter round and set off back the way he'd come. When he entered the open space of the piazza he lifted the front wheel onto the pedestrian space that ran from one side to the other, shortcutting the distance between him and the red bike slowly disappearing down the narrow street opposite. Tramps bellowed at him, brandishing their bottles of cheap beer, tourists licked their ice creams in silence, looking shocked and scared.

When he made it to the far side the bike was starting to edge its way towards the end of the lane at a steady, decent speed, one that wouldn't attract attention. Costa jerked back the throttle on his little machine until the twist grip would go no further, tried to ignore the screeching, high-pitched whine it made, and began to close the distance between them.

With no more than ten metres to go, the rider ahead noticed what was happening and began slowing to a crawl, one so leisurely he had to put down his feet to keep the big bike upright.

Costa had no weapon, nothing much that could change the situation. This was more than a little foolhardy. But he couldn't get those two bodies on the ground out of his head, and the nagging thought that he knew who one of them was, and could already begin to feel the pain that loss would cause.

The helmet on the bike turned to watch him, attentively, in a way that gave Costa pause for thought as he flew along the cobbled alley, bareheaded, wondering what would happen when they met.

The black-leather figure faced the road ahead and tore open the throttle on his machine. The powerful engine roared like a whipped beast. The front wheel lifted. The machine burst away towards the bridge with a turn of speed that seemed impossible. In a second or so it was already outpacing the rusty Vespa, increasing the distance between them. The front wheel came down, found purchase on the cobbles, then Costa watched as the red beast rode onto the steeply sloping pavement, using the incline as a ramp to leap high into the air, over the static stream of traffic locked on the choking Lungotevere.

It landed on the bonnet of a large black official looking Mercedes with a crash so loud Costa could hear it over the two-stroke engine beneath him. The bike rider kicked and fought to stabilize the machine as its heavy wheel punched deep indents into the bonnet of the vehicle beneath. With the skill of a stuntman he kept himself upright, then blipped the throttle again and lurched forward, working his way over the bonnets of two more adjoining vehicles, kicking at windscreens, levering his boots off doors and roofs and anything he could use to keep upright and get himself to the other side. Drivers opened their windows, shook their fists, furious, impotent as the rider used them as a pontoon across the broad riverside road.

As he got closer to the pavement the engine roared to its full extent again. The red shape and then the black-clad figure disappeared. Costa listened as the loud, violent voice of the bike ripped through the evening, diminishing with distance.

He took out his phone, called the control room, gave them the licence-plate number that he'd memorized when he got close enough.

At the bridge the bike could turn left into the *centro storico*, or right for the Via Garibaldi and the suburbs beyond. There were so many escape routes. Or . . . Costa was trying to think like a fugitive, aware it came naturally after all these years.

Or the rider would simply pull into some deserted alley nearby, leave the machine, take off the black leather suit and the helmet, dump them too, and stride off into the city, one more face among thousands, anonymous, invisible.

The control room said officers were already on the way. There was nothing else to do, no other chore he could think of that would delay the inevitable any longer.

He turned the scooter around and slowly worked his way back towards the Piazza Trilussa and the bar beyond. The street was packed with people, both scared and curious, the way the public always was in such circumstances. A uniform car was there already, blocking the foot of the alley.

He knew one of the cops.

'What should we do?' the officer asked when Costa turned up. 'They said it was a guy on a bike.'

'He's gone.'

Someone had placed blankets over the shapes on the ground. Rosa was on a stool by the door to the bar. Her make-up had run with the tears. She was clutching a drink that didn't look like soda water and ice any more. Her eyes never left him.

Costa walked over, put a hand on her arm and asked, 'Riggi?'

'What do you think?'

She looked down the little street, back towards

the river and shook her head. There was fury as well as shock in her face.

'How the hell did you know he was here?' she demanded.

'I put a trace on his phone and called him.'

'You might have told me.'

'Yes,' he agreed. 'I'm sorry. There wasn't time.'

I was thinking, he wanted to say. About Agata and what she'd told him. About fairy-tales and the curious, insubstantial nature of human belief.

'If we'd been here a couple of minutes earlier . . .' Rosa added.

He took the drink away, put it on the table, took her arms. She fought him a little, but not much.

'Then we'd be dead too. Don't you know that?'

She grabbed hold of the booze and took a clumsy drink.

'He was still a cop, wasn't he?'

Costa turned round, bent down, lifted the first sheet and saw Riggi's sour features beneath the fabric.

It was wrong to stop there and he knew it. So he walked round and removed the sheet from the second corpse. A woman in the crowd cried out, a shriek of shock mixed with disgust, and it sounded like a scream of protest, at him, for letting this ugly, bloody fact be seen beneath the fading light of a beautiful Roman evening.

A small red fire lit up in Costa's head. He turned round, saw the woman, saw the anger and outrage in her face, and said, 'If you don't want to see, Signora, I suggest you walk away.'

A few of them started to mutter. None moved. He didn't care any more.

Costa knelt down by the corpse and looked at the kid's face. Part of his scalp had been blown away, revealing bone and tissue. His glassy eyes seemed locked on something in the distance. The thin line of his mouth was pulled back in a rictus leer. Washed-out denim jacket, black T-shirt, cheap jeans, curly dark hair. The same clothes Costa had seen in the Lone Star bar the night before, when this same youth had led him to the house in the Via Beatrice Cenci, and the corpse of Joanne Van Doren, a suicide that wasn't.

Gingerly, he lifted the edge of the jacket, aware that Teresa would screech at him for this. But there was something in the inside pocket, a shape that looked familiar, and Costa knew he had to see.

A stash of notes. Eight euros, just enough for a meal and a drink or two. A small plastic bag with white powder in it. A single condom. A passport with the maroon cover of a European Union document, and the crest of the United Kingdom.

He opened it up and saw the same face he'd seen the previous evening, the same blank, surly expression too on the photograph beneath the clear security film, issued only six months before. And a name: Robert Peter Gabriel.

PART IX

CHAPTER 1

The first Thursday of September, a morning so hot it seemed summer would never leave.

A day and a half had passed since the murders in Trastevere. The gunning-down of a police officer and the missing Robert Gabriel had changed everything, brought a feverish anxiety to the headlines, the mood in the Questura, and the minds of the large team of officers now working on the case. It was rare for a member of the police to die on duty, an event that would usually demand some show of visible mourning on the part of the authorities.

The circumstances of Riggi's murder made this difficult. The media had quickly picked up the rumour that the dead man was under investigation for corruption. They soon learned, too, that Robert Gabriel had been in the pay of the Vadisi. When they coupled this with their existing fascination for the Gabriel case, and its links with the Cenci, they seemed to feel they'd found the perfect story, one that embraced everything that could sell news to a public desperate for both titillation and a source of outrage about the damaged state of the world. Murder, crime, sex – and the young, innocent-seeming face of Mina Gabriel, now grieving for her dead, wicked brother. The tale had it all.

The demonstrations outside the Questura had grown. Judging by their posters, their complaints now extended to police incompetence and inefficiency in allowing the suspect brother to be killed by a group of criminals who should have been arrested years ago, and thrown out of Italy as unwanted foreigners. Costa recognized this shade of public opinion. It was one that surfaced from time to time, when a case of injustice hit the headlines and touched some popular nerve.

The Gabriel case had unleashed a torrent of deep resentment towards the authorities over the state of law and order on the streets. It was a bad-tempered spirit, one that someone other than Leo Falcone might have exorcized the easy way, swiftly laying the blame for the murders of Malise Gabriel and Joanne Van Doren at the door of the dead son, closing that side of the case for good. Then, when the furore had abated a little, quietly working through a list of the known henchmen the Vadisi might have used for the hit.

But easy was never Falcone's style. The Gabriel case continued to concern him. The dogged inspector would not rest until he got to the very bottom of the strange and opaque event in the apartment in the Via Beatrice Cenci the previous weekend. As he made clear repeatedly in meeting after meeting, it was this that appeared to have triggered the series of tragedies which culminated in the shooting in the street two nights before. Truth never acquiesced to convenience in Falcone's mind. It was one of his defining characteristics, an awkward, staunch persistence that seemed ingrained in the man's personality.

Costa admired this, and could see and understand his reasoning. They now knew that Malise Gabriel's death was not accidental, as it was meant to appear. The loose scaffolding ties. The blood and tissue that had been revealed on Di Lauro's handkerchief, wiped from the radiator in Mina's room. The clear evidence that Gabriel was a difficult, argumentative man, one who had been conducting an adulterous affair with Joanne Van Doren in the secret photographic studio in the basement of her building.

All of these factors aroused suspicion. What irked Falcone most was the continued silence on the part of Mina and her mother, their mute response to his many questions, their unwillingness to become involved. This was irrational and odd, and Costa knew it too. He had told Agata that he believed Mina was an innocent party in what had taken place, perhaps an aggrieved one too, not that he had mentioned that. His words were only partly meant to reassure her. Some truth continued to elude them and it went beyond the curious silence on the part of the young English girl and her mother.

Then, as they assembled for one more case conference, Teresa Lupo summoned them suddenly to forensic. Finally, some hard evidence had, it seemed, been unearthed.

CHAPTER 2

In the Questure's largest forensic lab office Silvio Di Capua gazed at the grubby object in front of him, grinned and said, 'You've no idea how lucky we are. There are a million illegal dumps around Lazio and most of them would have this stuff in ashes by now. Behold.'

Forensic had tracked down some of the household material taken away by Joanne Van Doren's builders the previous Sunday. It had been found on a site near Latina, untouched since it arrived. Di Capua's attention had come to focus on a mattress from a single bed, one that looked depressingly familiar. The sheet was still on it, with the white and green mosaic pattern Costa and Peroni had seen when they walked into Mina's room the previous Sunday, before the place had been cleared.

'Why wasn't it burned?' Costa said.

Falcone looked at him and sighed. Judging by the expressions on the faces of Teresa and Peroni they found the question baffling too.

Di Capua shook his head.

'It was some crappy little place that was behind

schedule or something. Am I meant to care? Maria?'

The stocky young assistant who now seemed permanently attached to Teresa's deputy beamed as she showed them the marks left by her aerosol.

'Semen,' she said proudly. 'We've sent off a sample for analysis.'

Costa took a closer look at the mattress.

'Do we know for sure this is Mina Gabriel's?'

'Oh, come on,' Peroni objected. 'We were there. In the room. We saw this ourselves. It's hers.'

Teresa placed a gloved finger on the mattress and said, 'I'll be able to confirm it's the girl's from skin residue if nothing else. Mattresses are full of it. It might help if you can persuade her to give me a DNA sample we can match, of course.'

Costa wouldn't give up.

'If it turns out the semen was the father's, it could have been one more place he slept with Joanne Van Doren.'

The pathologist stared at him.

'His daughter's room? Why would he use that? He had his own secret little sex club in the basement. Why take the risk in the house?'

'Some people like risks,' Costa began. 'I don't know. Why don't we wait for some facts? Instead of trying to concoct a case to match some theory that keeps bobbing up in front of us every time we're stuck for an idea? Why . . . ?'

'Let's not allow our personal feelings to colour

this investigation,' Falcone interrupted. He nodded at Di Capua. 'Good work.'

'And another thing,' Costa began, then saw Falcone's stony face, gave up, realizing it was pointless.

Teresa Lupo was working her gloved hands along the side of the mattress, underneath the white and green sheet. She'd seen something that Di Capua and his assistant had missed. There was a fabric handle built into the side, for carrying and turning. It protruded a little more on one side than the other.

She raised the sheet, took out a pen and poked the end down the hollow cotton loop of the right-hand fastening. Something popped slowly out of the other side. It was a tiny USB memory stick, the kind people used for storing and moving files around computers.

'Well, what do you know?' Costa murmured. 'We're in luck again. Am I the only one who finds this steady stream of evidence a little . . . ?'

He stopped. They weren't taking any notice. Their eyes were on the memory stick, and they were listening to Di Capua wonder whether it would be protected by a password or not.

'Most people aren't sad geeks like you,' Teresa told her deputy, taking the thing in her gloved fingers over to a laptop on a nearby desk. 'They wouldn't even understand how to encrypt something. They'd think hiding it down a mattress would be enough.'

'A mattress!' Maria said gleefully. 'What kind of thing would you want to hide down there? Bad things. Dirty things. I wonder . . .'

Peroni gave her a filthy, judgemental look. She shut up. Teresa plugged the stick into the side of the computer. It wasn't encrypted at all. Not even protected by a password. A flood of images began to fill the screen automatically. Costa stared at a couple, understood what he was seeing, and turned away.

This part of the forensic department was at the front of the Questura, in a modern annexe tacked onto the original building in the seventies. It faced the cobbled Renaissance square of the Piazza San Michele. Before being turned over to the police in the late nineteenth century, the Questura had been a palace belonging to the Vatican, home to a famous Cardinal, one known for gambling and sexual licentiousness. The spiritual and the sensual were never far apart in Rome.

From his viewpoint he could see the gang of demonstrators milling around in the street. The protest had reached a lull. The figures outside were swigging bottles of water, wandering around in the heat, their faces sullen with boredom. Banners stood at half-mast. The mainly female crowd chatted mostly, barely remembering to hand out leaflets to those passing through the square on the way to the Pantheon.

He wondered what these same women would say if they could see the photographs being revealed on the nearby computer screen, stored secretly on a tiny digital device hidden in the crevices of Mina Gabriel's mattress. One more convenient clue, it seemed, pointing to the obvious conclusion.

'*Sovrintendente,*' Falcone barked. 'Would you care to give us your opinion?'

Costa took a deep breath and went back to the screen. There must have been thirty photos there or more. All of them, he felt sure, were of Mina Gabriel. Her face was visible in many. The shapes, the poses, the contortions . . . his eyes told him this was from the same photographer who took the pictures they'd found in the basement. In many she could have been interchangeable with Joanne Van Doren. Except these were more explicit, more visceral. More amateurish too, somehow.

Mina looked scared, tired, reluctant, even drugged in some, as if taking part in a perform-ance she was unable to refuse. There was only one part of the man that was visible, the predictable part, though in a single shot it was possible to make out the barest outline of a hand reaching out to the back of her head, pulling her face towards him.

'Well?' Falcone persisted.

'What do you want me to say?'

The inspector scowled.

'Malise Gabriel was committing incest with his own daughter while simultaneously conducting an affair with Joanne Van Doren,' Falcone said. He sounded more than a little disheartened and disgusted by what they'd found, but there was relief in his voice too, and determination. 'He kept his secret with the American woman in the cellar. He hid his abuse of his daughter in her own bed.' Falcone glared at the computer screen. 'Turn that off. I've seen enough.'

'Bastard,' Di Capua spat. 'No wonder they wanted him dead.'

There were no words left, Costa realized. No possible objections he could raise.

After a long pause Peroni asked Falcone, 'What do you want to do next?'

'I'm going to get an arrest warrant out of Grimaldi,' the inspector said. 'The girl and the mother. Mina Gabriel has to admit to what went on here. She's not leaving the Questura until I get that. We'll show them this . . .' His hand swept towards the screen. 'If we have to.'

'Do you think you have enough to justify a warrant?' Costa asked.

'Scaffolding tampered with on the roof?' Falcone asked. 'Cecilia Gabriel round there the very morning her husband died, clearing the place so quickly we don't get to look at what was there? Some kind of a struggle in the girl's room? And she never noticed a thing? Please.'

'And Joanne Van Doren?' Costa asked.

'Perhaps she found out. She must have known what kind of man Gabriel was.' Falcone looked at him. 'Try and distance yourself from this girl. Look at the facts dispassionately. We may not know the full story, but we surely understand the direction it's taking. Alone, or in concert with the mother and daughter, Robert killed them.'

Peroni was staring at Costa from across the room. The big old cop was, in some ways, one of the smartest people he knew, a man in touch with his own emotions and those of others, even if his physical appearance belied this fact entirely. At that moment Costa was sure Peroni was trying to share something, to say that he'd his doubts too.

A uniformed officer came through the door. He looked happy.

'Immigration got the Turk at the airport,' he announced. 'The one called Cakici. Riggi's contact. Picked him up waiting for a flight to Izmir from Ciampino. Trying to leave the country on a false passport.'

There was a contented murmur of approval in the room. Riggi was still a cop. People wanted his killer brought to justice.

'Fetch him,' Falcone ordered. 'This man murdered a serving police officer. I want him here. In the Questura.'

'They say we have to interview him there first,' the officer said. 'False passport. That's their territory.'

Falcone swore, pulled out his phone, was about to start yelling at someone, then thought better of it. The tall, thin inspector was thinking, finger on his tidy silver goatee, striding round the forensic room, silent.

He turned to Costa and Peroni, aware, perhaps, that they'd exchanged some unspoken misgiving a few seconds before.

'Go to Ciampino,' he told them. 'Get him out of their hands. You can leave Mina and Cecilia Gabriel to me.'

CHAPTER 3

The first Appian Way, the Antica, curved away from the gate of San Sebastiano in the Aurelian walls then ran south-east across Italy, past ruined tombs and temples, gatehouses and the debris of imperial-era barracks. Past Nic Costa's home too, where it was little more than a narrow cobbled lane surrounded by the detritus of a lost empire. The Via Appia Nuova, its modern equivalent, was very different, a broad, busy highway choked with traffic, its city stretch passing low, grey housing estates, supermarkets and furniture warehouses, the ugly façade of twenty-first-century urban life. It was this that took them to Ciampino.

They were passing a line of cheap stores not far from the airport turnoff, Costa driving, a habit he'd kept from the days he and Peroni were of equal rank. There was something in the older cop's silent, sullen mood that intrigued him.

Rome's second airport, originally a military and business installation, was now an unlovely provincial dump preferred by the budget operators unwilling to pay the fees of the flashier Fiumicino.

It was a few minutes away. Without being asked, the big man called ahead and made sure immigration knew to expect them, and to expect, too, that the Questura would send an armoured meat wagon to take the Turkish gangster Cakici back into their custody in central Rome before the day was out.

'Why are we blaming the Turks again?' Costa asked, fishing to get the big man talking out loud.

Without emotion Peroni repeated Falcone's reasoning. It lay in the flimsy intelligence they'd received from Rosa Prabakaran's superiors. Gino Riggi had been in the pay of the gang known as the Vadisi, the Wolves, that held the drugs franchise for the tourist dives around the Campo and Trastevere. The Gabriel kid had been the go-between for Riggi and the Turks. The fierce burst of publicity about the case had persuaded the Vadisi their operations could be jeopardized by the arrest of Robert Gabriel for murder. So they acted to save themselves.

'Would they murder two people, one of them a cop, for that?'

Peroni's jowly face contorted into a scowl.

'Seems a little excessive, doesn't it?' he said.

'Seems like asking for trouble,' Costa thought.

'I guess . . . Leo knows that too.'

They'd worked together for so long that they could almost read one another's moods. Falcone wasn't content with the explanations he was trying to use as a basis for this case, and his dissatisfaction made him cling to them all the more. Not out of arrogance or laziness. It was his way of testing a theory, pushing it until the flimsy structure fell to pieces.

'None of this fits,' Peroni muttered as he watched a couple of tourist coaches pull out from the entrance to the airport, cutting across a line of cars without thinking. 'Or maybe it fits too well. I hate this whole damned thing. I hate the thought of what that man did to his own daughter. Someone intelligent, cultured. Why? What would drive someone to do such a thing?'

'He was sick physically,' Costa suggested. 'Perhaps that made him sick in the head too?'

Peroni gave him a cold stare and asked, 'Do you really believe that?'

'Not for one minute. Mina loved her father. I'm sure of it. Would she feel that way if he abused her?'

'You wouldn't think so,' the big cop muttered. Then he cheered up briefly and asked, 'Did your father ever read you fairy stories?'

Costa laughed and said, 'You'd never have asked that question if you'd met him. No. He didn't.'

'Well I did. With my kids. Loved doing it. One day I picked up a copy of Grimm's tales, an old, cheap one at a church sale.' The smile left his face. This memory troubled him. 'Picked a story at random, sat down by their beds and read it out loud. They were eight, ten at the time.'

'And?' Costa said, prompting him when he fell quiet.

'It was about a king whose beautiful wife was dying. So she made him promise he'd never marry again unless he found someone who was more lovely than she was.' They stopped and waited for a tourist bus to disgorge its line of backpacking passengers. 'The mother never thought that would happen, of course. But there was someone more beautiful, to the father. His daughter. When the mother died, he became crazy with grief and told his daughter he'd marry her.'

Costa thought for a moment and murmured, 'This may be why my father didn't read fairy stories.'

'There was all the kids' stuff,' Peroni went on. 'The girl running away into the forest. Coming back disguised, working as a servant, trying to hide her true identity. But the king fell in love with her anyway, even though he'd no idea who she really was. And in the end, after a lot of stupid shenanigans, they married. Father and daughter. Happily ever after.'

He scowled at the vast car park, the lines of taxis waiting to get into Ciampino's overcrowded pickup area. '*Happily ever after*. And no one said a word. Last time I bought a kids' book at a church sale, I can tell you. Why can't life be just good and bad, the way it's supposed to be?'

Costa flashed his police ID at the car park and drove to the secure area. Peroni waited as he parked the blue liveried police car, a cheap, dirty Fiat, not the flashy Alfas the Carabinieri got.

'Still, I suppose I should be glad you left the Vespa at home,' he added, breaking the mood a little.

'Bit far for her,' Costa replied. 'But she's still as strong as an ox. A little ox. One day,' he pointed back towards the Via Appia Antica, 'I'm going to ride her all the way down there, into the hills. Want to come?'

Peroni laughed.

'I'll pass on that. You always said you were going to go there on a pushbike.'

'Too old. Too little time.' Costa looked at him. 'I've never worked organized crime, Gianni. Not seriously. Tell me something.'

'What?'

'How many ride-by killings do we get a year? Gang assassinations? Two? Three?'

'Not as many as we used to get.'

'And why's that?' Costa continued. 'Because it's an Italian thing. The Sicilians, the Neapolitans. They love all that show-off stuff. But they're not running these rings any more. They're more interested in easy, safe money. Bribery, corruption, skimming.'

'Riggi wasn't involved with the Sicilians.'

'Precisely. Here's another thing. If you're going to kill someone from a motorbike, surely you need two people. One to ride. One to shoot. Have you ever known a mob ride-by where there was just one person on the bike?'

Peroni was smiling and shaking his head.

'No, *sovrintendente*, I haven't.'

'And the small matter of the Ducati?'

Costa folded his arms. Just before they left they'd heard that the red motorbike had been located at four that morning, at an auto-strada service station on the route north to Florence. Two cops had performed a textbook arrest and taken a thirty-three-year-old man into custody. It took a local inspector only thirty minutes to realize he had a case of theft on his hands, not murder. The bike had been abandoned shortly after the shootings, left in a side street near the Via Beatrice Cenci with the keys in the ignition. The man in custody was a city bus driver who'd been on duty till midnight and seen the machine by the side of the street on the way home. He was planning to drive the Ducati north to a relative in Florence and sell it on. The original rider's clothes were still missing. The machine itself had fake number plates. No weapon had been found, no real clue as to the identity of the man who had killed Riggi and Robert Gabriel the previous night.

Peroni screwed up his flabby face and said, 'Even the stupidest gangsters I've met, and there've been quite a few, would never have left a machine like that in the vicinity, with the keys in the ignition. Why take the risk? They'd have whisked it out of Rome in a van or something. Taken it out into the countryside and burned the thing. Or repainted it, changed the numbers, and put it in an empty dope crate back to Turkey or somewhere. That bike's worth, what, seven, eight thousand euros? Either they'd destroy it or sell it.'

Exactly as Costa had thought. 'So?' he asked.

'So Leo knows all this. He's just working with what he has.'

'We're here to talk to this Cakici guy for no other reason than he was Riggi's contact with the Turkish mob?'

Peroni's bright blue eyes sparkled.

'A contact who was trying to flee the country on a false passport, remember.'

'Probably just scared we'd come looking for him. As we have. My guess is he's as innocent of these murders as Mina Gabriel is of the death of her father.'

'I hope your guess is correct,' Peroni said quietly, unwrapping a chocolate bar and taking a big bite of it. 'On the latter anyway. I truly do.'

Costa thought of the interview ahead.

'All the same, I don't like scum who sell drugs to teenagers,' he said. 'Let's make a point, shall we?'

CHAPTER 4

Teresa Lupo liked Toni Grimaldi, the chief resident Questura lawyer. He was a friendly, portly man in his fifties with a genial face and a walrus moustache rather amateurishly dyed black to match his full head of hair. His role was not always an easy one. He acted as the conduit between the police and the judiciary, the internal Questura expert who would tell an investigating officer whether he or she had sufficient evidence to merit a search warrant, an arrest or a charge.

Officers trusted Grimaldi, a man who'd worked in the Piazza San Michele longer than almost anyone else still serving. He rarely gave the green light to a case that would fall at the first hurdle, as many a young lawyer was wont to do. He was frank and open with his advice, sometimes suggesting routes of inquiry that had not occurred to the detectives concerned or, on occasion, the forensic team. Over the years he had become a vital cog in the workings of the Questura, an impartial eye who would not shirk from telling an investigating officer when it was time to give up. For this he was admired even if his advice was not always welcome.

Every last file Falcone possessed, and the latest information from the forensic department, had been in his hands for two hours. Teresa now sat next to Leo Falcone in Grimaldi's bright fourth-floor office overlooking the courtyard at the back of the building, waiting for his opinion. Much, she thought, as a patient waited for a doctor to pass on news of a diagnosis. There was the same nervous resentment, in Falcone at least. The same presentiment of bad tidings too.

Grimaldi took off his reading glasses, looked up at them over his desk and asked, 'Is this it?'

'Of course,' Falcone snapped. 'Do you think we'd withhold something?'

'Only if it damaged your case,' Grimaldi replied. 'And since you have no case . . .' He shrugged. 'What would be the point?'

'No case? No case?'

'We'll be getting more forensic, Toni,' Teresa said quickly. 'We've got the photos to show Malise Gabriel had a sexual relationship with the Van Doren woman. Once we get the report back from the girl's mattress we'll know whether he had sex in his daughter's bed too.'

'Malise Gabriel's dead,' Grimaldi pointed out. 'Can't put him in the dock. Even if you could you can't place him in the girl's bed or say he had sex with her.'

'Not yet,' she said.

He looked at her, frowned and said nothing.

Falcone added, almost calmly, 'The father's

behaviour establishes motive. On the part of the mother. On the part of the daughter and the adopted son too.'

'And the motive for killing the American woman?'

Falcone looked desperate for a moment.

'Jealousy? Perhaps she discovered something? I don't know. I want the chance to ask them.'

Grimaldi didn't answer. He shuffled the papers again.

'Who killed the son and this bent cop of ours?' he asked.

'Probably the drugs people they were involved with,' Falcone told him. 'We think we have a suspect out at Ciampino. Costa's talking to him now.'

The lawyer didn't look happy.

'It's a bloody old affair, isn't it? Families.' He shook his head. 'And drugs. You always hope the two won't meet.'

'Malise Gabriel wasn't murdered because of drugs,' Falcone insisted. 'He was having an affair and abusing his own daughter. Racked with a terminal illness. A monster.'

'Just like the Cenci father,' Grimaldi cut in. 'So the papers got it right.'

'Perhaps! But I need a search warrant for their home. I need to arrest the mother and the daughter and bring them in so we can question them properly. They're so damned slippery.'

Grimaldi's walrus moustache wrinkled. He stared at the papers in front of him and asked,

'On the basis of what I have here? Nothing more?'

'Precisely.'

'No,' the lawyer said straight out. 'You don't have the evidence. I'd let you bring in the son, but he's dead. Even if you can prove the father was abusing the daughter there's no live criminal case there for precisely the same reason. You surely aren't suggesting we try to prosecute her for incest instead? This isn't the Middle Ages. The monstrous regiment out there would riot in an instant.'

'Of course I'm not suggesting that!' Falcone insisted. 'I wouldn't dream of it. This whole affair is distressing. But we have to—'

'Leo!' Grimaldi looked cross. This was rare. 'Will you kindly try to see this with some perspective? The *commissario* has made it clear to me we must proceed with the utmost care here. The media. The public interest.'

'To hell with the media!'

The lawyer sighed.

'You're too intelligent a man to mean that. In order for me to approve a warrant I will require more than mere motive. I need you to establish an evidential link between the mother and the daughter and one or more of these crimes. Is there anything to suggest they were there when the American woman died? Quite the contrary. The mother has a firm alibi and a seventeen-year-old girl couldn't strangle a grown woman and then suspend her corpse from the ceiling. Is there any evidence that they, not the son, tampered with the scaffolding, or scuffled with Gabriel, causing his head to fall against the radiator and give you your convenient blood stain? No. In fact I see no evidence that anyone was with Malise Gabriel at the time of his death. He was drunk. He'd had sex with someone unknown earlier. Perhaps he stumbled against the radiator, and went outside for a cigarette as the daughter says. Nothing you have proves otherwise.'

He thought for a moment, then added, 'We've had cases before, you know, where disgruntled children have set traps for their parents. Accidents in waiting, ones that may never be triggered. The son, or the daughter, could have removed those stays from the roof, thinking, if this monster does walk out there for a cigarette he could tumble to his death. It's an easy, cowardly way out, isn't it? You leave the man's fate to chance or God. If he lives, you carry on. If he dies, you forgo the blame. In your own head anyway.'

'Let's leave God out of this, shall we?' Falcone replied.

'If you feel that's possible. The fact remains. You need to persuade one of these two to confirm your suspicions. To confess, perhaps.'

'Which is why I need to arrest them,' Falcone exploded. 'Without that they simply won't talk.'

'Then,' Grimaldi said, with a smile, 'you'll have

to go back to work and find me some real evidence to support these theories of yours. What you have is flimsy, circumstantial and insufficient. The crimes of a dead man, however vile, are insufficient to justify throwing these women into an interview room for twenty-four hours and leaving you to try to break them. This is not the sixteenth century. We are not the Pope's inquisitors.'

He closed the folder in front of him ostentatiously and looked at Teresa Lupo.

'More evidence please. Until you have I won't look at this case again.'

'You do realize I have yet to persuade these two even to set foot inside the Questura!' Falcone bellowed.

Grimaldi looked puzzled.

'What do you mean? They've been in to identify the brother's body, surely?'

Teresa shrugged and said, 'Not yet. We've asked them. The mother said she's still too upset. It's standard practice to leave the timing up to the relatives. It's not critical in this case. So I've never pushed them.'

The two men stared at the pathologist.

'They've got a dead son on a slab in the morgue and they don't want to see him?' the lawyer asked.

'Dead son, dead father,' she said. 'You'd be surprised, Toni. Sometimes people are like that.'

'Then . . .' Grimaldi extended a hand. 'There you have it, Leo. Tell them it's important you have an ID, however upsetting that may be. Once you have them here I bow to your improvizational skills. Just don't expect me to pick up any debris you leave behind. Consider yourself warned.'

CHAPTER 5

By the time they were back in the morgue, waiting on the Gabriels to arrive for the formal identification of Robert, Falcone was in an oddly foul mood. The nature of this case, and the way it had propelled him into the usually cherished role of antagonist, had come to haunt the man in some way. Peroni had told Teresa how Cecilia Gabriel had slapped him that day in the Casina delle Civette when he first broached the subject of incest. Falcone was thoughtful, intelligent and, in spite of himself sometimes, deeply sensitive. His personal distaste for the case was obvious. The very fact that its successful prosecution might depend upon his own resolute curiosity into these dark and disturbing secrets unsettled him, she felt. Grimaldi's comment – that success might lie in breaking Mina Gabriel or her mother – weighed on his mind. He was never happy or predictable in such moods.

'Can you tidy him up a little?' Falcone asked as he stared miserably at the body on the silver table, shifting on his shoes, uncomfortable. More from the prospect of questioning the family than any

389

squeamishness, she guessed. 'I don't want this to be any worse than it has to be.'

'We've done as much as we can,' she said. There was a folded sheet covering the gaping wound in the skull. The blood had been washed off his face. He had olive skin, and deep, sunken eyes. Seen like this she began to understand he could only be an adopted child. There was no physical resemblance at all to the young girl she'd seen in the news-papers. 'Let's get the ID out of the way and then I'll finish. It's not as if I'm looking for any surprises, am I?'

'I imagine not,' Falcone answered.

'I hate this part,' Teresa murmured, staring at the still, sad corpse. She liked to think of herself as a professional, someone who worked alongside the inevitable, death in all its forms, an officer of the state who brought, on occasion, some justice to the living. But comfort? That was rare, and slow to arrive if it ever did. Grief was the invis-ible spirit that rose from the dead, swiftly, bringing with it anger and resentment. She and Falcone had enjoyed many long conversations about the popular notion of 'closure' for the relatives of those who had died through violence, accident or any one of the everyday diseases that stole breath from the mouths of both young and old, most of whom who never dreamed for a moment that their lives would come to such an end, without warning, often without explanation or any rational need. Both she and Falcone hated the term, thought it a misnomer, an easy lie, like 'moving on'. The bereaved needed such fantasies, perhaps, as a way to allow them to survive the difficult days. But these were convenient lies that fooled no one, fabrications designed to hide the plain truth: death was a cruel intrusion, an ever-present ghost dogging the footsteps of the living as they trudged through the world.

Leo Falcone loathed this necessary legal ceremony as much as she did, even when he hoped to gain some insight from it. The tall inspector, serious in a darker suit than he normally wore, went out of the room then led Mina and Cecilia Gabriel back into the morgue. They looked like mother and daughter, Teresa thought, both tall and slender, with very English faces, classically beautiful in an old-fashioned way. She rather envied women like this: high cheek-bones, large, sad eyes, pale, perfect skin, a timeless kind of beauty, that of women from the pages of glossy magazines or canvases on the walls of galleries.

The mother's cheeks were a little hollow, her eyes and mouth surrounded by lines, as if marked with some long-standing pain. This was the first time she'd seen the girl in the flesh and she appreciated immediately how someone as careful and attentive as Nic would find her fascinating. The daughter had none of the detached, incurious disdain of her mother. She wore a simple black T-shirt and jeans. Her pale young face was bright, intelligent, alert, with sharp brown eyes that swept these strange, perhaps frightening surroundings, and avoided nothing. With her fair hair swept back her appearance seemed astonishingly close to that of the famous image of Beatrice Cenci that had appeared to be everywhere, on TV screens, in newspapers, on magazine racks, over the past few days. There was an intelligent, touching grief about her, not the blank, raging anger Teresa felt she saw in the mother.

There was a man behind them. He wore a dark navy suit, a pale pink shirt and a black silk tie, a little overdressed for a lawyer, she thought.

Falcone stepped forward and said, 'Signor Santacroce. This is a family affair, I think.'

'If they want me, Inspector,' the man said in a patrician tone that bordered upon condescension. 'I'm a family friend after all. But only if I'm needed.'

'Stay, Bernard,' Cecilia Gabriel announced without turning her head for a moment as she approached the corpse on the metal table. 'But don't look, please. This is distressing enough for us. It's not for you.'

The man nodded and stayed at the door, out of sight of the corpse on the table.

The two of them, mother and daughter, of similar height and stature, and the same stiff, upright English stance, reached the body and stood there in silence. Then Mina Gabriel reached beneath the white sheet, lifted the fabric and took the still right hand there, holding the fingers in

392

her own. Teresa watched and felt a deep, word-less sadness at this sight. The youth's cold flesh was, for a few moments, enclosed in her thin white fingers, those of a musician or an artist. Brother and sister, in name if not blood. They grew up together, must once have held hands this way as they walked down the street.

Teresa was conscious of Falcone, glowering at her. She stepped forward and took the girl's elbow lightly.

'Mina. I'm sorry. There are rules in these situations. Please. You mustn't touch.'

'He's my brother,' she said softly, staring at the waxy, frozen face on the table, and the folded sheet that covered the dreadful wound to the skull.

'He's a murder victim,' Falcone replied, quietly, respectfully. 'I must insist . . .'

Slowly, reluctantly, she placed the youth's hand back beneath the sheet then looked at her own fingers.

She went and stood closer to the mother. Neither said a word.

'Don't you want to know anything?' Falcone asked.

'About what?' Cecilia Gabriel said.

'About how Robert died?'

She seemed cold, unmoved almost, as if this were not quite real. Mina's arms were wound round herself. The girl was starting to weep in silence.

'My son was a drug dealer, Inspector,' Cecilia Gabriel said in very precise, clipped tones. 'You know that. You know, also, that in a sense we lost Robert a long time ago. He chose the kind of people he wished to be with. I'm sure you have a much better sense of how he came to die than I can ever begin to appreciate. Does it matter? He's . . .' Then the mask cracked, the real woman, a mother, Teresa thought, was visible, though there were still no tears. 'He's gone for good. I imagine you can heap on him all the blame you wish and none of us can object, can we?'

A brief touch of colour rose in Falcone's cheeks.

'I'm trying very hard to understand the circumstances of four violent deaths. Your husband. Your son. Joanne Van Doren. A serving police officer.'

'From what I've read in the papers about him . . .' the Englishwoman began.

'The papers,' he retorted, 'are full of material I find deeply questionable. I can't help but wonder where some of it came from.'

Mina Gabriel as Beatrice Cenci, Teresa thought to herself. He was making a good point. The girl's hair, her very manner, almost seemed to be modelled on that now infamous portrait. The publicity was inevitable, though the Roman media had picked up the connection very quickly indeed.

Santacroce intervened, in a mild, conciliatory tone.

'I was under the impression that Cecilia and her daughter were asked here to identify Robert,' he said. 'Nothing more. If that's the case, then I think this distressing, if necessary, appointment is concluded, isn't it?'

Falcone glared at Santacroce.

'No, sir. It is not. Mrs Gabriel, I would be grateful if you and your daughter joined me in my office. Alone. These are personal matters.'

'I came here to identify my son,' Cecilia Gabriel interrupted. 'That is all I intend to do.'

'Please . . .'

'You heard what Cecilia said,' Santacroce interrupted. 'If you've anything to say, then say it now.'

Falcone glanced at Teresa Lupo and she knew what he was thinking, understood how reluctant he was to take this step.

Then he walked over to the desk, removed the folder with the latest set of photographs, and handed it, unopened, to the mother.

'I'm deeply sorry I have to raise this in such a way,' he said. 'But you leave me with no choice. Please. Look at them.'

CHAPTER 6

Bedir Cakici was alone, bored, hungry and down to his last stick of gum. He'd been sitting in the immigration police's interview room for four hours. It was a small, windowless cubicle with noisy air conditioning that didn't work. The place was as hot as an oven and stank from the cooking fat of some nearby canteen drifting in from the single vent.

He shook his handcuffs and wondered again when there might be some avenue of escape. From here it was impossible. But they'd been making noises about the police wanting him, about a move to the city Questura. If he could make a phone call, get the right guy. If the men he knew were willing to take a couple of risks to spring an old friend from some sleepy cop car as it tracked down the Via Appia Nuova. Then he could do the smart thing, hide out for a while, work his way to the Adriatic, get across in one of the smuggling speed-boats that brought in contraband tobacco from Croatia.

If, if, if.

He couldn't believe they'd stopped him. Or that

he'd been dumb enough to use one of the oldest fake passports he carried. Life had been a little hectic since Tuesday evening. Now he was paying the price.

One of the immigration officers, a man who looked like a prissy schoolteacher, walked back in followed by a couple of surly-looking individuals in shapeless suits who announced themselves as state police. He believed this. They had that nasty, suspicious look about them. Nevertheless they were the oddest couple of cops he'd seen in a while, one youngish, slim, good-looking with features that seemed as if they ought to be pleasant, smiling, but weren't. He had dark hair and the kind of stance the Turk associated with sportsmen, football players and the like. The older one was tall, heavily built and ugly, a scary individual with a battered face that might have been through a windscreen once or twice. Yet the tough guy seemed strangely deferential around the younger man, as if he were the boss, not the other way round, as Cakici could have expected.

They didn't show ID. They just yawned, pulled up a couple of chairs at the table, then stared at the immigration officer.

'You want me to stay?' the man asked. 'I'm supposed to stay. That's what the rules say.'

The big ugly one had his huge hands behind his balding head and was giving him a very nasty look.

'I mean, I *think* that's what the rules say,' the immigration man added.

'Sir?' the big one asked the cop with him.

Sir? Cakici thought.

'No, we don't,' the younger officer told him. 'Isn't it your lunch time or something?'

The immigration man left, mumbling under his breath.

The one who'd ordered him out waited, then got up and walked round the room, examining things, ignoring Cakici entirely.

'There's a microphone here, sir,' the big cop said, pointing at a little plastic stick in the middle of the table.

'I don't think we need that, do we?'

The big guy reached over with one huge arm and ripped the mike out of its housing, wrapped the cable round the body, then threw the thing into the corner of the room.

The other had stopped in front of a video camera lens set high on the wall above the table.

He turned, still ignoring the Turk, and asked the old cop, 'Am I imagining this or is it chewing gum?'

Cakici's head came up from the table. This had been a bad day. He deserved a little respect. He didn't like being referred to as 'it'.

The huge one stared at him, as if examining some foreign object, and said, 'It is. Unbelievable.'

'It? It?' Cakici kept on chewing, all through his outrage. 'What am I? An animal or something? How about some courtesy around here? I got a name.'

The young cop came and sat down. So the Turk

398

had the big guy on his left and the shorter one on the other side, which didn't feel good.

'What name? Mickey Mouse?'

'Minnie more like,' the big one grumbled, staring at his pale linen designer suit.

'Real Armani, muttonhead,' Cakici told him, trying to stab a finger across the table, not that the cuffs let him do it properly. 'Guess you can't buy that on your wages.'

They went very quiet and then the young one said, 'You'd be surprised what we could buy if we wanted.'

The big cop shook his head, as if this saddened him deeply.

'I don't know,' he muttered in a quiet, mournful voice. 'You get some dope dealer with a fake passport. It's chewing gum. And it wants courtesy?' He opened his hands in a gesture of exasperation. 'Sir. This is so . . . unreasonable.'

The Turk sighed, struggled in the cuffs but finally managed to take out the gum, placed the damp lump on top of the shiny plastic table and began to say, 'OK. Do not call me 'it'. I got rights, I got . . .'

He fell quiet. The young cop, the boss cop, had picked up the gum in his fingers, stared at it with an expression of disgust. Then, as Cakici watched, bemused, he walked over to the video camera and placed the grey blob on the lens, patting it until the gum extended across the whole of the round glass eye, blocking the camera's view completely.

No mike. No video. This was an unusual interview.

The big guy yawned, pulled his chair up very close to Cakici, placed a gigantic arm around his shoulders and squeezed.

It was a bone-breaking hug and the cop smiled at him, quite affectionately it appeared, throughout. His breath smelled of mints.

The Turk was starting to sweat.

'First impressions count, you know. The gum was a bad start,' the cop told him. 'My *sovrintendente* has never liked gum. It offends him.'

He squeezed harder. Cakici let out a little cry of pain and said, 'I didn't kill nobody. Honest, I didn't. I was just going on holiday. There's this girl. I didn't want her to know . . . Women . . .'

The cop sighed, shook his head, removed his arm, shuffled the chair a short distance away and said, 'It thinks we're stupid now.'

The other one was patting his jacket absent-mindedly as if he'd lost something. The Turk watched, worried, unsure what to say.

'I know I've got it somewhere,' the young one said, still looking. 'Oh, wait a minute.'

He reached into his side pocket and took out a black handgun, a Beretta 92. Cakici knew his firearms. He had one of these himself, in the little armoury he kept in a safe in the garage.

'What is this?' he asked, laughing nervously. 'Some kind of a joke.'

400

The young one held the Beretta loosely, lazily in his right hand and leaned forward.

'Are we laughing?' he asked the other one. 'Did I laugh once since I came into this room?'

'No, sir, you didn't—' the big one began.

'Shut up!' Cakici screeched. 'Cut this out. All this "sir", and weird stuff. Gimme a little dignity, huh?'

They looked at each other then the boss cop asked, 'Dignity? How much dignity did Gino Riggi get? Dead in the dirt in a back alley in Trastevere, outside some lowlife bar where you sold junk to kids?'

The big one let go with another deep and sorry sigh then shook his huge bald head again repeatedly.

'Very little, it seems to me, sir,' he said. He smiled again and came very close to Cakici. 'And you know something? Gino was a nice guy. We liked him. We had beers with him. And pizza too. Pizza was Gino's favourite. He never mentioned us?'

'What? *What?*'

The gun waved at him lazily from across the table and the other cop asked, very slowly, 'Did he ever mention us?'

'Nic,' the big one said, then pointed a finger at his own barrel chest. 'Gianni. His best friends. Did he ever mention us?'

'No,' Cakici shrugged. 'Why the hell should he?'

Nic waved the gun around as if it was a toy. Cakici couldn't take his eyes off the thing.

'Gino was a good man,' the man said. 'Loyal. Trustworthy. Discreet. He had respect. He knew his place.'

He looked at the one called Gianni.

'I don't know why we're telling it this, do you? Something that chews gum when you walk into the room. Chews gum on public property.'

'That's terrible, sir. Shocking. It does not know how to behave.'

'Stop calling me that!' Cakici cried.

Gianni stroked his chin then, with his big right fist, he reached out and grabbed Cakici by the collar of his Armani jacket, dragging him close to that ugly, scarred face.

'Let me say this slowly so that your stupid little brain can understand,' the big cop intoned, one syllable at a time. 'Gino was more than a friend. He was our colleague. Our employee, if you like. You know those big guys who stand over you? Who tell you what to do? When to speak? When to go for a piss and when to wait? The people you listen to 'cos things go bad if you don't?'

Cakici was staring at the video camera lens covered in grey gum, as if that might help him.

'I want those immigration guys in here,' he muttered.

'Lunch break,' Gianni told him. 'No planes coming in for another ninety minutes. Long lunch break. Quite some way from here. Ciampino's a shitty little airport. Either empty or full, and right now it's as empty as a church on Thursdays. This is a place for poor people and the poor just get poorer, don't they? We never fly from here, do we, sir?'

'Beneath us,' the Nic character said.

'I want the immigr—'

'See,' the big man continued, ignoring him, 'we were to Gino what those guys were to you. Superior. Kings of our own little world, with Gino there like a little prince, doing as he's told. And now he's dead. And now . . .' He let go with a push. Cakici rocked back in his chair. 'Here you are.'

'It knows,' Nic said.

'I didn't! Not about you! Not a damned thing.'

'It knows now,' the young one added.

Gianni picked up Cakici's left hand and slapped his own face with it.

'Sir,' he said, in a hurt, young voice. 'It hit me. The prisoner hit me. I think it may be violent and dangerous. It may be trying to escape. I'm scared.'

Across the table the young cop yawned and murmured, 'That's terrible.'

Cakici shielded his eyes, whimpering, 'You can't do this. You can't . . .'

'Watch me,' Nic said, then pointed the gun in his face and pulled the trigger.

CHAPTER 7

Cecilia Gabriel flicked through a few of the photographs from Falcone's collection, her face stony, expressionless. Then she closed the folder, threw it onto a nearby desk and walked towards the door.

Falcone stretched out an arm to prevent her leaving the morgue. Teresa Lupo's heart sank. This was not a good sign.

'These questions need answers,' the inspector said.

The Englishwoman stared at him.

'What questions?'

He shook his head in disbelief.

'Are you serious?' he asked.

'Very.'

'I believe Robert murdered your husband,' he said straight out. 'And Joanne Van Doren. I believe—'

'No!' Mina cried, staring at the body on the sheet.

'Then who did? Robert was there. He had the opportunity—'

'Why!' the girl cried. 'Why would he do such a thing?'

404

'To protect you! And your mother! To stop us finding out what really happened the night your father died . . . And before.'

The girl's eyes misted with tears. She turned to Cecilia Gabriel.

'Mummy? What's going on? What photographs?'

'I can show her,' Falcone said, staring at the mother. 'If you like.'

'They're fakes,' Cecilia Gabriel insisted. 'Grubby, dirty little pictures. Perhaps you ran them up, Inspector. I don't know.'

'Oh, for God's sake,' Falcone cried. 'Why would we do such a thing? All I require of you, madam, is the truth. I know it's painful. I will ask a specialist officer to deal with you and your daughter. But we must put this case to rest.'

'You have no case,' the woman snapped.

'I do not *understand*!' Falcone shouted.

Teresa Lupo took a step towards him, touched him arm, and said quietly, 'Leo . . .'

But there was no stopping him. The wrong buttons had been pressed, and it was almost as if Cecilia Gabriel knew she was doing this. All the advice that Peroni and Nic had been quietly trying to give him about how to handle this family amounted to nothing when his temper reached such a pitch.

'When,' he demanded, 'is someone going to start telling me the truth?'

'We are . . .' Mina said, distraught, fighting back the tears. 'Why won't you believe us?'

405

'Lies!' Falcone snapped. 'None of this is credible. What happened between you and your father that night? And before?'

He turned on Cecilia Gabriel and barked, 'And you? Doesn't a mother want to know? Don't you even give a damn . . . ?'

Teresa cursed herself for waiting a moment too long and then stood in front of him, half-said, half-yelled, 'Inspector! This is my department, not a police interview room. If you wish to interrogate these people I suggest you take them there. I will not have you disrupting our work in this way. This is unseemly in the extreme. I won't tolerate it. Do you understand?'

She had never treated him in this fashion before, though there had been plenty of grounds in the past. But she did it for his benefit as much as anyone else's. Falcone's frustration with this difficult case was beginning to affect him, to depress him, she believed. It was written in the lines on his narrow, tanned face, and the weariness in his eyes.

The Englishwoman took a step towards him and said, 'What exactly do you want of me?'

There was a bleak look of stony self-hatred on Falcone's face. This outburst had shocked him as much as anyone.

'An honest answer. We have evidence, incontrovertible evidence, that your husband abused your daughter. Photographs. Physical stains on the mattress from her room. The mattress, I might add,

406

which Joanne Van Doren so hurriedly removed from your apartment before we had the chance.'

The mother's face was suffused in fiery anger. Mina Gabriel's hands went to her mouth. Her eyes were glassy with floods of tears.

'Oh, Leo,' Teresa murmured.

The wrong time, the wrong place.

'It is my belief,' he went on, 'that your daughter, your son and you conspired to murder your husband for this very reason, and make it appear an accident. That Joanne Van Doren died because of what she knew. That Robert—'

'Well, arrest me, then?' the Gabriel woman yelled at him. 'If that's what you believe. Do it or leave us alone. One or the other. Which is it?'

Falcone looked lost for words, for action, and there was an expression in Cecilia Gabriel's face that seemed quietly triumphant. She knows we're prowerless, Teresa Lupo thought. She expected this all along.

The stranger at the door intervened.

'This is quite enough!' Bernard Santacroce declared, stepping between them, his arms outstretched, his face a picture of outrage. He looked into Falcone's face. 'Have you no sense of decency, man? How can you make such accusations? At a time like this?'

'I am making them, sir, on the basis of the facts. Because it's my job.'

'Not here, Leo,' Teresa Lupo said firmly. 'Not now.'

The room had gone quiet. The forensic staff

were quietly staring at their computers and their instruments, embarrassed, unsure of where to look.

She strode forward and said, 'This is a mortuary. A place for the dead. I will not tolerate shouting matches. Nor will I allow it to be used as some kind of interrogation room. If you have anything more to say to each other, go somewhere else, please. This instant.'

The girl, Mina, looked as if she'd woken up inside some dreadful nightmare. Her hands were still at her mouth. Her eyes darted around the morgue, as if looking for something that was out of reach.

Nic, Teresa thought immediately. She needs a friend. From the way her gaze never strayed towards her mother it was surely clear there was little love, no amity there. Such secrets seemed to live inside these two, and Teresa Lupo realized she had no idea how they might be prised into the open. Or whether that was where they belonged.

'You're her mother,' Falcone yelled, wagging a finger at Cecilia Gabriel. 'Don't you want to know what happened? What he did?'

He got a slap from her for that. A good one. Teresa had already heard about the first. She wondered if that had been as hard and as painful as this powerful, vicious blow.

'Will you all kindly get out of here?' she insisted.

'Gladly,' Santacroce replied and placed an arm around the Englishwoman, beckoning her and her daughter to the door.

Then he ushered Mina and Cecilia Gabriel outside.

Falcone watched them, helpless, full of an internal, seething rage, a hand to his reddening cheek. There was an expression on his face that shocked Teresa Lupo. It wasn't the realization of failure. She'd seen that before, and knew he could deal with that, in time. It was some cruel moment of self-revelation, a realization of how desperately he'd tried to delve into the private moments of a family that, whatever the reason, was locked deep inside some painful, personal agony, one they never wished to share.

CHAPTER 8

The Turk didn't look too good. His hooded eyes were wide open, his brown, stubbly face taut with fear. There were sweat stains beneath the arms of his linen suit and he was shaking like a sick man.

Cakici opened his mouth and began to scream a loud and wordless plea for help. Peroni batted him once with a big fist, knocked him clean off the chair and spoke a few short, serious words. The Turk's noise dwindled to a whimper.

Costa pulled out the Beretta's magazine, shook it: empty. He looked at the gun, scratched his head and said, 'What happened? Did I forget to load it after the last guy we shot?'

'I think that may be the case, sir,' Peroni said, and plonked Cakici back in his seat.

The big man was enjoying this little game, which was going exactly as they'd planned.

Peroni patted his own pockets.

'I didn't bring a gun. Sorry. You got some shells of your own?'

'No.'

Cakici started to scream again. Just the threat of Peroni's fist stopped that.

'This is all your fault!' Costa yelled at him. 'I haven't slept a wink since you wasted Riggi and that English kid on Tuesday night.'

'For God's sake will you listen? It wasn't me!'

The two cops glanced at each other and shrugged. Then they looked at Bedir Cakici and Costa said, 'Haven't you grasped this yet? We're not here to decide whether you go to jail. We're here to decide if you live or not.'

'I didn't kill him!'

Costa shook his head and muttered something about going out to the car.

'I didn't . . .'

'Sir,' Peroni said. 'He seems . . . sincere, if I might say so.'

'Really.' Costa folded his arms. 'Then who did kill him?'

'I dunno.'

'The car,' he said, getting up.

'No, no.' The Turk looked ready to burst into tears. 'Maybe I can help.'

'Maybe?' Peroni wondered.

'Really. I can. It's just . . .'

They waited.

'I don't know names.'

Costa checked his watch ostentatiously. And Cakici began to talk.

It was an interesting story, and it made sense in some crazy fashion. At the end, when Cakici appeared finished, Peroni reached out and placed his gigantic arm around the cowering prisoner.

'Let me make sure I understand this properly,' he said. 'You're saying you weren't the only one shipping dope to all those foreign teenagers hanging round the Campo of an evening, thinking how wonderful it is to be free of their parents finally, and somewhere cool too?'

'You mean he didn't tell you?' Cakici asked.

'If he'd told us . . .' Peroni began.

'Sure, sure. Sorry. Hear me out. These last few months there's been dope turning up in places where I never had anyone. Colleges. Cafes. Language schools. Lots of it. Big money. I'm not so stupid I'd go there. You work the bars. That way it's all within the boundaries. You don't start handing out pills in public, just to anyone. What's the point? Asking for trouble. Gino knew that. He was the one who kept ringing me, asking what was going on. Like I knew.'

Costa asked, 'There was another supplier?'

'That's what I'm saying. And I got to thinking that Gino was locking lips with him too. All the gear was turning up in the places his people went. It made sense. Pretty soon we were going to have to talk.'

'Turkish?'

'Italian!' Cakici insisted. 'Gino told me he didn't know the name. But it wasn't one of ours. The kid told him about it.'

'The kid?'

'The English kid. The one who got killed.' The

Turk was getting a little braver. Peroni removed his arm. 'He was taking us all for a ride, if you ask me. Working both sides. Not a team player. Here's something else too.' Cakici leaned forward. 'The kid came to us. *To us.*'

He shook his head as if still unable to believe it.

'You know how we recruit these morons? Feed 'em a little dope. Wait till they owe enough money. Turn 'em round, send 'em back on the streets selling the junk. Pretty soon you've got an army of them. They make a little dough and steal what they want on the side. That's fine. We take the big margin. It's been like that for years. The system works. Why screw with it?'

'You're saying Robert Gabriel recruited Riggi in the first place?' Costa asked.

'That's what Gino said it felt like. He loved money, that kid. That was all it was about. Gino said he never even saw him using stuff. Always straight. Didn't even drink much. Got into a little trouble now and again. Arguments in bars. That goes with the turf. But he wasn't like the rest. Not at all.'

Cakici leaned forward. His cuffs rattled as he pointed a finger at Costa.

'You want to know who killed Gino Riggi and that English kid? Find this Italian guy. You do that and I'll take care of him. That's a promise. No footprints home. Guaranteed.'

The two cops exchanged glances.

'You've nothing to worry about from my end,'

the Turk insisted. 'Not a thing. I won't say a word. They won't pin Gino and the kid on me either. I got an alibi. A genuine one. My auntie was over from Istanbul. I was with her. *My auntie.*'

'Then why in God's name did you run?' Costa asked.

Cakici shrugged.

'I didn't like the feel of what was going on here. Gino called me on Tuesday. He was getting jumpy. About things. About the English kid. All this publicity. That kid murdering his old man. Something about his family. Gino had good instincts. If he felt this was all about to go bad, it probably was. Time to take a holiday back home and see what happens.'

He held out his hands and smiled.

'Now. Let me out of these then put me in a car back to the city with a couple of dummies. I can call someone. They can get me loose. You get me the name of that Italian, I'll deal with it. Then we're back in business. Whatever Gino passed on to you, I'll double it. You're the kind of guys I can work with.' He smiled and held out a hand. 'What do you think?'

'I think one way or another you're going to jail,' Costa said and they left the room.

The immigration officer was outside on a stool, with a bottle of San Pellegrino and a sandwich.

'Some interesting noises in there,' he said.

'We had a frank exchange of views,' Peroni told him.

'When do you want to send a van?' he asked.

'We don't,' Costa said. 'His auntie says he's innocent. Bust him for the passport. We've got nothing else.'

The immigration man's eyebrows lifted in an expression of surprise.

'All that shouting and screaming? And you got nothing?'

'You heard,' Costa murmured, wondering what was happening back in the Questura, wishing he could have been there instead.

CHAPTER 9

Not long after the Gabriels and Bernard Santacroce left the morgue Falcone took a call from Costa. Teresa waited, watching, and could see the disappointment in his face.

'Well,' he said when it was finished. 'One more blind alley to add to the rest.'

'Meaning?'

She listened as he explained what Costa and Peroni had discovered from the Turk at Ciampino.

'We'll check the alibi,' Falcone said. 'I'll get narcotics to search his home. There won't be anything there, of course. And the alibi will stack up. If it was him on the bike . . .' He scowled and shook his head. 'He wouldn't have said a word.'

'Drugs. Complicated business. Is it really surprising there's some grubby little war going on around the Campo? Or that our stupid little English friend on the table here put his own neck on the line by bringing all this attention to himself?'

Falcone muttered something foul and didn't answer.

Teresa Lupo came and stood next to him. In his own way the man had tried to be sensitive towards the Gabriel family, as best he could. But the job, the need to ask awkward questions, and his own difficult personality all intervened in the end. It wasn't his fault. This was who he was.

'You know,' Teresa Lupo said, 'it is just possible that everything here really is as simple as it seems. Robert realized what a creep his father was and killed him. Then the American too when she found out. Toni Grimaldi's right. Proving Malise Gabriel was having sex with his own daughter won't bring anyone to justice. It could just cause a lot more pain to people who've had more than their fair share. Gabriel was a very sick man, Leo. Whether he told his family or not, they will have felt the burden. Should we really add to it?'

'I know all this!' he replied, seemingly hurt by her accusation.

'I appreciate that.'

'I'm not here to spare their feelings. I'm here to find out the truth. If they'd sit down, look me in the eye, and tell me something I could believe . . .'

'They don't want to talk about it, Leo,' she said. 'Would you?'

He scowled. 'What have they got to lose? You know the way public opinion is at the moment. Even if I could prove they knew Robert intended to kill his father I doubt I'd get them in court.'

'Their dignity?' she suggested.

He took a deep breath and looked into her eyes.

'I've taken that from them already, haven't I?' he murmured.

She waited. He'd recovered himself again, was once more the maddening individual she'd grown to admire, to love in a way, over the years.

'I don't believe they're murderers,' he insisted. 'Not directly. The brother, yes. Not them. I don't see that they could have been involved in the American woman's death. But Malise Gabriel's? If they're innocent why don't they *look* innocent? Why do they act this way?'

'Perhaps they feel you're intruding into a part of their lives where you don't belong. Besides, if you could prove they weren't entirely innocent, that they somehow knew, would that be justice? Who'd benefit?'

He bristled and said, 'That's not my job. I don't make those decisions.'

'But you do. We all do. That's why we're here. Beatrice Cenci had the Pope's inquisitors. Mina Gabriel has us. We're kinder, I think. But are we really any different?'

'You can't pick and choose,' Falcone insisted. 'We're all equal under the law.'

'Unless you're rich or a politician or the friend of someone who knows someone.'

'They're all the same as far as I'm concerned. This is the first time you've seen Mina and her mother. You tell me. Am I mistaken? Do you really feel I'm chasing some ghost here?'

No, she thought. His misgivings were entirely understandable, the reaction of an intelligent, experienced detective. Mina Gabriel was genuinely distraught at her brother's death. But the mother with her cold indifference to everything, even the incriminating photographs . . .

'Grief isn't a predictable emotion,' she said. 'It shows itself in very different ways, and at different times, because that's how people are. They're not machines or Pavlov's dog.'

He pointed at the door through which the Gabriels had left and asked, 'Have you seen that way before?'

She felt so sorry for Leo Falcone at times. He had an insight into dark places, a sympathy with the pain of those he suspected of terrible deeds. This awkward, intuitive wisdom was beyond the ordinary men and women within the Questura. They were lucky not to have it.

'No,' Teresa Lupo agreed. 'Not that way. Do you really want to pursue this further, Leo? Toni Grimaldi doesn't. But you're the boss.'

'What about you?' he asked hopefully.

She shrugged.

'I don't know. If you asked the man in the street . . .'

'Then half the time they'd want to bring back hanging, and the rest they'd let the guilty walk away free,' he interrupted.

'Quite,' she agreed. 'It's so much easier to define crime than it is to put your finger on justice, isn't it?' She observed him, thinking. 'You're letting this get to you and I don't like watching that. You need to step back a little. See it from the kind of perspective we had in the beginning. When it was a dead man in the street, an intellectual man, a genius some might say. A man who loved science and reason and Galileo. And loved women and arguments and . . . life, I guess too.'

Teresa Lupo tried to crystallize her thinking. It was so woolly, so vague it was impossible. But doubts led to certainties sometimes, if only they could be viewed in the right light.

She took Falcone by the arm and said, 'You know the most illuminating conversation we've had about this curious little affair was last Sunday, in the ghetto, in Gianni's little restaurant.'

'True,' Falcone replied. 'We're in the middle of a murder inquiry. I don't have time for social events.'

She looked at her watch.

'We still have to eat. Listen to me. It's nearly four thirty. I doubt anything's going to happen our end today. I'd put money on it not happening yours. Why not?'

A thought had clouded his face. He glanced anxiously at his watch.

'Oh lord,' Falcone said. 'I forgot what date it was.'

He scratched his head.

'Dinner,' he said. 'That's a good idea. Very good idea, actually. Eight o'clock. I'll book a place I know.'

He was pointing at Silvio Di Capua and the work experience kid, who were head down in the corner going through some papers.

'Bring them along too.'

'Are you serious?' she asked.

'Why not? I'm paying. Finding that mattress deserves something.'

Teresa put it to the pair of them. They looked surprised. Horrified, more like.

'We're busy,' Di Capua said. 'The Ducati from Tuesday night's supposed to turn up any minute downstairs.'

Maria waved her gloved hands in their faces.

'We're going to rip it apart,' she said gleefully.

'But thanks for asking,' Di Capua said, and went back to work.

'Eight o'clock,' Teresa agreed. 'And now?'

Falcone scooped up his papers. He looked a little calmer, almost happier for some reason.

'I'm going for a walk,' he said. 'Some fresh air. I need to get out of this place for a while. Call Costa and Peroni. I'll meet you all there. And persuade Nic to go home and get a change of clothes for once. He's only ten minutes from that place of his. It ought to be easy enough.'

CHAPTER 10

'Leo? Gone for a walk?' Peroni asked, amazed.

They sat on the porch of Costa's villa near the Via Appia Antica, sipping Pellegrino, watching the birds pick at the black grapes on the vines. Netting, Costa thought. That might be what he needed if he ever got round to trying to put the vineyard back in order.

'He never goes for a walk,' the big cop went on. 'And this dinner? What's he playing at?'

'We don't know what Leo does when he's off duty, do we?' Costa said.

There'd been a time, once. When he was briefly in love with the woman from Venice. But then that fell apart, as his affairs usually did after a while. And Leo Falcone was back to being the man they knew: a dedicated and talented police officer whose life revolved around the Questura, and barely seemed to exist outside it.

'Suppose not,' Peroni replied.

He turned and looked at Costa.

'Is he happy, Nic? I mean, just a little bit. I'd never expect Leo to be really happy. Not like a normal human being. But a little bit. It would worry me if he didn't have even that.'

Some more birds – finches, he thought – had begun to descend on the crop of grapes. They looked better than usual this year. He ought to be making wine, inviting people round to pick the crop, take part in the entertaining ceremony of crushing them, turning the juice into bad wine, just as his father had done with his friends a generation ago when Costa was a child. But those times, that way of life, seemed gone now. Everyone was so busy. The hectic round of work and duty never seemed to offer the space, the opportunity for leisure, time with the people you loved. Then the seasons turned once more, summer to autumn, autumn to winter. Another year gone, lost forever, haunted by the ghosts of words unspoken, promises never kept.

'He'll be happy when this is over,' Costa said. 'Something about this case . . .' He knew what it was, and so did Peroni. There was no need to say it out loud. Falcone was haunted by the thought of Mina Gabriel's damaged innocence, and the idea that she might be punished for defending herself against the brutish attentions of her own father. 'It gets to him, doesn't it?'

'Gets to all of us,' Peroni said. 'Can I take the car? I need to change too. You can make your own way there?'

'Of course.'

The big man stood up and stretched a little

painfully. Both he and Falcone faced retirement in a few years. Neither, Costa thought, would find it easy to leave the Questura behind. It wasn't just the job. It was the people, the companionship, the notion of some shared sense of direction. The idea that, in some small way, their mutual efforts represented a glimmer of hope, a trace of humanity, in a world going bad.

'We need to get Leo out more,' Costa said without thinking. 'We need to go back to the way we were. When Emily was alive. When we felt like . . .' There was no other word, and he was a Roman so it was not difficult or embarrassing for him to use it. '. . . like a family.'

Peroni nodded.

'We do,' he agreed. 'Starting tonight.'

Costa watched him go, thinking all the time about Agata, what to say, how he might help her through this difficult transition. He became lost in his thoughts after a while. So much so that, when the time came to go, he simply walked upstairs, threw on the first set of clean clothes he found, then came back down, fell on the Vespa and kicked it into life on the first try.

CHAPTER 11

They assembled at the restaurant just before eight, Agata coming directly from work. Falcone had picked Al Pompiere back in the ghetto, just a few steps away from Sora Margherita, the humble little hole-in-the-wall they'd visited a few nights before. He arrived in a fresh grey suit, a carnation in his lapel, a smile on his face, looking so calm, so at one with himself, Costa wondered why, a few hours earlier, he'd been worried about the man.

They went up the staircase to the first floor of the restaurant, one of the best in the ghetto. A reserved sign stood on a secluded window table with a view back to the Piazza delle Cinque Scole and, on the small mound opposite, one face of the gloomy, sprawling Palazzo Cenci. Costa found the sight distracting: this tragedy was somehow rooted in the buildings around here. In the history of the Cenci family, in the rundown apartment block that Joanne Van Doren had been trying, unsuccessfully, to resurrect and turn into a gold mine, creating instead a bleak fortress of secrets, some of them still hidden.

The waiters danced around the inspector obediently. He was known here, though he'd never so much as mentioned the place. Falcone was a private individual, even as he went about his business in the throng of the city. There was a duality to the man, in the way he could be personable, and show great care and courtesy to those around him, then retreat into his own thoughts in an instant.

Sparkling Franciacorta arrived, followed by plates of zucchini flowers stuffed with mozzarella, battered salt cod, crunchy fried artichokes and bitter puntarelle shoots with anchovies. Finally the head waiter entered carrying a small gift box wrapped in beautiful velvet and placed it in front of Agata.

Falcone clapped, alone. The rest of them stared at him, wondering, until Teresa asked, 'Are we celebrating something?'

'A birthday!' he cried. 'I'm too much of a gentleman to reveal the age, naturally.'

Agata bent over her present, creased with laughter, hiding her mouth with her hand.

'I thought you'd forgotten,' she said.

'As if!' he retorted. 'You should tell a few more people, though. You're out here with the rest of us now. Not hidden in some cloister.'

'I was an orphan! After that a sister.' She watched as Falcone, then the rest of them, raised their glasses in a toast. 'Birthdays were never so important. One year older. What does it matter?'

'It matters,' Teresa interjected, 'because you get free food and drink, and presents. Or rather one present. Of course . . .' She glared at Falcone. This was why the cunning old fox had gone for a walk. 'Had we known . . .'

He squirmed on his seat at the head of the table as Agata opened the velvet box. She found herself holding a very ornate gold necklace. One, Costa judged, a little too ostentatious for her taste.

'It's beautiful,' she declared. 'Thank you. You don't need to do this, Leo.'

'Of course I do,' Falcone replied. 'I was your sponsor when you were a child in that orphanage. These ties come with duties. As does friendship.'

He gestured at the waiters. They came out with more gifts: boxes of expensive chocolates from a fancy store in Via Condotti.

'What exactly is going on?' Teresa began, in a tone that was only just short of being cross.

'It's my way of saying sorry,' Falcone said quickly. 'To all of you. I've behaved badly of late and I know it. I took my anger out on the people around me. That was wrong. I want to apologize. Come on.' He pointed a lean index finger at the menu. 'Pick the best they have. Lamb and artichokes. Wonderful. Beef with citron. Fish. Nic, they'll cook anything a vegetarian can want.'

Peroni was staring at Costa from the other side of the table, a meaningful and deeply suspicious expression clouding his customarily friendly face. They all knew Falcone well by now.

427

'This is very kind of you,' the big cop said in clipped, measured tones. 'Given that we're in the middle of a rather nasty murder investigation.'

'Happy birthday to me!' Agata announced with a touch of despair, raising her glass to them. 'Why did I end up with police officers for friends?'

'Because you were lucky,' Falcone told her. 'Who better to help you find your way into the real world?'

'Who indeed?' she murmured. Agata looked almost as doubtful about this impromptu party as Peroni did.

'Tell us about work,' Costa said quickly, trying to change the conversation. 'Yours. How is the college? Your students?'

'My students,' she said, laughing. 'Is that what they are? Most are just children and don't know it. Children with parents who've more money than sense and think that, by sending their offspring to Bella Italia, they will come back transformed. Adults. Civilized. Made into the human beings they should be, by strangers like me.'

No one said anything. The mood, her mood, seemed terribly fragile.

'Being a teacher's never easy,' Teresa suggested.

'I imagine not,' Agata replied. 'But the truth is, I don't like some of them. They're coarse. They come late into class in the morning. Hung over. You can see the alcohol in their eyes. The drugs. The lazy licentiousness. That's their response to being given their freedom. To throw it away in some bar in the Campo.'

428

'Drugs?' Costa asked.

'The other teachers talk about it as if it were nothing. I'm sorry.'

'And the director? Bruno? He knows?'

She put down her glass and toyed with the beautiful necklace.

'This is my night, isn't it?' Agata Graziano asked.

'Every second of it,' Falcone declared with a theatrical flourish.

'Then let's not talk about the Collegio Raffello. It's . . . boring. I have to go to some convention on Sunday evening. Four nights. I didn't expect this. Milan.' Her dark face became still and thoughtful. 'With Bruno.'

'Milan has its beautiful parts,' Peroni suggested.

'No,' Agata insisted. 'Enough. Tell me something. The truth, now. I have to ask, since it's in all the papers. On the TV. This awful story has my students, such as they are, more enthralled than any old paintings I can throw at them . . . The Gabriel family. Well?'

Falcone smiled at her very pleasantly and asked, 'Well what?'

'When will it come to an end, Leo? When can I open a newspaper or turn on the TV and not see that poor girl's face staring back at me? Soon, please. Tell me that.'

'Soon,' he agreed. 'Tomorrow, in fact.'

They all stopped and looked at him.

'Yes,' he went on. 'Tomorrow. I've decided. This has gone far enough. I shall file my report to the *commissario*. It will say no more than the obvious. Malise Gabriel was the monster the papers have been painting him to be. He was murdered, with some guile, by the son, who also killed the American woman. Perhaps because she was involved somehow. Or she found out. We'll never know. Only the dead could tell us that. The brother himself was murdered by this unknown Italian drugs outfit we learned about today from the Turks, as was his crooked policeman friend. This is not unrelated. Had he not killed his father and brought such publicity on himself . . .'

A thought crossed Falcone's mind, one he kept to himself.

'That side of the case I shall pass to another inspector who can attach himself to narcotics in order to pursue it fully. I've seen enough of this tragedy, as I'm sure have you. So.' He chinked his glass with Agata's. 'Consider it done with. Despatched, all neat and tidy.'

'And Mina?' she asked. 'Her mother?'

He paused for a moment.

'I shall say that, while we have plenty of evidence to suggest both of them had good reason to fear and hate Malise Gabriel, there's no evidence to implicate them in his death, or that of anyone else. The case will be closed.'

There was silence around the table. Then Agata brightened, chinked her glass all around and said, 'That's the best birthday present I could have hoped for. The very best.'

Falcone watched her. In his face was the pride of a parent, Costa thought. And some relief too, some satisfaction that, in his own head, a turning point, a decision, had been reached.

CHAPTER 12

The red Ducati was, as Maria had promised, in pieces. The wheels, engine and frame lay scattered over the downstairs forensic room, each element tidily labelled with a tag. She and Silvio Di Capua stood next to the bits, along with a couple of forensic assistants they'd called in when the labour became too physical. The Rome number plates were on the desk. Fakes, naturally.

He felt wiped out. They'd been working twelve hours a day for almost a week. He needed a break. But the discovery of the mattress had energized the young woman next to him. Perhaps she saw it as a way into a job in the Questura. More likely, Di Capua thought, she just loved the challenge. For all her clumsiness and over-exuberance Maria Romano was a natural forensics officer: doggedly curious about everything. Even matters she didn't begin to understand.

'Remind me. What exactly are we meant to be looking for again?' he asked, half wishing he'd accepted Falcone's strange invitation to dinner.

'Clues, silly!'

Di Capua's initial disdain had transmuted to desire a few days before. Now it was slowly changing again, into a grinding, subterranean sense of annoyance.

'Yes,' he said testily. 'But what kind exactly?'

It was a rhetorical question. He knew the answers by heart. Prints, stains, smears from leather boots or gloves. If they could find the helmet or some other clothing they might identify an individual who'd ridden, or worked on, the bike. But there was nothing, only a few marks that would take days to interpret. Scuffs on the paint. Some fabric – wool and cotton, it looked like – trapped around the tank filler cap. Corroborating material. Nothing that would put a name or a face to the man who had gunned down two people in public on a hot Roman night.

Maria still had evidence bags to sort through. Judging by the bright and energetic expression on her face she seemed willing to work through the night if necessary.

She pulled on her shiny black hair and looked at him, realizing this was a test.

'We've got blood.'

There was some, on the right-hand side, the frame, the seat, the composite casing behind the carb.

'It's smear,' Di Capua said. 'I told you. We'll type it but it's not from the rider. It's from one of the poor bastards he shot. Look.' He pointed to the tell-tale points of soft tissue on the black metal and scarlet paint. 'Spatter too. He was still bleeding badly when he fell. It's the brother or the cop. The brother would be my bet. There was some smear on his clothes that suggested he'd come into contact with the bike.'

'Why would he do that?' Maria asked.

'I don't know! Does it matter?'

'Maybe. We've got the drugs.'

She'd retrieved two small plastic bags containing what looked like cocaine from the little compartment where tools were kept. Di Capua had had to scream at her when she seemed about to lick her little finger and taste the stuff. Too many bad movies. He'd had to point out the obvious: why would anyone do such a thing? What if it wasn't cocaine but something poisonous? And how was she supposed to know what cocaine tasted like anyway? This was so often the problem with the work-experience kids. They thought they knew more than they did.

'The drugs don't give us a name,' he said. 'That's what we're looking for. Some form of identity.'

Still, she was supposed to be there for training.

'What about the road tax?' he asked.

'It's gone.'

There was a clean spot on the frame where the licence should have been displayed. A rather feeble attempt to hide something, it seemed to him. Why not burn the entire machine to make sure?

'Is there any other way we can identify this bike?' he asked.

She looked blank.

He got down on his knees and poked around at the frame.

'All vehicles come with a serial number somewhere,' Di Capua told her. 'Usually you need the manual to know where to look. We can get in touch with Ducati tomorrow and ask them where to find it on this one. I've spent enough time scrabbling around on the floor. It could be anywhere.'

'Anywhere?' she asked.

'Well,' he corrected himself. 'On the frame usually, I think.'

'The engine,' said one of the assistants, a youth with long, lank hair and an unfortunate, cadaverous face. 'You normally get a Ducati number on the case. My brother had one.'

Maria crouched down too and said, 'The engine's very big.'

Di Capua felt his eyes were going wrong. Everything was a little blurry and it was impossible to focus.

'What about this?' Maria asked. She was pointing to a patch on the right hand case, beneath the cylinders. The metal looked different, recently scoured or scratched.

He got as close as he could, then asked for a magnifying glass. They were all watching him.

'Amateurs,' Silvio Di Capua said, shaking his head. 'They should have just torched this thing somewhere. Or got it out of the country. Rank amateurs.'

'What is it?' she asked.

'They tried to file off the number. Terrible job. Even you could have done better.'

Her blank young face went pink with a touch of anger.

'Get a photograph,' he said to one of the assistants. 'Put it on the system upstairs. I can make out three numbers just looking. Given we know the model I'm guessing we could identify it from that. Tomorrow we'll call Ducati and track down the dealer who sold it.'

'I'll stay behind and call them now,' Maria said.

Di Capua sighed.

'It's the evening. Motorbike companies don't work evenings. They're sensible people. Tomorrow.'

'So what can I do?' she asked.

'I don't care. I'm going home to bed.' He bent down and stared into her wide, guileless eyes. 'And nothing any of you can do will stop me. I feel old. I feel tired. I feel stupid. I feel . . .'

To his amazement she'd pulled an evidence bag out of the items tray on the bench beside the Ducati. It contained a phone, with some kind of gadget strapped to the base.

'You got that from the bike?' he asked.

'No. The dead boy. The brother. It was in his jacket pocket. Dead like him. Remember?'

'Dead like him,' he repeated.

Forensics staff had to be around the bereaved on a regular basis. He wondered how on earth he'd train her for that.

He remembered the phone. The battery was flat.

'I asked for someone to take out the SIM so we could look at it.'

She shuffled and said, 'I know. But there wasn't anyone around and I have this neat charger thing for my iPod. You plug it into your USB socket and then, when it's full, you plug it into the phone. You get plugs for phones, iPods, all kind of things. Ten euros down the market . . .'

'Maria!' he barked. 'Enough information! Tell me something or I go.'

'The battery's full,' she said, holding up the evidence bag. 'I set it to charge while we were working. That way we'd get things sooner.'

The bars on the Nokia were all there.

'We don't get things off phones any more,' Di Capua scoffed. 'It's got to have a PIN code on it. You can't just recharge the thing and . . .'

She pressed the power button. It came to life straight away. No PIN, no password. These really were the worst bunch of crooks Silvio Di Capua had encountered in a very long time. Either that or, more likely, there was nothing of value on the phone.

He watched Maria Romano working the keypad with that eager ease the young had, one that made him feel old at the age of twenty-nine. He knew from looking at her face that once again he was about to be proved wrong.

The girl tapped a few more times then broke into a broad, toothy grin.

'Tell me,' Di Capua said.

'It's a cool phone. No messages. No call records. But it's got the Internet. Look. This . . .'

The brother had been using it for email. There was a single message in the inbox, received from Mina Gabriel the previous week. Two days before the death of her father. A little paper clip by the side indicated it had an attachment.

He took the Nokia from her and looked at the message. There was no subject and the body didn't add up to much either. It just said, 'You'll need this.'

The attachment was a large pdf file, an image or a document or something. He tried opening it on the phone but it was too slow and the file was too big to be practical on the little screen, even if his eyesight would allow him to see. So he wandered over to the nearest laptop and beamed the file over. Maria was behind him following every move, purring all the time.

The thing was so large it took almost a minute to transfer. When it finally arrived in its entirety Di Capua hit the enter key. The pdf opened straight away: a big technical document, the kind companies posted on the web for their customers. Line drawings of wheels and pulleys and stays, and how they had to be joined together in order to be safe.

'What,' Maria asked, sounding a little disappointed, 'is that?'

He knew at once, could feel the excitement that

came from seeing two seemingly unrelated circumstances finally joined together by some ridiculously serendipitous connection.

'It's a set of instructions on how to erect the brand of suspension scaffolding used on the roof of the Gabriels' apartment. Or, if you like, how not to erect it. How to remove the right pieces to ensure it'll come toppling down if you throw a body out onto the platform.'

'Ooooh.'

Her eyes were wider than ever. Her fleshy hands performed one little clap then fell still under the gravity of his gaze.

'Are you going to call the boss?' the girl asked.

They were all out for dinner. He didn't want to spoil that. Teresa deserved a break as much as any of them. Besides, she was off duty, unlike him. His first point of reporting was clear. Falcone never really rested.

Di Capua checked his watch, told them what to do with the evidence, and what tasks to prepare for the following day. Then he bade them good-bye and walked outside. The night was still sultry and stifling. Usually he loved this time of year. September was when Rome began to wake after the hazy stupor of August. Life returned. They hadn't got there yet.

He didn't feel elated by Maria's discovery and he wondered why. Perhaps because a part of him had always hoped that everything they suspected about the Gabriel girl would turn out to be wrong. From what he'd read, from looking at her pretty, intelligent face in the papers, she seemed a nice enough kid, one who'd suffered under the nightmare of an abusive and terrible father. She deserved a few more hours of freedom before the storm cloud that had been gathering around her bright young head broke with a vengeance.

All the same, he knew he had to make the call. Not now, though. Now there was time for a beer and some solitary thinking. A Baladin. A cigarette. Some respite from the sea of questions, doubts and posibilities that refused to stop running through his overactive mind.

CHAPTER 13

They left the restaurant just after ten, happy, well-fed, a little drowsy from the long day. Costa offered to walk Agata home but she declined, making an excuse he didn't believe. Something was wrong in this new life of hers. It was obvious, just as it was clear she didn't want to discuss it.

He watched her go. Teresa and Gianni Peroni stood, arms linked, at the edge of the Piazza delle Cinque Scole, laughing and joking with one another. The night had brought an unexpected revelation. Leo Falcone really had abandoned a difficult case, one they all suspected was more complex than it seemed. This had never happened in all the time Costa had known the man. There were failures, plenty of them. Cases that fell down in court or, more often, investigations that simply went nowhere. But he couldn't recall a single instance where Falcone had decided that he would accept the obvious, the status quo, and no longer pursue an inquiry that, in all probability, still had some way to run. Even the matter of the brother's death and the murder of Gino Riggi would now be handled by some other officer. A part, the private, personal part, of Costa wanted to welcome this decision. The professional side of him was quietly appalled.

They said their farewells. Teresa and Peroni wandered off looking for a cab. Costa picked up his helmet. He'd had just a single glass of wine. It was fine to ride home. He wanted to. The city became too close, too constrictive at times, particularly in the narrow lanes of the ghetto. He'd parked the scooter near to the tiny arch beneath the Palazzo Cenci, a grim, dark alley with a small shrine supposedly marking the location of an ancient murder.

'Safe journey,' Falcone said, emerging from the dark and still amused by the idea of the Vespa. 'I never had one of those things, you know. Straight from a bicycle to a car. Nothing in between.'

Costa hesitated.

'Is everything all right, Leo?'

'Of course it is. Did Agata enjoy herself? Shouldn't we be worrying about her?'

'A little, I imagine. But she's like you. She'll never tell you when something's wrong. You have to learn the signs. Then pluck up the courage to say something.'

He left it at that. Falcone didn't.

'And you think that came from me?' he asked.

'You were the only outside figure in her life when she was in the orphanage, weren't you?'

The older man leaned against the restaurant wall and stared back into the piazza.

442

'I was a kind of father, I suppose. A very poor and distant one. I remember realizing, when she was seven or eight, that she saw me that way. I retreated a little after that. Frightened. Yes, I was frightened by it. The dependence. The closeness.' He shrugged, amused at his own frailty. 'Some of us aren't cut out to be family men.'

'I think you did more than you realize. More than you accept.'

'Perhaps.' His face had grown long and gloomy again. He was tired. They all were. 'How could a man like Malise Gabriel do something like that? To his own daughter? *How*? I don't understand. That's not sexual desire, is it? It's power. Bullying. Violence. Just one more form of rape. A worse form, if that's possible. And that girl. That child . . .' He shook his head. 'I think she actually feels guilty herself.'

These questions troubled Costa from time to time. There were crimes that sprang from comprehensible sources. Greed. Jealousy. Hatred. Despair. But not this one.

'We can't see inside the minds of everyone we deal with.'

'We see inside the minds of their victims though, don't we?' He began to walk towards the square, and the place where Costa had left the scooter. 'You know . . .'

The night was beautiful when they reached the open space of the piazza. There were lights in the apartments of the Palazzo Cenci, faces at the glass, some blank, a few happy, staring out at the sea of cars parked on the cobblestones.

'I stood in the Questura today and did everything I could to try to force Mina Gabriel to talk. To get that young girl, woman, I don't know, to tell me the truth. Or rather confirm the truth. That her father abused her. And somehow everything we've seen – the deaths, the agony – followed from that terrible, disgraceful act. Why did I do that? Who benefits? If she, and perhaps her mother, were accomplices, what will happen? A lengthy and expensive trial. A few months in jail at the most. Probably not even that. And . . .' He shook his head, as if scarcely able to believe he'd left the most important point till last. 'More than anything, the pain. The agony I put them through. Why? Because it's my job. Because, as I so pompously told Teresa, we're all equal under the law. Are we?'

Costa could see the scooter now, against the wall by the low, dark arch. Malise Gabriel had died on the cobblestones beyond. 'We can't afford to make choices.'

Falcone stopped, put an arm on his and said, 'We can, Nic. We do. All the time. It's pointless pretending otherwise. I chose to pursue this case because their reticence offended me. Almost as much as the idea that a father could do such a thing to his own child. I felt there was something here that deserved punishment, and it was my job to deliver that. But there's no one left to punish, is there?' He looked into Costa's eyes. 'God knows, haven't they suffered enough already?'

'They have,' he agreed. 'I'm still not sure . . .'

'Well, I've thought about this long and hard and I am.' He pointed at Costa in the dark. 'When you become an inspector remember this case. We need to be conscious of our humanity too. That's more important than the law sometimes. Just don't ever quote me on that. Especially in the Questura. Now . . .'

His phone rang. Falcone apologized, seemed ready to ignore it, then saw the number on the handset.

'Excuse me,' he said, and stepped away to stand by a parked car.

Costa waited. It seemed necessary for some reason. The call was short. Falcone barely spoke at all, though he listened intently, nodding all the while, his face a picture of introspective concentration. Something else too. It was difficult to tell in the dark, but it seemed, to Costa, to represent a return of the bleakness he'd seen in the man these last few days, a desolate gloom that had been dispelled by the time they arrived at Al Pompiere that evening.

Finally Falcone ended the call with a curt *'grazie'*, no more.

'Thank you for coming,' he said and patted Costa on the shoulder, not looking into his eyes for one moment. 'I'm glad you did.'

'Something from the Questura?'

'Don't worry about it,' Falcone replied immediately. 'Routine stuff. Come in tomorrow and tidy up the papers. Then take some days off. Go back on holiday. Enjoy yourself.'

'Holiday?'

'Speaking of which,' Falcone added, 'I won't be at my desk in the morning till around lunch time. Some . . . personal matters to attend to. Please tell people not to contact me. It's rather delicate.'

'I see,' Costa replied, in a tone that said he saw nothing at all, and would happily be enlightened.

'Good,' Falcone said and then loped off into the night, a tall, solitary figure striding through the ghetto, head down, thinking.

PART X

CHAPTER 1

The Questura felt odd the following morning. Falcone, as he promised, was nowhere to be seen. The murder detail had turned up to work only to discover they were to stand down from the Gabriel case until further notice. This puzzled Costa deeply. Falcone had assured them the investigation was finished. No one else had been told that. It simply seemed to be on ice.

Peroni felt equally baffled, so the two of them gravitated to forensic and the morgue, mooching around the staff there, trying to find some answers. No one knew why the case was in limbo, neither dead nor alive. Or if they did they weren't telling.

Then Silvio Di Capua and the young work-experience girl, Maria, who seemed permanently attached to him, wandered in complaining loudly, a furious-looking Teresa Lupo behind them.

The pathologist eyed Costa and Peroni. Then she said, 'My office. Now.'

They followed the three forensic staff into the glass cubicle overlooking the rear of the Questura and the crammed police car park. The demonstration outside seemed to have picked up momentum again. Marked police vehicles were struggling to get out through the crowd. A line of ten or so blue Fiats was backed up against the fortified gates trying to find an opportunity to make their way into the street.

'Did you know about this last night?' Teresa demanded, staring at Costa.

'Know about what?'

She ordered Di Capua to tell them. Costa listened as he explained the discovery of the email on the dead brother's phone, the document detailing the structure of the scaffolding, and where it had originated. Falcone's distraction the previous evening, after the odd call he'd taken in the piazza in the ghetto, started to make sense of a kind, and he told her so.

'So where is he?' she demanded. 'His phone's off. He's not returning calls. I sent someone round to his apartment. He's not there. We need to talk to him. Where the hell has he gone? To see the Gabriels?'

'He wouldn't go there on his own,' Costa said.

'Well, then where?'

'Leo's a grown man,' Peroni retorted. 'We're not his keepers.'

'Women,' Teresa said. 'That's it usually. Who's the current one?'

'Search me,' Costa added. 'Leo doesn't talk about his private life unless there's a reason. I've no idea if there's a girlfriend or not. Anyway, why do you need him so urgently? This can wait, can't it?'

She scowled at Di Capua.

'That rather depends on what he's up to. The information this department . . .' There was an icy stare at her deputy. '. . . provided last night was not as full or as accurate as I might have liked.'

'Mail headers,' Maria chipped in. 'You have to look at the mail headers. They're not right.'

Peroni, never a man happy with technology, was squinting at her, mouthing, 'What?'

'I've got this friend in America,' she went on. 'He knows mail headers inside out. I tweeted him and he took a look. Had to repeat tweet of course which is not good twittiquette. You can't get a whole header over with just a hundred and forty characters. He was in a bar in San Diego.'

'San Diego? Headers? Twittiquette?' Peroni asked. 'What in God's name are you talking about?'

Teresa told him. A little of the heat drained from his face.

Costa thought about what she'd said. The header was some hidden information in the email that revealed the name of the server from which it had originated, and the path by which it had reached its destination, Robert Gabriel's phone. Usually this was predictable and tied to whatever mail service was used for the individual email address. But in the case of the email on the phone, the server was part of an anonymous service designed to hide the true origin of the message. It could have come from anywhere and the sender must have deliberately used this route in order to disguise his or her identity.

'This doesn't make sense,' he said. 'Why would Mina Gabriel use an anonymous service and still put her name on the message?'

Di Capua cleared his throat, glanced at Teresa and said, 'She probably didn't.'

Maria took out her phone and ran her fingers across the keys.

'Look,' she said. 'I just sent a message to that address. What happens? Boing. It gets bounced. Either it's not a real email address. Or the server is down. Unlikely. Or it's a real email address that's expired. Or . . .'

'What does it all mean?' Peroni demanded

'It means that either Mina Gabriel is a very poor criminal,' Costa said, 'or someone is trying to frame her for the murder of her father. Which, if true . . .'

His mind was starting to race. Sometimes investigations ran on assumptions, through the process of trying to transform an invented truth developed from hypothesis and plain guesswork into some form of reality that one could touch and turn into an arrest, a conviction. It had been troubling him for some time that the assumptions they had about the Gabriel case had scarcely changed from the outset, even though in the very beginning they were based on the flimsiest of observations. Cases normally developed, shifted, changed shape and character with time and a growing sense of perspective. This had been the same from the start: a case of murder stemming from incest. Just like that of the Cenci family.

'We need Leo,' Teresa began.

'He's not here,' Costa said. 'I'm in charge in his absence. I'll deal with this.'

Teresa's eyebrows rose. Her plain, friendly face wore a wry, amused smile.

'Well, sir,' she said. 'What do you want us to do?'

'Is that it?' he asked. 'Is that all you wanted to say to Falcone?'

The forensic team exchanged another set of maddening, silent glances.

'Not exactly,' Di Capua replied.

CHAPTER 2

'Semen,' Teresa's assistant said. 'That's the problem. We expected—'

'Don't tell me what you expected,' Costa ordered. 'Tell me what you found.'

The forensic officers glanced at one another.

'Perhaps we won't miss Leo after all.' Teresa mused. 'The honest truth is we've found nothing. Because of the holidays and the stinking budget cuts we've got to use an outside lab for DNA sampling. Takes time. Saves money. The latter seems more important than the former, at least to the bean-counters upstairs.'

'On with it, on with it,' Peroni urged, waving a hand at her.

She took a deep breath then said, 'We don't have a positive ID for any of the semen yet. The reports that came back from the outside lab aren't usable. I've rejected them and said they need to be carried out again. They won't get round to that until tomorrow.'

'Wonderful,' Costa muttered under his breath.

'The best case you can come up with will still fall in court if the defence can question the DNA,'

Teresa said. 'It's happening more and more. I can't take chances.'

'We've been waiting days!'

'I know.' She paused to add a little drama, the way she always liked on such occasions. 'The problem is the data we've got back doesn't match. It's close. But it's not identical, as it should be. I think this is because it's been handled badly. But there is an alternative explanation.'

She took another deep breath then said, 'It's just possible that we have semen specimens from two men, not one.'

The two cops didn't say anything.

'We didn't look at the results until this morning,' Di Capua said. 'It's probably a mistake.'

Costa looked at Teresa Lupo and said, 'Probably?'

She frowned.

'Look, I hate this as much as you do. I want certainties. We don't have them. The most likely answer is that the lab screwed up. If they didn't . . .' She shrugged. 'Then we have two men involved in sexual encounters. One of them, I assume, is Malise Gabriel. But I can't tell you which yet. Or who the other might be.'

'The son?' Peroni asked.

'That was my first thought,' Teresa replied 'It seems logical. As logical as anything else in this case. I've sent off a sample to check. Tomorrow . . .'

'I don't want to wait till tomorrow,' Costa insisted.

'Well, you'll have to,' she said, shaking her head. 'Go shout at the bean-counters. There is a problem with the son, though. These two samples are different but similar, which is why we assume there's been some mistake and really it's two samples from the same man, contaminated somehow.'

Peroni growled and said, 'Make this simple.'

'If these do turn out to be from two different men, then I'd hazard a guess that they're probably related.'

That pause again. She gazed at Costa.

'Are you absolutely sure Robert Gabriel was adopted?'

'Mina said so. The mother too.'

'Quite. Are you *sure*?'

He thought about it and said, 'There's no physical resemblance. Robert was nothing like her. His habits. His personality.' He nodded. 'I'll get someone to check.'

Everything needed to be re-examined. Every last piece of evidence they'd lazily taken for granted.

'While we're at it,' he said, 'let's look at those photographs again, shall we?'

CHAPTER 3

'**A** deal?' Toni Grimaldi asked. 'What kind of deal?'

They sat at a quiet table outside the Caffe della Pace, not far from the small temple-like church of Santa Maria. When the place was quiet Falcone liked to use it for such meetings. It was close to his old home near the Piazza Navona, a pleasant, ancient establishment with an atmosphere conducive to the kind of frank conversation that was, on occasion, impossible inside the formal corridors of the Questura.

He'd called the lawyer that morning, catching him on the train in from Ostia as Falcone had hoped. Timing was important in such matters. It was vital to plant the seed of this idea early, outside the office.

'A deal that suits us all,' Falcone said, picking at his breakfast pastry. 'This case is damaging everyone. The Questura. The family. The judiciary, if we allow it to get that far . . .'

'You sound very different from yesterday,' Grimaldi noted. 'Then you wanted me to give you carte blanche to throw these two women into a cell and leave them there until they signed a confession to murder.'

'Yesterday was yesterday.'

'And today you have firm proof the girl was involved in the death of her own father! Now you wish to pardon her! Please.'

That was not what Falcone was suggesting. He repeated the idea. Grimaldi listened, nodding. He was a good, decent man, one who would stop at nothing to put a criminal in the dock. But a solid Catholic, with a large family and a happy home life too. An honest, hard-working citizen with an open mind. The kind of individual the Questura depended upon.

'I want this to go away,' Falcone continued. 'We all do. Unless that happens, we'll have those people demonstrating outside the Questura every day of the week. Headlines in the newspapers. Officers engaged in fruitless inquiries.'

'Fruitless? You still have two unsolved murders. That's if we apportion the brother and our friend Riggi to this drugs gang. You're not suggesting we forget them, are you?'

'Not for a moment. The deaths of Malise Gabriel and Joanne Van Doren are not unsolved. Robert was responsible for both. That's what I'll put in my report. But this new evidence. The email linking the daughter to her father's death. Much as I'd like to, I can't bury it. She, perhaps the mother too . . . there needs to be a statement. An admission of some prior knowledge. She can say she never knew why he wanted the information. I don't want an admission of guilt, but I do require an explanation. In return . . .'

Grimaldi finished his coffee. His walrus moustache bristled.

'In return what?'

'An agreement that the case will go no further. You tell me. You're the lawyer.'

The man opposite thought about this for a while.

'If there was a prosecution she'd never go to jail, you know. The daughter. Even if you could gain an accessory conviction on the basis of a simple email. And the mother? You've nothing, have you?'

'Nothing. I know all this, Toni. Why do you think we're having this conversation?'

It was a beautiful morning. The air had the first breath of autumn in it, a subtle chill beneath the heat that had pervaded Rome night and day for weeks. This harsh summer would come to an end.

'There are four people dead, Leo. Even if one of them was a crooked cop. Another a murderer. The third some kind of monster.'

Falcone wished Grimaldi hadn't said that. Mina Gabriel did love her father in some way, he believed. This was one reason, an unspoken one, why he didn't wish to pursue the case. He feared what else it might uncover, to no one's benefit.

'All the more reason I'll be happy if we can close this for good today,' Falcone said. 'That would be best for all of us. No one need suffer more.'

Grimaldi nodded.

'So be it.'

'What? A pardon? A caution? What?'

The lawyer laughed.

'A pardon? I'm a Questura lawyer. Not a judge. I can't hand those out. Besides, I want this girl, the mother too, to understand we know they've been less than frank with us. That we're choosing not to take this any further. I want to hear Mina Gabriel acknowledge that email you found and tell me, in her own words, she didn't know why Robert wanted it. I'm no priest, Leo. I don't offer forgiveness to the guilty. For our sake and for theirs I want to hear some word, some expression of responsibility on their part. If I get that, they'll hear no more from me. I'll concur with you that there's insufficient evidence for anyone else to be charged. Which is probably true, by the way.'

Falcone recalled the difficult meetings he'd had with Cecilia Gabriel and her daughter.

'I'm not sure how easy that's going to be.'

'The girl hasn't even admitted there was abuse, has she? Even with those photographs you have.'

'True, but—'

'No,' Grimaldi cut in. 'I won't move on this. If she won't give me even this small thing, you must continue the investigation. Find more evidence than a single incriminating email. I can't bury four murders without a reason. It's not as if I'm asking for some sign of complicity. Only a brief and understandable explanation. In return they may be getting away with murder. Or at the very least being party to one. You asked for a deal. How good a deal is that? The best they're likely to have.'

Falcone scratched his tidy silver beard, thinking.

'The trouble is,' he asked, 'how on earth do I sell that to them? I haven't managed to have a civilized conversation with Cecilia Gabriel since we met. She's slapped me in the face twice. I don't know . . .'

'You need a lawyer with you,' Grimaldi told him. 'We possess what those bright young things in human resources call a different skill set. Come.' He looked at his watch. 'I can make the time. Let's walk round there now. This House of Owls sounds an interesting place. We can have a full and frank conversation, just the four of us. No notes. Nothing formal. A little chat, one that in legal terms doesn't even exist. I will make the situation plain. All I require is a little candour on their part. In return I shall see that the file goes no further on the grounds that a prosecution would not be in the public interest.'

He opened his hands in a very Roman signal of generosity.

'What more can I offer, Leo? Please. Tell me.'

Falcone thought about this. It was what he'd hoped for, though he still felt uncomfortable leaving his team rudderless that morning.

'I should call Costa and explain.'

'That,' Grimaldi said, 'is the last thing you're going to do. Trust me. With arrangements of this

461

nature you do not involve the Questura. Not till the deed is done.'

The lawyer tapped the side of his bulbous nose.

'Agreed?' he added, though it was not, in truth, a question.

CHAPTER 4

The prints were spread out over the desk in two separate heaps. No one had looked too carefully at these, Costa realized. There hadn't been time and they all quietly shared Falcone's distaste for the prurience of this case from the outset. No one wanted to peer too closely at such material unless there was a very good reason. That seemed absent. Everyone involved, police and forensic, thought they knew what was there.

'These pictures are different,' Costa said.

'Technically, they're bound to be,' Di Capua piped up. 'The ones in the basement are taken using film. That nice old Hasselblad we found. That's why they look so much better. That and my processing skills. The ones on the USB stick are from some digital camera we still haven't located. From the EXIF on the jpeg I can tell you . . .'

Peroni uttered a long, loud sigh.

'We know from the data,' Di Capua went on, 'it was taken with an inexpensive Fuji pocket camera. It couldn't possibly look as good. If—'

'I'm not talking about quality,' Costa interrupted.

He steeled himself to stare again at both sets of photographs: the ones of Joanne Van Doren, the shots which were, without any doubt, of Mina. It was nothing to do with sharpness or depth of field or anything else photographic. They were entirely different in nature, in the way they'd happened, the story they were trying to tell.

'These,' Costa said, indicating the Hasselblad prints, 'are posed. As if Gabriel was trying to take shots to order. For a pornographic magazine or something. I don't know. Also . . .'

He understood very little about photography. But he remembered the way his own father had struggled to take family portraits using the awkward clockwork timer on their ancient Kodak. It rarely worked. There were always shots that caught the cameraman walking back to the group, back to the lens, arriving too late. It was messy and unpredictable.

'The ones in the basement. I'm not even sure it's just him, is it?'

They crowded round and stared hard themselves.

'Oh God,' Teresa groaned. 'Why didn't we see that?'

'We weren't looking,' Di Capua grumbled.

They had all assumed that it was Malise Gabriel in this set of shots because he appeared, full face, in a single frame early in the sequence. That one picture showed him on the bed with the American woman, poised over her, as if they were about to begin making love. But they weren't even touching,

464

and the expression between them was one of false lust, theatrical expectation. All the other prints were principally of the woman, and they were different. Real. Visceral. Full of a bleak animal heat, the way pornography often was.

'How,' Costa asked, 'could Malise Gabriel have taken those shots on his own? With a timer? She's having sex with someone. You can see that. How could you set up an old-fashioned camera, any camera, to take something as carefully shot as this? So that you can easily identify the woman but not the man?'

'They could have cropped it,' Maria said. 'Deleted things.'

'It's not digital,' Di Capua snapped. 'What's there is what was on the film.'

'A second man,' Teresa suggested. 'Either it's Malise having sex or he's behind the camera. We can look at what we can see of him and compare it with what we've got in the morgue. I can tell you definitely once there's a DNA report I can trust. Sorry, Nic. It just looked like one more white male having his fun. We didn't have any reason to think otherwise.'

Costa bristled.

'We had every reason not to make assumptions. Let's try to remember next time, shall we? And these . . .'

He stabbed a finger at the vile shots of Mina.

'It's the same, isn't it?' the girl said. 'You can see it's the daughter. You can't see who the man is.'

'It's not the same at all,' Costa replied. 'These are rushed shots taken by hand. Look.'

He held up his arm and pretended he was snapping off shots of himself.

'He's doing this while he's having sex with her. Camera in hand. Arm up here, just firing away. It's secret and squalid, as if he's capturing some kind of conquest, not something that's meant to be erotic. This is just for him. Or them.'

Di Capua was nodding. He could see this.

'Right,' he said. 'And he's bound to get his own face in there at some stage. Has to happen. So he goes through the shots afterwards, deletes the ones that identify him, copies the rest onto the memory stick then keeps it safe in her mattress.'

'Why would he do that?' Maria asked. 'It seems an unnecessary risk.'

It did too, Costa thought. One more unanswered question.

Teresa told Di Capua to get a team looking at the prints, trying to find some features that would enable them to identify any second individual in the frames.

Costa shook his head.

'We've been racing round Rome, yelling at Mina Gabriel and her mother. We didn't even look at what was here, right in front of us.'

'I said I'm sorry,' Teresa told him.

'I wasn't trying to blame anyone. We're as guilty as you. It's as if . . .' He wasn't sure what he was saying himself. 'As if we were meant to be chasing these ghosts.'

Maria had her hand up, like a schoolgirl with a bright idea.

'Yes?' Teresa said.

'I got a tweet about the Ducati a couple of minutes ago. The company never got back to me. Some geek dealer in Milan's got the records database.'

'Tweet?' Peroni asked, aghast.

'Don't ask,' Teresa told him. 'And?'

'It's not Italian at all.'

They waited.

'It's an export model,' Maria said. 'Made for the British market. Never sold here or anywhere else.'

CHAPTER 5

By eleven the teams were in place and looking at the details that Costa had ordered them to explore: the red Ducati, the photographs found in the basement of the house in the Via Beatrice Cenci and the ones secreted in Mina Gabriel's mattress.

Peroni was heading up the police group pressing the UK authorities for more information. Di Capua had brought in a photographic expert he knew to help with the pictures. No one had even mentioned Falcone's name in a while. There was too much work to do, too much interest in what was beginning to emerge.

The expert turned out to be a gruff and burly individual from the city's paparazzi pack. After twenty minutes spent poring over the prints through an eyeglass the man stood up, massaged his back, casually inquired whether it was OK to smoke, grunted when this was refused and said, 'Don't you people take your clothes off sometimes? These shots . . .' He indicated the prints from the basement. 'They're two different men. Isn't it obvious?'

Peroni walked in, looking busy.

'Am I interrupting something?' he asked.

'Bear with us,' Costa told him.

'Yes,' Teresa said, glaring at the paparazzo and Di Capua in turn. 'We do know that. Is there nothing else you have to tell us?'

'He's hiding his identity. The second man. Not *him*, obviously.' He placed a fat thumb on the face of Malise Gabriel, hovering over the naked and rather drowsy-looking Joanne Van Doren. 'The other one. He doesn't want to be seen. I've done a little porn in my time, who hasn't?'

Teresa put up her hand and smiled at him.

'What I meant was, who in the business hasn't? Sometimes you have to keep people's faces out of the picture for obvious reasons. Men usually. Women don't mind too much. Or if they do, they don't say. It's not easy either. If they're pros, maybe. They know how to pose. But when you've got amateurs performing, and this woman *is* an amateur, trust me, it's difficult to stop them getting carried away.'

He leaned down and looked at the picture again.

'Though not her. She looks drunk to me. Or stoned or something. Not good. Where's the joy? Where's the passion? You could never sell these.'

'Are we learning anything here?' Teresa asked.

'You're learning what I think, lady,' the paparazzo said. 'Two different men, one of them doesn't want to be seen. Miserable woman. Though quite hot on a good day, I'd say.'

'And the other pictures?' Costa asked, indicating the ones of Mina Gabriel.

The photographer's face wrinkled with disgust.

'Please. There are standards, you know? This is different. Horrible, dirty stuff. No self-respecting photographer would get involved in something like that. It's just plain grubby. The kind of thing kids take with their phones. Sexting, they call it. Yuk.'

Teresa put a finger on the earlier prints, the ones from the Hasselblad.

'So you're saying these are good?' she asked.

'Pretty good, yes. They're well posed. They do the job. No face except the woman. No obvious identification. You've got all the frames?'

The pathologist glared at Di Capua and said, 'Most. There was a little accident.'

'Well, if he managed to shoot a roll of film without any obvious identification in there, he knew what he was doing. An amateur wouldn't manage that. Even a good one. Of course, someone set up this guy for the first shot.' He pointed at Malise Gabriel. 'Then changed places for the rest.'

'You mean this man,' Costa pointed to Gabriel, 'could have taken the rest of the pictures? Even if he didn't know what he was doing?'

'Fix a tripod and a monkey could use a camera. That kind of shot, it's focus, lighting, frame. The real guy screwing the woman could just shout out when he wanted, I guess. Odd thing to do.'

He scratched his head.

'You know the worst thing?' He picked up the

shots of Mina Gabriel. 'Someone *would* pay money for these. Some creep somewhere. That's the kind of world we live in.'

'I suppose,' Teresa said glumly.

'That's all I can tell you,' the man added.

'Not much, is it?' Costa complained. 'I hope we're not paying you well.'

'I do it as a public service,' the paparazzo said. 'Just a hundred euros will do.'

He held out his hand. No one took any notice.

'Well?' Costa asked Peroni.

'Robert was adopted. The story about the kid who died? It's all true. We found the inquest.'

'It could still be Robert on those sheets,' Teresa suggested. 'Let's wait for the DNA.'

'We'll have to, won't we?' Costa said. 'At least we know Mina Gabriel told us the truth about him.'

'Seems so,' Teresa agreed.

Costa looked at Peroni. He was remembering the conversation with Mina at Montorio, the story about St Peter and a dead magician. Simon Magus. A story that came from her father.

'Mina said she had an uncle in England,' he said. 'A banker. She thought he was called Simon. Didn't get on with Malise. She'd never even met the man. See if you can track him down.'

Peroni's face creased.

'The police in London didn't say anything about any relatives. I asked them if they'd been to see next of kin. You'd expect it in a violent death. They said there wasn't any.'

'Simon Gabriel,' Costa repeated. 'Go back to them. Ask.'

'Will do.'

'Anything else?'

Peroni looked at his notes and frowned.

'The Ducati was bought from a dealer in London nine months ago. Reported stolen one month later. The Metropolitan police said there'd been a lot of thefts of fancy motorbikes recently. Some kind of ring operating.'

Costa wasn't convinced.

'A ring stealing Italian motorbikes and shipping them back here? Why?'

'When it's stolen,' Di Capua said, 'who knows where it's going?'

'Doesn't work like that,' Costa said. 'Who did it belong to in the first place?'

'Some . . . Englishman . . .' Peroni stuttered, checking his pad. 'Name of Julian Urquhart. Lived in Hampstead. No current address. He moved not long after he reported the bike stolen.'

Costa took fifty euros out of his wallet, gave it to the paparazzo, and said, 'Thank you.'

'Fifty?' the photographer asked.

'On an hourly rate you're still beating any of us. Good day. Sir.'

He waited until the man had left.

'Urquhart was Cecilia Gabriel's maiden name,' Costa told them. He looked at Peroni and asked, 'Are you in the mood for coincidences?'

'No,' the big man said.

'Good. Me neither.'

There were so many questions that should have been asked. A stray thought occurred to him: Falcone had allowed his own personality, his distaste for the idea that the girl had been abused by her own father, to intrude into this case. That mistake had coloured everything.

'Forget about the DNA and the Ducati for the moment,' Costa ordered. 'The answers are in that family. Find out everything you can. Everything.'

He stopped. A memory came back to him. Mina Gabriel, pretty and distraught, pale-faced in the cafe near the Piazza Venezia, getting ready to play that haunting piece by Messiaen, one that brought tears to her eyes in the darkness as the organ of Aracoeli seemed to enfold her like a mechanical beast.

Before that happened she'd talked about herself and the Gabriels. Her father's maternal grandmother was Italian. Their arrival in Rome was not entirely by chance.

'Get someone who can work the births and deaths database,' he added. 'I want to know who these people really are.'

CHAPTER 6

Falcone and Toni Grimaldi walked to the Casina delle Civette, talking amicably all the way. Their route crossed the *centro storico*, from the Piazza Navona through the busy open space of the Campo dei Fiori, where tourists and locals alike were wandering through the market stalls, onto the back lane where the Palazzetto Santacroce lay. The lawyer was pleasant company as usual, frank, intelligent, interesting, and always willing to offer an alternative point of view. It was men and women like these, Falcone felt, who made working life in the Questura tolerable. The two were of the same age, on the cusp of retirement. The lawyer spoke openly about the country cottage he'd bought in Puglia to restore. Grimaldi was sufficiently sensitive not to ask Falcone about his plans for life after the Questura. No one could imagine that eventuality, certainly not the man himself.

The press pack had gone, bored by the lack of opportunities. So they were able to walk into the place unhindered, and deal with the caretaker in his cabin, Grimaldi making flattering noises about

474

the beautiful building, which was in truth more palazzo than palazzetto. Then Cecilia Gabriel came out to meet them and the three of them strolled beneath the courtyard arch into the garden with its palm trees, shady corners and gaudy beds of canna lilies.

She seemed a little more amenable than on the previous afternoon. The lawyer's charm could be considerable, Falcone realized. The woman was, perhaps, easier when she was not in the presence of her daughter too.

'Your home is so lovely, Signora Gabriel,' Grimaldi declared, sweeping his hefty arm across the green space in front of them. 'I've lived in Rome most of my life. I never imagined there was so much beauty hidden away in this grey corner by the river.'

He was smiling at her narrow, lined face. She wore a green shirt and dark slacks, more elegant than before.

'I'm sure you gentlemen didn't come here to talk about the garden,' she said in good Italian. 'This affair is growing very tiresome, Inspector. How many times do we have to have this argument?'

'Never again,' Falcone said. 'At least I hope not.'

'You mean you're not here to arrest me? Or accuse us of some terrible crime?'

'Signora Gabriel.' There was an old wooden bench in the shade beneath a well-trimmed orange tree, its branches heavy with fruit. 'Please. May we sit down and speak frankly? My colleague here is a lawyer, not a police officer, though he works for the Questura. However, this visit . . . I would wish you to regard it as private. We're not here on official duty, or official time even. Should nothing come of our discussions, no record will be made, no report written. I would like this dreadful affair to be brought to an end. Just as much as you.'

She beckoned them to the seat. Falcone was glad to take the weight off his feet after the long walk.

'I can assure you there's nothing I'd like more,' Cecilia Gabriel responded. 'But how? Whatever I tell you, you seem to reject it immediately.'

Falcone nodded. The two men sat either side of the Englishwoman. It was a beautiful day in this hidden little corner of Rome, a fragrant, private place, the air rich with the scent of orange and oleander.

'There are facts we cannot ignore,' he began. 'What I would like to do is find a way in which we can deal with them, set them to one side, and allow this case to be closed.'

He took her through the primary issues: the clear evidence that Malise Gabriel had abused his own daughter, and the new information he'd received from Silvio Di Capua the previous evening, about the scaffolding plans that Mina Gabriel had sent to her brother's phone by email.

The latter part was new. It didn't surprise him she rejected the idea immediately as ridiculous. Still Cecilia Gabriel listened, her eyes a little moist, with no small measure of repressed anger in her taut face.

When he was done she sighed and said, 'Inspector. The first time we met you brought out a private photograph of me, naked. An old and personal photograph taken when I was eighteen years old. One intended for my husband's eyes only. One you regarded, quite stupidly I must say, as evidence that my husband was having sex with our daughter. On the second you told me Malise was having an affair with Joanne Van Doren. Now some nonsense about an email. My daughter doesn't have an email address as far as I know. She's not like other teenagers. Haven't you realized that yet?'

The last part threw him. Di Capua was adamant the night before. The message had come from the girl.

'The evidence,' he began.

'What evidence? I've slapped you in the face twice now. I'm not proud of that, if I'm honest. But are you surprised?'

'I have a job to do,' he insisted.

'What you resolutely fail to appreciate,' she went on, 'is that I still do not believe any of these things. I knew my husband. I knew Joanne Van Doren. They were friends, acquaintances. Nothing more.' She hesitated, then said, 'My husband was very ill. He had been for some time. Sex wasn't easy for him, not without a little help.'

She stared at the tower of the Casina delle

Civette rising from the lawn, checking to make sure that her daughter wasn't at the window, Falcone assumed.

'There,' Cecilia Gabriel added. 'You have an intimate confession. I trust it pleases you. Whatever your photographs say I find it impossible to believe that Malise was engaging in some squalid tryst with Joanne.'

Yet Falcone remembered well the moment he'd suggested this.

'You turned on your own daughter and asked her if it was true,' he pointed out.

'I did. I was being an idiotic mother. Mina's a secretive girl sometimes. The way she doesn't look you in the eye. I don't know. It's probably me. Probably what any mother feels. Left out.'

She turned and stared at him intensely.

'I don't believe for one moment Malise abused Mina in any way. It's impossible. He could be a difficult man. An argumentative one. He had a terrible temper. But he was incapable of cruelty. The very thought of it appalled him. He loved her. He loved all of us. He adored Robert above all others, I think, because he was the most difficult of all to love. And now you're telling me he was some kind of a monster, and that Mina and Robert conspired to kill him.'

Grimaldi leaned forward and peered into her eyes.

'Signora Gabriel,' he said. 'You must understand. It will be difficult for me to end this case without some answers to these very real questions.'

'Answers?' she interrupted. 'Very well. Malise printed that first photograph of me from an older picture that was fading. He said he wanted to keep me that way. The way I was when I was eighteen or so.'

Her fingers toyed nervously with a twig of sprawling oleander falling over the back of the bench.

'The words on it, "*E pur si muove*" – I wrote them. You know where they come from already.' Her eyes fell briefly on the tower again. 'Galileo. You know the circumstances. It was Galileo's way of saying, "This I still believe, in spite of all the violence and pain you may bring to bear."'

Her eyes were glassy. She wiped them carefully with a tissue from her sleeve.

'That was the name of the project he was working on for Bernard. It upset him for some reason. He wouldn't tell me why. These last few months . . . I sometimes felt I hardly knew him. I hated seeing him depressed. The night before he died I found him rereading his own book, using that photograph as a bookmark. I wrote those words on the back of that picture. It was my way of saying the same thing as Galileo. In spite of all the pain and heartache, in spite of the fact Malise was very ill, this I still believed. That I loved him and he loved me.'

She took a deep breath and then looked at each man in turn.

'A few weeks ago Malise told me that he'd given

up on the treatment for his cancer. I knew already, I think, in my own heart. It was written in his face. The way he acted. The sadness. What little money we had was gone, which was what troubled him more than anything. The idea he would leave us alone, to fend for ourselves. He had a few months left, perhaps less. At some stage he would have to enter some kind of charity hospice. He wanted to spend his last few weeks rereading his own book, pointing out all the errors, all the statements he wanted to correct, to improve, to expand, and never would. He hoped I could sell it after his death.' She smiled. 'A ridiculous idea, of course, not that I told him so. All I wanted to say to him was that he was loved and always would be.'

'You could have told us that in the beginning,' Falcone pointed out.

'I could,' she said with a smile. 'But I thought it was none of your bloody business, Inspector. And I was right.'

Grimaldi shrugged and said with a wry smile, 'Signora, the bookmark is not a piece of evidence that concerns us any more.'

'Shouldn't it?' she asked. 'Doesn't it tell you something? What do you want of me? Ask. If it will bring this to an end . . .'

'There were photographs taken in your daughter's room,' Falcone went on. 'Evidence of sexual activity.'

'Not Malise,' she insisted. 'That's impossible.

Mina's seventeen. I don't own her. I never did. Besides, when they're that age these days . . .' She laughed at herself, lightly, briefly. 'Who am I fooling? I was sleeping with Malise when I wasn't much older. Everything happens so quickly. One moment you feel this life will never end. The next it's running through your fingers like dust.'

The two men glanced at one another. This had to be said. Falcone wanted the words to come from Grimaldi.

'We need your daughter to make some kind of statement,' the lawyer told her. 'It will never be made public. But the evidence that exists requires some kind of clarification.'

Cecilia Gabriel shook her head and stared at them.

'You still believe my son and daughter conspired to murder their own father, don't you? That this Beatrice Cenci nonsense in all the papers is true?'

'Your daughter knew all about the Cenci girl,' Falcone reminded her.

'That was for Joanne! Nothing else. Some childish fantasy, perhaps. Mina's a dreamy girl, not quite one thing or the other. It's impossible.'

'Signora Gabriel,' Grimaldi interrupted. 'We cannot sit here arguing forever. The fact is this. If your daughter is willing to tell us the truth, and it's a truth I can bury, then I shall do so. If, for instance, she confirms the abuse by her father . . .'

She swore, an English word, a common one.

'If she does this,' Grimaldi went on, 'and says,

merely, that she passed on this building information to Robert because he asked for it, that she knew nothing of any conspiracy, well . . .'

He watched her wringing her hands, waiting for the woman to calm down.

'Then,' he went on, 'we're finished here. I can write honestly that this is a family tragedy with an unfortunate conclusion. One with several victims. One that should not waste the time of the courts, since the principal perpetrator, Robert, is now dead.'

'You're asking her to tell a lie! To make out her own father was some kind of animal!'

They waited for a moment.

'We can only help the living,' Toni Grimaldi said eventually. 'I don't know if you honestly believe Mina has told you the truth. From what you say, I suspect not. Understand me, please. We're not here for her confession. We're here to beg her for sufficent information to allow us to declare this case closed in spite of the evidence that exists. Surely you understand it would be better, for you and for her, that this bleak episode is laid to rest? A brief conversation is all I ask. Just us, you, your daughter. No lawyers, no friends. No notes, no . . . commitments. Simply something I may use as a justification to end this once and for all.'

'Even if it's a lie?' she asked.

Grimaldi didn't answer. Falcone found himself looking into Cecilia Gabriel's clear blue eyes and admiring what he saw there. This woman wished to protect her daughter more than anything. As an individual he was deeply uncomfortable with the relentless bonds of family, the ties of closeness, which so often seemed unbreakable, resolute. From time to time Falcone had privately wondered what kind of parent he would have made. A bad one, surely, willing to abandon a wayward child in the end. In Cecilia Gabriel's stiff and determined face he saw something he could never possess: a fiery sense of protective loyalty, whatever the circumstances. In terms of the law this was awkward and problematic. Yet it seemed to him that there was, in such blind, unthinking devotion, a degree of decency and love that no law, no court, no sentence could possibly deliver. It was a private judgement, and one he would never commit to paper, but he was now convinced that no good would come of dragging any of these people into court if that eventuality could be avoided.

'Even if you feel it's a lie,' he responded. 'It's of no consequence. We cannot ignore the evidence we have. If Mina will give us reason to tell our own superiors that there is insufficient material to continue with the investigation . . .'

He waited for her reaction.

Cecilia Gabriel stared at him candidly.

'I'm rather sorry I slapped you, Inspector,' she said. 'We've all got a temper in this family unfortunately. Except Mina, of course.'

'I've had much worse,' he confessed, and found

himself wondering if he would encounter this woman again. Some time beyond the black mist of mourning and despair that had hung around her on every occasion they'd met, and would stay there until the moment Toni Grimaldi caused the fog to lift.

'I imagine you have.'

She then did something which struck Falcone as curiously English. Cecilia Gabriel clapped them both simultaneously on the knee, palms down, like some schoolmistress from a period movie who had come to some momentous decision.

'I'll ask Mina to talk to you,' she declared, standing up, stretching, a long, lean athletic figure under the sun. 'Just us. But I warn you now. I doubt she'll agree to some convenient fabrication. Not even to save herself.'

CHAPTER 7

They were back in the squad room. Costa stood behind one of the intelligence officers working a couple of huge computer screens simultaneously. Teresa and Silvio Di Capua were with him, liaising with forensic on the phone. Peroni was calling the UK, trying to locate Malise Gabriel's brother. Finally, Costa thought, they might be on the brink of finding a way into this case.

The young woman officer on the desk had just come off the phone to Scotland Yard. She looked at them and said, 'There's no one called Julian Urquhart at the address where the bike was registered. The police in London say they went back two months after the theft was reported. The apartment was rented to someone else. The new people didn't know anything about the previous occupant. There was no mail, no forwarding address.'

'Why would someone with a false identity want an expensive new motorbike?' Costa demanded.

She peered at the screen. Emails kept coming in almost by the second.

'A crook with money doesn't steal any old junk

off the street. You buy something new under a false ID then fake a theft to get it off the register. Take it abroad. Use it without running the risk of getting stopped for driving something hot. Also . . .' She tugged at her short dark hair. 'Crooks are normal too. They like nice cars. Nice bikes. You can do things to them. Tweak the engine. Build some compartment for explosives or guns or dope.'

Silvio Di Capua brightened.

'We found cocaine in the frame.'

'We know the bike's supposed to have come from a drugs gang,' Costa said. 'Where's the surprise there?' He stared at the screen, trying to think. 'We're back on the same assumptions again. I hate that. Give me some different ones.'

Teresa Lupo got the idea straight away.

'The photos in the basement were taken to incriminate or embarrass Malise Gabriel.'

'Good,' Costa told her. 'I like that. But why? He didn't have any money. He didn't have anything. He was dying.'

'The photos from the bedroom are real,' said Di Capua, ignoring the question. 'He's our man.'

'So who is he?' Costa wondered, not expecting an answer.

Di Capua's face was a picture of exasperation.

'Give us time, Nic! I told you. We'll get there.'

'Why is it,' Costa asked, 'that I don't think we've got time? We appear to be dealing with someone who can steal a Ducati in a different country and bring it into Italy without a soul noticing. Falsify photographs, force a man like Malise Gabriel into sexual situations, possibly against his will. Murder two people, one a kid, one a cop, in the street and disappear afterwards. Do you think he's waiting around for us to knock on the door?'

They went quiet. This was not Costa's normal, calm tone.

'No,' he went on. 'Forget that question. Let me offer another assumption. Someone's trying to put Mina Gabriel in the frame for her father's death. Take another step. If they're trying to do that, aren't they trying to set up her brother too? Easiest way in the world to cover a crime. Blame it on a dead man.'

'His sister can still talk,' Teresa added.

'Except she's too scared and has been all along.'

Ever since that night in the Via Beatrice Cenci, he thought. For any number of reasons. Fear. Shame. Something else. A terrified silence that would always, in the end, come to be interpreted as complicity.

'I still don't understand. Why do any of this?' he asked suddenly. 'If it's not for money . . .'

'For the girl?' Di Capua suggested.

Costa shook his head.

'If you've got this kind of money and control you surely don't need to go to all this trouble for a seventeen-year-old kid.' He tried another tack. 'What about the Italian connection? Gabriel's grandmother? She was called Wilhelmina something?'

'Wilhelmina something doesn't really help,' the woman at the keyboard told him. 'I've got someone trying to track back from the British births and deaths records to ours. It's going to take a while.'

'Is there anything that doesn't take a while?'

'*Sovrintendente*,' Teresa Lupo said firmly. 'We're all doing our best.'

'I know that. But why didn't we see this till now? Why?'

He knew the answer already: they thought they understood what this case was about. Beatrice Cenci brought back to life. Brute incest leading to murder. Even he'd begun to believe there was something in that story after a while.

The intelligence officer was still hammering the keyboard.

'What are you looking for now?' Costa asked.

'I thought I'd try the Europol database. It's pretty recent stuff. A bit rough at the edges in places. The best quick way we have of sharing records across the EU. I don't know.' Costa watched as she typed in the name 'Julian Urquhart'. The little icon on the screen span round slowly. Then nothing.

He wondered what Falcone would try in a situation like this. Much the same? Probably. There was little else one could do except carry on thinking about the questions that no one had yet asked or answered. There were so many, and he didn't feel close to penetrating any of them. Every step of this strange investigation, starting with the death of Malise Gabriel that night in the ghetto, had seemed oddly predictable, as if they were being guided towards the conclusion they sought. A conclusion, he reminded himself, that had been in his own mind almost from the moment he saw Mina Gabriel's pained, pale face as she bent over her father's broken body in the Via Beatrice Cenci.

'Nic,' Peroni said, interrupting this sudden reverie.

Peroni had a notebook in his huge paw and a pen behind his ear. His face, so human, so familiar, was full of the alert intelligence Costa had come to admire. Peroni didn't even cast a glance at the woman and her computers. He'd been doing what he did best, working the phones, working people.

'You've got something?' Costa asked.

The big man took a deep breath and said, 'I don't know. This younger brother.'

'Simon. Banker. Didn't get on with Malise.'

'I know,' Peroni continued. 'You told me that. You're wrong. That's not true. It can't be.'

'Mina told me. She said she'd never met him but her mother . . .'

'I don't care. I got nowhere with that name. In the end I phoned Malise Gabriel's old college at Cambridge. These university people keep themselves close. I guessed there had to be someone there who knew. Kept in touch.'

Costa laughed. It was so obvious. A phone call. A conversation. A stab in the dark, reaching out for another human being, not some record in a database.

'And?'

'They loved Malise Gabriel in Cambridge. In spite of everything. The professor I talked to was an undergraduate with him. Hadn't been in touch with the man for years. Seems Malise didn't want the company. I couldn't get this college guy off the phone. He wants to come to the funeral. That's how much they adored him.'

Costa tried to imagine what this meant.

'And Simon? The brother?'

'The brother disappeared years ago when he was still an undergraduate at Oxford. According to my Cambridge man it wasn't that Simon didn't get on with his older brother. He hated him. Malise was the bright one, the clever academic everyone admired. Simon was a wastrel, not so bright. He couldn't compete. All that trouble Malise got into, the pregnant student, the book, that was nothing compared to the brother. He was into student riots. Trouble. Drugs. You name it.'

Simon Magus. The magician. Flying through the air, taunting the world.

'We don't know where he is now?' Costa asked.

Peroni looked at his notebook and said, 'In Cambridge they think he changed his identity. Went to Morocco, Afghanistan, South America. Became some kind of dope king with a high-and-mighty English accent. The prof's emailing me some newspaper cuttings. Apparently the guy was a bit of legend in England ten, twenty years ago. The cops named him as one of their principal suspects for smuggling hard drugs into the country. Never caught up with him though.'

The intelligence officer hammered at her keyboard, waited a second and said, 'Let me try the narcotics records.' A flash of fingers. 'Simon Gabriel. Nothing, sorry.'

'According to my man in Cambridge he had lots of names,' Peroni said. 'These university types are fastidious, you know. He even had a cutting from a crime story in *The Times* of ten years ago. He read it out to me. Look.'

Peroni held up his pad. Costa scanned down the names, got to the last one and groaned.

'Have you got the Italian births and deaths database online?' he asked the intelligence officer.

'Of course.'

'Look up the name Wilhelmina Santacroce.'

The answers were starting to fall into place already.

'Married 1922. Address . . .' She blinked at the screen. 'It's that place you've been going to, isn't it? The palazzetto?'

He wondered how much of what Mina had told him was really the truth, how much lies that she'd passed on unwittingly from the stories and excuses she'd been fed.

The Santacroce palace once belonged to one side of her own family. When Malise Gabriel returned to Rome he was, in some small sense, coming home.

'Sir,' the intelligence officer said, bringing him

491

back to earth. 'That third name on the list. Scott Mason Nicholson. I've got him. I've got data.' She typed frantically again. 'There's a mugshot on the FBI wanted list.'

Costa looked at the screen and knew what he'd see.

'Peroni,' he called as he strode out of the room.

The big man couldn't keep up. When Costa got downstairs the traffic was backed up to the Questura rear gate. Noisy demonstrators were waving placards, yelling at the bored cops in blue uniform, waving banners about Beatrice Cenci and the cruelty of the police.

It didn't make sense that this case had generated quite so much heat. Someone had stoked it. He was starting to think he knew who and why.

There was no way he'd be able to get a vehicle out of this crowd. He shouted back to Peroni, now lost behind him, and asked for a patrol car with uniform officers to meet him outside the Palazzetto Santacroce.

Then he turned out of the Questura, pushed his way through the crowd and began to run, across the city, down towards the Tiber.

CHAPTER 8

There were just the four of them in the apartment in the tower of the House of Owls. Bernard Santacroce was in his rooms in the palace, Cecilia Gabriel said. They wouldn't be disturbed.

The girl sat in the centre of the living room on a chair tugged from the dining table. The rest of them formed a semi-circle around her. Falcone watched this happen, realizing, to his dismay, that they had so easily adopted the pose and the characteristics of an interrogation.

It was now nearly midday but Mina Gabriel still appeared to be in her night clothes: loose pink pyjamas, plain cotton, cheap. Her hair was uncombed and a little lank, her eyes listless and unfocused. Like a kid on the edge, unable to contain for much longer the black truth Falcone was convinced she held trapped inside.

The mother talked a little, in a calm, almost friendly voice. She did her best to reassure the girl that this was nothing formal. Not some kind of grilling. Not even a formal interview. There would be no notes, no pressure. And if it came to

nothing, then every word would be forgotten afterwards.

Mina listened, eyed each of them in turn then
asked, her voice brittle with hatred, 'Do you think
I'm an idiot?'

'We're here to help,' Grimaldi insisted.

'That's what they told Beatrice Cenci,' Mina
snapped. 'The Pope's inquisitors. The lawyers. The
torturers with their chains and pincers.'

'Mina,' Grimaldi said quietly. 'We're not those
men. This is not that time. You're not Beatrice
Cenci.'

Her pretty head lolled a little at that, as if she
was thinking. Falcone caught an expression on the
mother's face, one of shock, of revelation perhaps.
They didn't talk much, these two. Mothers and
daughters had a certain distance sometimes, one
that emerged in the early teens and, usually, would
have begun to dissipate at this point. He'd recognized that often enough even though, in his own
head, he still believed he knew little of families.

'What do you want?' she asked.

'The truth,' Cecilia Gabriel said quickly, before
either of the men could speak.

'The truth?' She looked at her mother and
laughed. 'Why?'

'Because . . .' Cecilia Gabriel closed her eyes for
a moment, trying to stem her tears. 'It's time, Mina.
This secret . . .'

Her voice had a frail, pleading tone. It didn't
appear to move the girl.

'What secret?' she asked.

'I don't know!'

There was a tension between them, one taut with intimacy.

'So this *truth*,' Mina hissed. 'You think it's going to set us free? Can't you hear in your head what Daddy would say to that? How he'd rip that coarse little cliché apart?'

'Daddy's dead,' Cecilia Gabriel told her. 'I can't hear him any more.'

'Can't you?' the girl spat at her.

Cecilia Gabriel pulled her chair over then placed her arm around Mina's shoulders. The girl stiffened, with all the false yet hurtful loathing that a child could sometimes display towards a loving parent.

'I'm sorry,' the woman said and kissed her cheek tenderly, then stroked her hair, the way one did with a child. 'I'm so very sorry.'

Mina pulled herself together and sat bolt upright, pushing Cecilia Gabriel away.

'You're on their side now, aren't you? You're one of the torturers too.'

Cecilia Gabriel stared at her daughter, her eyes full of sorrow. Falcone asked himself again: without some point, some hope of justice or redemption, was it worth inflicting this amount of pain on anyone? Even those stained with guilt?'

'Something's wrong,' the Gabriel woman whispered. 'I'm not blind, Mina. I've known since the beginning. *Something's wrong* and it's inside you.

I don't know what it is. I don't want to think sometimes.'

'You're my mother! You're supposed to defend me! Not ask questions!'

The woman closed her eyes. She seemed to possess no more words.

Falcone shifted his chair closer to the girl and tried to catch her eyes.

'No one's defended you more than your mother,' he said. 'You've no idea how hard it's been for us to get this far. But she needs to know, Mina. As do we. The law demands that we deal with these facts, and until you help us do that this will go on. It must, however much we'd like to end it.'

The girl was silent, thinking, her small fist tight against her lips, tears streaming down her reddening cheeks.

'Did you have any idea that Robert planned to kill your father?' Grimaldi asked.

She said nothing.

'This email we found on his phone.'

'What email?'

Grimaldi explained, adding, 'It has your name on it. It's an incriminating document.'

'It's an invention. Like everything.'

She bit her fist with her even white teeth.

'Did Robert feel he had good reason?' Grimaldi persisted. 'Because of what your father did?'

The skin on her fingers turned scarlet. There was blood there. Cecilia Gabriel uttered a cry of agonized despair and tried to force the girl's fingers away from her mouth.

'All we need,' Falcone added, 'is to know that you sent him that document because he asked for it. If you can just tell me that. The rest . . .'

He glanced at Grimaldi who looked deeply unhappy at what he believed Falcone was about to say.

'Inspector,' Grimaldi objected. 'There are limits.'

'If you say you sent him something because he asked for it,' Falcone continued, 'the rest I will deal with, Mina. I promise. This evidence, this apparent proof, I cannot hide. But I can choose to set it to one side.'

'I loved Daddy,' she chanted. 'Daddy loved me.'

The words came out like the lilting refrain from a child's song. Then again. And again.

CHAPTER 9

The guard on the gate of the palazzetto said he'd no idea where Bernard Santacroce was. But he told them they weren't the first police officers there. That Falcone and another man were with the Gabriels in the little tower in the distant garden.

Costa cursed his own stupidity. He told the uniformed officers to stay by the gate. Then he strode on through the courtyard, beneath the arch, through the exquisite garden, to the Casina delle Civette.

The ground-floor door was open. He took the stone steps of the circular staircase two at a time. They were in the living room of the second-floor apartment, silent, grim-faced, seated awkwardly around Mina. The harsh midday sunlight fell through the arched windows. The girl blinked at him, shielding her eyes against it, as he entered.

'Nic?' Falcone began, standing up as Costa entered.

'What is this?' Costa asked, waving at him to stay seated.

Cecilia Gabriel was a little way from her daughter,

distraught, face puffy with tears, a tissue in her hands, her eyes fixed on the floor.

'We're trying,' Toni Grimaldi said, 'to bring this matter to some kind of conclusion.' He sounded exasperated. Costa wondered how long they'd been here, throwing questions at the girl again. 'To get Mina to tell us just a little of the truth so that we can close this case for good. Unfortunately without some degree of co-operation, the evidence we have is too strong to be ignored.'

'What evidence?' Costa demanded.

'The photographs,' Grimaldi said, as if the question was ridiculous. 'The email to her brother—'

'The photos aren't what you think,' Costa interrupted. 'The email's a fake.' He glanced at Falcone. 'If you'd only left your phone on, Leo. If you hadn't tried to take this case on to your own shoulders . . .'

Falcone's lean, tanned face flared with fury.

'I am the inspector here,' he declared. 'I will decide the course of action.'

'Not now,' Costa cut in.

He pulled up one more chair from the dining table and set it next to the hunched young figure in the childish pyjamas, hugging herself in silence in the centre of the room, trying to pretend none of this existed.

Then Costa sat down, very close to her, tried to catch her eye, did so eventually and said, 'I know, Mina. *I know*. Not all of it. Not yet, and maybe I don't want or need to know everything. But

I know enough. I know you told us the truth when you said your father loved you. I know enough, I think, to understand your brother was not what we thought.'

'Aren't you the clever one?' she murmured in a thin, petulant voice.

'Not really. Not at all. I've been stupid. Blind. I just saw what I wanted to see. What *you* wanted me to see sometimes. And sometimes, mostly maybe, what I felt like seeing myself.'

She clutched herself and rocked backward and forward, staring into the space in front of her with damp, unfocused eyes.

'Where's your uncle?' he asked.

Costa watched both of the Gabriels avidly. Mina didn't react, didn't say anything, but Cecilia Gabriel's head came up and her acute eyes were clear and sharp with shock.

'I know it was him, Mina,' Costa continued. 'I understand, I think, the kind of pressure he must have placed on you. Why you felt you couldn't tell us, even though—'

'Even though what?' she snapped.

'Even though he killed your father.'

'Mina!' Cecilia Gabriel shrieked. The woman stood up, a tall, skinny picture of despair. The girl put her hands to her ears, closed her eyes, let her mouth droop in an expression of teenage disdain that didn't suit her, didn't seem real for a moment.

Cecilia Gabriel came and knelt in front of her

daughter, taking hold of her hands, trying to unwind the tight fists.

'What's he talking about? What . . . your *uncle*?'

The two of them were so close, they seemed to be a single person.

'You weren't supposed to know,' Cecilia whispered. 'None of that. You weren't supposed to . . .'

'Know what?' the girl yelled, her eyes suddenly alive and desperate, her face full of fury. 'That the mythical Uncle Simon in England didn't exist? I'm seventeen, mother. Do you not understand that?'

'Darling . . .'

'I wasn't supposed to know he lived here all the time, paying to keep us alive. And in return? Fucking you and Joanne and anything else that moved and you didn't dare say no, did you, because then . . . then . . .'

Her features contorted until they were those of an infant gripped by agony.

'Children shouldn't use words like that, should they, Mummy? Not a baby like me. Bright Mina. Obedient Mina. The good daughter. The one who was never any trouble.' She laughed and it was a dry, dead sound. 'You never saw me in my room with Bernard. He never got round to showing you those pictures he took. Not yet. He was going to. That was what came next. You and me. With him. Maybe Joanne. Robert. Daddy too if he was still alive. That would have been fun, wouldn't it?'

She leaned forward, stared into her mother's face and asked, 'Did he hurt you too? Not just here . . .' She snatched away her hands and tapped her fair hair. 'I mean *hurt*?'

'Oh God,' Cecilia Gabriel moaned. 'Oh God.'

Costa watched them both, wishing he was somewhere else.

'You could have told me,' Cecilia Gabriel murmured. 'You are my child. I would have done something.'

'What?' Mina shouted. Then, more quietly, '*What*?' Her fingers went to her mother's face.

'He owned us. You. Me. Robert. Daddy. We were just his playthings. We didn't have a voice. We weren't even human beings, were we? Just things. Do this or Daddy doesn't get his treatment. Do this or you're on the street.' She fell quiet, staring at her mother, then said very quietly, 'Things. Not people. You. Me. Robert. Joanne. Daddy. All of us. We were just his toys. And when he did it . . .'

The girl closed her eyes. 'He saw Daddy, didn't he? He imagined Daddy's pain, not ours. That was all it was about. Hurting him. Killing him.'

'What made your uncle hate his own brother so much?' Costa asked.

Cecilia blinked away the tears, then brushed at her hair.

'Because Malise was the brighter one. The happier one. Because, whatever problems we had, we were a family. Simon could never have that. He's a hateful, spiteful, avaricious man. Everything that Malise stood for – honesty, virtue, decency – appalled him.' She gazed at her daughter, trying to see something that wasn't there, and said, 'Why didn't you tell me?'

'For the same reason you never told me,' Mina replied. 'Or Daddy. Because I was frightened. Because I was ashamed.' She closed her eyes. 'Because I am ashamed.'

She shook her her head as if wishing away the memories.

'Daddy found out in the end. About me. Bernard told him. Bernard *boasted*. He couldn't stop himself, could he? All his conquests.'

'Stop it!'

Falcone sat stony-faced and shocked in his chair. Grimaldi had a hand to his florid face, thinking. Costa listened to every word, every syllable, making the links.

'Where is Bernard Santacroce now?' he asked.

'I don't know,' Cecilia Gabriel murmured, shaking her head. 'Really I don't.'

'He can hear,' the girl said. '*Everywhere*. He can hear us. He knows.'

'No, Mina,' Costa told her. 'He can't harm you.'

'Really?' The child again, scared, resentful. 'He said he'd kill Daddy and he did. He said he'd kill Robert and he did.' She looked at her mother. 'Then you. Then me. If I told . . . If I told . . .'

503

Gently, Costa took both her arms and tried to look into her lost, damp eyes.

'He's never going to harm anyone again,' he said. 'I promise.'

CHAPTER 10

It was like opening the floodgates on a dam that had been waiting to burst. When Mina Gabriel began to speak it seemed she couldn't stop. They sat and listened. Not making notes. It seemed unnecessary. Impertinent.

'I told you. I'm not *bad*,' the girl said. 'Robert wasn't either. He just wanted money. We all did. Bernard had so much. He seemed so generous.'

'When did you know he was your uncle?' Costa asked.

'The first time it happened,' she said straight away. 'It was his way of introducing the idea I suppose. His way of telling me how . . . why he wanted to . . .' Her voice changed, became sarcastic. '. . . *help*. I knew about Robert and the drugs. I never understood that, not till then. Bernard's generosity always came with a price. For Robert it was doing what he did down the Campo. Bernard said he had all the money in the world. Daddy could have as much as he needed so long as we offered a little something in return.'

She stared at Grimaldi and Falcone, both of them rapt, silent, horrified.

'Love, he called it. Love. That's what families are about, isn't it? For some reason, he and Daddy . . . it had never happened. So the rest of us made amends.'

Costa had fetched her a glass of water. She took a sip before continuing.

'It was supposed to be a game at first.' She shrugged. 'A touch. A silly little thing, nothing really. Horseplay. That didn't last long.'

Her eyes went to the window and the palm trees swaying idly outside.

'One day he took me to that room in the basement in Joanne's place and I realized it wasn't a game at all. He said he went there with Joanne too. That way he could keep helping her with all the debts on the building.'

She continued to stare at the bright blue day outside, as if she didn't want to see them as she said this.

'Then he told me.' She turned abruptly and looked at her mother. There was the briefest of smiles. 'That I wasn't the only one in the family. It wasn't just Joanne and me.'

'Oh God, Mina,' Cecilia Gabriel gasped.

'What was I supposed to tell you?' Mina asked. 'That I knew he was making you have sex with him? Just becasue he could?'

'You could have said!'

'No,' she said simply. 'I couldn't. Any more than you.'

She turned to Costa, steeling herself as if this was meant to be matter-of-fact.

'Daddy didn't know until the end. I wasn't enough for Bernard, you see. Nothing ever was. He hated Daddy. Wanted to grind him into the dust, make him crawl, make him miserable. A worm, he said. That's what your father is. Bernard would tell me all the things he made Daddy do.' Her mouth fell into a bitter, hard line. 'Things with Joanne. Cruel, hurtful things. It was either that or he lost his job, what money we had. Everything.' The briefest of sighs, a shake of her head. 'I don't know why he despised him so much. His own brother. He said it was like that from the beginning. From when they were little. Daddy was always the brighter one, the charming one, the child everyone loved most. Then when he had a little fame and notoriety for a while . . .'

She took a deep breath and the expression in her eyes was that of the girl in the portrait of Beatrice Cenci, exactly.

'That was years ago but Bernard still loathed him for it. This . . .' She looked around the room. '. . . was his revenge. Daddy dying. Penniless. Every day becoming more dependent on Bernard's charity, if you could call it that.'

Costa nodded and asked, 'And he told your father?'

'That was Bernard's final trick. He came straight out with it one day.' She glanced at the ceiling above them. 'In here. When Daddy pointed out some ridiculous error in that stupid paper. Bernard thought it was . . . funny. One more way of adding to his big brother's misery. "Listen, Malise. I'm screwing your wife. I'm screwing your daughter. And what can you do about it? Nothing, because you're a sick old man and soon you'll be dead. Can you guess what's going to happen then?"'

She glanced at her mother and said, softly, 'I'm sorry. Honestly.'

Cecilia Gabriel got up and stood at the window behind, a tall, thin figure staring out at the grounds.

Mina waited for an answer. When it didn't come she turned back to Costa.

'The evening before he died Daddy came to me and said he'd had enough. He said he'd told Bernard he would go to the police if it didn't stop immediately. I thought . . . I assumed that's what would happen. That night, while I was practising, I heard the two of them. Arguing.' Her eyes wandered. 'Bernard came to the building during the day. Joanne said he'd been on the roof for some reason. It puzzled her. I thought the two of them were just having a row. And then . . .'

Her lips trembled, she began to stutter, to struggle with the words.

'It all got louder. Shouting. Screaming. Something like bricks falling, I don't know. Bernard came to me in the music room. He said there'd been an accident. Daddy had fallen out of the window. I had to keep quiet, tell no one what had been going on. Because if I did it would be bad for all of us. We'd be the ones who'd get the blame. It would be like Beatrice Cenci all over again. We'd never escape, never be a family again. Never recover. It could kill us.'

She wiped her eyes with her sleeve.

'He told the truth there, didn't he? I think . . .'

The girl fell silent, unable to go on.

'He was determined to make sure the blame would come your way,' Costa said. 'The photographs. The way they were carefully doctored. The so-called evidence.'

He found himself looking at Falcone. The man looked horrified, perhaps as much by the gullibility they'd all shown in this case as anything.

Then something came back. The old Falcone perhaps. He got up and said, 'I'm sorry, Mina. We all owe you an apology. This man, Santacroce. Gabriel. Whatever his name is. I don't want . . .'

'I've got men on the gate,' Costa cut in. 'If he's here, he won't be leaving.'

Falcone had stopped and was staring at the palm trees outside. Cecilia Gabriel was no longer at the window. She seemed to have slipped out of the room, unseen, unheard, while they were engrossed in the final details of Mina's story.

Costa walked to the window.

He could see her in the garden, striding back towards the palazzetto where Santacroce kept his private apartment. Something silver glittered in her hand.

CHAPTER 11

The sun seemed too dazzling for September. Costa raced across the grass of the garden. The woman had disappeared beneath the grand courtyard arch, into the elegant building ahead.

The four uniformed officers stood by the gate, bored, a couple of them smoking. Costa barked at the caretaker, demanding directions to Santacroce's apartment.

It was on the first floor, the side of the courtyard facing back towards the river, overlooking the gardens and the tower. He ordered the men to follow him, found the broad stone staircase that led into the building, running through the double doors, up worn grey steps, past paintings and statues, tapestries and porcelain, the treasures of an old Roman family that had fallen, somehow, into the hands of a rogue.

An old story, Costa thought. A little like the tragedy of the Cenci after all.

He reached the first floor, found himself in a wide corridor with a polished wood floor. There was a door open at the end, light streaming through it, some elegant antique furniture just visible.

Three steps away, no more, he heard the first scream and he'd no idea at that moment whether it was a man or a woman, there was something so violent, so animal in that high, guttural shriek of pain.

'Sir,' said one of the uniforms, a fit man, faster than Costa, pushing in front of him, gun out, the way they'd been taught.

'You don't need that,' Costa told him, and elbowed his way back in front then got through the door. He found himself in a long, airy studio filled with light that danced off polished chairs and tables, tall walnut cabinets and gilt-frame paintings. A high rack of books ran one length of the room. At the end Bernard Santacroce sat at an ornate desk, his heavy body twisted round in a captain's chair, his face bloodied and racked with agony.

Cecilia Gabriel was over him, half on the desk, half on his knees, her right arm arcing backward and forward.

The only sound was that of the man's racked breathing and the repetitive slash of knife against flesh.

The uniform had his gun out again.

Costa glared at him and snapped out an order to put it away.

By the time he got to the desk it was over. Bernard Santacroce, Simon Gabriel . . . There was no

512

saving him. The woman's fierce torrent of hatred had taken his life just as surely as the cobblestones of the Via Beatrice Cenci stole away that of his elder brother. Now Cecilia Gabriel sat over him, the bloodied blade still in her right hand, gasping, from effort, from emotion, her blue eyes icy with fury.

'Signora,' said a voice from behind.

He turned. It was Falcone. Himself again, though his lean face looked a little more bloodless than usual. He was holding out his hand, staring at the woman locked above the dead Santacroce as if she were a partner in some bloody tableau, one disturbed before it had reached its final scene.

She dragged herself off the desk, off the man, walked towards them and placed the long, stained knife in Falcone's outstretched fingers.

'There, Inspector,' Cecilia Gabriel said. 'You wanted to find yourself a murderer. Now you have.'

Costa's eyes fell to the expanse of verdant lawn outside. The girl sat near the fountain at its centre, knees drawn up to her chin like a child, face hidden in her skinny arms, a tight, hunched bundle of misery struggling to withdraw herself from the bright, golden day.

PART XI

CHAPTER 1

Eight days later Costa found himself alone outside the tiny pink-washed church of San Tommaso ai Cenci, in the little square at the summit of the gentle mound behind the bleak old palace where Beatrice had lived. There were so many churches in Rome, and this one was unremarkable except for its connections.

He watched the small crowd of mourners, mostly women, dressed in black, enter through the narrow single door. When they were inside, and he began to hear the tremulous tones of an organ, Costa came out of the shadows and walked up to the façade, trying to remember enough Latin to decipher the inscription on the imperial tombstone set high on the wall, between two tiny circular windows that would surely have allowed in little light. The Cenci, who had built this terraced place of worship, seemed to thrive in darkness. He could read a name on the tombstone: Marcus Cincius Theophilus. Cenci. Cincius. One of their ancestors, or so the family had wished to think.

And four centuries on Romans still gathered here each year to mark the execution of Beatrice.

There were flowers on the Ponte Sant' Angelo that morning. Some worshippers would, he knew, visit the spacious interior of Montorio on the Gianicolo hill opposite, wondering as they prayed whether any trace of the Cenci girl still remained in the dun, dry earth beneath its marble stones.

No one would mourn the man who, in Rome, had called himself Bernard Santacroce. His body still lay in the Questura morgue, awaiting instructions, and would probably remian there for months to come. Cecilia Gabriel had made it plain she would not be responsible for any burial. No other relatives existed. The British and American authorities had expressed an interest in the case immediately Santacroce's true identity became known. Simon Gabriel, it seemed, was a man with an international reputation, wanted around the world for drug and people smuggling, money laundering, fraud, a litany of twenty-first-century sins. All of them pursued, for almost a decade, from behind the genteel walls of the Palazzetto Santacroce, a property he had bought back from a distant relative, apparently through legitimate means, and used as an opaque front for his activities.

The legal accountants were now poring over Santacroce's empire and finding, for the most part, little but obfuscation and mystery. The palazzetto itself had been signed over to the Confraternita delle Civette, the charitable organization he had revived in order to lend his presence in Rome some

518

plausibility. Control of that would now, ironically, fall to his sister-in-law, Cecilia Gabriel, the woman who had been charged over his death. She had been released on bail after a brief court appearance for manslaughter, a heroine it seemed to the Roman crowds, who had followed the story of this English family with the same voracious appetite that their predecessors, four centuries before, had shown towards the Cenci.

Some things never changed in this city, Costa thought to himself. Though there was, perhaps, a little more mercy now. Everyone knew that the Gabriel woman would never see the inside of a jail. She'd lost her husband, her son, and the honour and dignity of her daughter. The popular consensus was that she had done nothing wrong. That a crime committed in the defence of inno-cence was no real crime at all. Beatrice and her stepmother went to the scaffold; Mina and Cecilia Gabriel stepped onto the front pages of the news-papers and magazines, becoming a *cause célèbre* in the worthy fight against domestic violence and abuse.

Costa had taken Falcone's advice and gone back on holiday. The two men needed a little distance between them. Both had recognized this. Falcone himself had taken sudden leave and disappeared to Sardinia to stay with an old colleague from the Questura. This case had tested their closeness and left each a little wary of the future. The younger officer was growing, working towards the inevitable, the next promotion, a rank that would one day equal that of Falcone. He did not feel in any way in competition with a man he regarded as both mentor and one of his closest friends. Yet the Gabriel case had created difficulties that would not easily disappear. Falcone hated mistakes, in himself most of all. The hurt he felt for the way he pursued Mina and Cecilia Gabriel would, Costa judged, take some time to subside.

Investigations such as these always possessed some kind of aftermath, a lingering sense of doubt and failure. This one in particular.

He'd stayed at home as Falcone had suggested, calling Agata, who'd gone to the convention in Milan with her boss, with no success. Concerned, Costa had phoned her school repeatedly only to be told she wasn't there. The messages he left on her phone went unanswered until two days before, when a single text promised that she was fine and would soon be back in Rome.

So he worked on the Vespa, painting out more rust, tidied the garden, and paid a neighbour to harvest the vines and take away the grapes to be made into the usual soft red table wine, the humblest of vintages, that his field produced.

And from time to time he visited the Questura, forensic in particular, asking questions. He was the only one to do so. The matter was closed, with gratitude mostly. The tantalizing, un-answered details shelved. Why spend money out of academic interest? Bernard Santacroce, Simon

Gabriel, the monster at the heart of this tragedy, was dead.

The singing ceased in the church opposite. Someone came and threw open the shiny green wooden door into San Tommaso ai Cenci. Costa retreated back into the shadow beneath the wall of the vast, sprawling palace that overlooked this tiny piazza.

He barely recognized Mina when she came out. Her hair was cut short and dyed a chestnut colour. She wore large black sunglasses to hide her features, which was understandable since her face was now well known in Rome. With her black skirt, black jacket and white shirt she could have been twenty or more, no longer the child in pink pyjamas he'd seen curled into a close ball of agony on the lawn of the Palazzetto Santacroce a week before.

Without a word to any other mourner she set off on foot, back down the alley, towards the Via Beatrice Cenci and the river. The route to the tower of the Casina delle Civette, the place that, in spite of all its memories, still seemed to be home.

He followed her from a distance, across the busy Via Arenula where she waited for a tram from Trastevere to pass, then on into the dark nexus of lanes that led towards the Campo dei Fiori. When she went back into the palazzetto he found his courage failing.

In a tiny cafe near the footbridge across the river

he drank a macchiato slowly, called Agata again and got no answer. Then he walked out to the road by the river, thinking of the point a little further along where Beatrice had died four centuries before by the pretty bridge of the Ponte Sant' Angelo, with its marble angels bearing the instruments of both ecstasy and torture.

The funeral cortege would have passed close by. He could almost imagine that he saw it crossing the Ponte Sisto with its ragged beggars hunched on the ground and their mongrels tethered with string.

Costa called Agata. When there was no answer he walked back into the darkness, knowing he needed to see Mina Gabriel again. One more time. One more.

CHAPTER 2

The girl was alone in the living room in the upstairs apartment of the Casina delle Civette, curled up on the sofa with a book in her hands. Her adult black business suit had been replaced by fashionable tight slacks. Mina Gabriel wore a long-sleeved cotton shirt with a beaded necklace. This close he regretted the loss of her young, blonde hair, its replacement with a short, stylish cut, more sophisticated, more adult. The young, distressed girl he'd met that dark hot August night seemed to be gone for good.

It was just past midday. Bright, sunny, cloudless. The palms shimmered in the heat beyond the windows. The room hummed gently to the tune of the air conditioning.

He took the chair opposite her and asked, 'Where's your mother?'

'Sorry? I was deep in the book.'

She showed him the title: *The Fall of the House of Usher and Other Writings* by Edgar Allan Poe.

'"*Mon cœur est un luth suspendu: sitôt qu'on le touche, il résonne*",' she recited, reading from the page in front of her.

'I'm afraid my French isn't so good,' he said.

Mina screwed up her nose. For a moment she was childlike again.

'I suppose you could translate it as, "My heart is a silent lute, touch it and it sounds." Poe uses it as an epigraph, misquoted unfortunately. I think I prefer *The Tell-Tale Heart*, to be honest. Usher's a bit . . . I don't know. A bit *too* creepy.'

Her words trailed off into silence.

'You've done something?' he said, indicating her hair.

'You like it?' She bobbed the side with her long fingers. 'Photographers. I had to do this magazine shoot. What a pain! They said I couldn't look like a schoolgirl. Not that I ever was one. Apparently it was some famous cutter. I don't know. And these clothes. I don't care much for them really. Appearances.'

'Your mother?'

'She's seeing the lawyer again. Everyone's so kind in Rome. I'm glad this happened here. Anywhere else . . .'

Something he remembered brought a shadow of a smile to Costa's face.

'What?' she asked.

'A friend of mine from Turin says all Romans are children, really. We spend our days luxuriating in one long daydream, trying to imagine we're in a world that's always beautiful, one without pain and grief, cruel reality. That if we were left to our own devices everything, ourselves, Italy even, would fall apart.'

'It's a compliment, isn't it? We'd all stay children if we could.'

He nodded and said, 'Perhaps. How is she?'

Mina Gabriel frowned.

'Mummy will survive. We're good at that. Plenty of practice. The lawyers say she won't go to jail. She got bail easily enough. I don't know who put up the money. Why am I telling you all this? You're a policeman. It can't be news.'

He was aware of the details. They were insignificant.

'A million people would have put up the money to keep her out of prison,' Costa said. 'If it was left to most Romans she wouldn't be in court at all. She'd be getting a medal. A heroine. The mother who stood up for her child against the man who violated her. It's as if the Cenci case happened all over again. Only this time we got it right.'

She put down the book and sat upright on the sofa.

'I never thought of it that way.'

'I'm sure you didn't. Will you stay here? In Rome?'

'I haven't decided yet,' she replied immediately, shaking her head. 'When Mummy's free to travel again and they've sorted out wills and ownership and things, she thinks we might sell this place and move to New York. I'm supposed to need a college education.' She grimaced. 'I keep getting all these offers. Talking. Writing. Media. Why? Because I've something to say? I don't think so. They just want to stare at me and say: so that's what she looks like. That's the one it happened to. Perhaps they want to . . .' She hesitated a moment before continuing. 'They want to picture it in their own heads. I'm theirs now, aren't I? I belong to them. They can imagine whatever they like.'

'It's not easy being in the public eye,' he said.

'I'd be an idiot to turn it down, though, wouldn't I? I've never really been outside my own family before. I ought to see what's there. And I get paid.'

He looked around the beautiful apartment.

'Everyone needs money,' he agreed. 'Independence. Self-respect. It's when we deprive people of these things . . .' He thought of the many troubled individuals he'd dealt with over the years. How difficult it was to reconcile the evil they inflicted with their own ordinariness. There were no monsters. Every murderer he'd ever met, however vicious, however cruel, was someone who would never turn a head on the subway. 'The miracle is how often we treat others badly, how people suffer with poverty and hatred and cruelty and still turn out sane and decent in the end. Not everyone, though.'

'What makes the difference?' she asked, suddenly interested.

'One unkindness too many. Some brutal act that goes beyond the pale. I don't know. I don't think those it affects understand either. They feel the pain and the anger and crave some way to release it, to let all that disappear by passing on the hate to someone else. And then they're a little happier for a while. Not cured. Not quite. But free for a time. Able to pretend that it was all someone else's fault, another man's evil.' He thought about it a little more. 'In a way it is, I suppose. Mine. Yours. Everyone's. I think we created the Devil for a reason, a selfish one. He makes it easier for us to accept the imperfect, fallen state we're in. He allows us to shrug off the blame.'

The sun edged into the line of the window. A shaft of piercing golden light fell on her face. Her hand went to her eyes. She shuffled along the sofa, looking a little uncomfortable.

'Why did you come?'

He reached into his jacket pocket and took out the deep red document.

'I brought back the passport I found in Robert's jacket.'

'Thank you.'

Costa held it up, open at the photograph: a young man with dark hair and a sullen, dusky face.

'Who is this?' he asked. 'Who is it really?'

CHAPTER 3

Mina Gabriel leaned forward and said, 'Excuse me . . . ?'

'The young man in the photo. The one who died. My guess . . .'

He pulled out the photo he'd got from Ciampino two days before. The immigration officer he'd met when he went to see the Turk, Cakici, had let him run through the departure camera records. He only had the old photo of the brother to use, and a tentative link.

'. . . is that he's an Albanian kid called Arben Dosti. Someone of Robert's age flew from Ciampino to Tirana using a passport with that name. It's on a low-level drugs-watch list we have. Not sufficient priority to stop him. He was leaving anyway.'

He showed her the picture taken at the immigration control booth and said, 'That's Robert, your brother. Using the passport of the young man we have in the morgue, identified as him.'

Mina Gabriel's face contorted the way he'd seen in so many teenagers: marred by an angry disdain at the apparent stupidity of the question.

'What are you talking about? Robert's dead.'

He relaxed in the comfortable chair and threw the passport across the table, towards her. She didn't pick it up.

'No. That passport's been tampered with. It's genuine enough. It *was* Robert's. I asked a friend in forensic to take a look at it. Someone clever. Discreet. So it's just between him and me. He said someone had changed the photograph. They did a good job. I imagine that, through Santacroce, Robert had some contacts in the drug trade who could do that kind of thing. Arben was one more dope dealer in the ring. For Santacroce maybe. For Cakici. Does it matter?'

Costa studied her icy, frozen face for some sign of defeat.

'He's still out of the country, Mina, isn't he? I don't think you'd dare allow him to stay here. Not right now.'

'Nic! You know it's Robert. You met him in that bar in the Campo.'

'I briefly saw him,' Costa said, stabbing the passport on the table. 'You made sure of that. One more piece of bait along the trail. Arben got paid to pretend to be Robert. To carry one of his phones. The one you'd set up with the incriminating email. He thought it was all part of some scam. And it was. You'd worked it out in advance, just as you'd worked out everything else.' He stopped, remembering that night. 'The kid I saw in the bar never spoke English. I just got a message on my phone. That seemed odd at the time. When

I was in the building, with Joanne Van Doren's body, that really was Robert, which was why he wouldn't let me see him. He couldn't. That would have broken the spell.'

Her eyes turned wide and limpid, the way he had come to recognize.

'You set up this Albanian kid,' he went on. 'Just as you set up Bernard Santacroce. It was very clever, very calculating. Why would we check his identity? You'd confirmed it. I'd seen him. We *knew* it was Robert.'

'My brother's dead!'

'No,' he insisted. 'He's not, Mina. You wanted us to think we were trying to unravel some scheme to kill your father. That way we'd never notice that the real plot had only just begun. That was to give your mother the opportunity and the motive to murder Bernard Santacroce, Simon Gabriel, the uncle who'd really been abusing you, all of you, one way or another. A plot you planned very carefully, minutely, step by step. From the time your father died in the street to the moment your mother stabbed Santacroce in his study here. You brought the suspicion on yourself, you left us the evidence that would first incriminate and then clear you. And when we reached the conclusion you'd concocted for us, your mother murdered him, as you'd planned all along, knowing that public sympathy would keep her out of jail.'

'Why are you saying these awful things?' she asked in a voice that was beginning to break. 'I don't know what you're talking about. Please. Haven't I been through enough?'

Her arm came up to her face, wiping away the tears. She was the teenager once more, the damaged innocent pleading for understanding, for mercy.

'You tried not to lie, I guess,' he said.

'I told you the *truth*!'

He pushed the passport closer to her.

'Look at the picture,' he ordered. 'Look at it and tell me that's your brother. Lie to me now, Mina. I want to see what that looks like.'

She was thinking, he guessed. Scheming. Wondering what avenues were left to her now. There were none. None he could think of anyway.

Mina snatched the passport, got up and stumbled to the bright windows, staring at the palm trees moving in the placid breeze. The years had fallen from her. This was the girl he first saw, beneath the street lamps of the Via Beatrice Cenci and later, lovingly feeding the cats in the ruins where Julius Caesar had lost his life. Young, bright, pure.

She was crying, half-sobbing, clutching the document to her, unopened. Then she tucked it beneath her arm and rubbed her eyes with the back of her fists, trying to recover her composure.

'I can't believe you're saying all this . . .'

'Look at the photograph!'

She wiped her face once more then opened the pages of the familiar red document and stared at it.

Costa got up and walked to stand by her side, peering into her face.

'Is that your brother Robert?'

'I didn't do this,' Mina Gabriel cried. 'Any of it. Robert must have . . .'

She looked up at him, her glassy eyes full of fear.

'Please, Nic. Believe me. You. Of all people.'

'Sorry,' he said simply. 'It doesn't work.'

'But . . .'

'If I'm honest,' he added, 'I'm not sure it ever did.'

She placed her palm on his chest, held it there and asked, 'What do you want?'

He glanced out of the window. September in Rome. Heat, lethargy, people too tired, too lazy or too honest to wish to witness the deceit that lay beneath the city's radiant façade.

'I'm not sure,' he said.

CHAPTER 4

There was a tall stool by the window. She climbed onto it, bleary-eyed but not crying any more, composed, with her arms wrapped around herself. Old again, he thought, wondering whether the other Mina Gabriel, the one he believed he'd first met, was a myth, a creation or just one more victim along the way. And whether she knew herself.

'We'd no money,' she said, staring at the palm trees and the ordered flowerbeds of Bernard Santacroce's garden. 'Everything we had went on Daddy's treatment. Robert even took to selling Bernard's drugs to make money. Working for other people too. He hated it. And Daddy was dying. Everything we had went on trying to save him but it didn't work.' She was hunched up, clinging to herself. 'There was nothing any of us could do. A few months. That was all he had. It didn't matter to him. We did.'

Mina sniffed and wiped her face with the back of her hand.

'I never knew him so unhappy. It wasn't like him. In Canada or England, even when he got fired, he could laugh at them, at their stupidity. *He was a good man*. He loved us. He read to me. Not kids' books. Real books. I was never just a child. He treated me as if I mattered. Someone with an opinion, a right to express it. When I was older he taught us. Literature. Languages. Science. Robert couldn't take it so he went away to boarding school. That was his choice. Daddy was everything to me, to Mummy, and then . . .' She gazed into the garden, remembering. 'We came here and he became someone else. So full of despair. For us, because we were going to be alone and penniless. In a city of strangers.'

She thought for a moment and said, 'He blamed himself for this. Not the cancer. Only himself. But Bernard . . .'

Mina closed her eyes for a moment and when she looked at him again there was something dark and savage there.

'He knew Daddy was vulnerable. That was why he invited him to Rome in the first place. He saw there was something to exploit. That was Bernard's talent. He could read people, see into their pain, and use it. The bastard.'

Her arm shot upwards, towards the office above.

'At first Bernard said he wanted Daddy to add some academic weight to the Confraternita delle Civette.' She cast a vicious glance around the room. 'It was a joke to him. He'd no idea what he'd resurrected. In memory of Galileo? Please.'

She stopped. He waited. These were thoughts

534

she'd never spoken before, and their release was both painful and cathartic.

'Daddy would have gone along with the charade of being his lackey, for our sake. It was either that or . . . God knows. But whenever you accommodated Bernard he made a note, smiled, and sooner or later he came back for more. Finally he put that idiotic paper he'd written in front of Daddy and said he wanted his name on the cover too. Not just as editor but as joint author. Bernard knew what he was doing. He was asking a man who was a million times his intellectual superior to renounce everything he believed in. To throw away his life. He even threw in his own little joke. The title. *E pur si muove.*'

Mina groaned at the memory.

'He wanted to be the Inquisition, making Daddy take back everything he believed in. And in return? They would have Galileo's own whispered denial on the front page. Along with the recantation of the heretic Malise Gabriel, a *mea culpa* the whole world could see. And that was just the start.'

Curt, dry laughter.

'Bernard got more pushy. I didn't really understand at the time, but we had to leave this place and move into Joanne's dump. It didn't make any difference. The pressure was always there, and Daddy getting sicker by the day. Then . . .' Mina turned and looked at him earnestly. 'Bernard decided he wanted more. He thought he was God's gift to women. He'd got Joanne into a corner over money or something. She wasn't enough. He could never keep his eyes off Mummy. He seemed to think we were . . . his right. Just like this place. He was born to be master of everything. So when he began to get really impatient over Daddy's stalling, he turned to Mummy instead. She didn't have a choice. None of us ever did.'

'Did your father know?'

She looked at him, surprised, and said, 'About Mummy? Of course. From the outset. We were a family, Nic. Trying to find some way through this mess, to survive. Why shouldn't she have told him? It was for all of us. Even poor, lost Robert, wasting away in those stupid bars in the Campo. Whenever Bernard got pushy Mummy would keep him quite for a while. Needs must. Then . . .'

Mina placed a finger in her shiny, chestnut hair, twirled the side, a little nervous perhaps.

'The problem was that Bernard was the kind of man who got bored rather easily. Mummy was a worthwhile diversion for a couple of months, no more. After that he was back again, demanding the paper, with Daddy's name on it. And games. Games with Daddy and Joanne, in that place of his in the basement. I don't think it was about sex. Not really. It was about power. About humiliation. That's what he wanted most of all.'

He knew what was coming and wondered whether he wanted to hear.

'Then you?' Costa asked.

She stared out of the window.

'I knew what he was thinking. I could tell from the way he'd started looking at me. One Thursday I was in here, alone, doing some work for Mummy. She had to be at a rehearsal. I can type. I can file. I can be a menial when required.' She pointed to the sofa. 'I was there reading some more of his interminable manuscript. He came downstairs and sat next to me. It was the afternoon. I think he'd had wine for lunch or something. I could smell the drink on his breath.'

He watched her, fascinated, horrified.

'Bernard asked me what Mina was short for. Whether I was Wilhelmina, like someone else in the family. I told him I was Minerva. He knew that already. It was all a part of the game.' Her hand twitched nervously over her lips. This was a difficult memory. 'He said, did I know that this place was called after me? The Casina delle Civette. The owl is Minerva, you see. The goddess of wisdom.' Mina's voice fell a tone, as if talking to someone else. 'Of warfare too, Bernard. Perhaps you should have remembered that.'

She beckoned to Costa to come closer, then she took his hand and placed it on her thigh.

'Then he touched me like this and said, "You're wise like her, Mina. She was a virgin goddess." I can remember his face. The smell of his breath. The stupid leer when he grinned me at me and whispered . . .' Her voice fell away, but not enough to disguise the sardonic tone. '"Are you?"'

537

Costa took away his hand and sat on the cushion on the window sill, looking up at her.

'"Are you?"' she repeated, gazing out at the cloudless blue sky. 'It wasn't a lot to give really. Not when I thought about the consequence of saying no. Bernard was a . . . frantic little man at times, though he didn't get bored with me quite so quickly. I imagine the novelty was greater. Coming to my room with his little camera. I managed to get the card out of that. I thought it might come in useful. It was only afterwards that he told me he was my uncle. I think that was meant to seal the secret between us somehow. Make me as guilty as him.'

'Your family . . .'

Clear-eyed and frank again, she gazed into his face.

'I told you the truth. Bernard boasted about me to Daddy, just a few days before he died.' The faintest glimmer of pleasure crossed her face. 'Daddy said he was going to come round here and eviscerate the bastard with a bread knife. We had to hold onto him. Mummy, me, Robert. Weak as he was, it wasn't easy. He wanted Bernard dead that instant. It was only when we thought about it . . .'

She raised her shoulders in a gesture of acceptance.

'When *he* thought about it. Daddy was going to die anyway. What he wanted more than anything was a secure future for us. If his death delivered that, and we got rid of Bernard too . . .' She cast an arm around the apartment. 'Mummy checked Bernard's papers. He was an arrogant sod. He hadn't even made a will to cover all this, all his legitimate money. That meant everything would come to us in the end. There was no one else. You have to admit it has a certain delicate symmetry. Besides, we had all the evidence we needed right here. It was simply a matter of placing it, and waiting. Then when the moment arrived . . .'

Costa pointed at the passport and asked again, 'Who is he?'

'Some stupid riff-raff that Robert got to know on the street,' she said with a shrug. 'He was willing to pretend to be Robert for a few hundred euros, not quite knowing what the consequences were. I'm sorry, Nic. That was Robert's doing. I'd no idea it would happen. I suspect Robert didn't think things would turn out that way either. I imagine he felt he had no choice.'

'And all of this was your father's idea?'

'Not all of it,' she said quickly. 'It was *our* idea. The family's. It was our way of surviving. Of making the best of what we had. It seemed simple in the beginning. Daddy killed himself. We pushed you first towards us, and then towards Bernard. And one day Mummy killed him. But . . .'

Her eyes strayed outside again.

'"The best laid plans of mice and men . . ."' she murmured. 'Things began to change. Joanne helped us at first and then became scared. Robert was frightened she'd go the police.'

'So he killed her? And the Albanian. And Gino Riggi.'

'I knew nothing about those things until they happened, I swear,' she insisted. 'I'd never have allowed him to hurt Joanne. You've got to believe that. But by the time it was done . . . We'd become part of the trap we set ourselves.'

Costa remembered seeing her the day after the American woman's death. She was truly distraught, he believed. That was not an act.

'The problem,' she said, 'is that you take one small step on the path of righteous wickedness, and the next seems to happen of its own free will. One that isn't righteous at all. I'm sorry. That's what we did. Why we did it. Do you still not understand?'

'Not really,' he said and went to the window.

She joined him there, standing so close he could feel the sweet heat of her breath.

'I used you, I know,' she whispered. 'I had to. We needed someone who'd follow the trail. If they didn't, what was the point?'

He remembered her pale, frightened face in the night, outside the house in the Via Beatrice Cenci. Costa had known from the start there was something she wanted to tell him. Yet it took all this time.

'I never realized it would be someone I'd like so much,' Mina said quietly. She sidled up to him, brushed against his body.

'The passport, Nic. You haven't done anything

with it, have you? No one else in the Questura has a clue?'

He didn't want to answer. She knew anyway.

She took his hand and wound her fingers in his. 'Why is that?'

Costa could see the bend in the Tiber, the miasma rising from the water in the heat, could imagine the dome of St Peter's just out of view, and ahead of it, near the Castel Sant' Angelo, the bridge with its blind angels, and the patch of road where, centuries ago, a young girl had been brutally executed.

Her lips moved to his cheek, to his ear. Mina kissed him once, biting lightly. Her hands ranged over his chest. She took them away and pulled the half-unbuttoned shirt over her head, the lazy, easy way a child did, then pushed her small breasts against him.

'I know what you want,' she murmured. 'I saw it in Bernard's eyes. I see it in yours . . .'

He tried to push her away.

'I saw it in Daddy's face. That last night. When he was sitting on the bed, crying, scared as hell, half-drunk, head bleeding because he'd tried to go outside once and fallen at the window, failed. He was scared. Ready to back out. To go whimpering all the way back to Bernard and offer to put his name on that testament of lies after all. Let Bernard do what he liked to the rest of us so long as he got enough money to live a few more weeks. When we'd worked so hard for this. So hard . . .'

He tried to say something. He didn't want to hear more.

Her voice was hot in his ear. Her lips worked damp and warm against his skin. Her fingers fought to drag his to her small, taut breast.

'So I sat down on the bed and kissed him. Told him I loved him. I always would. That I'd prove it for him and I did. And he stepped out of the window and I watched him fall.'

Costa wished he'd never come to this lonely hidden tower in the garden by the river. That he'd taken the advice of Falcone and buried this case deep in the ground until it was as lost as the scattered remains of Beatrice Cenci.

'Was that one of your guesses, Nic? Did you dare go that far? I don't think so. It wasn't Joanne Van Doren with Daddy. Not that night.'

Closer, closer.

'Are you glad you were right in a way? I was Beatrice after all but willingly, lovingly. It was his last moment on earth. He was frightened and lonely and desperate. I owed him all that and he wanted it. Besides.' She kissed his ear, biting the flesh. 'There was no going back then, was there?'

She had the stance of some cheap coquettish model. He watched as she pushed the red passport down the front of her slacks then placed his fingers there, on the warm skin of her stomach.

'You want your evidence, Nic? Take it. That's why you came, isn't it?'

He withdrew his hand, bent down, picked up the cotton shirt from the floor and gave it to her. 'No,' he said. 'It's the last thing on my mind.'

Out in the garden, among the lilies and the orange trees, beneath the shadow of the tower of the Casina delle Civette, he found himself looking back towards the window, unable to prevent this last backward glance. She stood there, a little hunched, still half-naked, clutching the shirt to her pale skinny chest, watching him leave.

He was too far away to read the expression on her face, and for that Nic Costa was grateful.

CHAPTER 5

He rode the rattling turquoise Vespa all the way to Montorio, mostly following the route that the bier of Beatrice Cenci had taken four centuries before. Then he parked outside the church where her remains lay hidden, scattered by time and the cruelty of man.

The place was deserted. The day was still terribly hot. Costa perched on the wall and realized there were two calls he could make. One to the Questura. One to another destination. The first would be irreversible. Perhaps the second too, though in a different, more subtle way.

At least one of these decisions could be postponed. So he phoned and waited until finally there was an answer.

Almost thirty minutes later he saw Agata Graziano walking up the hill below and waved to her from the wall, smiling, his heart full of some inexplicable joy.

She trudged round the long, winding hilly corner and joined him as he sat on the brickwork, looking back at the city the way Mina had once done when they came here.

'Hello stranger,' she said, and hitched herself up beside him, letting her legs swing, childlike, over the edge.

'Am I?'

'What?'

'A stranger?'

She was back in old jeans and a T-shirt, hair free and wild, no make-up on her dark, interesting features. There were a couple of crease lines round her eyes. He liked them.

'Flowers,' he said, and pulled out from behind the wall the expensive bouquet he'd bought in Trastevere. It was a little battered from the journey up the hill, clutched in his hand as he rode the scooter.

She took them, smelled the fragrant blooms, and smiled.

'I felt you were a stranger. For a while,' she said.

'Sorry. I never meant it that way.'

She watched him with her keen and glittering eyes. Agata had changed again, he thought. Gone was the insular, intransigent sister he'd first met, and the lecturer dressed like one more Roman businesswoman. Perhaps she was finding her real self. It seemed a struggle.

'It was the girl who got in the way, wasn't it?' he asked. 'Mina. Mina Gabriel?'

She shuffled closer, frowned and toyed with some moss in the brickwork, tugging it out of the cracks.

'I wish you weren't so eagle-eyed sometimes,' she complained.

'It was a guess.'

'Really? You still don't know, do you? I saw you with her. That Monday after her father died. My first day at work. I was in the Piazza Venezia and you two whizzed past on that silly little scooter of yours.' Agata's eyes fell to the machine on its stand beneath the trees. She shook her dark head. He watched the way her hair moved, ever more grateful it was unruly, untamed once again. 'I was so mad. So jealous.'

'Jealous?' He laughed, couldn't help it. 'She's seventeen years old.'

'There she was. Holding onto your waist. Young and beautiful. Free as a bird, riding through Rome as if there was no tomorrow. And me trudging to work, wondering what I'd let myself in for.'

Something had happened. He knew it.

'Mina was a very troubled young girl. I thought that, perhaps, I could help. Nothing more.'

'I know. But she was so young. So beautiful. Flying through Rome on a scooter. Holding onto you.' She turned and stabbed him in the chest with a short, dusky finger. 'I wanted that to be *me*. Not her. Not anyone else. Me.' She looked at him. 'Perhaps if I hadn't spent most of my life inside a convent . . .'

'You're young,' he said. 'You're beautiful.'

She raised a single eyebrow and stared.

'I mean,' he insisted quickly, 'you should never look back. Not like that. There's nothing there you can change.'

'I know that. But you can still yearn for something, even if it's just a dream.'

She kicked her legs against the wall, glanced at him, shrugged her slight shoulders then looked at the view, the forest of spires and great buildings, the distant peaks of the Sabine Hills.

'I quit the college last week,' she said. 'While I was in Milan. At the so-called conference.'

Costa scratched his head and said nothing.

'It seems,' Agata added, 'the job entailed certain duties Bruno had never mentioned at the interview. Bastard. It was like working with an octopus.'

'Any . . . plans?'

She didn't look at him when she answered.

'A friend of mine at the Barberini has got me a six-month stint at the Metropolitan Museum in New York. They'll even pay the air fare and find me somewhere to stay. I'm waiting for the confirmation letter. I should be gone in two weeks. Time enough to get out of Bruno's little love nest in Governo Vecchio. I wasn't the first, it seems.'

He didn't know what to say. Or what to feel either.

'Why did you phone me?' Agata asked.

'I wanted to see you. I wanted to ask your opinion. To tell you a story.'

'What kind?' she asked, a little alarmed. 'Not the usual? You know . . .' She ran a finger across her throat and made a cutting sound. 'That kind?'

It was the story Mina had told him. About St Peter and Santa Francesca Romana, the church by the

Forum, its campanile just out of sight, in its wall a strange stone with what looked like knee marks set in the centre, guarded by iron to save them from the fingers of the curious. He knew that. He'd checked, walking into its cool, dark interior, chatting to the polite and talkative priest he'd found there. It was one of the places on his list for the last few days.

She listened as he told her about the magician called Simon Magus and the saint whose prayers dashed him onto the rocks of the Forum, in front of the Emperor Nero. An act that brought about Peter's own martyrdom, for murder not faith, on a cross, upside down, no more than a few steps from where they now sat, if the old stories were to be believed.

As he reached that part of the story her eyes travelled to the church and then Bramante's Tempietto, trapped behind its bars. A steady stream of people, women mainly, were wandering into Montorio. He knew why, and told her. That this was the day of Beatrice Cenci's death, a day some still marked in sorrowful remembrance.

'An interesting story,' Agata said when he was done.

'I thought so.'

'And?'

He blinked and asked her what she meant.

'What is the question you want me to answer?'

'I'm not sure,' Costa admitted. 'Who killed Simon Magus, I imagine? Who stole the old magic

548

from the world? Peter? Or God?' He tried to find the right words and found they remained as elusive as ever. 'Who, I suppose, was responsible? In the end?'

'It's a fairy-tale, Nic. You shouldn't read too much into it.'

He thought of the story from the Grimm brothers that Peroni had remembered when they went to see the Turk at Ciampino. Of the bereaved father who fell in love with his own daughter, and pursued her until she gave in.

'Stories mean something,' he said. 'They're how we express ideas, fears we have that we can't talk about any other way.'

'Fairy-tales,' she repeated, glancing at the door of the church where a group of seven or eight women had arrived in dark dresses, bearing bouquets. 'Like Beatrice Cenci. A convenient myth around which to build our lives.'

'So you told me,' he said, watching the stream of visitors too. 'But it doesn't matter, does it? That it's all a myth?'

'It didn't matter to you. I told you it was all fantasy. The painting by Guido Reni. The idea that Beatrice was some virginal teenager, like that English girl. And what did you do with it?'

'Nothing,' he said quickly.

'Quite.' She smelled the flowers again and smiled. 'It was terrible the way that story ended. The English girl, I mean. But at least she was vindicated, wasn't she? Both her and her father.

It was that horrible man, Santacroce. Or whatever his name was.'

She hadn't really listened to the fairy-tale about St Peter and Simon Magus, and perhaps that was for the best.

'It was that horrible beast all along,' she went on, then said, very firmly, 'If it had turned out that young girl was guilty, as the papers said, I couldn't have borne it. I would have gone back into that convent. This world of yours . . .'

'. . . of ours.'

'This world of yours is hard and cruel and too, too real for me at times. I held that girl in my arms that dreadful night her father died. I felt her innocence as surely as I feel the presence of God when I walk into church. I would not have stayed and watched her punished like some common criminal. You know that, don't you?'

He nodded.

'I had an idea.'

'Good. And now it's past. What next?'

He reached into his pocket, took out his phone, and made a point of turning it off.

Then he picked up the second helmet he'd brought and held it out in front of her.

'The sights,' he said. 'From here to the Aventino, then . . .' His arm swept the glorious panorama in front of them, the campaniles, the hills, the monuments he loved so much.

'I know all those places already!'

'Not from the back of my Vespa. And then Baffetto. Pizza.'

'Pizza?'

'The best there is, or so they say.'

She leaned forward and kissed him on the lips, slowly, gently, amused by the clumsiness of his response.

'You're worse at this than I am,' she told him. 'Why is that?'

'Lack of practice,' Costa replied with a shrug. He dangled the helmet once more. 'Shall we go?'

'Not yet.'

She jumped off the wall and strode to the church, the bouquet in her hand. Costa followed, watched in silence as she bowed and made the sign of the cross. Agata Graziano walked to the altar where Beatrice Cenci's shattered corpse had once been interred and gently placed his roses, lilies and gardenias alongside the mass of colourful blooms laid there earlier.

Then she knelt in silence, her hands in prayer. He watched, unable to respond, to think, to envisage any way to touch this part of her.

In a minute or two they were outside again, struggling to put on their helmets, laughing, happy, carefree, if only for a little while.

The Vespa started first time. He knew this little machine now. Slowly they rode to the summit of the Gianicolo hill then wound their way down to the city below.

AUTHOR'S NOTE

Most of this story is invention. But not Beatrice Cenci, who was executed in Rome on 11 September 1599, by the Ponte Sant'Angelo, in front of a distraught crowd of citizens praying for her reprieve. Visitors to Rome can follow the Cenci trail outlined by Mina Gabriel, from the portrait by Guido Reni in the Barberini, to the bridge, her supposed resting place of Montorio, and the artefacts, including the executioner's sword which is said to have taken her life, in the Museo Criminologico in the Via del Gonfalone. The Beatrice legend is still a matter of some debate among those who follow such stories. Many believe the Shelley version, which portrays her as a young innocent fighting for her own rights and dignity. Others tend to side with the the real-life nineteenth-century historian Antonio Bertoletti who discovered that, whatever the provocation, the girl was not as young or as blameless as many have since assumed. Nevertheless her death is still marked in Rome by a small number of faithful followers, who do indeed hold a mass in the Cenci church near the former family palace.

I've taken the liberty of including three actual

restaurants in the Roman ghetto in these pages – Sora Margherita, Al Pompiere and Da Baffetto – for no other reason than personal pleasure. They are among my favourites in the city. The story of St Peter and his conflict with the magician Simon Magus is, as the narrative says, taken from the apocryphal Acts of Peter. The church of Santa Francesca Romana is real, and a delightful diversion near the Roman Forum. The supposed marks left by Peter's knees when he brought the magician crashing to earth can be found in the wall at the right of the nave, protected by an iron grating.

Galileo's murmured words to the Inquisition – 'and yet it moves' – are equally apocryphal, though believed by many. The Brotherhood of the Owls and the Palazzetto Santacroce are entirely fictional and bear no relation to the real-life Accademia dei Lincei – the Academy of the Lynx-Eyed – which was formed to support Galileo's pursuit of science in 1603. The organization was suppressed by Mussolini but resurrected after the Second World War and now proudly styles itself as the oldest scientific organization in the world.

David Hewson